Acclaim for Nina Marie Martínez's

¡CARAMBA!

"As mesmerizing as acrobats in Cirque du Soleil and as rich as a double-fudge chocolate cake. . . . Riotously funny. . . . Quite a trip." —*The Miami Herald*

"Other than being a beautiful book to look at . . . *¡Caramba!* is a beautiful book to interact with, getting us to connect with the symbols that often feed our cultural and artistic experiences." —*San Antonio Express-News*

"A comic tale of two cultures. . . . [The heroines] encounter a born-again mariachi, assorted miracles and picaresque experiences that would have made even Cervantes envious." —*Chicago Sun-Times*

"Hilarious. . . . Eruptions—volcanic and otherwise—promise the constant transformation of landscapes and individuals. *¡Caramba!* creates humor out of what Martínez convinces us are the all too serious matters of language, authenticity, and folk wisdom." —*The Women's Review of Books*

"A lighthearted homegirl epic. . . . Crammed with bright Lotería cards, maps, and letters, the volume bursts with color and high spirits." —*Entertainment Weekly*

"There's a lot to love in Nina Marie Martínez's *¡Caramba!* Its heartwarmingly bizarre characters, from the most despicable scoundrels to the most steadfast heroes, never fail to win the reader's empathy." —*The Montreal Gazette*

"A wild ride of a novel that will remind many readers—with its rash of characters caught in high drama—of the oh-so-popular telenovela dramas on Spanish-language television. . . . Pure adrenaline and lots of fun." —*Santa Cruz Sentinel*

"Riotous. . . . [Tells of] a fictional California town, where the women's lives are as unpredictable as the nearby volcano." —*Latina*

"*¡Caramba!* is a jubilant celebration of story, language, and the fabulous in the familiar. Martínez weaves a vibrant magic around divine women and men striving for divinity." —Katherine Dunn, author of *Geek Love*

"A smart, antic, sexy and funny frolic. Martínez both celebrates and pokes fun at Mexican traditions as she asks what it means to be a man and what it means to be a woman and considers how we cope with loneliness, make the transition from romance to love, and age with grace." —*Booklist* (starred)

"[An] effervescent, luminous debut. . . . Martínez, in a bubbly mix of English and Spanglish, draws on magical realism, kitschy humor and tongue-in-cheek clichés. . . . But there's truth behind the zany humor . . . serious truth telling about love and happiness in life and death." —*Publishers Weekly*

"*¡Caramba!* is about six characters in search of a volcano. It's *Thelma and Louise* on the border. And Nina Marie Martínez really knows her stuff: zanier than a telenovela, funnier than a Mexican-cowboy western."
—Sandra Cisneros, author of
The House on Mango Street and *Caramelo*

"Essential. . . . A manic first novel . . . imbued with magical realism, about the wacky goings-on in small Lava Landing, CA. . . . A great read."
—*Library Journal* (starred)

"Dreams—both the day kind and the night kind—are at the center of *¡Caramba!* A wild book and it's funny, too. . . . Martínez has a unique writing style; when you're reading the conversations between characters, you'll feel almost as if you're eavesdropping. . . . *¡Caramba!* is muy bueno."
—*Savannah Morning News*

"Magical realism meets *la cultura de K-Mart* in Nina Marie Martínez's lively, beautifully observed *¡Caramba!* The tone of a Tom Robbins book, fueled with a chicks-rule sensibility. . . . Natalie and Consuelo are more fun than a barrel of axolotls." —John Sayles, author of *Los Gusanos*
and director of *Casa de los Babys*

NINA MARIE MARTÍNEZ
¡CARAMBA!

Nina Marie Martínez was born in San Jose, California, to a first-generation Mexican-American father and an American mother of Germanic descent. A high school dropout, she holds a bachelor's degree in literature from the University of California at Santa Cruz. In addition to writing novels, she is also a vintage clothes enthusiast and dealer and an avid baseball fan. She currently resides in northern California, where she is at work on her second novel.

¡CARAMBA!

¡Caramba!

A TALE TOLD IN
TURNS OF THE CARD

NINA MARIE MARTÍNEZ

Anchor Books
A Division of Random House, Inc.
New York

FIRST ANCHOR BOOKS EDITION, SEPTEMBER 2005

The Library of Congress has cataloged the Knopf edition as follows:
Martínez, Nina Marie.
¡Caramba!: a tale told in turns of the card / Nina Marie Martínez—1st ed.
p.   cm.
1. Women—California, Southern—Fiction. 2. Mexican-American Border Region—Fiction. 3. California, Southern—Fiction. 4. Female friendship—Fiction. I. Title.
PS3613.A7865C37 2004
813'.6—dc21
2003056192

Anchor ISBN: 0-385-72152-8

Book design by Peter Mendelsund and Johanna Roebas

www.anchorbooks.com

Printed in the United States of America
10 9 8 7 6 5 4 3 2 1

FOR MY FATHER, WHO ALWAYS
GAVE ME ENOUGH ROPE TO HANG
MYSELF, BUT WAS THE FIRST TO
RIDE TO MY RESCUE EVERY TIME.

Sabe más el diablo por viejo
que por diablo
            —un dicho Mexicano

The Devil knows more from age
than from being the Devil
            —a Mexican adage

THIS BOOK CONTAINS

LA LOTERÍA:

A game of chance, not unlike bingo, only the cards come with images as well as numbers and dichos to make the wise wiser. In México, La Lotería is one of the most popular and traditional games. One person "sings" La Lotería while the others cover their tablas with a handful of beans. The one who fills the tabla first, or makes the designated line, wins, yelling, ¡¡¡LOOOOOTERÍA!!!

¡CARAMBA!

(What you say when you don't know what to say): A tale told in turns of the card featuring a volcano, an ugly beauty queen, a prophecy, a handful of Born Again Christian mariachis, a crew of curanderos, a couple of convicts, a saint, and a whole bunch of like-minded individuals.

THE ARTIFACTS:

Companions to the novel proper featuring, amongst other things, letters for the archivist, maps for the armchair traveler, and paper dolls for the little girls, boys, and cross dressers in us all.

Tabla 1

AN INTRODUCTION TO THE PLAYERS

Tabla 2

THE DECK IS SHUFFLED

Tabla 3

THE CARDS ARE CUT

Tabla 4

THE PLAYERS PLACE THEIR BETS

Tabla 1

An INTRODUCTION *to the* PLAYERS

El Paraguas

The Umbrella

PARA EL SOL, Y PARA EL AGUA

FOR RAIN OR SHINE

LIKE-MINDED INDIVIDUALS

Natalie and Consuelo were best friends since the second grade when the latter stuck a piece of ABC gum in the former's hair while they were engaged in a fistfight over a boy whose name neither of them could remember. When Natalie had to cut her then waist-length hair up to a chin-length bob, Consuelo followed suit. Both girls realized at the early age of eight, a man is the last thing that ought to come between friends.

On a Saturday night Consuelo called Natalie, not for any of the usual reasons, but to inform her that she had just killed a man. This scared Natalie even more than the time she was shoe-jacked by a mental ward escapee who made off with her favorite pair of black platform slides. Consuelo forwent the details, but implored Natalie to "come quick."

Natalie ran to her closet and pulled out her favorite dress, which was long and black with spaghetti straps, and her favorite sweater: a pink mohair cardigan with pearly buttons. She threw on a strand of faux pearls she had bought after watching *Breakfast at Tiffany's* on late-night TV—trouble she normally wouldn't have gone to, but it was a Saturday night, and if it really was true, if Consuelo really had committed the crime she had spoken of over the telephone, then it was all the more reason why the girls ought to have a good time while they still could.

On the way to Consuelo's, Natalie considered herself lucky to have eight cylinders on her side. She had worked every summer between the second and ninth grades either picking or cutting apricots, and sometimes both, in order to earn enough money to buy the car of her dreams: a 1963 convertible Cadillac Eldorado. As she pulled into Roscoe's to fill up, she was struck by a sense of pride and sentimentality. In that day and age as well as any other, a girl needed all the advantages she could get, and Natalie was happy to have a car that was on the one hand beautiful and elegant, and on the other, responsive and powerful—characteristics she strived for in herself. With that sentiment in mind, she eased into the full-service island and said to the attendant, "I'll take a tankful of Super Unleaded, and be sure to top it off, please." Common sense and the movies told her that when two girls go on the lam, a full tank of gas is an essential starting point.

The dust followed Natalie down the back roads while Eydie Gorme y Los Panchos hummed "Mala Noche" from the AM radio. When Natalie arrived, she was surprised to see Consuelo sitting on the wooden steps which led to her front porch, idly smoking a cigarette. Consuelo did not appear the least bit vexed, her composure failed to resemble that of a murderer or even a man slaughterer. With her long black hair parted down the middle and sectioned into two neat ponytails, she wore a white tank top and a pair of red terry cloth shorts.

As Natalie approached Consuelo, she looked into her eyes and tried to find the dancing devils Consuelo's mother insisted dwelt within, but all she saw were two mossy puddles. Consuelo claimed her mother was crazy, a point Natalie wouldn't argue against, but the fact is, most Mexicans don't get green eyes, so when one does, it's a big deal.

Natalie remembered something Consuelo once told her. When Consuelo was four years old, she met her tía Concha for the first and only time. Taking the child's chin in her hand, Concha looked into Consuelo's eyes saying, "You only get one life, chica. Live it up." With those words, claimed Consuelo, it was as if Concha had planted a seed within her, then, momentarily opening her up, she had shed sunlight and rainwater upon it, causing it to grow and grow, wrapping its vines around her innards, seeking its escape.

Consuelo considered this her most formative moment. She would always remember her tía with a strange mixture of reverence and fear, as if Concha were a member of the clergy who commanded respect while inciting fear, and was so close to something so powerful and irresistible, it could not be overcome. It might have been completely coincidental, but Concha had single-handedly been responsible for the defrocking of seven priests in her hometown of Culiacán, which is in the Mexican state of Sinaloa. A devout sinner, but a Catholic, Concha believed in confessing her sins as well as the other Sacraments. It might be relevant to mention, Concha also had green eyes.

"Consuelo," said Natalie taking a deep breath. "I got a whole tank of gas if you feel like gettin on out of here."

Consuelo took a long drag off her cigarette. Natalie scooped up the soft pack of mentholated Marlboro®s, removed one, and let it dangle from the corner of her mouth. A nonsmoker but a fidgeter, it gave her solace to have something to chew on.

"I may have gotten you more worked up than the situation calls for," said Consuelo. "Not to say that it ain't shockin, because it is. Only it ain't probably nearly as bad as you're thinkin."

"Give it to me straight and start from the beginnin," said Natalie, tossing her long, naturally curly and naturally auburn hair.

"¿Promise not to laugh?" Consuelo began.

Natalie crossed her fingers, held them up, and nodded, then sat down on the steps next to Sway.

"A few days ago I decided to start exercisin. In case you haven't noticed, I'm growin quite a gut and I just can't imagine givin up the finer things in life such as menudo or carne asada." Consuelo pinched her abdomen and held it. "So, I figured I'd start out slow. Maybe just walk around the block or somethin. It's hard for a girl like me to know where to begin when it comes to a thing like physical fitness. For starters, I ain't got no walkin shoes, so I put on my most comfortable pair. ¿Member them suede platforms I got on sale last spring at Leroy's?"

"Think so," said Nat.

"Well I don't own no sweats either, so I put on a pair of cutoffs and a T-shirt. No makeup mind you. You might say I was keepin a low profile. I'm about to walk out the door when I start hearin the voices." Consuelo scanned Natalie's face for a reaction, seeing none, she continued. "¿You ever hear voices, Nat?"

"Not usually. Which isn't to say I haven't, because I have. Only mostly I don't usually hear voices unless somebody's talkin to me, and even then it's questionable."

Consuelo moved closer to Natalie and lowered her voice. "Sometimes I hear voices, and usually it's my momma that's speakin. My tía Lila says it's a gift, the voices that is, but I'm not so sure about that. I'm on my way out the door when I hear my momma as if she's standin right behind me and she's sayin, 'A girl dressed like you can't have no good intentions, you little sinvergüenza.' It shocks me, but only for a second, because it ain't the first time I heard my momma say that, and it don't matter that she's gone to that other world either."

"Geez, Sway, that's purty incredible and a bit creepy if you don't mind my sayin so," said Natalie.

"Not in the least. The best things in life are just a little creepy," said Consuelo. "I walk out the door and around the corner. Purty soon I notice this guy slowin down in his car to take a look, but I don't pay him no mind because I'm thinkin about all them calories I must be burnin. Plus I got my Jackie O shades on, which always makes me feel sorta protected. The eyes bein the windows to the soul and all, I prefer to keep the shades drawn. I was mindin my own business."

"And the world would be a better place if everybody did the same," contributed Natalie.

"Out of nowhere there's a screechin of the brakes, and the next thing I know, there's a dead man in the street," said Sway. She bit her bottom lip, then elaborated, "There was this little old guy tryin to cross the street and he got himself runned over because some pervert was busy checkin out my nalgas. He was even usin the crosswalk." Consuelo dropped her cigarette to the dirt, stretched out one of her long long legs, then extinguished the Marlboro® with the wedge heel of her sandals.

"¿That's it, Sway?" said Nat.

"I'm afraid so," said Consuelo. "¿Were you expectin somethin more action-packed?"

"Oh, no," said Natalie swatting at the air in front of her. "Well I hope you're not feelin bad about it, because it ain't by any means your fault. That's just the price of bein purty."

The girls sat silent for a moment staring off into the not so distant fields where a slight breeze rattled the pepper plants.

"You know it's funny," said Nat. "People turn the wrong way down one-way streets all the time, but that don't always spell disaster."

"No it don't," said Sway. She knew precisely what Nat meant: that the world was a place where anything could happen and everything did, and that even the most simple and well-intentioned acts could provoke disaster.

"May the good Lord rest that poor man's soul, but it's Saturday night, and I was just wonderin, ¿what's the plan, chica?" said Nat.

"Was thinkin maybe we could head on out to the racetrack for some watch and wager horse racin," said Consuelo.

"¿You feelin all the sudden lucky?"

"Not hardly, but that ain't never stopped me before. Wait on me while I go in and change," said Consuelo rising to her feet.

"Before you go, I just want you to know that you really scared me there for a second," said Natalie waxing suddenly sentimental. "I figured you'd be sent up and I'd be lucky to see you maybe once or twice a year. And with your fear of public transportation and long car rides, you might go crazy on the bus ride over. It ain't often a person runs into a like-minded individual, least not as like-minded as I consider you."

"Don't worry about a thing," said Consuelo. "I ain't goin nowhere except to change, then we can hit the road. Chin up, chica," Consuelo shouted as she ran up the steps and into the house.

CONSUELO'S DILEMMA

Consuelo's given name was Consuelo Constancia González Contreras until, when she was eighteen, she legally changed it to Consuelo Sin Vergüenza. She had been told so many times that she was shameless, which is what sinvergüenza means, that not only did she believe it, but she came to consider this alleged shamelessness her most admirable attribute.

Her most practical problem in life was this: She was afraid of public transportation and long car rides. With Natalie behind the wheel, Consuelo could get into the Cadillac and go around the corner to the grocery store, or across town to the flea market. She could make it to bingo, to the baile, or anywhere else, just so long as it was within her thirty-mile travel zone. Why she was even known on occasion to hitchhike. But board a bus, never. Much less a train.

Consuelo's father, Don Pancho Macías Contreras (Q.E.P.D./R.I.P.), was runned down by the midnight freight train from Guanajuato. He drove a white Chevrolet pickup truck he called El Caballo Blanco to which he sometimes sang the legendary song of the same name. Like any complex character, Don Pancho was filled with contradictions. He loved his wife, but not nearly as much as the collective charms of his many mistresses. Seven days a week he worked hard, long hours at numerous jobs, only to gamble his money away. He was concerned with physical fitness, ran several kilometers a week, yet he undermined his health by drinking every night.

To get right straight to the point, Don Pancho was a real parrandero—he liked to live it up drinking, dancing, womanizing, gambling, and barroom brawling.

One evening, while on his way home from the cantina, Don Pancho forgot to cross himself as he passed the village church. He was sure this would bring bad luck, so he stopped quite literally in his tracks. (The realization of his oversight occurred just as he attempted to cross the train tracks.) Don Pancho put the Chevy in reverse, but it didn't wanna go backwards. He put it in first gear, but it didn't wanna go frontwards either. It didn't wanna go at all.

DP didn't get out, pop the hood, and try to figure out what was the matter. Nor did he push—that truck was far too heavy for just one man. Going for help crossed his mind, but he had heard enough corridos to know that a real man never leaves his horse, and while the only horse he'd ever had he'd lost in a poker game, he still considered his trusty white Chevy the next best thing. So instead of getting out of the saddle, he took off his sombrero, set it on the bench seat beside him, killed the engine, then began to sing. He sang "El Corrido del Caballo Blanco" over and over. Drunk as he was, it wasn't long before he fell asleep. Nor was it long before the train swept him away.

Back home, Don Pancho's wife, Doña Luisa, was fast asleep in bed. In dreams Don Pancho came to her. "Forgive me, vieja," he said with his sombrero in hand. "I always loved you more than any of the others. Leave me where I have fallen. I don't deserve more."

Doña Luisa knew something was up, because Don Pancho spoke to her in English, and she understood every word of it. She also knew that her husband was gone for good, as opposed to just spending the night with another woman. So when the men showed up at her doorstep with Don Pancho's lifeless body dangling over the back of a burro, Doña Luisa told them to take him back where they found him, and that he had wanted it that way, then she went back to sleep. Don Pancho might have been the father of her six children and the one on the way, but it's hard for a woman to get all broken up over a man who spends most of his time and all of his money womanizing. And besides, Doña Luisa needed her rest. She was less than a month shy of her due date.

Don Pancho had it his way. He was put under with little ceremonia in approximately the same spot where he had taken his last breath, but he really didn't know what he was getting himself into. In Don Pancho's home state of Sonora, a man buried in unsanctified ground without the benefit of a priest saying fancy words over his body is known as a tiradito, and some tiraditos can perform miracles.

Many might jump at a prospect like that, but Don Pancho hadn't exactly behaved himself like a good Christian during his earthbound existence. After DP's vices and virtues were weighed, he was promptly relegated to Purgatory where he was forced to learn English by the low-ranking Saints and Angels Who ran the place.

Due to his status as a tiradito, Don Pancho was, however, given one special power: the ability to show up in dreams. At night he would visit the women who had been his lovers, whispering sweet words in their ears, just as he had in life. With his honey-colored hands clasped together, he would drop to a knee and say, "Por please, pray for me, chatita. It's the only way I can reach my destiny." The women would smile, stretch and sigh, then roll over in their sleep. So captivated were they by Don Pancho's many charms, prayer was the last thing on any of their minds.

Twenty-five years later, the mercury on the Prayer-o-Meter® had scarcely moved; DP was right where he started from. Watching those women grow old and fat was just about as depressing as being in Purgatory. One day Don Pancho turned bitter, dropped his gentlemanly bedside manner, and began telling those ladies just how it was. His voice would begin as a sultry whisper, then escalate to a shout, saying, "You ain't the hot mamacita you once were, ¡gordita! Get me outta here ¡or else!"

Now, instead of praying for him, the women would curse him, quickly depleting what little reserve he had accumulated in his prayer tank.

It would take twenty-seven years and twelve days before Don Pancho finally had enough courage to show up in Consuelo's dreams. Every full moon after her twenty-seventh birthday (a connection Consuelo would never make), she would see her father sitting in the doorway of the old stucco house where she was born, wearing a straw hat, strumming his guitar, looking handsome and just like a man should. The dreams were black and white, except for his guayabera and eyes, which glowed blue. To Consuelo, Don Pancho would strum his guitar and sing the most beautiful songs.

The thing about Consuelo Sin Vergüenza was this: She was five-foot-eleven and three-quarters in her bare feet, light-skinned, black-haired, and green-eyed. Being that she was from Sonora, she looked very much unlike most of the rest of the people from her mother country since Sonora is the land of the Yaqui, one of the few peoples the Spanish never conquered. Had it not been for Don Pancho's torturous, albeit infrequent nighttime visits, Consuelo might have forgotten about her homeland completely, especially since she was transplanted from there at the delicate age of three.

But the very most difficult part of Sway's dilemma was this: She needed to give her daddy some kind of goodbye. She was the seventh child still in the womb the night Don Pancho's life was cut short by the midnight freight train from Guanajuato. And not only did DP show up in her dreams to strum his guitar and sing her songs, but to implore her to return to Mexico where she was to lead the people first to the train tracks, then in prayer on his behalf so that he might be released from his Purgatorial place. The thought of her father being stuck anywhere, much less in Purgatory, bothered Sway more than it otherwise might have, since, due to her theretofore insurmountable fear of public transportation and long car rides, there was not a lot she could do to help him out. And that therein concludes this, an introduction to Consuelo's dilemma.

OTHER FISH TO FRY

After they got all dolled up in their Saturday night best, Natalie and Consuelo headed out to the racetrack as planned. They got there shortly after post time for the seventh race, a bit late by most people's standards, but in ample time to get in on the last daily double. "Looks like the Devil's on our side tonight," said Natalie spying a parking spot right in front.

"I'd put my money on the Devil anyday," said Consuelo as Natalie maneuvered the Cadillac between the white lines.

It had been a long-shot day at the racetrack. Losing tickets littered the concrete floor and the grandstand was nearly empty because more people lose their money quicker when the long-shots come in. Natalie and Consuelo turned their heads and covered their eyes as the horses paraded by. They believed it was a bad idea to look at the horses unless they were racing. On various occasions when she had accompanied an amateur to the racetrack, Natalie had explained why:

"Say you have a good feelin about number four and an even better feelin about number three. So, you figure you're gonna go up to the booth and ask for a 4-3 exacta box. Then comes the parade. You see number one, and he looks like he can really fly. Then number two relieves himself, so you figure he's lighter. Then your mind is set on 1-2, until number seven relieves himself in more ways than one, so you figure he must be even lighter, so you're stuck between one, two, and seven. Purty soon you're up at the booth askin for a 1-2-7 exacta box. And ¿what happens? The four and the three do their thing, and you're stuck holdin a losin ticket. You see they just parade the ponies by the public to get them confused, and it works every time. Always, always, trust your intuition in horse racin or anything else."

The girls found an abandoned program on the ground as they walked in. They took a seat in the grandstand and looked over the entries. Number seven was a three-year-old maiden called Other Fish to Fry. The girls had such a good feeling about this horse, they pooled their money, came up with fourteen dollars, and put it on the seventh entry to win. Other Fish to Fry was ridden by Altamira Suárez, a jockey who had made his way into racing history as the losingest rider of all time. "Least he's consistent," commented Natalie.

"And persistent," said Consuelo. This realization made the girls more confident in their selection. As they saw it, if a person hung in there long enough, the world would eventually give out.

Natalie picked up a discarded copy of the *Racing Journal*®, opened it up, then turned to an article about Altamira Suárez. With three minutes to post, Other Fish to Fry was showing 53 to 1 on the tote board. The girls settled in and read about Altamira. When he was two, his father ran off never to be seen or heard from again. His mother, a manic-depressive, was killed when she threw herself in front of the Giant Dipper roller coaster at the Santa Cruz Beach Boardwalk while Altamira stood by, leaving him all but orphaned at the age of four. As a final insult, Altamira would be forever forbidden from boarding the Giant Dipper, since he would never reach the fifty-inch height requirement.

Natalie set the journal aside and shook her head. "When the whole world is against you like that, only consolation is knowin it don't play fair."

"Small constellation that is," said Consuelo. Consuelo spoke English and Spanish, but neither to perfection. Hence she often minced her words.

The girls looked out onto the racetrack. The remaining spectators had gathered near the fence. The horses were in their gates. It was post time. Other Fish to Fry was the last horse out. At the quarter pole, she was in last place with no hope in sight. Knowing the race is won at the wire, Nat and Sway showed no concern. A horse called Swashbuckler was leading the pack with three lengths on the closest contender. Around the final turn and heading toward the stretch, Altamira Suárez swung Other Fish to Fry to the outside, and she made her move. Sprinting, exhibiting great speed, she passed the pack and the grandstand heaved. Altamira whipped Other Fish to Fry all the way to the wire, winning the race by a length.

Natalie and Consuelo gleamed with pride. Not only were they proud of their good judgment and intuition, they were happy for Altamira, who was on his way to the winner's circle.

They cashed their ticket, $782, then set $20 aside for the general coffer. That left $381 apiece. Slipping the money into her purse, Natalie said, "This'll give me plenty to get that VCR out of layaway at Kmart."

"¿Don't you just love layaway?" said Consuelo. The girls were headed for the parking lot.

"Poor person's salvation. Everybody ought to have somethin to look forward to no matter how little money they got, or how bad their credit. Matter fact," said Natalie, "I would even contend the world's a more civilized place for it. It gives people somethin to strive for."

"Never really thought about it like that," said Consuelo pulling out a pack of Juicy Fruit®, offering it to Natalie, then taking two pieces for herself. "There's this pair of boots down at Leroy's I got my eye on," continued Consuelo. "Triple-tone. Red, white, and black. These are about to shed," she said, looking down at her snakeskin boots. "But I just hate to give them up."

"I'm the same way, Sway. I get too attached to things, it's mostly people I can do without."

"Night's still young," said Consuelo. And indeed it was only a little after 9:00 p.m. A sliver of a moon glowed over the racetrack parking lot.

"¿You feel like stoppin for a tequila float?" said Natalie.

"Might as well, it's on the way," said Consuelo.

THE BIG FIVE-FOUR

Natalie and Consuelo arrived at The Big Five-Four and took a seat at their favorite booth. Their friend Javier Solís was there with his Born Again Christian mariachi band. Mariachi de Dos Nacimientos drifted from a bolero to a huapango and Natalie let out a sigh. "Just amazin what the alleged love of the Lord has done to that boy. He's a far cry from the kid that stuck his hand down my panties on the bus ride home. ¿Member that, Sway?"

"Sure do."

At the time, Javier was president of their third-grade class. When Mrs. García, the third-grade teacher, caught wind of Javier's bad behavior, he was promptly impeached and made to clean up the playground for the rest of the school year. It was an abrupt end to his political career.

"You got to admit, he sure is good to look at though. Especially in that get-up," said Consuelo taking a sip of her tequila float.

"Must have taken Lulabell a year's worth of Sundays to throw that one together," said Natalie referring to Javier's mother, who had taken to working only on the day of the Sabbath out of spite for her former Lord Jesus Christ. There are all sorts of reasons why a woman would turn her back on the Lord, and Lulabell's are too numerous and complicated to mention at this point, but it should be known that she had only agreed to work as seamstress for Javier's musical quintet because, as she saw it, Mariachi de Dos Nacimientos was expending far more souls than it was saving, and nothing made her happier than the thought that Jesus was accumulating red ink in His debit column.

"Well at least he has Jesus," said Consuelo pausing to think on it, then continuing, "Which is more than I can say at any given moment."

"Suppose you're right about that one. I'll have to think on it and right now I've got to pee too bad to give anything serious contemplation." Natalie slid across the red-upholstered booth, then headed for the ladies' room and walked through the swinging door marked DAMAS.

Natalie flushed with her foot, a habit she had formed after reading the Cowgirl's Manual which cited as rule number four, "Always flush with your foot." She could hear the muffled sound of the jukebox, which had taken over for Mariachi de Dos Nacimientos. She washed her hands, then two-stepped her way to the door to the sound of F37, "Hey Baby, ¿Qué Pasó?," a Tex-Mex tune she was particularly fond of. ("Guide to the Rockola at The Big Five-Four" follows.)

Consuelo was gliding around the dance floor with Cal McDaniel. Cal was the owner of The Big Five-Four as well as The Big Cheese Plant where Nat and Sway worked part-time. He was five-foot-four, "but a big five-four" which made him an unlikely dance partner for Consuelo, who stood five-foot-eleven and three-quarters in her bare feet. Cal believed that with ingenuity a man could make an advantage out of any disadvantage, and at that moment he was in the process of taking advantage of his disadvantage as he and Sway two-stepped their way around the dance floor—her wiggling and giggling, him nearly going cross-eyed trying to keep her attributes in constant view. The song ended, but Consuelo kept going—her shoulders cha-cha-chaing, her breasts demonstrating Newton's First Law of Motion. According to Sir Isaac, a body at rest or in motion along a straight line remains in that state unless acted upon by a net outside force, and it was Cal's oversized, pockmarked nose that acted as that force as he buried it in Consuelo's chest, bringing his science lesson to an abrupt halt.

Natalie walked over to the bar and ordered another drink. Mariachi de Dos Nacimientos were sharing a pitcher of root beer. She pulled up a chrome-legged barstool next to Raymundo, who was, according to Javier, the youngest member of the musical group. Raymundo was sixty-seven, but had experienced his second birth just two months before, making him the infant of the group, whose remaining members had all been born again years, if not decades, before.

"All good things come in threes," said Javier holding up that many fingers. "That's why the Lord has three embodiments. In honor of the Holy Trinity, we will be performing three songs for every request."

"I don't mean to interrupt," said Natalie doing just that. "But I thought you guys only had two songs."

"Fact is," said Javier. "We just about worked out our own version of the

José Alfredo Jiménez classic 'Si Nos Dejan,' only we're calling it 'Si Dios Deja.' As you might have gathered from the title, it's a song about the willingness of God and the plight of sinners such as ourselves." The other four mariachis nodded in agreement, each nearly losing his sombrero in the process.

"As I was saying before I was so rudely interrupted," said Javier giving Natalie an evil eye. "Jesus says that if a man asks that you walk with him one mile, you should go with him two. But I say three's a better number and that's why the Lord comes in three ways."

"A body's lucky if he comes in one way," said Cal as he and Consuelo pulled up to the bar. He gave Consuelo a firm but painless pinch in the ass.

"Speak for yourself baby," said Consuelo repositioning her long black hair with a swing of the head. Cal rubbed his hands together like a Boy Scout in front of a campfire—he had been sweet on Consuelo ever since the day he made her acquaintance, roughly ten years before. The jukebox cut to G47, Freddy Fender's "Wasted Days and Wasted Nights."

"¿How about another twirl?" said Cal holding a hand out.

"¿What is it you want?" said Consuelo demurring.

"I'd like another dance with you, you sweet thang. ¿Whatta you say?"

"I say yes if you promise you're gonna like it real well." Consuelo slid her tongue across her top four incisors before heading back out to the dance floor.

Javier leaned toward Natalie, shook a finger in her face, and said, "There's a reason that girl's middle name is Sin"—something Natalie always knew, but never before had she heard that sentiment so succinctly articulated.

Guide to the *Rockola*

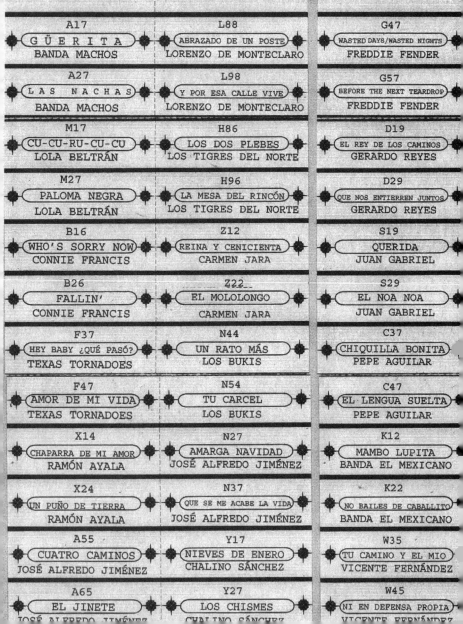

A17	L88	G47
GÜERITA	ABRAZADO DE UN POSTE	WASTED DAYS/WASTED NIGHTS
BANDA MACHOS	LORENZO DE MONTECLARO	FREDDIE FENDER

A27	L98	G57
LAS NACHAS	Y POR ESA CALLE VIVE	BEFORE THE NEXT TEARDROP
BANDA MACHOS	LORENZO DE MONTECLARO	FREDDIE FENDER

M17	H86	D19
CU-CU-RU-CU-CU	LOS DOS PLEBES	EL REY DE LOS CAMINOS
LOLA BELTRÁN	LOS TIGRES DEL NORTE	GERARDO REYES

M27	H96	D29
PALOMA NEGRA	LA MESA DEL RINCÓN	QUE NOS ENTIERREN JUNTOS
LOLA BELTRÁN	LOS TIGRES DEL NORTE	GERARDO REYES

B16	Z12	S19
WHO'S SORRY NOW	REINA Y CENICIENTA	QUERIDA
CONNIE FRANCIS	CARMEN JARA	JUAN GABRIEL

B26	Z22	S29
FALLIN'	EL MOLOLONGO	EL NOA NOA
CONNIE FRANCIS	CARMEN JARA	JUAN GABRIEL

F37	N44	C37
HEY BABY ¿QUÉ PASÓ?	UN RATO MÁS	CHIQUILLA BONITA
TEXAS TORNADOES	LOS BUKIS	PEPE AGUILAR

F47	N54	C47
AMOR DE MI VIDA	TU CARCEL	EL LENGUA SUELTA
TEXAS TORNADOES	LOS BUKIS	PEPE AGUILAR

X14	N27	K12
CHAPARRA DE MI AMOR	AMARGA NAVIDAD	MAMBO LUPITA
RAMÓN AYALA	JOSÉ ALFREDO JIMÉNEZ	BANDA EL MEXICANO

X24	N37	K22
UN PUÑO DE TIERRA	QUE SE ME ACABE LA VIDA	NO BAILES DE CABALLITO
RAMÓN AYALA	JOSÉ ALFREDO JIMÉNEZ	BANDA EL MEXICANO

A55	Y17	W35
CUATRO CAMINOS	NIEVES DE ENERO	TU CAMINO Y EL MIO
JOSÉ ALFREDO JIMÉNEZ	CHALINO SÁNCHEZ	VICENTE FERNÁNDEZ

A65	Y27	W45
EL JINETE	LOS CHISMES	NI EN DEFENSA PROPIA
JOSÉ ALFREDO JIMÉNEZ	CHALINO SÁNCHEZ	VICENTE FERNÁNDEZ

♫ at the Big Five-Four

B13	V41	U68
LA LÁMPARA	AMIGO BRONCO	MI CASA NUEVA
CHELO	BRONCO	LOS INVASORES DE NUEVO LEÓN

B23	V51	U78
DOS GOTAS DE AGUA	QUE NO QUEDE HUELLA	ROSALINDA
CHELO	BRONCO	LOS INVASORES DE NUEVO LEÓN

R24	T24	L42
VOLVER, VOLVER	CHICA DE MIS SUEÑOS	LA HIJA DE NADIE
VICENTE FERNÁNDEZ	JORGE LUIS CABRERA	YOLANDA DEL RIO

R34	T24	L52
SI ACASO VUELVES	TOMA MI CORAZÓN	TUS MALETAS EN LA PUERTA
VICENTE FERNÁNDEZ	JORGE LUIS CABRERA	YOLANDA DEL RIO

B33	M26	I19
LUCES DE NUEVA YORK	MALDITA MISERIA	COMO TE EXTRAÑO
SONORA SANTANERA	MERCEDES CASTRO	LEO DAN

B43	M36	I29
LOS ARETES DE LA LUNA	UN CACAHUATE	ESA PARED
SONORA SANTANERA	MERCEDES CASTRO	LEO DAN

Q19	E51	J84
COMO QUISIERA DECIRTE	BESOS Y COPAS	YO
LOS ANGELES NEGROS	CHAYITO VÁLDEZ	JOSÉ ALFREDO JIMÉNEZ

Q29	E61	J94
MURIÓ LA FLOR	LA NOCHE DE MI MAL	QUE SUERTE LA MIA
LOS ANGELES NEGROS	CHAYITO VÁLDEZ	JOSÉ ALFREDO JIMÉNEZ

F62	C19	L36
BEHIND CLOSED DOORS	AMOR PROHIBIDO	I FALL TO PIECES
CHARLIE RICH	LOS RIELEROS DEL NORTE	PATSY CLINE

F72	C29	L46
THE MOST BEAUTIFUL GIRL	NO VOLVERÉ	WALKIN AFTER MIDNIGHT
CHARLIE RICH	LOS RIELEROS DEL NORTE	PATSY CLINE

T47	J43	O24
UNA AVENTURA	VAMÓNOS A FIESTA	SERENATA HUASTECA
BANDA LA COSTEÑA	BANDA EL RECODO	

T57	J53	O34
PALOMA QUERIDA	SEIS PIES ABAJO	PA' TODO EL AÑO
BANDA LA COSTEÑA	BANDA EL RECODO	JOSÉ ALFREDO JIMÉNEZ

El Músico

The Musician

EL MÚSICO TROMPA DE HULE, YA NO ME QUIERE TOCAR

THE MUSICIAN WITH HIS PLASTIC HORN NO LONGER WANTS

TO PLAY FOR ME

EL MARIACHI

Javier had always been moved by mariachi. His mother, Lulabell, would recall that his first genuine smile was provoked by Jorge Negrete singing "¡Ay! Jalisco No Te Rajes" over the AM radio. The mother learned quickly how to calm the child: She dusted off classic records and played them for Javier. Seeing the infant cooing every evening in his crib, she would remark with equal parts fear and reverence, "¡Ay! ¡qué muchacho tan raro!" Javier was indeed a strange child.

A solitary youngster by choice, the only company Javier sought was that of his record player and his Bible. Lulabell might have predicted the half of it. Javier was born on April 16—an insignificant date aside from the fact that it was that day that Javier Solís, one of the most memorable mariachis of all time and Lulabell's favorite singer, had left the world in a most gentle way.

Javier Solís was best remembered as El Rey del Bolero Ranchero. He was a handsome man, ¡un guapetón pues! but he was handsome in a way that bypassed sexuality and headed for something more profound. Seeing him in his traje de charro, the love he promised seemed divine. If there were any doubt of this, it quickly dissolved when he opened his mouth in song.

A devoted and sincere man, Javier Solís was passionate about every aspect of his life, right down to his favorite meal. Javier was crazy about tacos. He loved them the way some men love their women: with a nice, hard, firm shell. While many men have fallen to the wayside on account of a woman, it is hard to imagine a taco unraveling a man the way it did Javier. After simple surgery to remove a cyst from his gallbladder, one of Javier's best friends snuck him a couple of hard-shelled tacos. He propped himself up in his bed, the green of his hospital pajamas matching the lettuce in his taco, smiled wide, and dug in. After a good meal, he thanked the Lord for his many blessings, including such good friends, then laid himself down to sleep never to wake again. The taco shell had ripped his stitches as it went down. Javier Solís bled to death.

It was almost just as well. Javier was the sort of man you wished could die in his sleep after a good meal. If only he would have waited at least another fifty years. He was not even thirty-five. Upon hearing the shocking news of Javier Solís' sudden demise, Lulabell went into labor seven weeks early. Her son was born healthy, and without further complications. Seeing a thing begin bad, but end successfully, Lulabell named her son after the singer she so adored. While she was at it, she even snatched his last name. It was really no matter. Javier's father had left in the first trimester of her pregnancy. He had done the kind of leaving from which there is no coming back. Lulabell knew this to be true because the Lord had told her so. But that was back when she and He were still on talking terms. Now, either the Lord had quit talking to her, or she had just quit listening. Either way, the effect was the same: She didn't hear Him whispering in her ear, which was fine with her because she didn't have much to say to Him anyway.

The Lord had been right all along. Javier's father never did return. The only male guidance the young Javier got came to him through his record player and his Bible. From Jorge Negrete, Javier learned to be proud of where he was coming from. José Alfredo Jiménez taught Javier that art involves more than interpretation, and it was Don José Alfredo who had inspired Javier to write his first song at the age of nine. Mostly, Javier learned from his namesake. While following in the footsteps of deserving idols is never a dishonorable pursuit, Javier knew he had to create his own good thing, and he saw Mariachi de Dos Nacimientos as just that.

With the formation of his Born Again Christian mariachi band, Javier combined his two great guiding forces. It was a natural progression, since it was through the legends of mariachi and the Word of God that Javier became what is commonly referred to as a man.

It was Sunday afternoon, and Javier was getting ready to set out on a soul-saving serenade at the Lava County Women's Correctional Facility—a minimum-security unit housing mostly first-time offenders. Even Johnny Cash, figured Javier, must have started out small. He couldn't have played his first benefit gig at Quentin.

Javier buckled his Bible belt, a simple strip of black leather engraved with his favorite verses from Scripture. He looked in the mirror and straightened his sombrero. Dressed in his traje de charro, he was no longer himself. He was a mariachi and all a mariachi stood for. In a world full of evil, Javier had long considered the mariachi the last honorable emissary of good.

He removed his sombrero, then knelt beside his twin bed for a little chat with the Lord. When he closed his eyes, he pictured there, up in the clouds, all the great men and women of mariachi who had passed on, dressed in white trajes de charro, cradling instruments carved of pearl, smiling subtly, surrounded by the Saints and Angels. Javier did not doubt that St. Peter Himself had been a mariachi, probably from the southern state of Veracruz where the harp is a staple instrument. This vision included Jesus seated at the right hand of God Whose enormous sombrero cast a huge shadow over the entire entourage.

Javier prayed:

Dear Lord,
On behalf of myself and my honorable Mariachi de Dos Nacimientos, as well as the detainees at the Lava County Women's Correctional Facility, I ask to be invested with the Holy Spirit to aid in our mission of bringing wayward souls to Your side. Knowing Your glories and learning more of Them every day, I would not feel right keeping Them all to myself. They must be shared.

Javier ended his prayer with Verse 6 of Psalm 86. "Give ear O Lord unto my prayer, and attend to the voice of my supplications," then said his Amen.

He got to his feet, replaced his sombrero, grabbed his guitarrón, and headed for the door. He put the instrument in the trunk of his metallic brown 1976 Chevrolet Monte Carlo alongside a box of Bible pamphlets. The mariachis were meeting at Raymundo's. Javier looked at his watch. He was on time.

In honor of the Holy Trinity, Javier pumped the gas pedal three times before taking off. He got onto Highway 33. His big black Sunday sombrero lay on the vinyl seat beside him.

It was the month of July and the sun was beating down hard, as was its custom in Lava Landing that time of the year. On the northbound side of the road there was a walnut orchard shady and inviting. On the southbound, nothing but brown brush. The walnut orchard faded into a bell pepper field bordered by the campos, a sprinkling of shacks and trailers where the field workers lived.

Up ahead on the opposite side of the road was a group of orange-vested men and women picking up trash. Javier lamented their disrespect for the Sabbath, before realizing that they were convicted drunk drivers paying their debt to society. Javier had recently been instrumental in the rehabilitation of an individual who had been the perpetrator of the same ugly crime. Their orange vests flashed in the rearview mirror like warning signs.

Javier unwittingly brought the Monte Carlo up to 90 mph and let it sit. Down the highway he sped, the wheels of salvation spinning in his head. He jumped at the sound of a sudden siren. Checking his mirrors, he realized he was being summoned to the side of the road by the red light of a Lava Landing law enforcement officer. He mumbled an ut-oh, then swung the Chevy to the shoulder.

Javier sat tight while the officer made his way to the Monte Carlo. He knew better than to ask the Lord for His assistance in such a matter, even though the financial repercussions of a traffic citation would infringe upon the funds of his ministry.

Javier was a make-do-with-what-you-had man. In Lava Landing, the primary sources of employment were in the fields, the cannery, The Sausage Factory, and The Big Cheese Plant. Javier felt lucky to have his job as a garbageman. In spite of his divine mission, Javier considered himself a person of the people. He wanted to be as close to his disciples as possible, and he considered his intimacy with their garbage a step toward this end.

Javier stepped out of the Monte Carlo, freshened his traje de charro, stood straight, and offered his hand to the approaching officer. "Good afternoon, Brother," said Javier.

The officer merely nodded, then said, "I pulled you over for exceeding the speed limit."

"And, indeed I was," admitted Javier. "However, it is within the Vehicle Code of the State of California that a driver may exceed the speed limit in the interest of safety." Javier smiled. He was proud of his excellent memory and his well-spoken nature and considered both glories of God.

The officer, who wore badge number 5784, pulled a toothpick out of his shirt pocket, and stuck it in the corner of his mouth. "So, ¿you're telling me that you were speeding in the interest of safety?"

"Exactly," said Javier recycling his earlier smile.

"You'll have to explain that one to me."

Javier began to pace with the nervous energy of the devout. "You see, Officer. I am a mariachi. But not just any mariachi. My mariachis and I are ambassadors of the Lord. Our music sings the praises of Jesus Christ Who is in Heaven. As I was driving down the road seeing my Brothers and Sisters who have fallen to the wayside, the Lord revealed to me the direction in which I must lead my mariachi. I was in a hurry to get the word to the boys. You see, any highway is safer if the drivers are on the pathway to the Lord."

5784 tossed his toothpick to the ground. He was a man who realized a threat when he saw one, and Javier was a danger to no one. He decided to let Javier go with a warning.

Javier sent Officer 5784 off with a thank-you, a handshake, and an invitation to next Sunday's services at The Church of God and His Son Jesus Christ, then honored the speed limit all the way to Raymundo's. Once he arrived, he thanked the Lord, then ran up the stairs and across the concrete walkway, before entering the apartment without knocking.

"Pardon me, Brothers, for barging in, but the Lord spoke to me while I was on the way showing me the direction in which he would like us to proceed," said Javier.

The mariachis scurried into position. They wanted to hear what the Lord had said. They convened on the mismatched couches. The one-bedroom apartment was home to four men—all of the mariachis except Javier. Aside from a brass cross hanging above the front door, the white walls were bare. A thirteen-inch television set sat poised on a milk crate in the distance. In front of the couches, a coffee table scattered with the breakfast paper plates and Bible pamphlets, and in the center of things, a free-standing chalkboard.

Javier grabbed a chalk stub and wrote the words "elimination" and "rehabilitation" on the blackboard. During Mariachi de Dos Nacimientos' conception, Javier had envisioned a two-pronged attack upon sin. The mariachis would first try to eliminate as many sins as possible. When the mariachis were unable to eliminate the sin they set out to squelch, they would come in as rehabilitative agents of the Lord, seeking to save the souls of the wayward in a mission not unlike the one they were about to set out upon at the Lava County Women's Correctional Facility.

"The Lord has shown me that our two-pronged attack upon sin is not sufficient, especially since the Devil's pitchfork is three-pronged," said Javier. The other mariachis sat wide-eyed and listening.

"We can never eliminate sin," continued Javier. "We can try, but we are just men, Brothers, and only five at that. But we can prevent it." He wrote the word "prevention" in capital letters, set the chalk stub down, then dusted his hands off. "¡We must come to the counsel of our Brothers and Sisters as they teeter on the threshold of sin and entreat them not to follow in the Devil's ways!"

"¡Amen!" said the mariachis.

Everyone grinned wide and long, their smiles competing in broadness only with the lips of their sombreros.

Javier crossed his arms with the exhaustion of one who has outdone himself. In a moment of silence, the mariachis heaved a collective sigh as they realized the gravity of the task that lay ahead.

Since you can sometimes know a thing without realizing the extent of its implications, the mariachis all learned an important lesson. The world was infested with sin. It always had been and always would be. Even still, the men could try to prevent sin, a realization they all found empowering and enlightening.

If idealism is to be effective at all, it must be tempered with a dose of realism. The mariachis loaded their instruments into the Monte Carlo and settled into their seats with just this form of realism, along with the sadness that must always accompany it, and headed toward the Lava County Women's Correctional Facility.

La Sirena

The Siren

CON LOS CANTOS DE SIRENA NO TE VAYAS A MAREAR

WITH THE SONGS OF THE SIREN, YOU WON'T SET SAIL

LAS SERENATAS

In old Mexican movies, there is the beautiful girl and the hand-
some man. They can both sing remarkably well and use this talent throughout
the film to express their innermost sentiments. The handsome man loves the
beautiful girl, so he gathers men, who gather instruments, and place themselves beneath her window. This is the serenade.

The beautiful girl is really, really beautiful. Because of this, her father has
placed bars across her window. Also, he has not yet realized that she is a
woman. The beautiful girl places her hands on these bars while the man and
his mariachis serenade her. She holds these bars so as not to fall over from
flattery or love, which, in certain manifestations, are the same thing anyway.
She places her forehead on the bars of her window and smiles. She wants to
be as close to the man she loves as possible.

It was in a similar fashion that the detainees at the Lava County Women's
Correctional Facility embraced their bars, albeit for a far different reason, as
Javier and his minstrel mariachis provided them with a strolling serenade. The
women wanted to see what kind of weirdness had come through their front
door.

Mariachi de Dos Nacimientos was in the house, bringing with them their
limited, though diverse, repertoire. The mariachis only performed three
songs, but they sang them in three different languages: Spanish, English, and
Spanglish, and to a variety of different rhythms including, but not limited to,
huapango, son, bolero, and jarocho. The lady prisoners looked on in awe as
the mariachis filed into the prison block. The men walked with the slow deliberate gait uncomfortable attire creates and the women had to wonder what
good behavior had earned them this reward.

The mariachis were all dressed in the traditional traje de charro: snug pants, a short jacket, a pair of botines, a large moño or tie, and a sombrero. But while a regular mariachi would have worn shiny silver buttons on the side of his pants, Mariachi de Dos Nacimientos wore a series of gold and silver crosses.

The men began with a huapango, and some of the ladies began to stomp out a zapateado. The shock of the trumpet with the steady guttural sway of the guitarrón, and the sweetness of the violin alongside the crispness of the vihuela, combined to get the women moving, but things were brought to a halt as Javier began to sing his Tex-Mex version of "Jesus Loves Me."

During the course of the song, the men and their music became less of a source of entertainment and more of a source of wonderment. Javier segued the other musicians into "Just a Closer Walk with Thee" sung to a bolero rhythm.

The inmates cut out their dancing and stuck to their bars.

"I'd love to take just a closer walk with thee," yelled an inmate. The mariachis were unfazed by this insinuation. Javier had counseled his musicians to always keep a straight and solemn face when singing the praises of the Lord.

"Just as Jesus suffered persecution, so too do those who sing His praises," Javier had reminded his quintet prior to their arrival at the women's facility. They kept that in mind as the ladies hooted, hollered, and projected profanities their way.

Hoots and hollers, better known as gritos, have always been welcome by the mariachi. They are the best indication that he has reached his audience. He even resorts to them himself when his pent-up emotions can sit still no longer. Excitement, happiness, drunkenness, patriotism, and sadness are all expressed with different variations of the same single syllable: ay. But the kind of hoots and hollers happening at the Lava County Women's Correctional Facility were meant to poke fun at the musical missionaries.

It was just past lunchtime. The women, two and three to a cell, banged on their bars with spoons—forks and knives were not allowed inside. Seeing that Javier and the boys were only interested in the salvation of their souls, the ladies took to dancing with one another. Cheek to cheek the women swayed. The music acted as an aphrodisiac and kissing prisoners could be seen throughout the facility. In cells that held three inmates, tempers flared. No one wanting to be the odd inmate out, several skirmishes arose.

From a distant cell came a heartfelt grito. The mariachis looked at one another, then moved their music down the concrete aisle to cell B47.

"Good afternoon, Sister," said Javier sniffing the air. The cell in front of him was neat and orderly and had just been mopped.

"¿Pueden complacerme con una canción?" said the inmate.

The mariachis had received their first request of the afternoon. Inmate G3742, aka Lucha, wanted to hear "Bonito Tecalitlán," a tune that sang the praises of the tiny town which had raised the world's greatest mariachi, Mariachi Vargas de Tecalitlán.

The mariachis looked toward Javier for direction. They were faced with an even greater dilemma than the kissing prisoners; they were being asked to play an agnostic number. Javier heaved a sigh. It wasn't as bad as it could have been. The song was a tame one which mentioned nothing of drinking, fighting, or gambling, and very little of romantic love.

The mariachis huddled to contemplate their predicament. Dressed in his traje de charro, Javier considered himself 51 percent missionary, and 49 percent mariachi. Even though the Lord claimed controlling interest, the mariachi always had his say. "Brothers, I am not sure I see any harm in our performing this song for our Sister," concluded Javier.

"I thought we only play songs about God," said Pablo. The other mariachis nodded.

"Yes. But Jesus did say, 'Give unto them that asketh of thee.' This is a challenge for us, but I believe if the Lord Jesus Christ were still on this earth, He would give the Sister her wish. We are here not only to bring the word of God to those who most need it, but to comfort them as well."

Javier's words were well considered and the vote to fulfill the inmate's request was unanimous. The mariachis paused for prayer, then redeposited themselves in front of Lucha's cell.

Pablo's trumpet signaled the first few notes of "Bonito Tecalitlán," and Lucha let out a grito. The music reminded her of her hometown, a place she hadn't seen since the age of nine, more than fifteen years before. She cut into the second verse of the song, giving Javier a chance to rest his vocals and his mind. He strummed his guitarrón and gazed at her. He might have been a missionary and a mariachi, but he was foremost a man and he couldn't help but notice what a beautiful woman she was. She wore her dark hair in a single braid. Her prison blues set off the amber in her eyes, which stood out starkly against her dark skin. And as for her singing voice, it sounded just as pretty to Javier as any of the old-time Mexican singers they always played on the Sunday morning radio program.

At song's end, the mariachis surged suddenly into their Tex-Mex version of "He's Got the Whole World in His Hands." Lucha clung to her bars making ojitos at Javier. As she batted her eyelids and licked her lips, goose bumps rose beneath Javier's traje de charro. Overcome with ever-increasing fear and excitement, Javier too let out a grito.

"¡¡Sí, Señor!!" exclaimed the mariachis. The ladies screamed and hollered as well, but the act of throwing gritos is an art not easily learned—the women's efforts were amateur at best.

The entire block was under the influence of mariachi.

Seeing a chance to save some souls, Javier led the mariachis up the cement aisle to a strategic position, removed his sombrero, and directed the other musicians to do the same.

He introduced his fellow musicians: Raúl on violin; Pablo on trumpet; Raymundo on guitar; and Kiko on the vihuela. "My name is Javier y estoy a sus órdenes."

The inmates pointed, whispered, and giggled. Mariachi de Dos Nacimientos ranged in age from nineteen to sixty-seven. The ladies had little trouble finding a mariachi within their age range to set their sights upon.

"Jesus is on His way," said Javier.

"And He has been for a long time," taunted an inmate.

"Maybe He's takin the bus," speculated another.

Javier replaced his sombrero and tightened the neck strap as if he were about to mount his horse and ride off into the sunset. The other mariachis followed suit. The sombrero being a source of great pride and tradition, the men felt more capable with theirs on.

Lucha seemed the only willing soul in the place; Javier gravitated her way. She appealed to him in every aspect. As a missionary, he was interested in her soul, which he sought to save then more than ever, and the mariachi in him considered her his equal.

As he placed himself and his mariachi directly in front of her cell, Lucha tied her shirt ends in a knot, thereby exposing her navel. Feeling desire creep up on him, Javier looked upward through the vents of the ceiling searching for the sky, but finding only slivers of it, he bowed his head. The other mariachis followed suit, commencing their own private prayers.

Javier knew he was being tempted, something that had never happened to him on such a grand scale. Sure he had been enticed, but with the delicacies of childhood: candy and quiescently frozen desserts. But now Javier found himself being tempted by sins of the flesh, and by a criminal no less.

Javier asked the Lord for all the strength He had to give, then said his Amen. The sombreros popped up one by one.

Lucha beckoned Javier closer. He went right straight up to the bars of her cell and leaned in as close as he could while the other mariachis looked at one another with a mixture of fear and confusion. "Thank you," she said reaching out toward Javier through the bars of her cell to caress his cheek. "You have reminded me of my home."

So she was from Tecalitlán. Javier's Adam's apple bobbed as he swallowed hard. His eyes projected admiration.

"I get out in two weeks," said Lucha holding up the appropriate number of fingers. Her tone had all of the sudden switched from sweet and sentimental to perky and practical. "¿You sign for me?"

Javier's countenance revealed confusion. He was not versed in prison procedure, but Lucha was quick to explain that she needed a U.S. resident over the age of eighteen to vouch for her so that she could be released into the custody of an entity other than that of the state. Lucha was due to be set free at 9:00 a.m. That would give her and Javier plenty of time to make it to the Church of God and His Son Jesus Christ for ten o'clock services. As the mariachis made their way out to the parking lot, Javier thanked the Lord for this small grace and others as well.

La Lonchera

The Lunch Truck

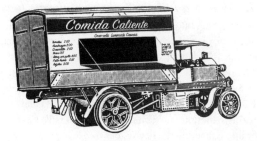

LO QUE TODOS VAN A VER CUANDO TIENEN QUE COMER

WHAT EVERYONE WILL SEE WHEN THEY HAVE TO EAT

LUCHA'S DILEMMA

When Lucha was a little girl, she was always having her hand slapped for sneaking into the candy jar. As adolescence set in, Lucha began to feel like the candy jar—everywhere she went, men were reaching out for her as if she were filled with orange slices and marshmallow circus peanuts, Lucha's favorites. It was during this trying time that Lucha solved both problems with the implementation of a single sudden insight. Lucha learned how to get what was inside the candy jar, by posing as the candy jar.

With this experiment, Lucha started out small. First she charmed the paper boy into delivering the newspaper free every morning, even though the only thing the residents of the household read was *¡Alarma!*® and *Telenovelas*®. Next, she got the paletero to push his cart up her porch steps, where he would offer her her choice of ice cream bars. At the service station the men ran to fill her tank with Super Unleaded and check her oil, as well as top off all other vital vehicular fluids.

All indications were that the experiment was a success. But when Lucha's mother, Violeta, saw the effect her daughter was having on these men, she slapped Lucha's hands harder than ever. But that was before Lucha got in with the guys at the carnicería. When Doña Violeta saw all of the pork, beef, poultry, and fish products Lucha brought home, she stopped slapping Lucha's hands and went out and bought an extra freezer. She was grateful for this small relief.

Violeta had struggled economically to raise Lucha alone after her husband, Lucio, had been killed at The Sausage Factory where he worked as head of quality control in the chorizo department. One day while in the course and duty of his employment, the machine that places the small but sturdy staple at the end of the chorizo went wild, pumping Lucio full of the metal stapling devices, leaving Lucha fatherless at the age of nine.

Of all her benefactors, Lucha's favorite was Ezequiel, the owner and operator of the best taco truck in all of Lava Landing. When Lucha went out dancing at El Aguantador every Saturday night, Ezequiel was always waiting outside with Lucha's favorite meal: tacos de lengua con chilito y limón and ice-cold guava juice to wash them down.

The taco truck was chromed out and as sexy as its owner/operator. After dancing the night away, Lucha would stand in the nightclub parking lot looking at her distorted reflection in the chrome paneling. She would arrange her hair and fix her lipstick, then watch longingly as Ezequiel reached up and used his well-formed biceps to power down the zarape-patterned awning. He would open up the side compartment to a wide array of pan dulce, fruit juices and sugary sodas, mangos on a stick and cups of sliced cucumbers slathered with chile and lime. On the counter he would place three globes of agua fresca in the most common flavors: tamarindo, jamaica, y horchata. Next to that sat a vat of thick pickles, and another of pickled pig skins. He sold durritos, those orange wagon wheels fried to frittery perfection, churros, ice cream bars de la marca La Michoacana®, bags of peanuts, pistachios, and pumpkin seeds, homemade potato chips, and all sorts of sweetness in the form of candy bars and prepackaged pastries. But the real magic occurred inside the lonchera proper where the burritos, tacos, and tortas were prepared from recipes passed down through the generations from all parts of the republic.

Early mornings, around 2:05 a.m., Ezequiel's taco truck became, for many, the last hope for a successful night. It was there, in the nightclub parking lot, that the men made their final tries to charm the women, the women their last attempts to avoid them, and in the course of this interplay, a fistfight was always inevitable. Female behinds were grabbed, male faces were slapped. Men in various stages of frustration and/or drunkenness asked in different ways to be taught a lesson, and Cheque, as Ezequiel was known for more reasons than one, often became their instructor.

One evening, a few years back, during the time in which the mariachi turf wars were going on, a fight broke out in the nightclub parking lot. Mariachi Macho had come from the other side of the valley where they were put out of business by other marauding mariachis. They had heard that there was an all-girl group playing El Aguantador and had the ladies made out for an easy target. What Mariachi Macho didn't know was this: The all-girl mariachi that went by the name Mariachi Maricón was made up of a band of drag queens, beautiful, elegant ladies whose true gender was as indiscernible in their appearances as it was in their voices.

So when Los Machos tried to box it out with Los Maricones, they got more than they came for. The Maricones quickly sent them packing, but in the process Lucha got smacked upside the head with a guitarrón. Her nose began to bleed all over her new pink and white dress. She looked at Cheque, who could see the tears which had welled up in her eyes from the pain.

Seeing his Luchita in such a state, Cheque didn't waste any time. He put his tongs down, untied his apron, stepped out of the lonchera, and went after the Macho who had done this to his beloved. As Cheque and the offending Macho boxed it out, Mariachi Maricón sang a suitable corrido. And then, his business finished, he took Lucha in his arms and kissed her, bloody nose and all, as Mariachi Maricón drifted dizzily into the José Alfredo Jiménez classic "Qué Bonito Amor."

It was there, under the full moon and beneath the awning of the taco truck, that Lucha fell hard for the taco man, and this time it was for real. Theirs was a lovely courtship. That very evening Cheque packed up the lonchera and drove Lucha home, walked her to her doorstep, kissed her softly on the lips, said he'd call, and did.

The two began to see a lot of one another. On Friday and Saturday nights, Lucha and Cheque would get dressed up, hop into the lonchera, and head out to the baile where they would dance all night.

About 1:30 a.m., Cheque would exit the dance floor in order to get things stewing in the lonchera. Lucha would head for the bathroom to pull her hair up into a netted bun so as to comply with Health Department regulations. She would board the lonchera, put on her floral apron, then help Cheque scoop menudo, wrap chile verde burritos, and fold lengua tacos. All the while, the dance floor energy between the two was still building, albeit at a slower, though steady pace, so when the crowd died down and they folded up the awning, and turned off the boiling pots and the placa, and put all the meats with their different descriptive names to rest in a single refrigerated place, they were more than ready to fall into one another's arms.

Now Ezequiel was better known as Cheque for a couple of reasons. In the first place, Cheque is the common diminutive of the name Ezequiel, which sounds markedly different in its Spanish as opposed to its English pronunciation. Secondly, Cheque also ran a check-cashing business out of his taco truck. The word "cheque" meaning check in Spanish, his nickname suited him in more ways than one.

It was the check-cashing aspect of Cheque's business that got the feds curious. ¿How, they wondered, did a taco man have enough cash on hand to cash several thousand dollars' worth of checks every week?

Under observation, they discovered that in addition to his wide repertoire of tacos and burritos, Cheque also sold an awful lot of tamales. His tamales came in two varieties: red and green. This explained nothing to the feds. They learned a little more when they considered that Cheque sold the vast majority of his tamales to a single individual.

During what appeared to be a routine traffic stop of said individual, the feds discovered that the tamales were filled with neither chile colorado, nor chile verde, but were in fact stuffed with polvo blanco y mala hierba, or, if you prefer, perico y gallo, or cocaína y marihuana. Como quieras.

In the great tradition of drug traffickers, Cheque lit out in his truck when the chota came for him, but with Lucha at the wheel. During the course of their courtship, Lucha had learned to maneuver the lonchera quite well. As she screeched around corners and sped through red lights, things began to make sense to her. Lucha remembered a conversation she and Cheque had once had which went something like this:

"¿Sabes qué es un cuerno de chivo?" Cheque had questioned.

Lucha, unversed in the secret language of drug traffickers, said, "It's a ram's horn. ¿Qué no?"

Cheque pinched her on the cheek like a girl after his own heart and said, "No, mamacita. It's an AK-47," then proceeded in pulling the aforementioned semiautomatic weapon out from under the cabinet where they kept the extra tortillas, caressed its handle, and said, "Remind me to show you how to use it sometime."

This made Lucha's heart beat faster. It scared her. Not that she thought that the taco man would ever do her any harm. On the contrary. He was her mero mero pistolero, her pan de Michoacán, and it didn't even matter that he was from the state of Guanajuato either. At Cheque's side, Lucha felt safer than she ever had, it made no difference that she was in the process of trying to outrun the feds in his trusty catering truck. What Lucha most feared was that part deep inside her that was excited about the gun that lurked in the tortilla cabinet. She knew it was that part of her that would one day get her into the kind of trouble that couldn't be gotten out of. As Cheque hung out the side of the taco truck firing round after round from his cuerno de chivo, the pavement became splattered with horchata, then jamaica, then tamarindo as the lonchera lost globe after globe of agua fresca, it became increasingly apparent to Lucha that she was more than likely already in just that kind of trouble. But it was obvious that this was the case when the lonchera landed on its side and Lucha and Cheque found themselves surrounded not only by stray corn and flour tortillas, pickled pig's feet, chile peppers, and brightly colored pieces of pan dulce, but also by agents of the DEA.

Lucha had always suspected that the taco man had been up to what many would consider no good, but she was not entirely aware to what extent Cheque was living fuera de la ley.

In the end, Cheque was sent to Folsom where he was sentenced to twenty-five years to life and learned how to sing Johnny Cash songs with a bad accent. He expected to get out in half the time due to good behavior since he never bothered anyone, and when somebody messed with him—an inevitability of prison life—Cheque would break out into "A Boy Named Sue" or "I Walk the Line," and something about the drug-trafficking taco man from the Mexican state of Guanajuato singing Johnny Cash's greatest hits always made the would-be offending inmate walk the other way.

Lucha was, for a time, heartbroken. It was as if her heart had began to beat at a different rhythm entirely, one she could never get used to, so that she felt nervous all the time and completely forgot what calmness and tranquillity felt like. Cheque had exited her life, but he had left her with some unfinished business to take care of, by way of a suitcase full of high-grade cocaine, and two shiny, silver pistols—business put on hold by the fact that the People of the State of California had considered the lonchera the getaway car, and since Lucha had been its driver, they considered her an accomplice. And it was in that manner that Lucha, at the age of twenty-four, had landed in the Lava County Women's Correctional Facility in the first place.

El Diablito
The Little Devil

PÓRTATE BIEN CUATITO, SI NO TE LLEVA EL COLORADITO
BEHAVE YOURSELF WELL, LEST THE LITTLE RED ONE
MIGHT CARRY YOU AWAY

LULABELL'S LEISURE

In Lava Landing, it was a well-known fact that Javier's mother, Lulabell, was a practiced and capable witch. For the vast majority of her life, she had laid her immense powers dormant in favor of devout pursuit of the teachings of her once Lord and Savior Jesus Christ. But after a series of misfortunes and a single bona fide tragedy, Lulabell eventually gave up on the Lord, His ways and teachings, and pursued what she had been born with: a natural knack for witchcraft.

That Wednesday morning, she pulled her shiny black 1977 Cadillac Seville into the parking lot of the Lava Landing Lumberyard. Cadillacs mean different things to different people, and while to Natalie and Consuelo they represented elegance and power, to Lulabell her car was a throwback to the days when she could depend on her husband's income. He was a self-employed mechanic, and even though he'd run off with another woman nearly twenty-five years before, Lulabell still respected the hard work he'd suffered in order to buy her the car, so she did her best to keep it clean and in prime running condition.

It was just a little after 6:00 a.m., but Lulabell was wearing a tight-fitting, sleeveless, knee-grazing, rayon-spandex blend dress, seamed stockings, and high heels. Her long black hair was braided and spun into two tight chonguitos, one at each side of her head. A black crocheted shawl rested across her shoulders sheltering them from the morning cold.

In order to maximize their shot at a day's work, the day laborers began arriving at a little after 5:30 a.m. The men lined the sidewalks adjacent to the lumberyard, and scattered themselves throughout the parking lot. They huddled in groups of three or four, chitchatting and drinking their morning coffee.

Lulabell swung the Cadillac into a parking space where she could have a good look around. She touched up her lipstick in the rearview mirror, then disembarked, her candy-apple-red lips glowing triumphant in the early morning light. She headed toward the most handsome man the labor pool had to offer.

Gilbert Espinoza did not like to work. He was relatively new in town and he entered the parking lot each morning, smoked half a pack of Marlboro® Light 100s because he was cutting back, but doing it on his own terms, then headed home.

Gilbert might have been lazy, but he was a good-looking man with a generous mustache and hair that was meant to pompadour. His frame and height indicated he would never be overweight. Upon receiving his first eyeful of Lulabell, Gilbert smiled wide.

Lulabell made her way to Gilbert's side of the parking lot. "¿Lookin for a day's work?" she questioned. Gilbert lit one cigarette from another, before looking up at his prospective employer. He shrugged and followed Lulabell to the Seville. He wasn't looking for a day's work, but since it had found him, he didn't see much choice other than to go along with it.

Gilbert didn't say much on the way to Lulabell's, but she didn't mind. The work she had cut out for him didn't require any verbal exchange. They reached her home in just a few minutes.

The house wasn't big per se, but it was nonetheless impressive, with an unparalleled newness and luxury to it. The front yard displayed a blend of young and old growth, a mixture of completed and thwarted landscape design motifs, and an assortment of statuary.

The well-groomed lawn featured a fountain-fed pond with a wooden bridge above it. Its borders were lined with dwarf Japanese junipers (*Juniperus procumbens*), their creeping, wide-spreading branches kept in check by scalloped concrete garden edging.

The walkway consisted of newly laid patio pavers with an occasional mosaic stepping-stone. Owing to their arrangement, Gilbert could have sworn he recognized the handiwork of Ted Rojas, a local landscaper upon whose crew he had recently spent a few days.

The exterior of the house was stucco and painted powder pink with wrought iron window boxes overflowing with begonias. The latticed porch was overgrown with grapes and blue passionflowers (*Passiflora caerulea*) in full vulvic bloom. They reached the front door, a ten-foot freshly lathed number with a wrought iron handle. Given the surroundings, Gilbert was left with the distinct impression that Lulabell was loaded. Actually, Lulabell eked out a just-get-by existence working part-time as a waitress at the Lava Landing

Bowling Alley Café, but over the years she had made so many connections in the Lava Landing Lumberyard parking lot, she got most of her labor and a good portion of her materials free.

As they walked through the front door, Gilbert didn't notice anything that might need his assistance. The entire place looked like it had recently received a fresh coat of paint. Gilbert sniffed the air and what he smelled confirmed this. A less obvious household ailment such as a clogged garbage disposal or a stubborn washing machine must require his expertise, he concluded.

Lulabell led him to the sofa, which was in no need of reupholstery, hooked an arm around his neck, pulled him close, and kissed him hard on the lips. Shocked by Lulabell's sudden seduction, Gilbert's lips and other oral accoutrements lay dormant. But acquiescence gave way to wholehearted participation, and the duo was soon strewn on the couch. Apparel fell to the floor—a pair of brown, faded, paint-splattered Ben Davis® here, a pair of pumps there. When Lulabell took Gilbert's sizable and growing penis in her hand, she smiled with all the delight of one touching the bread and realizing it's still warm.

Gilbert hung on to Lulabell's chonguitos as she satisfied herself atop him. Her agility amazed Gilbert almost as much as her audacity. She spun and shifted while he did his best to hold on to her chonguitos, which seemed her most stable part. No matter what position she swung herself into, they clung firmly to the side of her head.

Within no time, they both arrived. Lulabell smiled and sighed, then headed for her bedroom. When she returned, she was wearing her favorite huipil, a long shapeless cotton dress with brightly colored embroidered flowers. Gilbert sat speechless and blank-faced on the couch. Lulabell placed a hand over her mouth to conceal her laughter, then said, "The shower's down the hall on your right. Extra towels and soap under the sink."

"Thanks," said Gilbert. He needed a shower, more than anything to relax and think about what had just happened. It was the first time he had been unfaithful to his wife and he wasn't sure how he felt about it. It wasn't that he was dedicated to his spouse. Far from it. As mentioned earlier, Gilbert did not like to work, and he considered womanizing a sizable chore.

In the kitchen, Lulabell began to cut, dice, and chop while she sang along with the AM radio. She was a considerate employer who always fed her workers. If one of her employees proved especially skilled, she wanted him back for another day's work. To ensure that he would be available for further services, Lulabell snuck a few extra ingredients into his meal. This culinary secret she had learned from a brujo in Manzanillo, Colima.

The state of Colima had always captivated Lulabell. With its hazy, foggy, always overcast but sizzling climate, Lulabell had it pegged for the Devil's resting place. Only the Devil never rests. He had been at her service since she was a child.

One summer Sunday after church, when Lulabell was just eight years old, the Devil jumped inside of her. She knew this to be true, because there, within her, emerged a voice which steered her every action with a knowledge beyond that of human beings. Lulabell began to see the future, though not in any great-scheme-of-the-world sort of way. You might say her powers dealt in the simple details of ordinary life: She always knew what time of day it was down to the minute without ever looking at a clock, she knew when her father's trusty work truck would break down, and she was adept at choosing which horse would come in first at the County Fair—a skill she would carry into adulthood.

Initially, Lulabell's mother, Doña Eugenia, considered her daughter's powers "God's gifts." But her opinion soon changed. There came a time when Lulabell couldn't even so much as touch a Bible without feeling nauseous making prayer and Mass completely out of the question. Seeing this change in Lulabell, Doña Eugenia tried to cure her with special teas and herbs. But she only made things worse. If Lulabell's mother was trying to evict the Demon from within her soul, she was only tickling Him, for Lulabell could feel His laughter within her, and at night, in her dreams, she could hear it along with His footsteps, getting closer and closer.

Lulabell's mother's seven sisters were eventually summoned, along with a priest who still believed in the ancient art of exorcism. With one of her aunts holding down each of her limbs, the other three praying at her bedside along with the priest, and her mother crying in the corner, they all tried to exorcise the Demon from Lulabell's frail and ravaged body.

Early indications were that the exorcism had been a success. Lulabell was able to continue her Catechism, make her Confirmation, and conquer the other Sacraments as they came along. But even the rigorous religious study imposed upon her by Doña Eugenia could not fill the spot inside of Lulabell the Devil once occupied. Without Him filling her up, Lulabell felt as if the wind had been knocked out of her, like the time when she tried to do a cherry drop off the double bars at school and fell flat on her stomach.

The Devil had been laid low, there was no doubt about it. But a volcano can lie dormant for decades and still remain active. And like anything that takes a breather but doesn't go away, the Devil returned with the determination and tenacity of one making up for lost time. The Devil had taken a room within Lulabell's soul all right, and every indication was, He was renting to own.

Presently, as Lulabell slid her secret spices into a boiling pot of albóndigas, she called upon His assistance.

Gilbert entered the kitchen with a white towel around his waist. His hairless chest was particularly attractive to Lulabell. Seeing him in such a state, she more than ever wanted him to take part in the meal she had prepared. As Gilbert ate, Lulabell buttered his tortillas, and wiped the corners of his mouth when they needed it. Her breakfast guest was impressed with her culinary skills. It would not have pleased Lulabell if she knew that Gilbert was reminded of his mother's cooking back home. He didn't look more than twenty-two, and Lulabell was forty-seven—more than twice his age. Things being as such, she would not have reacted favorably to being compared to his mother in any capacity. But Gilbert would have been far less happy if he had known that Lulabell had spiked his meal with a pinch of her feces and a dash of her menstrual blood. Oh, yes. In Loo-Lee's home state of Guerrero as well as the five states which border it, this was a common method to get a man and keep him. If Gilbert had been from this part of Mexico he would have known better than to eat at the table of a strange woman. But Gilbert was a norteño, from the northern part of Mexico, a dozen states in the opposite direction.

As Gilbert scooped his last spoonful, Lulabell embarked upon another trick known as ojito y piojito. She looked deeply into Gilbert's light brown eyes as she rubbed and tugged at his thick black hair while picking at his scalp. Allegedly, this procedure was sufficient to ensure a man's dedication, but just in case, Lulabell thought it wise to snatch a few hairs from Gilbert's head. The spells which could be conducted with a patch of hair were countless. Gilbert jumped as Lulabell pulled a swatch from the crown of his head.

He dropped his spoon in his soup. "¿You got some work for me, lady?" he said.

"Your work is done," she said. With great relief Gilbert made his way to the living room and got dressed.

On the way back to the lumberyard, Lulabell slipped Gilbert a crisp fifty-dollar bill, a sum she considered reasonable, if not generous. From the look on his face, he agreed. As they pulled into the lumberyard parking lot, Lulabell asked Gilbert his area of expertise. He was an experienced layer of hardwood floors. Lulabell had always been bothered by carpet. The idea of having an unwashable fabric stuck to the floor disgusted her. After walking Gilbert back to the spot where she had found him, she moseyed into the lumberyard and sought assistance in the hardwood floor department where she bit her nails trying to come to a decision between oak and maple finishes.

El Salón de Belleza
The Beauty Salon

DONDE TODO SALE BONITO

WHERE EVERYTHING TURNS OUT BEAUTIFUL

THE AGE OF ELEGANCE

That same Wednesday morning, Natalie showed up at True-Dee's Tresses fifteen minutes shy of her scheduled appointment. "¿That you, Nat?" hollered True-Dee from the back room.

"Yep. It's me."

"Be with you in a minute. Soon's I give Miss Miranda a rinse. Iced tea in the fridge if you want some."

"No thanks," said Natalie.

She took a seat under a vacant dryer, picked up the latest issue of *Re-Vamp*® magazine, and flipped to the cover article entitled "Let's Bring Back the Beehive." The photo layout featured a full-page picture of women of every age and hair color with their hair all done up in beehives.

True-Dee high-heeled her way across the black and white checkerboard floor and out to the lobby. Miss Miranda sauntered behind, stopping every few steps to shake herself. True-Dee had just given her a triple process—a bleach, tint, and tone, making her the only platinum blonde poodle in Lava Landing, and perhaps all of Lava County.

True-Dee stopped behind Natalie and peeked over her shoulder. She put a hand over her mouth, inhaled deeply, looked Natalie in the eye, and shook her head. "Oh, no. You're not thinkin of doin that," she said, pointing at the picture in the magazine.

"Just passin time."

"It's a good thing because I got just the look for you, sister." True-Dee reached for another issue of *Re-Vamp*® and flipped through the pages. When she found what she was looking for, she held the open magazine to her chest, spoke the name of God, smiled and said, "¡Brace yourself!" She took another look at the page. "¡It's so elegant, so classy . . . so glamorous!" She held the magazine out for Natalie to see. The picture showed a girl with chin-length hair all done up in pincurls. "¿Isn't it stunnin?" said True-Dee. "No need to hide behind all that hair," she said picking up a lock of Natalie's already curly long auburn hair, then dropping it.

Even though, technically, True-Dee had been born a man, when it came to personal appearance, to the exciting world of fashion, Natalie trusted True-Dee's opinion second only to Consuelo's. Natalie, like Dolly Parton, had often thought that if she had been born a man, she would have been a drag queen. With these sentiments in mind, Natalie said, "Do with me what you will."

True-Dee led Natalie to the chair. She picked up a smock with two of her French-manicured fingernails and wrapped it around Natalie. Miss Miranda lay down on the floor at the foot of the chair. "Problem with the world is this," said True-Dee grabbing her scissors and pointing them at Natalie. "There is just no femininity left. I tell you, sister, the age of elegance is dead and gone and nobody's even mournin. I haven't heard of anybody out there lookin for the next Greta Garbo either. ¿Have you?" True-Dee didn't give Natalie a chance to answer. "¿You see what the girls are wearin nowadays? Jeans and tennis shoes. I'm tryin to do my part to bring some pride back to the female species one head at a time. But it's downright shameful what's occurred. No sense of pride, no sense of fashion. ¿Whatever on earth is next? Sister, you are a sight for sore eyes." True-Dee stood back and admired Nat from afar.

"That's what I like to see. Two things that define a lady, a decent handbag and quality shoes," said True-Dee admiring both.

Natalie caressed her handbag, then said, "Clothes come and go, but a purse is forever. And when it comes to bein a lady, good manners don't hurt either."

"They sure don't," concurred True-Dee, but she couldn't take her eyes off of Nat's shoes. She whistled, then said, "Quality craftsmanship and fashion united. ¿Wherever on earth did you get them snazzy platforms?"

"Me and Consuelo got them last summer on sale at Leroy's."

"¿Consuelo? ¿However on earth is that girl? ¿She ever get rid of them split ends of hers?"

"Far as I know."

"Those things are worse than fleas once the initial infestation sets in. Tell her to come and see me. You two are quite a duo. Makes it tough on the rest of us gals, if you know what I mean."

Natalie looked down. Her hair was scattered all over the floor. She wanted to see what she looked like, but True-Dee kept all the mirrors in her salon hidden behind heavy hot pink velvet curtains. There was nothing she anticipated more than the look on a client's face during the "unveiling." It was that moment that True-Dee felt the most gratification in her line of work.

"About forgot to tell you. Racine's sold enough Mary Kay® to get one of them snazzy new pink Cadillacs. Sister, we're gonna ride in style now."

Natalie was glad she hadn't contributed to Racine's success. There were few things Natalie liked less than mail-order cosmetics.

"Just about through with you," said True-Dee fluffing Natalie's curls. "Let's ask Miss Miranda what she thinks." The blonde poodle got to her feet, raised her ears, and wagged her tail. "Miss Miranda likes what she sees." True-Dee pulled a hot pink tasseled drawstring and revealed a mirror. She swung Natalie around and said, "Take a look at the real you."

"It feels weird without all that hair," said Natalie shaking her head. Her hair ringleted around her heart-shaped face bringing out her light brown eyes, and emphasizing the sprinkling of freckles across her nose. True-Dee put her hands over her mouth momentarily, then reached for a tissue from a poised box of Kleenex®. She dabbed at the corners of her eyes and announced, "You don't like it."

"Sure I do," said Natalie reaching across to give True-Dee a hug.

"Me and Miss Miranda wouldn't be able to sleep if we thought you didn't. Why we think you look as pretty as Ava Gardner."

"Thanks," said Natalie. She paid True-Dee and gave her a hearty tip.

"Tell all your friends to bring their messes to True-Dee's Tresses," True-Dee shouted as Natalie headed for the door.

Natalie turned around to see True-Dee standing in the doorway holding the screen door open. As she opened her car door, Natalie heard her say, "Stay in touch, sister. Us girls got to stick together."

El Volcán y Su Reina

The Volcano and His Queen

CADA VOLCÁN, SU REINA

TO EACH VOLCANO, HIS QUEEN

WHERE THE LAVA LANDED

April May had been named Miss Magma of Lava County for nine years straight and running, but not for any of the usual reasons. April May was ugly, but in a third-grade sort of way, which is to say, the kind of ugly she had looked like it might be outgrown. But at the age of twenty-six, April May was only getting uglier. Her freckles continued to multiply, her teeth became more crooked with time, her skin more pimple-ridden, and her feet had never stopped growing. Her eyes were big and bright blue, but the irises and whites were extremely disproportionate to one another, favoring the latter. April May was so pale her veins showed through her skin like a black bra beneath a white T-shirt. If ugly and time were having a race, ugly was clearly winning.

What made April May Miss Magma for so long wasn't beauty or even her funny name. (Miss Magma had stuck her head out into the world at 11:59 p.m. one April the thirtieth, but it wasn't until 12:00 a.m. May the first that she had fully exited the birth canal.) It was April May's hair that made her so hot. She had the brightest, reddest hair in all of Lava County. So, when the would-be float-riding, crowd-waving, tiara-wearing, bikini-clad contestants came out and strutted their augmented stuff, the judges were less than impressed. Sure, the ladies later appeared in the panel's private thoughts, but it looked like no one could dethrone April May as queen of Lava County. There was something about all that red hair spilling out of the crater and onto the side of the volcano float every year during the Lava County Labor Day Parade that got the judges every time.

Now Miss Magma was not without talent. She was an expert roller skater who made her living at the Lava Landing Roller Palace where she emceed the

Hokey-Pokey, Redlight-Greenlight, and other rink classics. She reprimanded gum chewers and speed skaters, and taught the willing how to jump, spin, and rex, regardless of their abilities. So after the bikini-ed blondes came out and sang their songs and twirled their batons, and the brunettes winked and wiggled to tropical music, April May would come out in her one-piece with the red, orange, and yellow flames shooting up the side, the same one she wore every year, and she would do a skate-dance routine to the 1957 Billy Lee Riley rockabilly hit "Red Hot," which aptly stated "My gal is red hot, your gal ain't doodley-squat."

April May was always last to exhibit her talent. The moment of truth would come. The would-be beauty queens would cross their fingers and flash their expensive smiles, then one by one carefully curtsy so as not lose their imaginary halos. April May, for her part, would peel back her lavender lips and show her crooked teeth, then fluff her fiery hair. The drums would roll and the blondes and brunettes (redheads knew better than to go against April May and her head of hair) would bow their heads and pinch the bridges of their noses. And when the judges would announce that once again April May had been named Miss Magma of Lava County, the losing contestants would ball up their fists and show their chagrin. Some would break out into tears, causing their less than Marathon® mascara to run down their cheeks.

April May's nine-year stint as Miss Magma had immortalized her. But ¿was it really enough to have one's name and accomplishments in the County Annals? Lava County wasn't called that without reason.

The county was located at the base of a dormant volcano known as El Condenado and was made up of three municipalities: Craterville, Caldera, and Lava Landing. The volcano had been born one afternoon in 1837 back when Lava Landing was known as San Narciso and was situated in California, then a part of the Mexican Republic. The city had been named for a priest famous for his ability to predict the outbreak of disease and natural disasters, and infamous for his undue familiarity with the village women.

Legend had it that one night as Padre Narciso lay in the arms of one of his mistresses, Jesus came to him in a dream, dressed as a peasant, wearing huaraches, and with His hair in two braids. Jesus didn't say anything. He just filled His cheeks with air, pointed to a smoking hole in the ground, clapped His hands, then fell over. Upon waking, Padre Narciso knew a volcano was on the way.

By sunset that very same day, the volcano measured twenty meters in height. The volcano grew exponentially, rising to over four hundred meters within a week.

The town eventually had to be moved out of Harm's way. The people

fig. 1 TIMELINE OF THE VOLCANO

1857 El Condenado goes dormant.

1849 California Gold Rush

1848 Mexican-American War ends. California and
all or parts of nine other states are ceded to U.S.

1846 Mexican-American War begins.

1841 City of Las Sergas becomes the
municipality of San Narciso.

1838 First major eruption followed by mass
exodus to Altamira, 20 miles away. Townspeople
promptly name the volcano El Condenado.

1837 June 14, volcano emerges, becoming
the second new volcano to be formed in
the Americas during Historical Time.

1837 June 13, Narciso predicts a volcano.

1834 Narciso enters priesthood.

1832 Narciso fathers first child.

1830 Narciso enters the Seminario Diocesano.

1821 Mexico gains independence from Spain.

1819 Narciso accurately predicts livestock outbreak at the age of five.

MEXICO

1813 Narciso Gómez Polanco born December 14 at Las Sergas

1887 Padre Narciso makes series of deathbed predictions.

1888 Death of Padre Narciso

1902 City of San Narciso is renamed Lava Landing.

1917 First Lava Landing Labor Day Parade

1921 Parade committee votes to include the
selection of a beauty queen. They agree to call
the title "Miss Magma."

1923 First Miss Magma, Beatrice Arnold, is crowned.

1942 Labor Day Parade canceled; U.S. at war

1953 Miss Magma, Ailene Stuart, is stripped
of her crown when it is discovered that
she was pregnant during competition.

1973 First meeting of "Doomsday Cult," Sons
and Daughters of San Narciso

1982 Lava Landing adopts Orizaba, Veracruz, as Sister City.

1984 Lava Landing Little League team, the Vulcanologists,
falls one game shy of reaching Little League World Series.

took to calling it El Condenado, which, in its most savory translation, means the God-forsaken one. They had lost so many cows, pigs, mules, horses, donkeys, and chickens to its eruptions.

And then one day, perhaps two years after, the volcano just went to sleep. No one, not even Padre Narciso, could explain why. Volcanoes are crazy that way. But since San Narciso was a town full of beautiful women, and the men naturally spent their spare time serenading them, the people came to believe that it was all the serenatas that had eventually lulled the volcano to sleep.

By the time April May won her first title, El Condenado had been dormant for more than 150 years. But a dormant volcano is not an extinct one, meaning that the volcano could wake up one day and wipe out all of Lava County, taking its archives and April May's notoriety along with it.

Like its predecessor, Lava Landing was known for two things: pretty women and mariachis. This gave April May solace, because she, like countless others around town, believed that it was all of that sweet mariachi music that kept the volcano sound asleep. Needless to say, she was more than a little worried when banda gained in popularity for she was sure that the tuba y tambora that banda is famous for would wake the volcano up. April May only asked for one more title, to bring her reign to a full decade. With this goal in mind, she behaved herself as best she could, and prayed on a nightly basis to someone known as God Who sometimes went by Jesus, and all of His highest-ranking Saints and Angels.

La Mano

The Hand

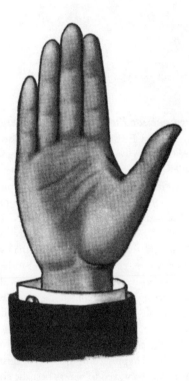

LA MANO DE UN CRIMINAL

THE HAND OF A CRIMINAL

LUCHA'S RELEASE

Javier waited outside the administrative wing of the Lava County Women's Correctional Facility, pacing and checking his watch more often than necessary. The two weeks leading up to Lucha's release had passed with uncharacteristic slowness and had been riddled with unrivaled anticipation. Javier had looked more forward to it than even a church gathering. His limited experience with bureaucracies told him that the process would take some time, and he was anxious to whisk her off to services at the Church of God and His Son Jesus Christ. Javier recognized salvation as a time-consuming pursuit, and he intended to get cracking on Lucha's soul ASAP.

Javier held a bag of clothes for the soon-to-be-released. He had spent two agonizing, indecisive hours in the women's department of the Lava Landing Kmart trying to find something suitable for Lucha, and nearly another hour second-guessing her size. He finally decided on a peach-colored, ankle-grazing, rayon dress, and a white cotton cardigan.

Javier looked through the prison panes to see Lucha as she was led down the hall in handcuffs. He pressed his nose up against the window. Catching a glimpse of Javier, Lucha waved to him as best she could.

Javier was finally let in, frisked, then led to a corner office where Lucha was already waiting. It was dull and dank in there. A robust prison secretary sat behind a steel fortress of a desk. She already had the proper paperwork in order.

Javier signed on the dotted line, and Lucha emerged a free woman, even though she was on probation. ("Conditions of Lucha's Probation" follows this chapter.)

Javier handed Lucha the blue plastic bag he had been holding on to all morning.

"Thank you," said Lucha. The bag was wet with sweat around the handles. She rushed off to the bathroom to change.

Those clothes were way too big for her. She looked as if she had gained twenty pounds, and her sweater hung in bulky cuffs at her wrists. Notwithstanding, Javier took one look at her and his cheeks turned bright red. "You look pretty," he said.

"Thanks. Now take me to eat. The food in this joint tastes like shit."

"First we go to church. Today is the day of the Sabbath. We must keep it holy. But after, I will take you to the restaurant of your choice," said Javier opening the door for her.

"Right," agreed Lucha. She had little say in the matter.

Once they boarded the Monte Carlo, Lucha slid up close to Javier. She had been incarcerated ninety-two days, had served just a little over half of her six-month sentence. The jury was convinced that Lucha had only been Cheque's accomplice in the making of tacos, burritos, tortas, and the like, but they did manage to convict her of Eluding an Officer, in the third degree. In addition to her six-month sentence, she would be making payments on a $1,000 fine and performing two hundred hours of community service.

Lucha had been looking forward to short-term pleasure for what seemed a long time. She stroked Javier's thick, wavy black hair. Javier hadn't the faintest idea what to do, and it didn't help that La Lucha was looking at him with those big brown eyes either. Javier'd never been so come-hithered. In his nervousness, he turned on the radio. Out popped a romantic ranchera. Lucha sang along, her caresses keeping rhythm with the languid beat. Javier switched to talk radio. Lucha said it bored her and she laid her head in his lap. Around that time, they pulled into the church parking lot.

Lucha stayed put with her head in Javier's lap even after he killed the engine. "Sister Lucha, I need to ask you something."

"Go right ahead." She gazed straight up at him.

Javier stared down at her and swallowed hard. "¿Just what were you in the Lava County Women's Correctional Facility for? ¿What was your crime?"

"Oh that," she said sitting up. "Just tryin to outrun the cops. It was no big deal."

"I suppose it could have been worse," concluded Javier, then he raced around to Lucha's side, and opened the door for her in a way he imagined a gentleman might. But the truth of the matter was this: Javier didn't know so much about men, much less gentlemen. In the absence of his father, Javier had always tried to be the man of the house, and in so doing, didn't have much chance to be a boy, or an adolescent, and having skipped so many steps along the way, Javier was left feeling around in the dark for the light switch when it came to that ever evasive thing called being a man. And now he had embarked upon the delicate ritual of courtship, even though the only thing Javier would readily admit to courting was Lucha's soul.

They entered the church arm in arm. The other Mariachis de Dos Nacimientos were already there and had saved them a seat in the foremost pew. The choir was in the midst of its opening hymns. Lucha sang along, nary missing a word. It should have come as no surprise. Mariachi de Dos Nacimientos were not the first missionaries to enter the women's correctional facility.

The pastor noticed a new face amongst the parishioners, and approached Lucha intent on welcoming her. Javier beat him to it. He stood and addressed the congregation. "Brothers and Sisters, I am proud to introduce a new member of our most holy church. Lucha is here to accept Jesus Christ as her Savior and to walk in the light of the Lord."

Amens echoed throughout the parish.

"She has renounced her once evil ways," said Javier with an inflection fit a missionary.

"Thanks be to God," declared an unidentified worshiper.

"On this day, the very day she was released from the women's correctional facility, she has come to the side of the Lord."

Hallelujahs, Amens, Praise the Lords, and Thanks be to Gods tumbled from mouths everywhere.

Lucha threw herself to the floor, then crawled to the large crucifix at the head of the church. She begged the Lord to accept her as one of His children and to forgive her sins, which were many and varied.

After, she rose to her feet and led the entire church as they sang "Just a Closer Walk with Thee." As she walked up and down the aisles shaking hands with the devout of whom she was now amongst their ranks, Javier had this great revelation: Lucha would be the next singer for Mariachi de Dos Nacimientos.

Several gospel songs later, Lucha took the podium and delivered the following extemporaneous, yet moving speech:

The Devil's ways are myriad as are sins of the flesh
The world is full of temptation and runnin low on holiness
But the Lord is my Savior now and forever
With His strength I will succeed and join Him in Heaven
A sinner I once was
But now I know Jesus
His commandments to the wayside I threw
My sins were many and my virtues few

Now I have seen the light
To the Lord I run, from the Devil I fly

She had also learned to write poetry in prison. Tears flooded the faces of various parishioners. Lucha returned to her pew and bowed her head in feigned quiet contemplation. The pastor resumed the podium, thanked Lucha for her inspirational words, then excused the gathered.

Once inside the Monte Carlo and homeward bound, Lucha snuggled up to Javier and hung her head on his shoulder. He rubbed her temples to ease the fatigue he assumed she suffered subsequent to her interlude with the Holy Spirit.

When they arrived curbside in front of her home, Lucha embraced Javier tenderly, and said, "Thank you so much for all you've done for me." She broke away from him slowly, but stopped to give him a soft, closed-lips kiss on the lips. This display of understated affection required a great deal of restraint on her part. She was immensely attracted to the handsome Javier, who reminded her in appearance of the great Mexican actor Manuel López Ochoa. Ochoa had captivated her mind during most of her prison escapades with her cellmate, Eusebia, making them bearable, if not enjoyable. Eusebia was as ugly as her name, but she had a way with the pads of her fingers that Lucha found physically pleasing.

"Bye," said Lucha. She slammed the Chevy door and headed up the steps that led to her family home. A lesser man might have asked for her phone number. But Javier knew what he had to do. As he drove off, he had this one satisfaction, along with the kiss which lingered upon his lips, the shivery stomach that accompanied it, and an intense approaching gravity of the task that lay ahead.

IN THE CRIMINAL COURT OF *LAVA LANDING, LAVA CA.*

STATE OF

VS   NO: 21085

Lucha Monossa Gomez
DEFENDANT

Conditions of Lucha's Probation

ORDER

• You shall report to your Probation Officer each month or as instructed by your Officer. You will make a full and truthful report to your Probation Officer on the form provided for that purpose or as instructed by your Officer.

• You will pay to the State or County supervision fees in a specified amount as determined by the court.

• You will not change your residence or employment or leave the County or State of your residence without first obtaining the consent of your Probation Officer.

• You will not use any intoxicants to excess or possess any illegal drugs or narcotics unless prescribed by a physician.

• You will not visit places where intoxicants, drugs, or other dangerous substances are unlawfully sold, dispensed, or used.

• You will not possess, carry, or own any firearms or weapons.

• You will not associate with any persons engaging in criminal activities.

• You will submit to urinalysis, Brethalyzer, or blood tests as directed by your supervising Probation Officer to determine the presence or use of alcohol, drugs, or controlled substances.

• You will live without violating the law. A conviction in a court of law shall not be necessary to constitute a violation of your probation.

• You will maintain gainful, lawful employment and support any dependents to the best of your ability.

• You will promptly and truthfully answer all inquiries directed to you by the court and your Probation Officer

• You will allow the Officer to visit you in your home, at your employment site, or elsewhere, and you will comply with all instructions given by your Officer.

IT IS THEREFORE ORDERED, ADJUDGED AND DECREED that the petition filed herein be, and the same is GRANTED.

ENTERED this _14_ day of _June_ _____ 20_15_

_____
JUDGE

FILED_____

El Queso Grande

The Big Cheese

EL QUE MANDA

HE WHO CALLS THE SHOTS

THE BIG CHEESE PLANT

The following Tuesday was the third of the month, and as such, it was tour day at The Big Cheese Plant. That afternoon, Natalie and Consuelo were to lead Mrs. Burnette's second-grade class on a tour of the place. The children would have much preferred a trip to Lava Land, the nearby theme park, for their year-end school outing, but things had been tight for the district.

Very little significant retail construction had gone up in Lava Landing in more than five years. This wasn't good for the school district, which got most of its funding from building permits. Sure there was the occasional housing going up here and there, but Craterville and Caldera had gotten a new Target and Wal-Mart, respectively. It seemed things were growing all around, but in Lava Landing the only things that grew were the vegetables in the fields and the fruits and nuts on the trees.

Downtown, there was the usual retail upheaval. The Knickknack Shoppe had gone under to be replaced by a cartoon character specialty shop. The Bingo Supply Store stood next to the movie theater, and next to that, the Western Store, the bowling alley with its attached coffee shop, Benny's Pawn 'n' Go, Leroy's Footwear and Apparel, True-Dee's Tresses, El Aguantador nightclub where you could dance the night away in Spanish, and The Big Five-Four where you could do it in English and Spanish. At one end of Main Street was the indoor swap meet which featured a panadería, frutería, tortillería, a florería, and several discotecas and jewelers, and next to that, El Charrito Market. The placita, all green and well groomed with a gazebo as its centerpiece, stood on the other side of the street. To one end of the plaza was a small office building which held an insurance company and a small law practice. There was a drugstore—Whapple's Drugs—the Nothing Over 99 Cents store, Taquería La Bamba, Discoteca El Indito, neighbored by its English-speaking counterpart, Big Al's Records, Panadería Mazatlán, Gunnels, a secondhand store, Sew Sweet, a sewing and notions shop, and Roscoe's. On a parallel street stood St. Mary's Church, and across the street from that, a bike shop.

Further away from Main Street were the county buildings, and in front of them, The Weenie Wagon. Once you headed out of town and toward the volcano, you would find La Kmart, La Family Bargain Center, K&S Market, The Church of God and His Son Jesus Christ, Calderón Garage and Tire-ía, the Humongous Bargain One Dollar Store, Eduardo's Furniture, the Lava Landing Roller Palace, a series of fruit stands, the flea market, Lava Land, the County Dump, and, eventually, The Big Cheese Plant.

The Big Cheese Plant was inspired by the Pennsylvania barn and was painted red and white. All of its accompanying structures followed this lead, except for the gift shop, which was stuccoed in the volcano's likeness. The BCP did not stand alone. Its cohorts included a gift shop, fruit stand, ice cream and candy shop complete with an old-fashioned taffy stretcher, a café, home of an alleged cup flipper, a playground, petting zoo, and a series of bathrooms. A makeshift locomotive motored around the green grounds. There was a small pond complete with many mosquitoes, a great quantity of axolotls, and an occasional duck separated the playground from the snack bar. All things considered, The Big Cheese Plant was not such an unlikely field trip destination.

The Lava Landing Grammar School bus had already parked in the lot beyond the Processing, Cutting, and Packaging Plant and the kids had begun to disembark. Natalie and Consuelo were bonneted and waiting in their light pink sanitary slickers and rubber boots. The girls shook Mrs. Burnette's hand while the children pointed and laughed. Natalie and Consuelo were used to that kind of grade school ridicule. They had been leading tours for five of the ten years they had worked at the BCP.

The children, and their entourage of adults, were off the bus. "¡Into the vats!" announced Natalie.

The kids marched behind Natalie mimicking her clumsy rubber boot gait, while Consuelo brought up the back of the line.

First stop, the Sanitary Station where Natalie and Consuelo handed out light blue and pink slickers, bonnets, and boots as if they were roller skates before a Saturday afternoon session.

Once the children and their various guides were scrubbed down and otherwise sanitized, the procession proceeded into the vats. It was pure stainless steel for as far as the eye could see.

As the children moaned their surprise, Natalie got perky with her presentation. "Each day at The Big Cheese Plant we produce two thousand pounds of cheese." Consuelo randomly translated Natalie's commentary into Spanish.

"In order to make two thousand pounds of cheese, we need twenty thousand pounds of milk," continued Natalie.

"That is an amount equal to about ten thousand Super Big Gulp® sized Slurpee®s," said Consuelo. It was true. Natalie, Consuelo, Cal McDaniel—the owner of The Big Cheese Plant—and a calculator had collaborated on the math.

The children ooed and awed.

The Big Cheese Plant used open vatting, enabling everyone to see things mixing and churning right before their eyes. The children got close. A big, fat, bald, mustached man was pumping milk into the vats. He gave his first five volunteers a hand at holding the hose.

"A bacteria is introduced into the milk," said Natalie. She had to shout to conquer the noise in the place—imagine the sound of a hundred Maytag®s stuck in their spin cycle.

"Bacteria gives you cancer," announced a child. She was tall and lanky, her brown hair bluntly bobbed.

"No," said Natalie raising a finger in the air. "Some bacteria can make you sick, but not all bacteria is bad. Especially not our bacteria. Cal McDaniel, our head cheesemaker, graduated from the Wisconsin Center for Dairy Research where he was named a Wisconsin Master Cheesemaker®. He knows what he's doin.'"

"I want to be a cheesemaker when I grow up," said a little boy. He was shorter than the rest of the kids, with red hair, freckles of the same color, and the sort of distinct look he would never outgrow.

Natalie bent down to his level and said, "I'll grab you an application on the way out." He swallowed hard.

The mass advanced. The floor was concrete with pink and blue rubber daisy nonslip decals every few inches. "We introduce an enzyme into the milk which helps it change from a liquid to a solid," said Natalie.

The kids kicked one another with their rubber boots, peeled off their bonnets and flung them by their elastic bands. The premeditated presentation had hit its usual low. Aside from the redheaded future cheesemaker, the group had lost interest.

The children would have to wait until the Alfomatic® for more hands-on fun. In the meantime, Natalie talked more about enzymes and an important cheese-making substance called rennet, which consists of a mucous membrane from the stomach of a calf.

They reached the curd station where Natalie stuck a hand down into the viscosity consisting of certain distinct curds and a lesser substance known as whey.

"Whey is a cheese-making by-product often found in candy bars," explained Consuelo in English and Spanish. Children and adults alike wrinkled their noses. The stench at the station was unbearable.

At last, they came upon the Alfomatic® where the children were allowed to participate in the draining and salting of the curds. Everyone was industrious, putting their sanitary attire to good use, but there was something sad about seeing those children who should rightfully have been two to a seat climbing the volcano on the roller coaster at Lava Land up to their elbows in a mixture of curds and whey.

Next stop, the Block Forming Tower. But it was no tower at all. Just a bunch of waiting molds on a stainless steel assembly line. The line did go up, up, and away, somewhere out of sight. Perhaps the tower lay on the other side. Neither Natalie nor Consuelo knew. They had never gone that far.

"Here we fill the molds," said Consuelo.

"Just like makin Jell-O®," said Natalie picking up a stainless steel pitcher, then dumping its contents into a waiting mold. "Easy as pie."

The children were all given a turn. It was the final leg of the tour. On their way out, everyone was stripped of their sanitary slickers and given a complimentary pound of the cheese of their choice. Amongst Cheddar, Monterey Jack, Havarti, Pepper Jack, Swiss, and Mozzarella, Pepper Jack was a clear favorite.

As the guests made their way to the picnic tables, Nat and Sway headed for the break room. Against the west wall stood a huge three-hundred-gallon aquarium. With neither clay castle, nor faux flora waving in its waters, it was an ugly aquatic statement. The aquarium was filled to the hilt with guppies, who were the axolotls' favorite snack. Nat and Sway grabbed a pitcher apiece, took turns filling up with guppies, then stepped outside.

The pond had been Cal's idea, but the axolotls were solely Nat and Sway's doing. They were introduced to their first specimen by the reptile man during a routine visit to the flea market. The girls were so taken by the handsome axolotl with its big happy face worthy of cartoon characterization, its tiny eyes, feathery gills, and its little hands and feet so disproportionate to its robust belly and capable tail, that they promptly talked the reptile man down from his twelve-dollar asking price, to their ten-dollar purchase price. Their money in hand, the reptile man plopped the infant axolotl into an empty clam dip container, instructed them to feed her flake food, then wished them luck. And so began Nat and Sway's love affair. Consuelo took it upon herself to call the tiny creature Chiníquina—the first thing that flew off the top of her head—which meant absolutely nothing, but sounded "darned purty." They poured her into a vacant goldfish bowl that same afternoon, whispered sweet nothings to her for six months before they truly discovered her magic.

At the library they read up on her species and in so doing discovered the story "Axolotl" by an Argentinian writer, Julio Cortázar. It was a tale open to interpretation about a man who had bonded with, was somehow tied to, or had somehow become an axolotl. Which they weren't sure, but Natalie and Consuelo read it to one another in awe over cups of hot chocolate in the dead of summer. There was something mysterious about the story, about the axolotl itself, that gave them goose bumps.

Shortly thereafter, the girls convinced Cal to fill his cheese-side pond with axolotls. It was an easy task since they were cheaper per specimen than the Japanese koi with which Cal had originally intended to stock the pond.

Natalie and Consuelo approached the pond. The axolotls had been there for more than five years and had multiplied several fold. And though it had been extremely difficult, Nat and Sway had even retired Chiníquina to the pond where they were sure she still lurked in its muddy waters. Surrounded by grassy knolls upon which to picnic, the pond's rim was made of polished rock which jutted out just enough to form some semblance of a bench. Nat and Sway had a seat, leaned over, and dumped the guppies into the water. The axolotls subsisted almost entirely on whey—that smelly cheese-making by-product that was pumped into their pond twice daily. But the guppies were by far their favorite food item.

The axolotls bobbed to the surface, then floated, waiting for a guppy to get close enough to gulp. *Ambystoma mexicanum* was their Latin name. The creatures, native to Lakes Xochimilco and Chalco, near Mexico City, had once been sold in great quantities at market. A soup is still made of them in the greater reaches and depths of the same region. Prized by science for their robust embryos and healing powers, they can even regenerate a limb. But most interesting to science is the fact that the axolotl exhibits the phenomenon known as neoteny, making it no ordinary amphibian, since it does not metamorphose. Rather, it lives its entire life in its larval stage.

Nat and Sway were so busy watching the feeding frenzy, they didn't notice Thomas, the redheaded aspirant cheesemaker, who was sitting right next to them. "¿What are you doing?" he said. He was eight going on nine, Natalie and Consuelo would have guessed.

"We're watchin our friends the axolotls," said Nat.

"¿What are they?" he said. He couldn't take his eyes off Natalie.

"An axolotl is an animal that doesn't change into what nature first intended it to be. It's like a child that gets bigger, but doesn't grow up. It doesn't metamorphose and as such it's neotenous." Natalie was chewing gum and she blew a big, fat bubble.

"¿What's metamorphose mean?" said Thomas.

"That's when somethin changes from one form to another. Like a caterpillar changes into a butterfly." Natalie rubbed his head, smacked her gum, and smiled big at him.

He smiled big too, and shuffled his feet.

"Speakin of metamorphosis, today's Tuesday," said Consuelo. "We gotta get home and rest up for tonight."

"That's right," said Natalie. The girls would be heading out to El Aguantador nightclub later that evening, along with their friend Lulabell, to root for True-Dee, who was set to make her debut as Thalía in the show transvestis.

Nat and Sway headed for the lunchroom to retrieve their time cards and punch out. As they walked off, Thomas looked so sad at their departure, Consuelo leaned in and whispered to Nat, "I bet that boy goes crazy for the first girl he comes across that reminds him of you."

Consuelo might very well have had a point. A little boy can fall in love at any age.

Everyday outfit with
striped *enredo* (wraparound skirt)

943

The axolotl *(Ambystoma mexicanum)* is an amphibian belonging to the Caudata/Urodela order of the salamander family. Carnivorous with typical carnivore anatomy except for its pedicalate (short, cone-shaped) teeth, it grips and positions its prey before swallowing it whole. Its heart is three-chambered. Like all amphibians, the axolotl is poikilothermic—its body temperature is determined by its surroundings.

The axolotl is neotenic, living its entire life in larval form, never undergoing metamorphosis. The most circulated theory regarding this metamorphic failure contends that at one point during its existence, the axolotl found its aquatic environment so stable and relatively benign, the easiest way for it to avoid the harsh surrounding terrestrial habitat was to forgo metamorphosis altogether.

Endangered in its native habitat but bred in high numbers in captivity, the axolotl is an asset to the scientific community. Its embryos are large and robust, making them relatively easy to handle under laboratory conditions. And while other animals depend upon the growth of scar tissue to heal their wounds, an axolotl can actually regenerate a limb or even part of its brain.

Your typical axolotl is fully aquatic, but does possess a set of rudimentary lungs and is known to rise occasionally to the surface for a gulp of air. And though it is extremely rare, some axolotls do metamorphose into a creature resembling the Mexican subspecies of the tiger salamander, *Abystoma mavortium valasci*. In this metamorphosed form, the axolotl is no longer merely aquatic but is free to roam on land and, some may contend, to be preyed upon by the world, or, seen in another light, to conquer and establish new habitats.

Samantha Borgnine
Curator, Axolotl Colony at Clearwater University

Tabla 2

THE DECK *is* SHUFFLED

El Ajolote
The Axolotl

NO TIENE BARBA PERO MIRA QUÉ BIGOTE

HE HAS NO BEARD, BUT LOOK AT THAT MUSTACHE

NEOTENY VS. METAMORPHOSIS

Natalie turned onto Main Street. She was in the company of Consuelo and Lulabell, the mother of their grade-school (and beyond) class-mate, Javier. To say that Nat and Sway were friends with Lulabell would have been an understatement. The trio had been playing bingo together ever since Nat and Sway could pass for eighteen, the legal bingo-playing age in the County of Lava, and nothing seals a friendship like bingo. Lulabell might have had twenty years on Nat and Sway, but she was like el pino, Number 49 of La Lotería: fresca, olorosa, y en todo tiempo hermosa, which is to say, fresh, fragrant, and always lovely.

The women were on their way to El Aguantador—the Mexican dance club/bar/taquería in town with the mechanical bull, smiles that yielded gold-and silver-capped teeth, beer posters with dark-skinned beauties, men with cowboy boots and hats, fancy belts, jeans, and gold jewelry, women with rayon dresses, long curly hair, or las chicas vaqueras with their pantalones Wrangler®, fancy belts and boots, just like their male counterparts, except for the frilly blouses, a banda, a conjunto norteño, a grupo, mariachis that some-times showed up and sometimes didn't, video screens showing cockfights and rodeos, un show transvestis, y un bikini show. The bar served beer in bottles with lime slices stuffed into their lips, tequila, and margaritas, Nescafé® if you drank too much of the former, and Squirt® if you drank none. Nothing else. At El Aguantador you could win the cumbia, quebradita, hombre más sexy, or the Million Dollar Legs contest, depending on the day of the week, or where your talents lay.

The women walked into El Aguantador, one behind the other, with Lula-bell at the lead, then took a table near the dance floor. The mesera arrived and placed a white square napkin on the table in front of each of the women, then said the obligatory, "¿Algo para tomar?" They ordered three Modelo® beers.

No sooner did their Modelo®s arrive than there was a drum roll and further dimming of what little light the place held. A man dressed in a light blue polyester suit and with a microphone in his hand welcomed all of the damas y caballeros to another noche del espectáculo.

The first female impersonator of the evening strutted out from behind the pink satin curtain. She wore a gold lamé fishtail hem spaghetti strap dress and high heels, and quickly cut into Laura León's hit "Acapulco." The audience clapped along to the cumbia while Ms. León scanned the crowd, searching the assembly of Stetson®s for a stray Señor to rub up against. She chose one of the front-row watchers, an all-cowboyed-out vato with a generous mustache, a macho man por cierto.

She cumbia-ed up to him, her breasts doing the majority of the to-ing and fro-ing, and placed her makeshift boobis right under the macho man's nose. He sat still for a moment, but anticipation soon got the best of him. He grabbed her by the shoulders and covered his nose and mouth with her chichis, then did his best to suck on them while she shook them for all they were worth, which was plenty—they were the result of a combined hormone and silicone regimen. Laura León turned her routine around, performing a lap dance with her backside in front of the mustached man before she headed back to the stage to lip-sync the rest of the song.

The macho man reached for a waiting shot of tequila, drank it down, then let out a grito.

Go figure. All those men watching a bunch of guys parading as ladies and enjoying it. Natalie and Consuelo had tried to figure out that contradiction on numerous occasions. All of the major Mexican bars in the tri-city area that was Lava County had a well-attended show transvestis. ¿How, wondered Nat and Sway, did they do it? I mean, Mexican men are amongst the most macho, ¿qué no? The girls had concluded that the only way a woman could be that sexy, i.e., as sexy as the transvestites, and not be called a slut or worse, was either by having her own telenovela, or by being a man. And when the men all went out to see the sex-spectacular show that was el show transvestis, they didn't feel the need to stuff dollar bills in the performer's panties, or even make up excuses for their wives or girlfriends whom they always left conveniently waiting at home. They were, after all, going out to watch a bunch of men perform, at least chromosomically speaking.

After Laura León took her finishing bows, there was yet another drum roll, followed by the announcement that damas y caballeros alike had a special treat in store, an all-new act featuring Mexico's very own, very lovely, and very talented Thalía. The crowd roared. They couldn't wait to get a glimpse of Mexico's most beloved telenovela star turned singing sensation turned telenovela star.

True-Dee emerged. She was wearing a salmon-colored, ostrich-feather-adorned bikini with a tiara on her head to match. Nat, Sway, and Lulabell stood tall and applauded. True-Dee's hair (actually it was a wig) was dirty blonde and swept up into a French twist. In that manifestation, she did look a lot like Thalía as she lip-synced and wiggled to "Amor a la Mexicana."

When the instrumental section of the song arrived, True-Dee writhed her way over to the audience and got up close with a middle-aged man in a silky, yellow western-tailored shirt. True-Dee looked him in the eye, dipped two fingertips into her panties, removed the ostrich feather fan that rested there, then began to wave it directly in front of his face. She grabbed his bottle of beer, took a swig, and let some spill down into the valley of her cleavage, then leaned over and offered that man a drink. He obliged. After the drinking was done, True-Dee cumbia-ed up to the stage where she gave the audience a backside view. She had forgotten the words to the song, but no one seemed to mind as they watched her shake her nalgas back and forth as she made her way across the stage. Her thong rode high as she took her finishing bow from the same position.

The crowd clapped, it cheered, it raised its drinks in the air, then drank. Nat, Sway, and Lulabell wasted no time. They got to their feet and headed backstage to congratulate True-Dee on a job well done.

It was dark back there, and humid. The entire place had benefited from a woman's touch and the ingenuity that a lack of money requires. There were makeshift dressing areas with lime green velvet curtains, makeup stations with many-bulbed overhead fixtures, and mirrors everywhere. The concrete floor was painted black, the brick walls of the old building, blood red.

True-Dee stood in one of the dressing areas with the curtain only partially drawn—she had never been very modest. She emerged in a flash wearing her street clothes: a red and white gingham baby doll dress.

"You were breathtaking," said Natalie giving True-Dee a hearty hug.

"¿You really think so, hon?"

"We know so," said Nat, Sway, and Lulabell.

"Well that's just terrific, because they've promised me the role of Paulina Rubio to boot," said True-Dee, her tone rising accordingly—¡Paulina Rubio was Mexico's hottest pop star!

"You girls are a sight for sore eyes," said True-Dee taking time to hug each of the three women. "Fore I forget, havin me a Tupperware® party this Saturday and I expect y'all to come. Let me give you the invite."

She rushed off to her dressing area and returned with a fuchsia background leopard print bag into which she dipped her acrylic nails and came out with three different-colored pastel envelopes.

Nat, Sway, and Lulabell took them in hand and said thanks.

"Oh, you have to open them right now," said True-Dee balling her fists up.

The women did just that to reveal three different invitations, each showcasing a Tupperware® product. All four ladies agreed that Nat had come away with the cutest one, which featured a large pink pastel tumbler on a royal blue background. The women said their good nights to True-Dee, congratulated her yet again, and promised to attend her upcoming event.

"Hasta mañana," said True-Dee to Nat and Sway, who had appointments to have their eyebrows waxed in the morning, then to Lulabell, "And good night to you, Doña." She leaned in and gave Lulabell a kiss on the cheek.

After dropping Lulabell off, Natalie and Consuelo headed for Consuelo's. Natalie pulled into the driveway, then killed the engine. A night of adventures in the books, the girls sat silent for a moment.

Natalie had a faraway look in her eyes. "You know, Sway, sometimes I wish I knew everything that ever happened in the entire world." She gulped big gulps of air before each "e."

"Well then maybe you ought to go back to school," said Consuelo. She stared down at her macramé slides. Macramé, the ancient art of knotting. Nat and Sway had recently watched a documentary about that. Sway loved to watch documentaries. It was the only way she ever got to go anywhere.

"I might consider going back to school," said Nat, "but I know you'd never go with me, and things just ain't the same without you."

Consuelo slipped her shoes off, put her toes up on the dashboard, and flexed them until the knuckles of both big toes cracked, then said, "Nope. I got my GED, that's plenty enough for me."

Natalie nodded. "I can understand that," she said. And indeed she could. Neoteny, the choice not to metamorphose. If it was good for the axolotl, then it was good for Consuelo. But ¿was it good enough for Natalie? She sat and wondered.

La Muerte

Death

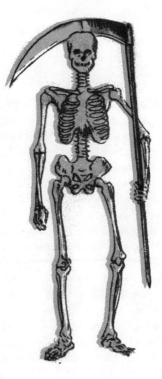

PELÓN Y FLACO

BALD AND SKINNY

CONSUELO'S DREAM:
A PRESENT-TENSE ACCOUNT

That same evening, after Natalie leaves and heads for her own home, Consuelo changes out of her dancing clothes and into her favorite spaghetti strap nightgown. She opens her bedroom window to the barely existent nighttime breeze, sighs at the full moon, then slips into her bed, which is king-sized, but fit for a queen. There is plenty of room for her long legs no matter what position she stretches or folds them. Tonight it's the fetal position into which she scrunches herself before falling asleep and dreaming of her father, Don Pancho Macías Contreras.

Her dream is set in the midst of a great apricot orchard in full bloom. The trees are grander than any she has ever seen and she has seen many. Every summer, as children, when she and Nat cut and picked, Sway was always the swiftest cutter, the only one who could split the fruit in two and remove the pit with a single flick of the wrist. For Sway, picking and cutting was the difference between new and used school clothes and shoes.

Now she sits atop a huge, overturned stainless steel bucket wearing a yellow and white striped dress, lace-trimmed bobby sox, and patent leather Mary Janes. She looks just like a little girl sitting there with her legs swinging and her hair in two braids.

Her father approaches then lifts her from her resting place with a single huge and gentle hand before setting her firmly on the ground. While in motion she gets a strange feeling in her stomach she might compare to that of being on the downhill of a roller coaster had she had that frame of reference, but roller coasters bear far too much in common with trains for Consuelo to have ever boarded one.

Don Pancho looks at Sway and says five words she never tires of hearing. "Mija, soy yo, tu papi."

"Te perdono," whispers Sway. It has recently occurred to her that that's something that ought to be said, that needs getting out of the way.

"¿You forgive me for what?" says Don Pancho.

"For not lookin both ways and for whatever else," says Consuelo.

"Thank you very much, mija. I really appreciate it."

"Your English is very good," comments Consuelo.

"I have been practicing bien-very-mucho."

Consuelo stands beside her father. Her head raised in an exaggerated tilt, she is looking up at him, smiling.

Don Pancho has a busy night ahead of him. He has to make it quick. The Saints and Angels Who run Purgatory were clear about one thing when They gave him his boarding pass to the nocturnal world of dreams: He has to be back to the Perg before dawn, lest he might turn back into his usual purgatorial self—a wrinkled and hunchbacked man with stringy white hair and yellow fingernails so long, they curly-q back toward his wrists.

Consuelo all of the sudden opens up. "Papi, I wanna go home to México, to see the place I was born, to visit my family and so I can learn more about you. I want to help you, but I can't."

"I know, mija, and that's why I'm here. I have come to say goodbye." He holds his hands out long and wide, proud of himself because he is about to do what he considers the right thing. "I won't be showing up in your dreams nunca no more. It's too much of a tormenta for you, cariño. Enough is enough. Sometimes you just gotta say basta."

"But, papi, this is only our fourth meeting. We have barely gotten to know each other. And besides, I will miss you. You can't leave me." She shakes her head and her eyes narrow as if she is about to cry.

"I will always be with you, mi niñita," he says stroking her hair. "I will be in you, bien dentro de tu corazón." He pounds his chest.

"But I wanna see you sometimes, papi. I wanna hear you sing me songs. ¿Where's your guitar?"

"I left it at home. Listen, chiquita, I gotta go. Don't be sad. We'll meet again someday, in the futuro when all is well, but in the meantime do me a favor."

"Anything," says Sway.

"Find yourself a nice young man con mucho dinero. Somebody who will take care of you. You are beautiful, mija. What your tía Concha told you was la pura verdad. You only get one life, live it up."

"But, papi . . ." says Sway. But it is too late. He is gone and all of the sudden her dream switches tracks. She is knee-deep on a muddy trail littered with precious and semiprecious jewels. She stops to pick up a marquise-cut aquamarine since that is Nat's birthstone, then forgoes all of the diamonds, rubies, sapphires, and opals. Consuelo is looking for an emerald.

THE HIGHEST BIDDER

When Lulabell got home that evening from the show transvestis she was surprised to find Javier sitting at the kitchen table, eating cookies and drinking milk. Lulabell would have never guessed, but Javier was thinking about a girl, and such a thing certainly didn't allow him to sleep.

Lulabell walked over and magneted True-Dee's Tupperware® party invitation to the refrigerator. She removed the big silver coquetas from her ears, set them on the table, grabbed a cookie, had a seat, and said, "The Lord says we should have no graven images of Heaven or Hell, but it seems we spend our entire lives creatin either or both right here on earth." She took a bite of her cookie.

Javier kept his mouth shut.

"I don't know if it's Heaven or Hell I'm creatin. I don't know if I oughtta give my soul to the Devil, or to Jesus, or to neither." She was feeling unusually pensive and being uncharacteristically vocal about it.

"¿Give?" said Javier with his mouth half full. "Momma, you'd sell your soul to the highest bidder, Lord forgive me for saying so." Javier dusted the crumbs from his hands, then wiped the corners of his mouth with a pastel napkin.

"Lord'll forgive you for anything, ¿ain't that the point?" said Lulabell.

"The Lord makes mercy and forgiveness His fodder," said Javier.

"Son, sometimes I think you forget. I know a thing or two about the Lord and His ways," said Lulabell. She put her feet up on a nearby chair and waited, anxious for some serious discourse on the matter, but Javier sat idly crunching his cookies.

Indeed it was true. Lulabell knew plenty about the Lord. She had spent the majority of her life in His loving arms, and had it not been for the death of her eldest son, she might very well have stayed there.

When Lulabell's husband ran off leaving her all alone to raise their two children, she did her best to provide a strong male example for her sons. And ¿what better example than Jesus Christ Himself? She got her boys involved in the church at an early age, insisting they attend all of its fund-raisers, outings, and outreaches.

One autumn afternoon, they went to a church picnic. Lulabell sat on a plaid blanket wearing a mint green polyester pantsuit and vinyl flats keeping an eye on the just toddling Javier while her eldest son, Ricardo, then four and a half, rode the swings at the nearby playground.

That afternoon, many ex–gang members were in attendance, which was nothing out of the ordinary—former gang members accounted for a sizable percentage of the congregation, and Lulabell herself had been instrumental in a number of jailhouse conversions.

Lulabell would always remember the color scheme of that blanket: red, orange, yellow, gray, and black, colors that didn't seem to match, but somehow did. She stared down at the blanket, bored, but afraid to admit it, with Javier's tiny hands in her own. Things all of the sudden began to happen very fast. There was a series of shots she mistook for she knew not what, then the sound of an eight-cylinder engine accelerating, its wheels screeching, followed by screams.

A crowd gathered at the playground. Lulabell picked Javier up and ran. She forced her way through. She could see Ricardo, who was lying face down in the sand. He was bleeding, but only a little. Lulabell thought this was a good sign. If Ricardo were hurt really bad, she reasoned, he would bleed profusely. Lulabell didn't know that a small amount of blood can indicate a diminished or nonexistent heartbeat.

As she held Ricardo in her arms, she made a manda with God promising that if He spared him, she would offer Him Javier in service as a Christian soldier. Lulabell didn't know it, but Ricardo was already gone.

The Lord took Lulabell up on her half of the bargain anyway. He swept Javier away just as sure as He did Ricardo, for in his time of need, Javier stepped straight into the loving light of the Lord, while Lulabell gave up cheap pantsuits and flats, and went fleeing back into the arms of His archenemy the Devil.

Lulabell finished off Javier's glass of milk, then stared off in the distance at two walls' worth of out-of-date Mexican calendars. The women depicted were so beautiful that Lulabell could never bring herself to get rid of the calendars once they expired. There was the Aztec princess, market mistress, girl in waiting, woman serenaded, la revolucionaria, the loving mother, or La Malinche, the unknowing traitoress being carried off on horseback to start a new race. Lulabell particularly loved La Pajarera, a brunette in braids with her peasant top seductively sliding off her shoulder (back then they didn't wear bras, ¿o, qué?), with a red bird in her hand. Lulabell had once felt as if she held her whole world in her hands as if it were that little bird. Not the world itself, but Lulabell's world, her children, her husband, her beauty, her God. But now everything was either gone or fleeing and La Lulabell was more apt to cast herself in the calendar scene "La Cruz de Palenque." Just a woman y su agonía leaning up against a wooden cross with the bones of the past at her feet, eyes closed, hands clasped casually (¿in prayer?), her braids shamelessly undone.

Lulabell looked at Javier. He was big and strong with the kind of thick black hair that mothers and lovers alike love to run their hands through. Little did he know that Lulabell's soul was at a crossroads, sitting there second-guessing itself, lingering like a face-up shiny penny on the asphalt waiting to be picked up. Lulabell considered the Devil and Jesus men like any others, who would naturally desire her, but inevitably leave her, and things being as such, she switched accordingly between the two. Now, at that juncture in her life, Lulabell was wondering if she had made the proper choice. ¿Should she try to tiptoe her way back to Jesus, or was she right to remain in the Devil's loving arms?

"Good night, mijo," she said rising to her feet. She stooped to give Javier a kiss on the head, then headed for her bedroom. Once under the covers, she thought about the evening in summary. After the show transvestis wrapped up, there was an hour's time before the nightclub closed and the women headed home. Lulabell had initially attracted a bunch of young men to her table, but as the evening wore on, they branched out finding other, younger dancers, leaving her with the eldest, shortest, least desirable of the bunch.

Lulabell had to wonder: ¿Was she losing her effectiveness with men? It reminded her of baseball, her favorite sport. It was always so sad for Lulabell when she watched the man at the plate being walked intentionally so the pitcher could get to the less effective batter after him. Lulabell felt bad for that man on deck. He was likely an old slugger who, in his time and day, had struck fear into the hearts of pitchers in both leagues, but time had taken a little something from his swing, until one day he was watching from the on deck circle as the catcher called for four wide ones and the pitcher obliged. Lulabell always pulled for him, always wished he'd hit a home run and show them all. Now she was beginning to see a little bit of that old slugger in herself.

Lulabell rolled over, did her best to clear her mind, and eventually fell asleep.

"¡Ay! papi," said Lulabell when she got a look at the handsome man in the blue guayabera who had shown up in her dreams. He wore a straw sombrero and carried a guitar at his side.

Lulabell and the stranger were in the center of Lava Landing at the placita. It must have been a Sunday because there were people everywhere. But with all of the activity, it was almost as if Lulabell and the handsome man were alone.

"¿Who are you?" she said looping her arm in his.

"I am Don Pancho." There was a ring to his voice, to the announcement of his name, which indicated that while he might have been a nobody, he was about to be a somebody. They began to walk the plaza in a counterclockwise direction.

"¿What do you do?" said Lulabell sizing him up. He was clean and sweet-smelling. After he exited Sway's dreams, he was headed for Natalie's to do a midnight fly-by, but something had gone wrong. A series of rights instead of lefts and he ended up clear across town in Lulabell's dreams.

Don Pancho paused and thought about it. "For starters, I got runned over by the midnight freight train from Guanajuato, and now I'm stuck in Purgatory."

"That don't seem fair," said Lulabell.

"I couldn't agree with you more, lady, but ¿what did you call me here for?" said Don Pancho.

"I didn't call you," she said.

"Then ¿what am I doing here?"

"¿How am I supposed to know?"

"It's your dream," said Don Pancho. "You must have done something because I was on my way to see a girl named Natalie, and somehow I ended up here."

"¿Natalie, as in Natalie and Consuelo Natalie?" said Lulabell.

"That's her. ¿You know her?" said Don Pancho.

"I have known her all her life. She and my son went to school together. She is a good girl," said Lulabell.

"I know," said Don Pancho. After vowing to never again torment Consuelo with his nighttime visits, Don Pancho decided that he would make one final plea for help. His plan was to surprise his daughter's best friend in her dreams and ask her to help free him from Purgatory.

DP and Lulabell sat down on a blue bench. The lonchera had just shown up. "¿You want some jamaica?" said Lulabell. She stood up and began to fish for change in the pockets of her skirt.

"No thanks. I have had enough jamaica to last a lifetime. It's the drink of choice in Purgatory. They say you have to get to Heaven to have horchata."

"We can have some horchata if you like," offered Lulabell.

"Thanks, but I should get going," said Don Pancho. He stood up and smoothed his slacks.

"Wait. Don't go," said Lulabell grabbing his arm. There was a tinge of desperation in her voice.

"¿What do you want?" he said, his voice fraught with impatience.

"I know you're stuck in Purgatory, but that's closer to God than I've ever gotten, and I was just wonderin if you could hook me up with Jesus," said Lulabell.

"Listen, lady, I got lots of problems of my own and I don't know what you're talking about. You can speak to God whenever you want." Don Pancho began to walk off and Lulabell followed.

"But prayer is not a direct line to God. I wanna talk to El Gran Señor myself, so He can tell me if He is just mad at me, or if He doesn't love me anymore."

The vendors were selling mangos con chilito y limón, Don Pancho's favorite. He was getting hungry. He wanted to get rid of the crazy woman so he could eat before he went out to look for Natalie.

"The Lord loves everyone, Señora."

"That's what They say," said Lulabell referring to the Prophets. "But I know if a man hates anything, it's a two-timer, and the Lord can't be happy with all the time I've been spendin with the Devil."

"You've got to decide which way you're gonna go. I've been in Purgatory for more than twenty-seven years, and one thing I learned is, nothing good ever happens in limbo. God and the Devil go by all sorts of different names in all sorts of different places, and there's impostors everywhere, so ¡watcha!" said Don Pancho, and with that, he ignored his appetite, clapped his hands, and disappeared.

The sound of Don Pancho's hands coming together woke Lulabell up. In a just conscious state, she decided she would put her soul in the hands of some capable deity or other and leave it there, learn His or Her rules, and follow them. But ¿in whose hands would Lulabell lay her soul? She rolled over and looked at the clock. It was 3:52 a.m. I will sell my soul to the highest bidder, thought Lulabell, before curling up into the fetal position, and falling back asleep.

In the morning, Lulabell woke up and headed straight for the kitchen table to draft the ad for the most important event of her lifetime: the auctioning off of her soul.

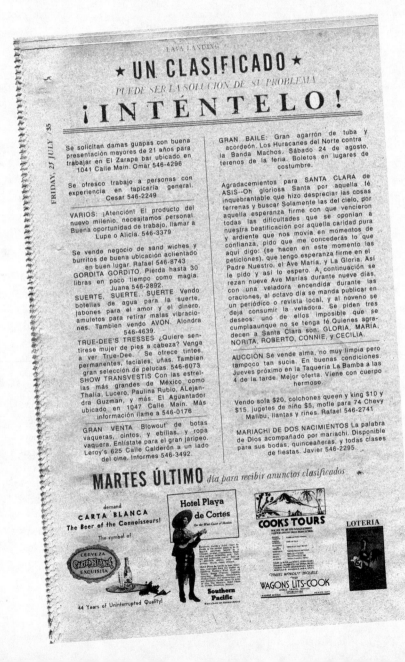

NATALIE'S DREAM

At first, Natalie thought those two beers and that shot of tequila she consumed at the show transvestis were to blame for the strangest dream she had ever had. But once the dream got rolling, she knew she was experiencing something beyond tequila and markedly different, that she had never, and might never see the likes of again.

Nat's dream, like Sway's, took place in that same immense apricot orchard, and she too was amazed by the size of the trees. She sat on the hard, dry ground with her feet folded under her. A man approached in the distance. Tall, with honey-colored skin, blue eyes, and black hair, he was the handsomest man she had ever seen.

He reached down and pulled Natalie to her feet, removed his sombrero, then said, "Soy Don Pancho Macías Contreras, deceased father of Consuelo Constancia González Contreras."

The resemblance was there. His eyes were gray-blue the way Sway's were gray-green, and he was oh so tall. "I know who you are," whispered Natalie.

"Good," said DP. "Then we can get right down to business. I came here to thank you for taking care of Consuelo all of these years. For understanding, but never judging her, and for making sure she always gets enough calcium."

"We saw a movie about a hunchback once. *La Jorobada* with Yolanda del Río. It really scared us."

"I have seen the same movie," said Don Pancho. He stretched his arms straight out, then back behind him. He was having a hectic evening. He had forgotten how difficult it was to fit so many women into such a small time frame.

He looked much younger than Natalie had imagined him. Even though Consuelo had never met her father, she still talked about him plenty. He was forty-four years old at the time of his death, plus the twenty-seven years he had been dead. That would make him seventy-one, and here he didn't look a day over thirty-five.

"Listen, mija, I need to ask you to do me a favor. Un favorcito bien big," said DP. "And I don't have a lot of time either."

"Go on," said Nat keeping her distance. He might have been handsome, but the sweat circles on his guayabera extended clear across his chest and met in the middle. He smelled like sour milk and body odor.

"I'm stuck in Purgatory and the only way for me to get out is if somebody goes to the train tracks where I was killed, and they get the people together to pray for me. But before you say yea or nay, I will let you think about it while I perform my favorite number for you."

Without further delay, Don Pancho began to sing the same song he had serenaded Consuelo with so many times in her dreams, but somehow on the way from Lulabell's dreams to Natalie's, he had lost his guitar. In its absence, he began to clap his hands to a rhythm known only to himself. Pretty soon, he couldn't help but dance to that rhythm. His arms and legs moved in unison with one another as if attached by a string. He looked so ridiculous, Natalie was embarrassed on his behalf.

After his song was up, Don Pancho stood bent at the waist, out of breath, holding on to his knees. Natalie approached. "¿Are you all right?" she said.

"¡No! I am not all right." He turned suddenly stern.

A strange and scary thing began to happen. Don Pancho's hair began to gray and grow. His skin wrinkled and sagged. His fingernails jutted out, then retracted into tight curls, like a Christmas ribbon under the tension of a thumb and the straight edge of the scissors.

The day was dawning and DP was in big trouble.

Natalie leaned up against the sturdy trunk of a nearby tree. She wasn't so much frightened as she was intrigued, but she played it safe and kept her distance.

"I can't take it no more," said Don Pancho. "They make us practice English day and night, and since even after twenty-seven years, I haven't lost my accent, They make fun of me."

"¿Who?" said Nat.

"The Saints and Angels, that's Who."

"That's not very nice," said Nat. She got close, hoping her presence would comfort him.

"No, it's not. They're not, and now I am really gonna be in trouble. I am late and They are gonna take everything away from me. Shit. Shit. Shit," said Don Pancho stomping his feet.

"I will never be able to appear in anyone's dreams ever again." He began to walk the floor as best a hunchback can. "Maybe in another twenty-five years They will give me another chance. Twenty-five years. That's a grain of sand in Their hourglass, but to us humans, that's a big piece of living." He looked down at his huaraches, which were covered with dust, then looked to Natalie. "You gotta help me. If you don't, if I don't get out of here, this life, it's not worth living."

Natalie was suddenly struck with a horrible thought as she looked at Don Pancho's fingernails and the way they curled back, headed straight toward his wrists. Natalie remembered learning about the circulatory system in her twelfth-grade anatomy class, for unlike Consuelo, she had finished high school. She knew there were plenty of important veins and arteries under the skin.

She placed a hand on his hunchback and said, "¿You're not thinkin of whackin yourself, are you?"

"¿Whacking?" repeated Don Pancho. After all of those vocabulary lessons imposed upon him by the Saints and Angels, he was surprised to come across a word he wasn't familiar with.

"You know, killin yourself. ¿You're not thinkin of committin suicide, are you?"

"I am already dead," declared Don Pancho.

"You are only kind of dead," said Nat sizing him up. His skin was gray, his eyes cataract-ridden, and in that state, he was more decrepit than anyone Nat had ever seen, even at bingo.

"I hadn't thought about killing myself," he said mulling it over. "That might be a very good idea."

"¡No! You can't." Nat grabbed him by an arm. "¿Haven't you ever heard of going from bad to worse? You could go from where you are now, right straight down to Hell, and Sway won't see you never, not in this world or that other one either."

"Hell," said DP. "¡Hah! ¿Who's to say it ain't a better place?"

"Tell me what I have to do," said Nat.

He huddled in close and brought his voice down to a whisper as if the visiting team were listening, then said, "¿Do you know my story, mija?"

Mija. The word warmed her. "Yes, I do," she said. "Consuelo told me all about you. At least as much as she knows, about how you died, and where you were buried, and how maybe someday you could do miracles."

"Yes it is true, mi niña." He ran his scraggly fingernails through her hair as she peered at him through a few ringlets which had fallen into her line of vision. "The Saints and Angels have promised to allow me to try my hand at working miracles, but I need your help. You must go down to México, to my hometown. Consuelo will tell you where it is. Once you get there, get all of the people together and go to the railroad tracks where I was killed and pray." At this point, Don Pancho picked up a stick from the ground and used it to draw in the dirt. He made a few lines, then an X, which marked the spot of his burial, then tossed the stick aside.

Nat gave it some thought. "But I don't wanna go by myself."

"You can make friends when you get there. Everybody from my pueblo is very friendly, and once they know who you are, they will welcome you with open arms. Now get," he said slapping her on the backside.

"I want Consuelo to go with me." It was a prospect she had imagined for years. She and Sway on the open road. Or in the open air. She supposed they would have to fly.

"Oh no," said DP. "Consuelo isn't cut out for a trip like that. Hence her fear." He chuckled in a way that betrayed his cunning and led Natalie to suspect that Don Pancho Macías Contreras had something to do with Consuelo's unreasonable fear of public transportation and long car rides.

"¿What do you know about her fear?" said Nat squinting.

"Nothing. Just that it serves her well by keeping her in one place and out of trouble."

Natalie had to ask herself if she could begrudge a macho comment like that coming from a man of DP's generation.

She answered his male chauvinism with this proposition: "And, ¿what if I cure her, then what?"

"She cannot be cured," said DP, just as sure of himself as ever.

"That remains to be seen," she said. Then in defiance not just of Don Pancho, but of all men who try to keep a girl down, Natalie woke up, leaving Don Pancho, as the saying goes, con la duda, to his own devices, and asking himself a few questions of his own, mainly: ¿Was La Güera de la Natalie gonna come to his aid, or not?

El Camarón
The Shrimp

CAMARÓN QUE SE DUERME SE LO LLEVA LA CORRIENTE

SHRIMP WHO SLEEP WILL BE SWEPT AWAY BY THE CURRENT

LA PURA NETA

After Natalie skipped out on DP and returned to the waking world, she had to wait two long hours for a decent hour before she could pick Consuelo up. The girls usually spent the night at one another's houses, but the previous night had been a to-each-her-own night, and hence found them at their respective dwellings.

By nine o'clock, Natalie had already scheduled a 10:30 appointment with Maestro Salomé, a local curandero who, according to his ad in the weekly magazine *La Guía,* handled emergencias.

By 9:15, Nat was on her way to Sway's, and at 9:22 she was walking through the front door saying, "Sway, wake up. We got things to do. Places to go."

"¿What's up?" said Consuelo nonchalantly. She was propped up in bed watching Marta Susana, who was featuring a panel of compulsive gamblers, shoppers, and liars.

"We have an appointment," said Nat.

"That's not until 10:30," said Sway thinking of their brow-waxing session at True-Dee's Tresses.

"We have a different appointment. One to get you cured. I've been thinkin about it for years, Sway. That fear of yours is unreasonable. And it's time we did somethin about it. For a while I thought maybe we needed to see a doctor. But if we turned to modern medicine, they'd likely direct us to their head-shrinkin branch and try to cram a bunch of pills down your throat, and I think we need somethin more esoteric. That's why I made us an appointment to go and see Maestro Salomé. Now get ready." Natalie folded her arms and rocked back and forth on her feet.

"Esoteric," said Sway. "¿Isn't that a brand of soap?"

"No, it's not. We're goin to see a brujo."

"All right," said Consuelo. "Just so long as he's not too far away."

"Hurry up," said Nat as Sway rushed to get dressed. "And we better drop by True-Dee's to let her down soft. You know how she hates cancellations."

"Whatever you say, mamacita," agreed Consuelo. She paused to study Nat, who was now sitting at the edge of her bed with a vacant look upon her face and her legs hung wide open in a manner unbecoming a lady. "There's somethin you ain't tellin me," said Sway taking note of it all, then sitting back down, waiting to find out what Nat was withholding.

"Shit, Sway," said Nat. "You know me far too well. I didn't wanna tell you so as not to make you worry, but your daddy came to me in a dream last night sayin that if we don't get the people together to pray for him so that he can get out of Purgatory, he's gonna whack himself and for sure go straight to Hell."

"¡Holy shit, Nat! ¿You were thinkin of keepin THAT from me?"

"Well kinda, but like I said, only to protect you."

Natalie could see a bunch of sadness gathering in Consuelo's eyes.

"When he comes to me, Nat, he strums his guitar and sings real purty songs. Them dreams are beautiful, but they're damn tormentative as well," said Consuelo.

"I imagine they must be," said Nat.

While on their way to True-Dee's, Nat couldn't help but think of her own father, Mr. Edward Steven. He had died when she was just nineteen years old and she had been closer to him than she might otherwise have been since her mother had run off (with the butcher no less) when Nat was just three years old. When asked about the former Mrs. Steven, Nat would contend that she didn't remember too much about her, and when it came to missing her she would simply state, "You can't miss what you ain't never had, just wonder about it."

During his life, Natalie's father had been a man fascinated by the natural wonders of the world, so fascinated, that he once journeyed all the way to Ecuador for the sole purpose of standing in both of earth's hemispheres at once. In the last known photograph of him, he is shown doing just that, with one foot straddling each side of the equator. His smile is so wide, so joyful, one wouldn't have thought the disease had already set in. Or ¿was it a sickness? Disease spelt something long and prolonged, and it had set in and done its nasty deed in no time.

After Mr. Steven's remains were carried away, they were passed through a series of messengers, until they made their way to a burro that carried them deep into the Andes where they were dumped into another natural wonder, Lake Titicaca, the highest lake in the world, and the living Mr. Steven's next intended travel destination.

So Natalie, at the age of nineteen, had been left all alone in the world to fend for herself with the help of a janitor's pension, and a house that was paid for outright. Her father had worked for the school district and what they say about government jobs having good benefits is true, but Nat was still wanting for paternal guidance, and in essence, el cariño de un padre. Maybe that's why she was so sympathetic to Consuelo and Don Pancho's cause. But all things being equal, it takes a daddy's girl to recognize a daddy's girl, and Natalie knew that that's precisely what Consuelo was, even though, technically, she had never met her father "en carne propio" as the saying goes.

Natalie thought about her own father often and wanted to go to Quito someday, to be photographed just as he had. With a foot on each side of the equator, she would smile so wide for the camera, then she would go to the shores of Lake Titicaca to feel his presence. But ¿who would go with her?

When the girls got to True-Dee's Tresses, Consuelo waited in the car while Natalie went in and explained everything to True-Dee, who was so moved by the circumstances of Consuelo and Don Pancho's dual dilemma that she decided to accompany the girls to Maestro Salomé's.

"It's gonna be all right, hon," said True-Dee climbing into the front seat beside Sway.

El Maestro lived at the edge of city limits, where agriculture gives way to the volcano. The women arrived and rushed to the front door and knocked. The maestro opened up and welcomed them in.

He was a well-kept man of perhaps sixty. His dark skin looked like a sun-tan since the hair on his face and head was completely white. Consuelo cringed when she got a good gander at him, for he was wearing a variation of what most men of his race and age at one time inevitably wear: a pair of comfortable slacks, a guayabera, and huaraches.

"A well-read man," commented True-Dee as the girls had a look around. The south wall of El Maestro's living room was completely covered with books in four languages, Spanish, English, Italian, and Portuguese. His home was an open-plan single-story. In the center of the living room, a cushioned wicker couch and love seat, a few scattered chairs, and on the floor a cowskin rug.

"Sit down, ladies," said El Maestro.

He looked at Consuelo. "This must be my patient," he said. It was plain to see. She was the biggest wreck of all. She sat on the couch with a blank look on her face, rapidly winding a strand of her long black hair around an index finger.

"¿Can I get you ladies something to drink?" offered El Maestro.

"No thanks," Natalie and True-Dee declined. Consuelo said nothing.

"A trabajar . . ." said Maestro Salomé. And with that, he got to work.

He took Consuelo by the hand, and said, "You have something floating around in your head that is not allowing you to face your destiny. To go where you need to go. God has a plan for us all, mija. We must do our part to complete it. Sometimes things get in the way, and now, we must do a reading to see what is getting in yours." El Maestro reached for his deck of cards, held it high in the air, then lowered it in front of Consuelo. "You must say, 'For my God, my spirit, and my house.' "

Consuelo did as she was told, then chose ten cards from the deck. The maestro eliminated five, then turned the remaining cards over before arranging them into the shape of a cross.

"You are sought by many men," said El Maestro. "And here, the double oars. This card represents distance. This card," he said pointing to another, "represents wisdom and age. There is a wise man very far away who wants to speak to you. ¿Do you know who he is?" El Maestro raised his eyebrows.

True-Dee and Natalie looked at one another knowingly.

"He is my father," said Consuelo.

"¿Are you ready to speak to him?" said the maestro.

Consuelo nodded.

"¡We must invoke the spirit of your father so he can help you!" The maestro held his hands high in the air. He was excited. What he thought would be a simple reading of the cards had all of the sudden turned into a séance.

"You love your papi, ¿verdad qué sí, mi amor?"

"Sí. Lo quiero mucho," said Consuelo.

"There is nothing to be afraid of. Now, all we need is a male medium. I will make a few calls and we will be underway in no time." El maestro got to his feet and headed for the kitchen telephone.

Natalie and Consuelo looked at True-Dee. She was wearing a denim skirt she prized for its versatility and a striped red and white scoop neck T-shirt. Her hair was parted down the middle and kept out of her face by two plastic Goody® red-ribbon-shaped barrettes.

True-Dee swallowed hard, raised a hand halfway in the air, demurred, and said, "Señor, Maestro, I think I can help you out."

"¿Yes?" said El Maestro. He had the receiver in his hand and had begun to dial.

"I have the physical attributes which allow me to be classified as a man," said True-Dee in her most resounding voice.

El Maestro lowered his spectacles to the bridge of his nose. "I see," he said. "Cada quien su camino," he added. It was an old Mexican adage which meant, to each his own road, and judging by the air of respect with which El Maestro had said it, he really meant it. He hung up the telephone.

"We must all four join hands," said El Maestro turning to Consuelo. "¿Do you have anything of your father's with you? ¿Perhaps something he gave you?"

Consuelo dipped into her purse and came out with a pair of minuscule huaraches. You see, the train that ran Don Pancho over had originated in Guanajuato, which is known for its shoes and, accordingly, was carrying nothing but. The collision was significant enough to derail the last two box-cars, causing them to spill their contents onto the roadway. The villagers who had hurried DP's lifeless body back home had also brought along several pairs of shoes for the family. As for the huaraches, Sway never got any practical use from them, seeing as how she was so long and lanky, she'd already outgrown them at the time of her birth. Even still, she would always consider those shoes the only thing her daddy had ever rightfully given her, and they had hung from the Cadillac's rearview mirror since the joyful day Natalie became its owner.

"These are very nice, mija." El Maestro took the huaraches in hand.

"Now we must all clear our minds as completely as possible," he said.

After several minutes of silence, El Maestro began to shake, subtly at first, then uncontrollably. Then, he regained his composure while True-Dee lost hers, as she began to wriggle and tremble. El Maestro opened his eyes, smiled, and said, "He's here," then headed for the kitchen. "¿Tea, anyone?" he shouted.

"Yes," said True-Dee in an unexpectedly manly voice with a Spanish accent.

Natalie and Consuelo looked at one another. They had never heard such deep tones emanating from True-Dee's mouth.

"No tengas miedo," said El Maestro returning from the kitchen. "Es tu papá. Háblale."

"Papi, ¿eres tú?"

"Yes, mija. It's me," replied Don Pancho Macías Contreras.

"Papi, quisiera preguntarte algo."

"Speak to me en inglés, mija. Tengo que practicar."

Consuelo let out a sigh that left her lips flapping. "I wanna go home to

San Luis Río Colorado, papá, to help get you out of that place, but I am scared of airplanes. Buses scare me too. Trains terrify me. Bein in the car a really long time makes me nervous too. I can go to the store or even across town, just so long as it's not too far. I don't know what to do. I am really scared." She started to cry and so did Natalie. If True-Dee were around, she might have too, only she was somewhere far away.

"Mija, if you want to go back home, you should go, but you can get a much better job here en Los Estados Unidos. That's why I am studying inglés. Besides, if I were you, I would never get into a bus, or an airplane, and never a train. Nunca. A lo mejor stay at home. You see what happened to me." Don Pancho looked down and realized he was wearing a skirt. He let out a scream. "¡Ay! no. ¡It is worse than I thought! You see, mija. You are much better off at home. Take my advice. Es la pura neta." Don Pancho looked at Natalie. "She is your friend." He pointed directly at Nat. "Send her. She will get the job done. Te quiero mucho," said Don Pancho.

"I love you too, papá," said Consuelo.

"Papi, I wanna ask you one more thing," said Consuelo.

"Anything," said Don Pancho.

"That night, you were runned over, ¿did you do it on purpose, did you commit suicide?"

Don Pancho took a deep breath. He gestured to freshen his nonexistent sombrero, but had to settle for running his hands through the long black hair that had somehow sprouted from his head. "I was drunk, mija. That's all there is to it. Nada más, nada menos."

"Drunk," repeated Consuelo at a murmur. She blinked three times, then squinted, and with that, Don Pancho was gone.

True-Dee let out a scream. She shook and wiggled until she came into her former self. She looked around, cleared her throat and said, "I wanna go home."

La Sirena

The Siren

CON LOS CANTOS DE SIRENA NO TE VAYAS A MAREAR
WITH THE SONGS OF THE SIREN, YOU WON'T SET SAIL

LAS SERENATAS II

Javier tried. He really, genuinely tried to stay away from La Lucha at least until Saturday, a day when dates traditionally take place and a boy can get somewhere with a girl, but come Thursday, he could stay away no longer.

That afternoon had found Lucha seated on her pink fuzzy bed looking just like a 1980s lowrider queen. Aqua Net®, Dial-a-Lash®, Strawberry Kissing Potion®, and a chrome teasing comb had all been a part of her private primping. With her halter top, her chinos bien baggy, her black bracelets spider-webbing up her wrists, and a pair of Mary Janes, she was quite a Teen Angel®.

She had been a free woman for only five days, but had already managed to hook up with a new vato. His name was Joaquín and he looked like a Mexican Yosemite Sam, but with tattoos. And now, for the third time in as many days, Lucha was out of her lowrider girl clothes, bien desnuda beneath the covers with Joaquín, who was in the process of making love to her despacito, muy despacito, when Javier showed up serenading her the song of the same name.

Lucha rolled out from under Joaquín, felt around for his nearby baggy T-shirt, and put it on. She walked to the window, pulled the curtains aside, and smiled. She had never been specifically serenaded.

Joaquín slid his boxer shorts on in a hurry, then got down on all fours. In his nervousness he hadn't realized that there was just one man and his guitar beyond the window. He imagined at least ten and macho ones at that for there is nothing more macho than a mariachi. Worse yet, there might have been twelve men out there, which is what a classic ensemble calls for.

Nothing which had come before in Joaquín's life had prepared him for that moment. Not even when he was way down Chino way and he found himself the object of seven inmates' affections, all in the same afternoon, and all at the same time. At least then he could pick and choose if he so chose, or stand up and fight if he didn't, but Joaquín was being assailed by mariachi, a force, in his mind, invincible.

Lucha looked down at Joaquín. "You look just like a dog down there, you pig. ¡Get up!" Joaquín placed a finger over parted lips signaling silence. His and Lucha's union might only have been in full force for less than a week, but her correctional facility had been his facility's sister facility, and they had been writing to one another for several months during which time he had come to consider Lucha his mera mera pistolera. As Lucha saw it, Joaquín might have been her main event, but Javier looked so cute standing there behind his guitarrón, she was thinking seriously of letting him slide in on her undercard.

At song's end, Lucha hung her head out the window and gave Javier the telltale kiss—an open-mouthed yet tongueless number that made the hair rise on the back of his neck.

With the serenade out of the way, Javier moved to number two on his to-do list: He invited Lucha on a date saying, "¿Would you like to go with me to Christian Music Night at the roller rink sometime? It happens the final Wednesday of the month and it's loads of fun."

"¿What the heck?" she said mimicking Javier's enthusiasm.

"Pick you up at eight," Javier shouted. "And don't be late," he added. He took off for the Monte Carlo. Such was his excitement, he drove all the way home with his sombrero on.

Once Javier was out of sight, Lucha plopped down on her bed. The serenade was having its desired effect and she was feeling more than a little frisky. Leaning back on her elbows with her head tilted to the side, she looked ready, willing, and twice as able. "Come here, chiquitito," she said.

Joaquín stared at her for a moment, then said, "¿Just how many others are there?"

"No muchos, but you're not the only one, carnal." She opened her dresser drawer, pulled out a cigarette, stuck it in the corner of her mouth, and let it dangle. "Such a gentleman," she said striking her own match, then lighting the waiting Marlboro® Red.

"I thought I was gonna take you to México so you could meet my mother and she could teach you how to cook," said Joaquín.

"Sorry, carnal," she said rolling all three "r's" unnecessarily. "I ain't that kinda girl. Thought you knew me better."

"You don't know me, ruca." He pointed a finger at Lucha, then got up and put his white undershirt on.

"It's early yet. Maybe I get to know you better." She took a long drag off her cigarette.

"I only want what's best for you, chiquita." He kneeled down at her bedside.

Lucha ran a hand through his thick, dark brown hair and said, "I'm thinkin about cuttin you in on somethin real big, only you gots to be a real good boy. ¿Me entiendes, Méndez?" She smiled. She was used to bringing a man to his knees, but it never ceased to please her.

"I always do good by you, mamacita."

"That's what I wanna hear," said Lucha. "So long as we understand each other. That way things go bien suave. And another thing, corazón . . ." She grabbed him tight by the forearm, then continued, "Hazme un favor."

"Anything."

"Try to stay out of the pinta."

Joaquín sighed. Lucha was well on her way to being the downfall of him and several other men, and if he didn't know it, he certainly sensed it.

El Tupperware®

The Tupperware®

QUE NO SE ECHE A PERDER LO QUE MAÑANA VAS A QUERER

DON'T LAY TO WASTE WHAT YOU WILL WANT TOMORROW

T-TIME

Natalie and Consuelo were headed south on Highway 33 at a brisk 75 mph, with the top down on the Cadillac, listening to Johnny Burnette and his Rock 'n' Roll Trio belt out the rockabilly hits of the 1950s—a decade, in their opinion, much preferable to their own.

Just three days had passed since the girls, with the invaluable help of True-Dee and Maestro Salomé, had evoked the spirit of Don Pancho Macías Contreras. Needless to say, the girls had plenty on their minds, but a promise is a promise. They were on their way to True-Dee's annual Tupperware® party.

Consuelo reached over and turned Johnny and the boys down to a murmur. "Certainly hope True-Dee don't push her Tupperware® too hard. Last thing I need is a bunch of Jell-O® molds," said Consuelo.

"Bet this is just True-Dee's excuse to get us to join The Cause," said Natalie. The Cause was True-Dee's crusade to save the female species from what she considered a conspiracy of the highest order designed to deprive women of their most volatile asset: their femininity. As True-Dee figured it, this conspiracy was planned, plotted, and enacted by none other than the leaders of the feminist movement.

The girls arrived at True-Dee's just a smidgen late. "A sight for sore eyes," said True-Dee as she opened the front door, embraced, then motioned them in.

Natalie handed True-Dee a platter of peanut butter cookies covered with Saran Wrap®. "Peanut butter. My favorite. And you made those cute little fork marks across the top," said True-Dee receiving the platter. She ran off to show them to Racine.

True-Dee was dressed like a geisha with her black hair spun up in a bun held in place by two crisscrossed pencils. She wore a green and orange satin kimono paired with green satin pajama pants which brushed together as she walked, causing them to static-cling to her thighs.

"Girls, girls, girls," said True-Dee clapping her hands together. "Come over and have a seat in the livin room."

The guests settled in on the velvety burgundy couch, its matching love seat, and a wide array of improvisational seating. The crowd segregated itself by hairstyle: the silver-haired shampoo-and-style set on the couch, the transvestites from the Tuesday night show on and around the love seat, the blonde tanning booth regulars on the floor, and the long-haired spiral-permed ladies were scattered about the room on folding chairs. With their elbows propped up, and their chins in their hands, Natalie and Consuelo had the kitchen table all to themselves—they were plenty disappointed Lulabell wasn't there.

True-Dee closed her eyes, took a deep breath, spread her arms as wide as she could, and announced, "¡It's T-Time!" as Racine wheeled in a cart stacked with Tupperware® of every shape and color imaginable. The ladies ooed and awed while Racine held up the little plastic jewel-colored canisters.

True-Dee pulled the pencils from her hair and tossed her head from side to side. She handed one pencil to Racine before using the other as a pointer to assist in her presentation. "Sisters, we are gathered here today to behold the genius of a man long gone, but never to be forgotten. DuPont scientist Earl Tupper did us all a favor when, in 1942, he created his revolutionary and nearly indestructible products," said True-Dee. She aimed her pencil toward the hallway as a large muscular young man emerged dressed only in a pair of bikini shorts. The women could hardly contain themselves as Leo stomped and pulled at the container. He put it in his mouth and growled before stomping back to his den.

"Leo will be back for more fun later," said True-Dee as she refocused the audience's attention on her sales pitch. "You ladies all know the virtues of Tupperware®. Plenty of you probably grew up on it." Racine held out a time line displaying the milestones of the Tupperware® Corporation while True-Dee rambled on. "From the lunch box to the pastel tumbler, Tupperware® is not a new commodity to any of you, but you might not be aware of what some of the forward-thinkin folks at the Tupperware® Corporation have come up with." True-Dee reached for one of Tupperware®'s latest marvels, but before she had a chance to share it with the audience, there was a knock at the door.

She set the translucent wonder down, excused herself momentarily, and walked to the door. Much to her surprise and more to her chagrin, it was

Javier Solís and his Born Again Christian mariachi band. The invitation to the Tupperware® party had been magneted to the refrigerator and Javier had been glaring at it from behind his cereal bowl all week. The mariachis agreed that a Tupperware® party given by a sinner of the highest degree was the perfect place to take their soul-saving message.

The mariachis, already in song, stormed the door before True-Dee had a chance to protest.

Natalie and Consuelo sat in their corner and giggled while the audience reveled in what they assumed was another one of True-Dee's surprises. The women clapped their hands in unison while Raymundo passed out pamphlets to the eager audience. Natalie and Consuelo shared one of the handwritten booklets. Across the front read the warning: "Don't just sit there! Repent! The Kingdom of Heaven is at hand." Natalie and Consuelo looked at one another then shook their heads. On the back side in small print was the sales pitch: "Mariachi de Dos Nacimientos: relentless as the Devil is unrelenting. We are available for weddings, birthdays, or any other event where the Word of God accompanied by music is needed." A telephone number and address followed.

True-Dee stood in the doorway, her head on Leo's thick shoulder, while Mariachi de Dos Nacimientos finished their song.

"The nerve of some people," pronounced True-Dee with her hands on her hips. "To go bargin in uninvited."

"Just putting my God-given gumption to good use," said Javier facing the audience.

True-Dee ran back to her bedroom and threw herself face first onto her king-size waterbed, while Leo stood in the hallway chewing on a carrot stick watching the drama unfold.

Javier addressed the assembly, "Ladies and others, I don't have anything to sell you this evening, but I do have something to give you. It is something that cannot be purchased in any store, or through any catalog. It cannot even be found on the Home Shopping Network®. It is salvation, and it is only available through the Lord, Jesus Christ."

"¡Amen!" declared the other mariachis.

"You may think you're living in the pink because the Lord hasn't caught up with you yet, but we are here to inform you that when He does catch up with you, you may have Hell to pay, because ¡the Lord charges interest!" warned Javier. There was a hush that overcame the audience as its various members put their hands over their mouths in realization of their insurmountable sin.

"Well, it looks like my boys and I have our work cut out for us." Javier scanned the audience, before continuing. "Never fear, we are here and we are ready to bring the Word of God to the unknowing unfortunate sinners of this small sect we call our home. Remember, Jesus gave His own life so that sinners such as ourselves could be saved." The audience heaved a sigh of relief at this revelation.

Javier took his sombrero off and tamed his thick black hair.

"If that boy wasn't so gone on Jesus, I don't know what I'd do," whispered Natalie.

"I do," replied Consuelo.

"Ladies, I am asking you to give up your lives of debauchery and come join us in being one with Jesus Christ. It would be my honor to accompany you down the road to righteousness," said Javier holding his right hand up in the air. "If we can be of assistance in directing you in finding God, you know where to find us." He pointed to the group's address and telephone number on the bottom of one of the pamphlets. "If we're not there, leave us a message and we'll get back to you. The world's ways are too wicked for us to be sitting around waiting by the phone, especially when the Devil's always got His finger on the speed dial. We hope when Satan calls for you you'll be wise enough to tell him He's got the wrong number because the only one that ties up your line is Jesus."

"¡Glory, glory hallelujah!" shouted one of the drag queens. She bit the knuckles of her right fist and licked her lips.

The ladies were overcome with longing and indecision. Javier and his handsome musical quintet were enough to lead them into temptation, not to mention Leo, who appeared capable of providing them with Heaven on earth.

"Well that's a relief," said Natalie as Mariachi de Dos Nacimientos, still singing, made its way to the door.

"We're lucky one of those dingbats didn't start speakin in tongues," said Consuelo. Natalie nodded in agreement as Leo hurried to catch up with the departing crusaders. He was just as enticed by the mariachis as the ladies had been. The women, seeing their dreamboat set sail, followed behind. Handbags flew as they vied for pole position. After they were all gone, Natalie, Consuelo, and Racine were True-Dee's only remaining guests.

True-Dee reemerged with mascara traces streaking her face. Miss Miranda sauntered behind. "Guess the Tupperware® party is over," she said taking a seat at the table with Natalie and Consuelo.

"No use in waitin," said True-Dee throwing her hands up in the air. "I called you all here today not just to share with you the advancements made by the Tupperware® Corporation, or even to try to get you to join The Cause, but because I have an important announcement to make." She paused, then continued, "I'm plannin on gettin the transformation. Thought about it for a long time and one thing I know is, nothin good ever happens in limbo." True-Dee was referring to the sex change operation she had been contemplating for a long time.

"Those are words of wisdom," said Natalie. She and Consuelo gave True-Dee a hug.

True-Dee gazed at Nat and Sway. "If I was a man I could kiss you both right now," she said.

"Good thing you're not," said Consuelo. "Because I got me a date tonight."

"And ¿who's the lucky fellow?" said True-Dee leaning in.

"Cal McDaniel," replied Natalie.

"Sounds like you got you a date with a real magnate," said True-Dee.

"A cheese magnate," added Natalie.

"I always have admired a girl unafraid to date the boss," said True-Dee. She winked at Consuelo.

El Pino
The Pine Tree

FRESCO, OLOROSO Y EN TODO TIEMPO HERMOSO

FRESH, FRAGRANT, AND ALWAYS LOVELY

LULABELL'S LONGING

Lulabell had loved the Lord and left Him twice. At the age of forty-seven, she was so set in her ways, she might never go back to Him, not even when Javier got home from True-Dee's party, spent from his constant crusading, but still bent on bringing one more soul on home to Jesus, threw his guitarrón down on the couch, stood up straight, spoke the name of the Lord, and said, "Momma, ¿won't you come on back to Jesus?"

Lulabell set her bag of extra-spicy pork rinds aside, ignored etiquette, and spoke with her mouth full. "¿What's in it for me?"

"Salvation, momma. Dios te ofrece salvación," said Javier falling to his knees. He placed a hand over Lulabell's knee. With her peasant top and long flowing skirt, Lulabell was in regional dress, although she didn't know from what region. She was about ready to head out to the Lava Landing Senior Prom, which explains her absence from True-Dee's Tupperware® party.

When she was in high school, Lulabell's parents couldn't afford the price of a dress, so she had to skip both her junior and senior proms. A missed prom could haunt a girl her entire life, so Lulabell tried to make her attendance an annual event. This year she was going with Simón, a music teacher and leader of the school mariachi. At forty-two, he was significantly older than the men Lulabell usually went out with, but he would suffice for the night. Since he would be donning his traje de charro, Lulabell was dressed more than appropriately. She had even gone to the trouble of braiding her hair and weaving in a couple of brightly colored red and orange ribbons— school colors. Owing to Lulabell's seemingly wholesome appearance, Javier figured he had a better shot than usual at saving his mother's soul.

"¿Salvation?" said Lulabell placing her hand over his. "And ¿what would I do with a thing like that, especially at this late date?" She gave Javier's hand a squeeze.

"Live forever and ever in the Glory of God," said Javier. He mistook his mother's rhetoric for willingness and squeezed back.

"Done enough livin in this life," said Lulabell.

"When the Lord comes a calling, momma, you'd be wise to listen."

"My soul's already spoken for," said Lulabell.

"The Lord'll take it back," said Javier reassuringly.

He was so full of hope, but so much in life is timing, and his was way off. If he had reached out to Lulabell's soul just four days before, he might have gotten somewhere. But now, Lulabell had decided to auction her soul off to the highest bidder and had, in fact, already put the ad in the newspaper for the event, which was just five short days away. Fearing she might sell herself and her soul short, she wasn't about to make any overtures toward the Lord.

"If the Lord's lucky, maybe I'll save the last dance for Him," said Lulabell. She let go of Javier's hand, and pushed him aside causing him to lose his balance and his sombrero in the process.

Javier got to his feet and replaced his sombrero. "You're more evil than we thought," he said, speaking not only for himself, but for the Lord. He picked up his guitarrón and marched off to his room.

Lulabell stayed put on the sofa watching her favorite weekly program, *El Mundo del Espectáculo*. Jorge Velásquez, the show's host, was introducing some singing guapo charro from the state of Jalisco, which is known for such things. "¡Ay! papi," said Lulabell as she got her first eyeful of Juan Ordóñez and the mariachi that accompanied him. In the young Juan, Lulabell couldn't help but see a bit of any one of a hundred different young men with whom she had danced and romanced over the years—the way he filled his traje de charro and what she figured lurked beneath it—a hairless chest reminiscent of his not too distant boyhood, flesh neither taut nor flabby and the way it clung to its frame, the legs a shade lighter than the rest of the body, the not yet filled out mustache (another reminder of not so long gone boyhood), and the more concrete reminders of manhood which always surprised Lulabell when she ran across them in her latest loves.

The truth of the matter was, Lulabell didn't know where boy ended and man began. Even in the alleged overage arena of bars and nightclubs, she often found herself in the arms of seventeen- and eighteen-year-olds, and the damage was always done before anyone knew otherwise. Both parties would begin by lying about their age. Lulabell would subtract twenty years from hers, the young man would add seven or eight to his, and for a time, everyone was happy, until Lulabell lost interest.

It was never the other way around. Lulabell would meet a fine-dancing, well-dressed young man at the baile on a Saturday night. By Tuesday he would be saying that he loved her—que la quería. By Friday, he LOVED her—que la amaba. Spanish being a language concerned with nuances, there are distinctions to be made in love and other things. It was at that point that Lulabell would take the young man in her arms and tell him that she was not really twenty-four, but thirty-three and that their union could not continue. He would be so devastated that within a week he'd be on his way home to mami, even if he had to cross at least one international border to get there, and it was in this manner that, in Lava Landing, Lulabell was responsible for the departure of more young ranch hands and day laborers than even the migra.

Lulabell dated mostly Mexican men with an occasional South or Central American here and there, thrown in for comparative purposes. Loo-Lee wanted to get to know a man from cada estado dentro de La República Mexicana, and in so doing gain a bit of knowledge of the land she was taken from at the age of six. Lulabell might not have broken Lava County lines in more than forty years, but she still missed her homeland because the thing about mother countries is this: They are like wristwatches or rings, forget to wear them for a day or two, but they still feel like they're on.

With a steady stream of young papacitos not just from her home state of Guerrero, but, potentially, the entire república at her disposal, Lulabell could hardly complain. If she smiled pretty and gave them a kiss when the dancing was done, she could rest assured that they would share a little about their mutual homeland.

Lulabell often recalled her sixth-grade Social Studies textbook and the climate maps that were inside—one area shaded light blue to indicate tundra, another bright green for grasslands, brown for desert. Lulabell was in the process of coloring in her own map. She had begun the project years before, but her pursuit was hardly climatological. It was purely anthropological.

Years of experience proved that a man from the state of Jalisco was more likely than any other to bring his girl serenatas, to show up under her window with his mariachi to either sing or wake her from sleep. But ¡aguas!, Lulabell might warn—Jalisco is also the state most inclined to raise or harbor a homosexual man.

As for loving, Lulabell knew a thing or two, or at least enough to know that men from her home state of Guerrero were the best lovers, but loving isn't everything, and for other things, namely dancing, the states of Nayarit and Zacatecas come highly recommended. Then again, the men from the capital, el D.F., were fine dancers, versed in the choreography of the cumbia, the nuances of salsa and merengue.

Now if a girl wanted a man macho and persistent, she would suggest the state of Michoacán. Then there was Sinaloa: It was a fine state, lovely Lulabell had heard, but there was something about the Sinaloan lisp that she didn't care for and the same could be said for the state of Chihuahua. Maybe it was the way they swallowed their "s's" and tripped over their "t's" that turned Lulabell off.

And that was the extent of her firsthand experience. She wanted to learn more, to shade her entire map, but all too often she found herself in the company of men from an already visited spot. Lulabell longed to be in the arms of a strange man, to ask him the telltale question, ¿De dónde eres? and have him say, San Luis Potosí or Nuevo León, but the push-and-pull factors of immigration had neither pushed nor pulled any of these men Lulabell's way.

Lulabell aimed the remote control at the television set as the credits rolled and Juan Ordóñez shook Jorge Velásquez's hand. She walked into her bedroom and sat down at the edge of her bed. A light blue makeup bag made of a silky oriental fabric, and a pink plastic-framed mirror waited at her side. She put on some bright coral lipstick, dabbing a bit onto the apples of her cheeks, and blending. Dressed as she was, she looked then more than ever as if she had just walked off of a Mexican calendar, as if she had been painted by the famosísimo Jesús Helgüera. With a bird in the palm of her hand, Lulabell would be La Pajarera. Put her on a horse and let her hair hang loose and long and she could pass for La Adelita.

Perhaps that afternoon it was the calendar scene of Las Mañanitas that Simón, Lulabell's date, had in mind when he showed up at the foot of her window with his mariachi. Hearing the first notes of the José Alfredo Jiménez classic "Serenata Sin Luna," Lulabell looked out the window and said, "Not another serenata." She was a divine woman used to the archaic ritual of the serenade, and perhaps a bit tired of it.

Lulabell hung her head out the window making her likeness to the woman in the calendar scene even more striking, and it did not even matter that there was no colonial architecture in the background, and for that matter, in all of Lava Landing.

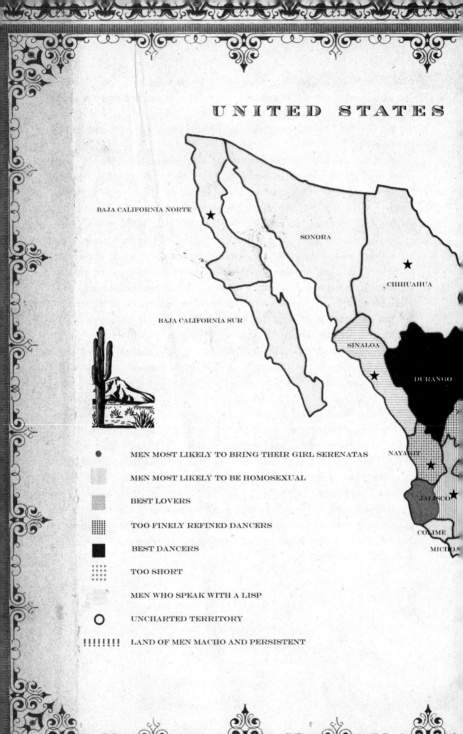

UNITED STATES

BAJA CALIFORNIA NORTE ★

SONORA

CHIHUAHUA ★

BAJA CALIFORNIA SUR

SINALOA

DURANGO ★

NAYARIT ★

JALISCO ★

COLIME

MICHOA

● MEN MOST LIKELY TO BRING THEIR GIRL SERENATAS

MEN MOST LIKELY TO BE HOMOSEXUAL

BEST LOVERS

TOO FINELY REFINED DANCERS

BEST DANCERS

TOO SHORT

MEN WHO SPEAK WITH A LISP

○ UNCHARTED TERRITORY

!!!!!!!!! LAND OF MEN MACHO AND PERSISTENT

El Cazo
The Pot

EL CASO QUE TE HAGO ES POCO

THE ATTENTION I PAY YOU IS LITTLE

EL BIG CHEESE

"Winona i don't you wanna come for a ride with me?" Cal sang as he combed his Grecian Formula®ed hair into place. He was getting ready to pick up Consuelo. Cal had been advancing on her every Tuesday and Thursday for the last seven of the ten years she had worked as one of his part-time employees at The Big Cheese Plant. That evening, Cal was feeling unusually proud of himself after convincing her to go on a date with him for the first time after he'd likened her to a dog that chases cars but wouldn't know what to do if it ever caught one.

He stepped lightly into his automobile—a 1964 powder blue Thunderbird he held on to as a token of his early success. Despite what his name implied, Cal was from Florida. He had come to Lava Landing in the summer of '73 in hopes of turning his cousin Rufus' then nearly defunct cheese factory into a sound moneymaking business. About that time, the Macías Brothers Dairy caught a bad bacterium, *Listeria monocytogenes* to be precise, which put them out of business and 105 people several feet under in what turned out to be one of the worst tragedies in dairy business history. As a token of his appreciation, Rufus handed over 49 percent of his business to Cal as well as the T-Bird. And if that wasn't gratitude enough, he dropped dead a few months later from a rare intestinal disease which turned his bowels bright green and burned a hole the size of a softball clear through his stomach. By decree of Rufus' Last Will and Testament, Cal became the sole owner of The Big Cheese Plant and it wasn't long before he worked his way into the hearts and pocketbooks of nearly every pizza maker in the state of California.

Aside from business prospects, Cal had come to California because he hoped that Lava Landing's dry air would benefit his health, which he considered failing at best. The humid Florida air had aggravated his eczema as well as his arthritis, not to mention what it had done to his respiratory faculties. As Cal figured it, every wayward carbon monoxide molecule in all of Miami had hitched a ride on the sultry air and now dwelt within the confines of his lungs.

At the age of fifty-three, the only thing Cal felt in full command of was his libido, which he considered his most virile faculty. Instead of waning with age, his sexual appetite had increased to several times what it had been in his earlier years. Cal attributed this to the fact that it was only during times of arousal that he was free of the aches and pains which plagued his daily life. As he put it, it was only "once the juices got flowin'" that the pain subsided enabling him to engage in his favorite activity: the pursuit of women.

Cal straightened his bolo tie in the rearview mirror. He pulled a can of Binaca® from the inside of his suit pocket, opened up and sprayed twice. On the way to Consuelo's, he listened to *Looney Bugsy McCray's Oldies Show,* a local radio program which featured a different theme every evening. That night Bugsy was spinning oldies about fast women. Turning the volume way up, Cal sang along to "Mustang Sally."

Cal pulled into Consuelo's driveway, took a look at his watch—a genuine platinum Rolex® with a diamond every three hours. He was a few minutes later than he said he would be. At the doorstep he took advantage of the brass lock set, arranged his hair one last time, and winked at his reflection before ringing the doorbell.

Consuelo came to the door wearing a velvet, zebra-striped, ankle-length, low-cut dress that could, perhaps, have been a size bigger so as to accommodate her attributes which were plenty, and a sparkly silver cardigan made of some multisyllabic synthetic fabric. One look at Consuelo reminded Cal of the second grade wherein and whence he had been given a cornucopia to color at Thanksgiving time. Back then, he had been plagued with the dilemma of whether to press hard throughout or to outline the figure, then softly shade its inside. As Cal looked at Consuelo, a similar predicament presented itself as he imagined what it would be like to take part in her horn of plenty.

As for Consuelo, she wasn't impressed. Cal looked older than his fifty-three years standing there on her doorstep. She generally dated older men, and didn't deny it either when Natalie pointed out that Consuelo was looking for a father figure.

Cal and Consuelo made their way to the T-Bird and headed for the Velvet Trapezoid, a twenty-four-hour, 365-day-a-year restaurant that boasted, "All you can eat, whenever you can eat it." For the occasion Consuelo had emptied out her biggest purse, the one she could fit three rotisserie chickens in.

As Cal sat beside Consuelo, he was beside himself. He put his hand on her knee, which had exposed itself by way of the slit in her dress. She straightened up, brushed the hand aside, and crossed her legs. As Cal suspected, her bark was worse than her bite. "Sorry, sugar cookie," said Cal. "Didn't know you was so bashful."

Consuelo ignored him, took her sweater off, and tossed it to the side, then rolled the window down.

"Find yourself some music you like," said Cal. He flipped on the radio. Consuelo turned the dial to her favorite AM Spanish language radio station, KAZA—La Casa de Los Recuerdos, a station that played nothing but classics of recent and not so recent memory. Consuelo sighed and put her hand over her chest when she heard the voice of her favorite female vocalist, Lola Beltrán, who was singing "Cucurrucucu, Paloma." Like all great ranchera singers, Lola sang with such emotion it was as if you could hear the teardrops in her voice.

Cal licked his lips as he caught a glimpse of the rise and fall of Consuelo's chest. With her eyes closed, Consuelo was completely caught up in the song. Cal's gaze rested on her breasts. He imagined what the cool nighttime air had done to her nipples and the thought alone forced him to shift his seating arrangements.

He shuffled around trying to get comfortable. With all the commotion his sharkskin suit made rubbing against itself, Consuelo opened her eyes and, much to Cal's chagrin, he was discovered.

Consuelo held her ground and stared at Cal's pants, which had levitated from where they ought to have been and stood suspended with no apparent foundation. She put her hand over her mouth and widened her eyes when she realized the cause of Cal's then present affliction and its possible effects.

She reached for her sweater, which, unbeknownst to her, was twisted around the shifting column. At first she tugged at it gently, but when it wouldn't budge, she pulled with all her might, putting the automatic transmission into neutral in the process. The engine raced as Cal swerved, knowing full well that R comes after N in the alphabet of automatic transmissions. A second later, the transmission was in reverse causing Consuelo, Cal, and his 1964 powder blue T-Bird to come to a screeching halt right smack dab in the center divide.

Mostly out of fear, Consuelo threw her arms around Cal's neck. Seeing the opportunity, Cal stuck his tongue in her nearest orifice—her ear—then climbed over and sat on her lap.

He stared at her for a fraction of a second before he kissed her. The things he did with his tongue amazed Consuelo in the same way it amazed her the first time she saw Bobby Trujillo wiggle his ears in the first grade. She unfastened Cal's bolo tie and the top two buttons of his shirt, then grazed her fingertips across his Adam's apple. Both she and Natalie had long held that this feature was the best indicator of the size of a man's sexual organ. Much to her surprise, it was about as big as the better half of a Big Red Delicious®.

Cal had the spaghetti straps of her dress untied and his face buried between her breasts. It was about that time that common sense overcame carnal desire and Consuelo pointed out that doing it right smack dab in the middle of the road wasn't such a good idea.

"This heat is gettin the best of me," said Sway wiping the sweat from her brow. "I could sure use me a Slurpee®." She scooted Cal to the side, then tied her spaghetti straps.

"¿A Slurpee®?" said Cal, fairly out of breath. He slammed his hands on the steering wheel.

Consuelo got out and started walking. There was a 7-Eleven just up the road. Cal hurried to catch up.

When they arrived, Consuelo soon saw that she was in luck as her favorite flavor, banana, was flavor of the month, and Cal was out of luck since, as he stood in the magazine section looking at the ghastly pictures in the most recent edition of *¡Alarma!*® magazine, Consuelo filled a medium Slurpee® cup, grabbed a special Slurpee® spoon-straw, then left a dollar on the counter, before she snuck through the prepackaged microwaveable food section and out the back door, then onto the street where she hitched a ride with a tall, dark-haired man in a big black truck with license plates from the Mexican state of Jalisco.

El Árbol

The Tree

EL QUE A BUEN ÁRBOL SE ARRIMA, BUENA SOMBRA LE COBIJA

HE WHO PROPS HIMSELF AGAINST A GOOD TREE

IS COVERED WELL BY THE SHADE

EL MAGO DE MICHOACÁN

The tall, dark-haired man with the big black truck with plates from the state of Jalisco was named Jesús Morales. Despite what his placas implied, he was from Caldera, the next town seven miles down the road.

Consuelo slid onto the bench seat.

Jesús opened his mouth and said the obligatory "¿Cómo te llamas?"

"Angélica," Consuelo said.

"And ¿where you headed?" said Jesús.

Consuelo did a double take. Chuy, as he was better known, had given her every indication that he was a non–English speaker.

"Home," she said.

"¿And where might that be?" he wanted to know.

"Lava Landin."

"¿You don't wanna stop nowhere on the way, to eat or maybe I could take you dancing?" He smiled big and wide revealing a gold-capped right bicuspid.

"No thank you," she said. "I've already exercised enough bad judgment for one night. I'd just like a ride home if it's on your way."

"It's not, but when I saw you walking down the road all alone, I just had to turn around."

Consuelo said nothing, but sipped her Slurpee® dry eliciting a sad burble from the bottom of the cup.

"Say, if you're not doing nothing tomorrow, maybe you wanna come to the rodeo. I'm riding in the first half."

Consuelo looked at him, remembered his license plates, and said, "¿Are you El Huracán de Jalisco?" The posters had been put up all around town for the upcoming rodeo, the first one of the season.

"Nope. I'm El Mago de Michoacán," he said.

"El Mago de Michoacán." Consuelo tried it on for size.

"That's this week. Next week I'm El Zorro de Zacatecas, and the week after, El Guerrillero de Guanajuato."

"But ¿where are you really from?"

"Caldera," he said. "It's marketing, you see. Every week we change our names, gives the people from all of the states somebody to root for."

They had arrived in town. "You can just drop me off at Roscoe's," said Consuelo.

"That's okay," said El Mago de Michoacán.

"Really," said Consuelo.

"I'd be more than happy to take you home," said Jesús.

"I'm more than sure that you would, only a girl can't be too careful," said Consuelo even though she knew as well as anybody that she'd been none too careful.

"If you insist," he said pulling into Roscoe's. "Now remember, if you feel like heading out to the jaripeo, this is what you do." He closed in on Consuelo, then continued. "Get there at 1:00 p.m. Go to the corrals and ask for Guillermo, El Güero de Polvos, and tell him Chuy sent you, and he'll let you in."

"All right," said Consuelo. She and Natalie would have liked to have gone to the rodeo. But they were otherwise occupied. They were going to have a yard sale where they intended to sell anything and everything they could in order to raise enough money to send Natalie on the trip south to try to free Don Pancho's soul. They had already put an ad in the *Lava Landing Lookout* boasting of antiques and collectibles, two things they were sure would draw a crowd and give them top dollar for their fine items.

"Thanks a lot for the ride," said Consuelo.

"Don't mention it," said El Mago de Michoacán tipping his Stetson®.

Consuelo stepped out, closed the door, and waved. El Mago de Michoacán disappeared into the night to take care of other business.

DOIN BUSINESS

"Last night I told my vato I got a gun under the seat of my truck, and he believes me. Rule number one," said Lucha holding up that many fingers, "never bring your cuete unless you're doin business, and last night I wasn't. Besides, este vato gots no idea what's goin on. He thinks he's my only one. Like he's my pan de Michoacán, mi piel de miel, mi mero mero pistolero. Pero así no es la cosa. He calls me all the time and tells me mamacita, chiquitita. He says I'm his luna, his estrella, his cielo. ¿Can you believe that shit?"

Fabiola nodded. Favy was Lucha's cousin and her all-around best friend. The girls were cleaning their guns, but had taken a breather to talk. Not that they were the sort that couldn't do two things at once. It was just that Lucha needed to pay special attention to Fabiola. Everyone thought that Fabiola was sordamuda, which is to say, deaf and dumb, but La Favy was neither, and she certainly wasn't stupid.

Favy's mother, La Lupe, had been a beautiful and generous young woman, too kind to say no to a boy. By the time she was fifteen, she was pregnant and didn't know who to rightfully blame but herself. She headed for the big city of Guadalajara to ply the only trade she thought available to her, prostitution.

As a child, Favy was a little girl with a big chip on her shoulder who liked to challenge her mother's customers to jalapeño-eating contests. By the time she was five she could out-jalapeño anyone in the neighborhood, and shortly thereafter she traded the jalapeño for its fiery cousin, the habanero.

One afternoon after church, Favy and La Lupe came home to find a customer waiting on their porch. As La Lupe went to the back bedroom to

change into something more appropriate for the occasion, Favy
the stranger, pulled two habanero peppers from the pocket of
bit the end off of one, then handed the other to him. He oblige

Favy didn't know what made him so angry, the way she had challeng—,
then one-upped him, or the way she laughed at his plea for water. But in his
rage, he took Favy right then and there and taught her firsthand the meaning
of a double entendre without even knowing it himself. You see, where he
came from, the word "chile" had an additional and vulgar meaning.

From that moment on, Favy hadn't said a word, not even to Lucha, the
person she loved more than anyone in the world. Favy stuck by Lucha
because she knew that Lucha would always take care of her, and what's more,
that she could, no matter what the circumstances.

It was a good thing too, because Fabiola was the sort of girl that came
with circumstances. She was tall and skinny with baby-fine, auburn hip-
grazing hair she parted down the middle. She had a weakness for Mexican
cinema of the 1970s, and dressed accordingly in bell-bottom blue jeans, high-
heeled cowboy boots, and weather permitting, halter tops. Otherwise, she
wore long- or short-sleeved western-tailored shirts she sometimes tucked in,
sometimes tied at the midriff, but never let just hang. She was big-busted,
wide-hipped, long-legged, light-skinned, and hazel-eyed. The fact that she
never got a word in edgewise made her seem, for some men, the perfect
woman. A thing like that often brought trouble, and when it did, one way or
another, Lucha took care of it.

"Este vato gots no idea what's goin on," continued Lucha. "Last night I
go to see him because he ain't got no ride of his own, just his bicicleta. A
thing like that don't bother me none, because the last thing I need is some
vato followin me around. That way he stays at home and watches his telenovelas. We're sittin in my truck listenin to music when he starts puttin his
hands all over me all kinds of places they ain't supposed to be. Usually I
wouldn't mind, but I wasn't in that sorta mood. Then he calls me chiquitita
and tries to do all the kinds of things that go with a word like that, so I tell
him, '¡Cálmate buey!'

"He laughs like he thinks it's real cute. A vato likes it when a girl gets
tough on him. Still he don't wanna listen, so I put my arm across his neck, lean
into it and say, 'Voy a sacar mi pistola.' I start reachin under the seat and he
opens his eyes up real big, but he don't know whether to believe me or not.

"I ask him does he think I'm stupid, and he does his best to shake his
head no. I push up against him real hard and say, 'Te parto la madre, cabrón,'
then let go."

Fabiola smiled.

"He moves up real close, but this time he keeps his hands to himself. He gives me a kiss on the cheek then says real suave, 'Tranquila, chiquita, tranquila.' Then he tells me somethin I ain't never heard nowhere before. He tells me chiquitiguapa."

Lucha smiled. "¿Anybody every tell you that before? ¿Chi-qui-ti-gua-pa?"

Fabiola shook her head. All of those years of not vocalizing her thoughts had led to an extremely expressive countenance, and she looked as though she were about to cry from disappointment.

"After he tells me that, I go soft on him, and I let him show me just what a mamacita he thinks I am, right there en la troca, and it don't matter who's watchin. Then I start to thinkin and feelin bad about my man Cheque. That vato was bad. Taught me how to shoot straight, and a girl don't forget a thing like that."

Lucha picked up her gun, a shiny silvertone .45, and slammed the cartridge into place. Fabiola followed suit.

Lucha put her hand over her heart. "I might give everything else away, but I'm savin this for Cheque, and it don't even matter if he's doin twenty-five to life." Then she got on her hands and knees, felt around under her bed, until she came up with the suitcase. "Eight kilos de la reina," she said opening it up. "Now all we gots to do is move it, and I know just how."

Fabiola's face moved into a question mark.

"It's rodeo season, prima, and we got a double date with a pair of bull riders. I let you choose which one you like better, El Mago de Michoacán or El Huracán de Jalisco. And don't worry if you don't like either one. The season has just begun and we're gonna move the merchandise one kilo at a time."

The first day of rodeo season in Lava Landing is traditionally kicked off with a charreada, the Mexican version of the rodeo. Accordingly, Lucha and Fabiola were on their way to the old charro ring just off of Highway 33.

"Good thing we got four-wheel drive," commented Lucha as they pulled behind the ring proper, to the area where the bulls and horses were kept.

The back of Lucha's Silverado was loaded. Cheque had taught her that every operation needs a front and this was hers: One idle weekend, Lucha and Fabiola had taken the six-hour trip down to Tijuana, switching turns at the wheel, to buy up a batch of hard leather flower-embossed purses, dozens of fancy belts, several hundred dangling huarache key chains, and a few pairs of exotic-skin cowboy boots. Lucha had violated the conditions of her probation, but so what. She was a criminal, and her soon-to-be drug-dealing ways were just part of a greater scheme of things. Lucha was gonna free herself from the throes of poverty into which she'd been born, and while she was at it, she was gonna get Favy the help she needed so that she could get her voice back.

The immediate plan was this: Lucha and Favy were gonna pass all of them imports to a pair of bull riders after the rodeo. And there, amongst the Mexican imports, the men would find another import, a Colombian one, stuffed in the right half of a pair of cordovan anteater boots.

The girls parked. Two flags flew up above, but neither sparked any patriotism within them. They could hear the banda playing beyond the fence, but could see none of the rodeo action. They could, however, see various vendors which lined the outside of the ring, trickling into the stands, some selling ice cream bars, others selling cut cucumbers and flowered mangos covered in salsa de la marca Tapatío®. Lucha pulled her binoculars out from under the seat and had a closer look. One enterprising individual sold tickets for the inevitable raffle. He held up a large rectangular cardboard box filled with what seemed the afternoon's greatest treasure: an Ezequiel Peña compact disc collection which, if you were lucky, could be yours for just a one dollar investment. Mr. Peña, Mexico's new cowboy, and his educated horses would be providing further musical and equine entertainment. (That's how they always billed his show: El Nuevo Charro de México con Sus Caballos Educados.)

But Lucha and Fabiola wouldn't stick around to see the handsome Ezequiel Peña ride into the ring atop one of his beautiful and civilized horses. With a microphone in one hand, the reins in the other, and a sombrero of unrivaled beauty and elegance on his head, Ezequiel would sing one of his heartfelt songs while his horse galloped to the beat and the girls in the audience screamed. Nor would Lucha and Fabiola walk along the promenade making ojitos at every handsome boy they saw. As the title of this chapter indicates, they were carrying their cuetes, and they were there to do business.

From the front seat of the Silverado, the girls could see El Mago y El Huracán recuperating in the corner of the bull pen. That afternoon, El Mago had stayed on the bull thirteen seconds and, in so doing, had outlasted El Huracán by a full five seconds. The Mexicans, unlike their norteamericano counterparts, don't strive for an even eight seconds, but aim to stay on the bull until it stops bucking.

Lucha and Fabiola stepped out of the Silverado and got close. The men looked at one another, dusted their hands off on their leather coverlets, then walked toward them.

"Soy El Mago de Michoacán," said El Mago de Michoacán. Something wasn't right. His accent was completely off.

"Cut the Spanish and let's get down to business," said Lucha rebuffing El Mago's offer of a handshake.

El Huracán stood aside.

Fabiola opened up her flower-embossed purse slow and easy. She had kept one of the handbags and insisted Lucha do the same. It was the closest the girls had ever come to breaking the cardinal rule of successful drug trafficking: Don't use the merchandise. Favy pulled out her polished .45, and poised it upon the tired bull riders. It was a moment of great relish for La Favy. Nothing made her happier than seeing a man in a vulnerable position, except being the one who had put him there. They were all alone. Ezequiel Peña had just entered the ring. The grandstand was in a roar.

The men were in their trajes de charro. According to regulation, and please be informed, the art of charrería is highly regulated, they were wearing the requisite pistols.

"Get your hands in the air," said Lucha. "I'm gonna grab at your belt, but don't get the wrong idea, boys." She licked her lips for emphasis and Fabiola did the same. Lucha unbuckled their belts, and their pistols et al. came tumbling down. She kicked them out of the way.

"They're fake," insisted El Huracán, his hands still raised high in the air.

"So's your act," said Lucha.

The men frowned, reminding Lucha of any one of a half dozen dumb sidekicks in any one of a hundred old Mexican cowboy movies.

Now my dear Reader, this is where I fear the narrative might prove disappointing. ¿Does the Reader think a drug deal would make for interesting prose? So it would seem, but all parties express their regret in informing the Reader that this is not the case. There was really nothing swashbuckling about it.

Imagine this if you will: two girls, two guns, a kilo of high-grade cocaine on one side, and on the other, two tired bull riders moonlighting as middlemen, as captivated by the beauty and daring of their business associates as by the bargain they were getting. At fifty grand a kilo, they were nearly getting wholesale on wholesale. The girls had priced the goods to go and that they did. Money and merchandise switched hands quickly and with little incident.

Fabiola kept tabs on El Huracán de Jalisco as he unloaded and inspected the merchandise while El Mago de Michoacán filled Lucha's favorite mesh Mexican shopping bag with cash, and the deal was done.

As far as the girls were concerned, the men could sell all those handbags, boots, belts, and key chains at next week's rodeo for all they cared. The grandstand noise wound down. Ezequiel Peña switched one educated horse for another and during this brief respite Lucha heard an all too familiar sound coming from the other side of the fence. Mariachi de Dos Nacimientos was strumming out its soul-saving message.

"Been a pleasure doin business with you boys," said Lucha. Their gratitude expressed, Lucha and Fabiola boarded the Silverado and promptly peeled out, leaving a trail of dust in their wake.

El Paraguas
The Umbrella

PARA EL SOL, Y PARA EL AGUA

FOR RAIN OR SHINE

UN BUEN SUSTO

"We're off to see a powerful lady that can help you," said Lucha to Favy once they were on their way.

She slid a newspaper ad Fabiola's way. Fabiola picked it up and gave it a look. Lucha was right. La Señora Linda was a spiritual counselor capable of reading cards and palms. With her psychic powers she could show you your past, present, and future. She could hypnotize you, give you a better tomorrow, teach you how to have fun, rid you of bad influences, fatigue, anguish, physical aches and pains, timidity, acne, obesity, sleeplessness, nervousness, frigidity, sadness, and depression. She could help you keep a good thing, or get rid of a bad one. ¿Does the one you love love another? La Señora Linda could bring your beloved to your side and all within twenty-four hours no matter the distance. ¿Does everything make you cry? La Señora could help you find happiness and a job. She could cure you of sexual impotence, unknown illnesses, and infertility, rid you of bad neighbors, clean your body and your soul, cure the evil eye, tell you the reason for your bad luck, repair your lost virginity, make your money go further, or show you the face of your enemy in a glass of water.

Fabiola set the newspaper on the seat next to her.

"Things are good all around, but they're only gonna get better," said Lucha pulling into a dirt driveway. Lucha tried to be optimistic, but it was hard. She hadn't heard her cousin's voice in more than fifteen years.

Lucha found a shady spot under a weeping willow and parked. Despite what La Señora Linda's super-psychic powers might have implied, she lived in a small single-story house in dire need of a new roof and a paint job. The girls walked to the door.

Lucha rang the doorbell. It didn't work. She knocked. La Señora came to the door.

"¿Es usted La Señora Linda?" said Lucha.

"That I am."

La Señora was a small woman, in an apron and cleaning clothes. Lucha would have guessed she must have been in her fifties.

"You must be my 6:30," said La Señora untying her apron. "Come in. I am only just getting home from work. There is not enough respect for my true profession. I have to work another job." She led the girls to the living room and offered them a seat on the laminated sofa. "¿You like Avon®?" she said dropping a catalog in Lucha's lap. "Maybe you look at this while I get everything ready." She walked to the back room.

There was no television set in the living room, just a coffee table, and plenty of baskets filled with dusty fake flowers. On the walls, a brass-toned clock, pictures of what the girls assumed were La Señora's children alongside framed prints of La Virgen de Guadalupe and the Sacred Heart of Jesus. And there amongst the household mundanity was a sign which stated plain and clear in English and Spanish: One swear word and you're outta here.

La Señora was back shortly.

"¿You see something you like?" said La Señora pointing to the Avon® catalog.

"A few things," lied Lucha.

"You take it with you, show it to your friends. I order it for you."

"Thank you," said Lucha.

La Señora paused to study Fabiola. "Estás bien bonita, mija," then to Lucha, "¿Does she prefer English or Spanish?"

"Either or," said Lucha.

La Señora took Fabiola's hands and rubbed them. "We are going to start with a limpia." La Señora looked over at Lucha for approval. She nodded.

An egg and a glass of water waited on the coffee table. "I am going to clean you, cariño, on the inside. Then I crack the egg in the water and the egg tells me what is wrong with you, then we fix you. ¿Está bien, mija?"

Fabiola nodded.

"You have to stand up for me." Fabiola did as she was told. La Señora held Fabiola's arms out in the form of a cross.

La Señora ran the egg up and down Fabiola's body, paying close attention to the temples, wrists, and heart. Lucha sat on the couch with her arms folded. That afternoon's drug deal might have made Lucha's heart race, but that was with excitement. As La Señora tended to Fabiola, Lucha's heart raced, but for fear this time. She was worried whatever Fabiola had couldn't be cured.

La Señora continued with the limpia. She used the egg to trace the shape of the cross over Fabiola's body what seemed, in Lucha's estimation, a hundred times, before she set the egg down, then picked up a branch from the pirul tree and ran it all over Fabiola's body.

"This is to purify the body and the soul. Here," said La Señora handing the branch off to Lucha. "You finish it up." Lucha hadn't expected such a hands-on approach.

La Señora Linda knelt down in front of the coffee table and carefully cracked the egg into the waiting glass of water. A gooseneck lamp waited. She turned the light on and positioned it over the glass.

"That's enough," she said to Lucha. "Sit down. Both of you sit down."

La Señora looked at Fabiola. "Pobrecita," she said.

"¿Is it bad?" Lucha wanted to know.

"Yes, mija. It is bad. Very, very bad."

Lucha put an arm around Fabiola.

"But ¿can you fix it?" said Lucha.

"What she has only she can fix," said La Señora.

"We have money," offered Lucha.

"I know you do."

"I mean we have a lot, whatever it takes."

"Money cannot fix this." La Señora shook her head. "You see, she can speak, sing even, like a beautiful bird. ¿Am I right?"

"Yes," said Lucha. "When we were children, en México, sometimes we wouldn't go to school and she would sing at the plaza where the mariachis play in Guadalajara. The people would give us pesos, and after, we would go to El Mercado de San Juan de Dios to spend them. ¿Ain't that right, Favy?"

Fabiola nodded.

"She would sing so purty. She would sing 'La Cigarra,' " said Lucha.

"That is a beautiful song," La Señora said to Fabiola. "And Guadalajara is a beautiful city. My husband is from there."

"And you, ¿where are you from, Señora?"

"I am from Sinaloa," she said.

La Señora squeezed Fabiola's hands in her own, looked her in the eye, and she, La Señora, began to sing softly. She sang "La Cigarra," a song about a cicada singing as it goes off to its death.

Lucha sang along with La Señora. The first verse went by without incident. During the second verse, Fabiola's lips began to move, no sound, just the movement of her lips, as if she were lip-syncing to two mismatched voices when her own was so beautiful.

It wasn't until the final verse that Fabiola made a sound, a whisper at most, but a sound nonetheless.

"You see, you can speak," said La Señora.

Fabiola nodded.

"I am going to tell you something you already know," said La Señora to Fabiola. "You suffered a trauma. Un buen susto. Something very bad happened to you many years ago, something you want to forget, but can't, something you had no control over. Something you could not fight off."

La Señora looked at Lucha. "Maybe you know what it is, maybe you don't. That was a long time ago, in a place far away."

"I know what happened to her," said Lucha. "Un hombre maldito se abusó de ella." She couldn't bring herself to say it in English. In Spanish it was more vague. All she had to say was that a bad man had abused her. She didn't have to go into the details for La Señora to know what she was talking about.

Fabiola looked at Lucha for a long time. Her gaze was so steady she didn't even so much as blink, and when she finally did a single tear rolled down each of her cheeks. Then she did something she hadn't done in so many years. She spoke. "You know," she said.

Lucha grabbed her by the shoulders. "Yes I know. I have always known." Lucha waited for Favy to say something more, but she didn't. "Favy, talk to me," said Lucha shaking her by the shoulders, but she wouldn't say a word.

La Señora pulled Lucha away, then turned toward Fabiola. "To deal with your pain, and to protect yourself, you took control of what you could. You decided not to speak."

Favy stared at La Señora as if in defiance.

"But ¿can't you fix it? Maybe you could make her forget. Hypnotize her or somethin," suggested Lucha.

"I could hypnotize her, but that would mean she would have to go back to that badness, and that would be too difficult for her."

Tears formed in the corners of Lucha's eyes.

"You love her and you protect her," said La Señora. By that time, she had Lucha by the hands. "And you always will." La Señora flashed a reassuring smile.

"But, Señora, you can do so much," said Lucha wiping her eyes and getting to her feet. She had shoved La Señora's ad into the back pocket of her jeans, and now she pulled it out. "You can do so much, you have to be able to do somethin to help her."

"Yes. It is true. I can do a lot," said La Señora, then she proceeded in rattling off her specialties in rapid Spanish:

"Embrujos, protecciones, exorcismo, maleficios. Le enseño la cara de su enemigo en un vaso de agua. ¿Tiene usted mala suerte en el amor? ¿Malas influencias? ¿Malos vecinos? Leo la mano, echo las barajas, limpias, impotencia sexual, timidez. Le reuno con su ser querido en solo veinticuatro horas.

Vicios, maltrato, enfermedades desconocidas, adicciones, depresión, tristeza, angustia, nervios, alcoholismo, drogas, obesidad, mal ojo. ¿Se siente perseguido? ¿No le rinde su dinero? Yo le puedo ayudar resolver cualquier problema por lo difícil que sea. Problemas con su pareja, en su casa, en su negocio, envidia, amigos desleales, males postizos o hechicerías, infertilidad, frigidez. Yo le puedo ayudar.

"Why I can even make a loose woman decent," whispered La Señora. She leaned in toward Lucha and waited to see if she would take her up on the offer.

"Thanks, Señora, but I was really hopin you could help my cousin."

"Sorry. I do not do susto. No one does really. Check the competition," said La Señora opening up the newspaper. Actually it was a weekly news magazine called *La Guía*. She turned to a competitor's ad. "You don't see susto on his list either. I can bury this for you," she said gesturing toward the egg in the water. The egg was La Señora's best indication of what was ailing Fabiola and she had studied it with the precision of a surgeon examining a piece of biopsied flesh. La Señora Linda didn't mention it, but she had never seen such an ugly egg in all of her years in practice. The yolk was bloody and it seemed to quiver as if it had a heartbeat.

"Viejo," she shouted down the hall, and her husband emerged from the back room. "Bury this for me, ¿ay? And deep."

He took the glass and walked out the front door.

"¿Are you sure there is nothin more you can do?"

"I am very sorry," said La Señora, then she did a strange thing. She grabbed Lucha by an elbow, pulled her near and spoke to her in confidence, saying, "As a woman and a Mexican national, I advise you to go back to México. In these cases, I find the only thing that really works is venganza. Understand this has nothing to do with my profession, but it is my advice to you." She flared her eyebrows, then let Lucha loose.

Lucha knew a good idea when she heard one. Revenge. ¿Why hadn't she thought of it sooner? She rubbed the spot where La Señora had put the hold on her and said, "¿How much do we owe you?"

"You owe me nothing, but if you would like to make a donation, I will leave you in privacy so that you can leave whatever comes genuinely from your heart." She pulled a decorative plate from behind the couch and set it on the coffee table, then grabbed Fabiola by the hands once again. "I wish you all the goodness in the world, y que dios te bendiga, que te cuide, y que te ayude ahora y siempre."

Lucha watched La Señora disappear down the hall, and turn into what she assumed was her bedroom, before she opened up her purse, removed a sliver of hundred-dollar bills, and set them on the plate.

¡CARAMBA!

Una Yarda, or Most Noteworthy Items Nat and Sway Had to Sell in Order to Finance Natalie's Trip South So That She Might Endeavor to Extract Don Pancho's Wayward Soul from Purgatory:

Papasan chair with pink-flowered cushion and matching stool

1970 Chevy Malibu model unassembled and in the box

Rooster-patterned tablecloth from the 1950s

Iorio® bass accordion

Wrought iron three-tiered plant stand

Belt buckle with petrified scorpion

Knife block with hand-painted rooster

Original zinnia-framed watercolor

1¢ bubble gum and peanut vending machine

Original Maid-Rite® washboard

Wristwatch with Marcasite® band

Mint green cinder bucket

Bingo bag with daubers and lucky elephant

Snakeskin attaché case

Stuffed animal poodle from the 1950s known as Inés

Monkey swing

Butterscotch Bakelite® bracelet

Aquarium with gravel, statuary, and fish

Silver belt buckle with bucking bronco and rider

Daisy decal decoupage nightstand

Genuine Brahma bull horns Nat and Sway considered attaching to the hood of the Cadillac during a weak moment

Wrought iron birdcage never used for its intended purpose

Three red-carved Bakelite® bracelets

1943 copy of *Terry's Guide to Mexico* complete with all original foldout maps

Replica silk bullfight poster featuring El Cordobés

Chinese curio cabinet

Original framed watercolor of matador and bull

Chartreuse Fiesta® teapot

Glamour girl head vase from the 1940s

Original movie poster for the Mexican film *El Hijo Desobediente* starring David Reynoso, Manuel López (¡ay! papi) Ochoa, and Lucha Villa

Original Bob's Big Boy® bank

Fully functional black panther TV lamp

Japanese pagoda jewelry box

Flamingo-in-pond candy dish

Lucite® ring holder in the form of a cat

Embroidered 1933 Chicago World's Fair flag

Bamboo deep-sea fishing rod with reel

Ceramic ashtray with matador wielding cape in front of charging bull from Tijuana

Mexican wrestler dolls and makeshift wrestling ring

Light green milk glass rooster toothpick holder

Chinese ceramic ginger jar

China girl ceramic planter

Pancho Arango cigar tin

Old Honolulu seashell box

Lucite® fruit salad bracelet

Seven-piece Bakelite® vanity set

Tapestry and Bakelite® purse

Bamboo wall divider

Amoeba-shaped coffee table

Tabla 3

THE CARDS *are* CUT

El Avión
The Airplane

NO ME EXTRAÑES CORAZÓN,
QUE REGRESO EN EL AVIÓN
DON'T MISS ME, SWEETHEART,
FOR I WILL RETURN ON THE AIRPLANE

GIRL TALK

The girls were able to raise $442.37 during their yard sale with- out having to part with any of their matador collection or chinoiserie. They also kept the petrified scorpion belt buckle, Inés, *Terry's Guide to Mexico,* the movie poster, and the flamingo-in-a-pond candy dish—items which had initially made it out to the front lawn, but with which they ultimately couldn't part. Everything else went and it was just as well. Since the girls had shrewdly purchased each and every item at yard sales and the flea market, they received dollars on the penny. In addition to these yard sale fondos, they were also able to secure a week's advance on their wages. It was in this manner that they had financed Natalie's passage south.

"I never really wanted much out of life by way of material things, except maybe to have enough of them satin-covered padded hangers to hang all my dresses on," said Natalie. She stood in front of her closet door, reaching in, pulling dresses, blouses, and skirts from plastic and wire hangers.

"That would be somethin," said Consuelo. Consuelo was seated atop Natalie's queen-size bed. The bed was covered with a pink and white pinstriped bedspread, two pillows cased in the same fabric, and another satin pillow shaped like a rainbow including a cloud and displaying all of the usual colors. Up against one wall stood a cabinet stereo, and next to that, three wooden crates of records—a collection of English and Spanish tunes made up of mostly Patsy Cline and Loretta Lynn on one end, and Lola Beltrán and Chelo on the other.

Consuelo was busy preparing a letter of introduction to her family about Natalie, stating the obvious as well as the not so obvious, the latter of which included the fact that Natalie spoke bad Spanish with a good accent, liked to dance and was good at it, couldn't stand avocados, was very clumsy, had weak ankles and loose joints, a low tolerance for alcohol, and a sensitive stomach. She shouldn't drink the water, and keep her away from unsavory men at all costs.

Natalie was flying out on a nonstop flight to San Luis Río Colorado, Sonora, where she would have five days and six nights to free the soul of Don Pancho Macías Contreras. While it might seem like a very short time to rescue someone from Purgatory, it seemed like an eternity to Natalie and Consuelo, who hadn't been apart for more than twenty-four hours in nearly twenty years.

"You gotta make sure and watch what you eat. Just stay close to my tía Elena. She'll take real good care of you," said Consuelo.

"¿Anything else I should know, Sway?"

"Most important, Nat, I need you to look around and remember everything that's important. Go and visit the place where my daddy's buried and bring a rock. That's how they do it over there. You see, if a man dies and he's put under with little ceremony and he doesn't have the benefit of a priest sayin words over his body that the Lord understands, people come by and stop for a minute. They pray for him and leave a rock just to show they were there. This is to help him get to Heaven if he hasn't already."

"I'll go there, Sway. And, I'll bring flowers and a couple of rocks," said Natalie.

"The most important thing is that you take care of yourself because I don't know what I'd do without you. Also you should know that you gotta be careful with the men over there. They ain't nothin like the ones over here. There's a good to it and a bad to it and that's what makes it even worser. You see, they teach a boy how to be a man from day one and that's the good of it. But if a man takes a likin to you, Nat, even if the feelin ain't mutual he's liable to haul you off and make you his the only way a man knows how. And you're not likely to get any help from anyone, because that's the way things are done. Unless he ain't the only one that wants you. Then your problems get bigger when they start fightin over you and stuff, so don't let it happen."

"¿How do you know all this?" said Natalie.

"¿Don't you never listen to the radio, Nat? Those songs ain't made up. They happen."

"¡Shit! I never realized."

Natalie got up and closed her suitcases. Consuelo reached around and took off her chain with the medallion of María de Lourdes; Natalie did the same. It did not matter that the medallions were identical and that the girls had both received them during their First Communion twenty years before. They exchanged necklaces, hugs, kisses, and a few tears.

"Remember," said Sway. "All kinds of crazy shit happens, in all kinds of places, so watcha."

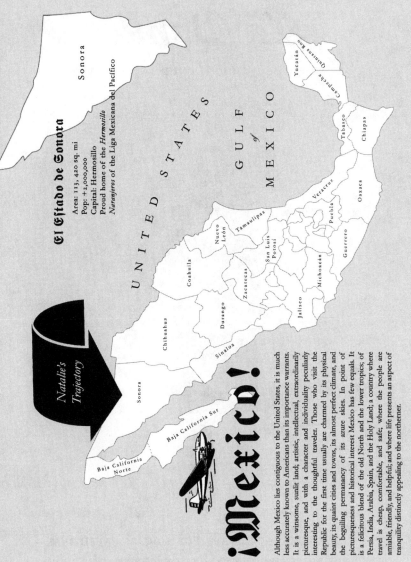

El Estado de Sonora

Area: 113, 420 sq. mi
Pop: +2,000,000
Capital: Hermosillo
Proud home of the *Hermosillo*
Naranjeros of the Liga Mexicana del Pacifico

Natalie's Trajectory

Sonora

UNITED STATES

GULF *of* MEXICO

Baja California Norte

Baja California Sur

Sonora

Chihuahua

Sinaloa

Durango

Coahuila

Zacatecas

Nuevo León

Tamaulipas

San Luis Potosí

Jalisco

Michoacán

Guerrero

Puebla

Veracruz

Oaxaca

Tabasco

Chiapas

Yucatán

Campeche

Quintana Roo

¡Mexico!

Although Mexico lies contiguous to the United States, it is much less accurately known to Americans than its importance warrants. It is a winsome, sunlit land; artistic, intellectual, extraordinarily picturesque, and with a character and individuality peculiarly interesting to the thoughtful traveler. Those who visit the Republic for the first time usually are charmed by its physical beauty, its quaint cities and towns, its almost perfect climate, and the beguiling permanency of its azure skies. In point of picturesqueness and historical interest Mexico has few equals. It is a felicitous blend of the old North and the lower tropics; of Persia, India, Arabia, Spain, and the Holy Land; a country where travel is cheap, comfortable, and safe; where the people are amiable, friendly, and helpful; and where life presents an aspect of tranquility distinctly appealing to the northerner.

T. Phillip Terry, *Terry's Guide to Mexico*, 1943

La Dama
The Lady

LA DAMA PULIENDO EL PASO, POR TODA LA CALLE REAL

THE LADY POLISHING THE STREET EVERY STEP OF THE WAY

LA CATRINA

In that land they would always remember Natalie as La Catrina because she was always dressed up, even when she was running in the street playing fútbol with the boys in a pair of borrowed tennis shoes and a chiffon dress from some distant decade, then running down the street to the plaza to fall down out of breath on a patch of damp grass and say, "I love to play el kíckbol." Men young and old of the pueblo would learn the sound of her high heels by heart and hearing them coming, they would drop work or play to rush to her side to assist her with the unpredictable discrepancies of the sidewalk. When people who did not know her name saw her coming up or down the street, they would remark sometimes to themselves and sometimes out loud, "Ahí viene La Catrina." And the men who knew her name would forget or otherwise disregard it, replacing it with mamacita, chula, linda, hermosa, güerita, or sometimes all of the above, repeated in such rapid succession, they sounded like a single word.

When night came, she would shower, shampoo, dry and further curl her already curly hair, put on a dress, high heels, a fur-trimmed sweater, costume jewelry, and lipstick, then loop her arm in the arm of some suitable chaperone such as Marta—Consuelo's older fat cousin—and they would walk down to the plaza where the boys would be walking counterclockwise, and the girls clockwise, until one took a liking to the other and, if the feeling was mutual, they looped arms and took to walking the same direction.

For a few days, this is how things would progress. The days would be filled with soccer playing and English lessons. She would line the school-age boys and girls up on the sidewalk each afternoon and say, "Repiten por favor," then offer them the numbers in proper succession, colors, seasons, months of the year, and days of the week. All of this would stop at five o'clock when the church bells rang and all together the people of the pueblo stopped whatever they were doing—the women gossiping over simmering pots of descriptively named meat dishes, the men smoking cigarettes or unhusked corn over the asador, listening to Vicente Chente Fernández sing over the AM radio, the children running in the streets, the hollering vendors pushing their wares, the early arrivers to the plaza walking their different directions. All together they would take off baseball caps, sombreros, and tejanas, then turn to face the direction of the town church and raise their right hand to hesitate first on the forehead, second on the chest, the right shoulder, then the left, blessing themselves en el nombre del Dios Padre, Dios Santo, y El Espíritu Santo because that is the way things were done in that land.

¿And the nights? They would be filled with plaza walking just as they had been for centuries. Those who had no reason to walk the plaza would gather around kitchen tables, gossiping and sipping cups of canela, or lie sleeping in their beds. But even in dreams, La Catrina would come to occupy the minds of just about everyone. The young men would have impure thoughts of her made pure by the fact that they all wanted to marry her, so when they imagined her in ways that young men will, they saw her not just as some stray mamacita, but as their wife. The older already married men would have no hopes of purifying their thoughts, but this was not without benefit, for they would act out these wishful thoughts with their wives and this put perpetual smirks on faces that had not genuinely smiled in years.

And now it was a Tuesday afternoon and the ladies of the neighborhood had all gathered and placed themselves on Doña Elena's porch steps. It was Natalie's second full day in the pueblo and already they were making demands. They wanted three things: to know who la norteamericana was and why she had come, and last, to get hold of one of her dresses.

Doña Elena invited the women in, poured them cups of Nescafé®, and began. Her name was Natalie. She was Consuelo's best friend and she had come to do an errand for her. ¿Did everyone remember Consuelo, la hija de Doña Luisa y Don Pancho? They did.

But ¿where was La Catrina?, Doña Ernesta, the most practical of the bunch, inquired.

"Está jugando fútbol," said Doña Elena.

"Oh, sí," said the ladies. They went on to try to convince Doña Elena to sneak away one of La Catrina's dresses. They would return it promptly. They only wanted to get down the cut and proportions so that they could be duplicated. But then, La Catrina walked through the door out of breath, pulled her borrowed tennis shoes off, smiled and said, "Buenas tardes."

"Buenas," replied the women.

Doña Elena introduced La Catrina by her Christian name, but not just as the best friend of her niece Consuelo (Consuelo's mother and Doña Elena were sisters), but as her niece, for Natalie had already taken a place in Doña Elena's permanent affections, and when such a thing happens with a Mexican woman, she naturally looks for some sort of title to make that person a constant in her life, and since la Doña had been blessed with seven daughters and therefore could not offer Natalie a husband, she did what she considered the next best thing.

With a smile Doña Elena said, "Les presento a mi sobrina, Natalie."

And then the women rushed to shake her hand and La Catrina in a cut-along-the-bias-since-it-flatters-every-figure dress and bare feet, still sweating from playing el kíckbol with all the muchachos of the pueblo, held her thin hand out with its poorly painted fingernails, since with all of the excitement and the constant callers she hadn't the time to see to the small detail of a manicure, and she said to one Doña after the other, "Mucho gusto, encantada."

And indeed she was, enchanted. And she could not have been more so than when the ladies as embarrassed and delighted as the day they celebrated their quinceañeras got up the nerve to ask her to borrow one of her lovely dresses, just one.

Later, with the dress in their possession, the women made their way back to Doña Cuca's where they reduced it to a simple mathematical equation, a ratio into which they entered their respective proportions, and in no time, the women would be showing up on Doña Elena's porch steps, asking to see La Catrina, for they refused to acknowledge her given name. Natalie would come out from the back porch where she had been feeding the chickens or watering the flowers. The Doña would pose for La Catrina, and Natalie would look down at her shoes, wave an index finger, shake her head, then point to her own shoes and say, "Doña, lo que usted necesita es un par de tacones."

"Oh, sí," the Doña would reply and she would be on her way to El Canadá to buy a pair of high heels.

Pretty soon all of the women of the pueblo had them: high heels and cut-along-the-bias dresses. In no time, El Canadá sold out of high heels and had to wire to Guanajuato for more. Things were changing all right. But soon, things would change for real. El Canadá would close down, like every other establishment in town, except for the jail and the church. The lights would go out and there would be no hot water, because all of the electricity would be harnessed for the specific purpose of honoring San Jacinto, el Santo Patrón del Pueblo. People would put on their best clothes and walk down the street to drink and dance the night away, to light fireworks, to bet on roosters, to ride bulls to the sound of la banda tocando, to sing with the mariachis, to eat tacos de birria, roasted corn con chilito y limón, to do all of the things they had done during the most enjoyable moments of the entire year, but this time they would do them all at once and in the space of three days, for soon it would time for la feria.

La Grúa

The Tow Truck

PARA UNOS AMIGO, PARA OTROS ENEMIGO
FOR SOME A FRIEND, FOR OTHERS AN ENEMY

THE DAY LULABELL
AUCTIONED OFF HER SOUL

While Natalie was trying to think of a way to spring Don Pancho's soul, Lulabell was getting ready to auction hers off. In Lava Landing, for some strange reason, it was raining. Lulabell wished she had spun her hair up into her usual chonguitos, or had worn it in braids since the rain made it frizz and she worried that this would bring down the value of her soul. The week before on the Mexican radio station, nine out of ten men had claimed that they preferred women con el pelo suelto, so Lulabell let hers hang loose and long.

She arrived at Taquería La Bamba a few minutes before 6:00, ordered a super-quesadilla de carne asada, no onions, and a large horchata, then pulled two tables together, and sat down. She was expecting a big crowd.

A mariachi played in the corner. The man behind the guitarrón had a goatee. Maybe he is the Devil, thought Lulabell. Then she remembered that Jesus also wore a beard. And while Jesus' hair was long, the Devil wore His in a pompadour. As for the mariachi, he wore a sombrero, but from what Lulabell could tell, he had that haircut that was once so popular with all of the Mexican soccer players. His hair was short in front and in that respect respectable, but left long in back. A man who wore his hair this way paid far more attention to the long part than the short, often even going to the added trouble of having it permed. He could also be counted upon to use way too much styling product. Lulabell had once met such a man at the baile, had danced with him all night long, but by the end of the evening, his hair had stained her dress.

Lulabell didn't know if the mariachi was the Devil or Jesus. To add to her confusion, he wore a gold ring on the middle finger of his right hand. The ring was both gaudy enough and big enough to look like a class ring, but in the center of the red rock that resembled a ruby, but wasn't, was a number three. Lulabell didn't know if the number represented the three prongs of the Devil's pitchfork, or the Holy Trinity Itself.

When her order arrived, she lifted the top tortilla of her super-quesadilla to make sure there were no onions. Lulabell's presence made the taco boys so nervous, they often messed up her order. She'd walk up to the counter and ask for carnitas and get tripitas. She'd order tamarindo and end up with jamaica. Onions or not, Lulabell wasn't sure, for there on the underside of her tortilla was the following message scribbled in guacamole:

Remember that I am everywhere all the time, even though I am not there with you now. If you wanna come home, the door to My house is always open.
JC

It was a good thing Lulabell had ordered a super-quesadilla. For one thing, the tortillas are much bigger, but more importantly, the super-quesadilla comes with guacamole. Lulabell guessed she could count the Lord out and lost her appetite. ¿How could she eat a holy quesadilla anyhow? She took a drink of her horchata and headed for the bathroom. She chose the corner stall and read the writing on the wall:

Lulabell,
Sorry. I got other things to do today. Suerte.
Atentamente,
You Know Who

Lulabell wiped. Leave it to the Devil to leave a girl high and dry. Well it looked like neither the Lord nor the Devil were going to show up, but at least they had RSVPed, concluded Lulabell as she washed her hands, then headed back out to her table.

But now she was no longer alone. Alberto was waiting for her. He had loved Lulabell ever since they were in the second grade and the teacher made them dance the Mexican hat dance together as a form of mutual punishment after Alberto pushed Lulabell into a mud puddle, and she pulled out a fistful of his hair in retaliation. Alberto was glad Lulabell had had the foresight to pull two tables together because he liked to eat with his elbows on the table, not elbows on the table to rest his chin to think, but elbows on the table spread out, with both hands hovering over his taco plate. Beto was eating menudo, which came with a condiment tray big enough to include fresh quartered limes, oregano, cilantro, chile seco, and onions, all of which took up space.

As Lulabell sat down, Alberto smiled revealing a piece of cilantro between each of his upper incisors. He wiped the corner of his mouth with the napkin he had tucked into his collar. He was wearing his best Sunday shirt and the menudo stains on the napkin indicated that he had avoided disaster. He tamed what little hair remained on his head.

"¿What are you doin here?" Lulabell wanted to know.

"I read your ad," he said.

"But ¿How did you know it was mine?"

"I have been watching you, mujer. I don't have much to offer you, but since my uncle Louie died, que en paz descanse, he left me his half of the towing business and now it's all mine. I've been able to buy a place at the trailer park," he said.

She grabbed his ear, pulled him toward her, pried his mouth open, and used her long magenta fingernails to remove the cilantro from between his teeth.

"Don't tell me you want me to go and live in a trailer with you," said Lulabell.

"Well yeah," said Beto. "With the way they make them nowadays, they look just like houses." Alberto sighed and shook his head from impatience. An uninformed observer might have thought he was jumping the gun, but he had loved Lulabell, and only Lulabell, for more than forty years.

Lulabell pulled out her lipstick and compact and put both to use. The bags under her eyes and the creases in her forehead, once easily concealed by the careful application of makeup, were becoming more pronounced. Lulabell was strongly considering bangs, a move that would painlessly and inexpensively solve half the problem.

"It's a real nice home, you'll see," said Alberto.

Lulabell held the compact up and fiddled with her hair. She could see Alberto's tow truck, which was parallel-parked out front, reflected in the mirror. The truck was yellow and blue. Along the door it said, "Ramírez Towing. We wanna be la grúa tuya." A telephone number followed. Lulabell closed the compact and slid it back into her purse.

She looked into Alberto's eyes, saw his desperation, recognized her own, leaned over her quesadilla, lowered her voice, and said, "If you wanna be my mero mero pistolero, then you've gots to do some hoochie coochie conmigo."

Alberto set his big spoon down. "¿Huh?" he said. He wasn't much to look at. Short, fat, and bald, Beto was a far cry from any young ranch hand she might meet on the dance floor. But there was something about his having waited for her for so long, and her then current state of mind that prompted Lulabell to give Beto the chance he'd been waiting for.

"¿You listenin, Beto? Because I'm talkin serious," said Lulabell.

"Claro que sí," said Alberto.

"There's not much I can do to help you, but there are things you can do to help yourself."

"¿Huh?" said Alberto.

"Look at you. You are pelón pelón cabeza de melón. You hardly even have any hair left."

"Tú me lo sacaste," said Alberto referring to the earlier described event wherein Lulabell pulled out a handful of his hair.

"That was forty years ago, and you have only been bald for thirty," countered Lulabell.

Alberto hung his head.

"That doesn't mean that there ain't nothin you can do to get me for you."

"¿You mean like brujería?" His eyes widened.

"Sure," said Lulabell. "¿You got a problem with that?"

"Oh, no," said Alberto. "I was just wondering is all."

"My real name is Lola Bella María Jacinta Flores," said Lulabell writing her name down on a napkin. She handed it to Alberto and said, "Take this, you need it."

Alberto stuck the napkin in the pocket of his silk shirt.

"At dawn take an apple from a tree. It must be a green apple and it must be at dawn. Cuando apenas está saliendo el sol. Remove the seeds from the apple and cut it in half. ¿Are you gonna remember all this?" said Lulabell.

Then she gave her long magenta fingernails one last look, and then, in a very unladylike and in that respect uncharacteristic move, she bit them all off. Since there were no clean napkins left, she ripped a piece of tortilla from her super-quesadilla and wrapped the fingernails in it, then handed it to Alberto. "Don't eat this," she said. Alberto put the fingernails and tortilla in his pocket.

"Now loan me your knife."

"¿Pa' qué?" said Alberto looking at Lulabell suspiciously.

"Just hand it over before I change my mind."

Alberto dug into his pocket and came up with a crude version of a Swiss army knife he'd found years ago at the flea market in somebody's dollar pile, then handed it to Lulabell.

Lulabell put her head down, letting her long black hair hang over the table, then reached back and cut a lock off as close to the roots as possible. A lock of hair was necessary for the spell she was helping Alberto put on her. According to the spell that Lulabell had used on numerous occasions since she had found it several decades before en *El Libro Supremo de Todas las Magias,* in a section entitled "To Love and Be Loved," and subtitled: "Secrets of the Ancient Magicians," the spell would make its subject fall madly in love. Lulabell figured she might as well do something with her body while she was figuring out what to do with her soul. She had heard that there was a thing called love that sometimes also included the exchange of souls. With all the songs that had been written about said phenomenon, she figured there must be some truth to it.

She handed the lock of hair to Alberto, who ran it by his nostrils before slipping it into his pocket. It smelled even better than Pert Plus®, like vanilla, coconut, and cinnamon, probably because Lulabell's hair being as long as it was, couldn't help but fall into the horchata on its flight across the table.

"You must put everything I have given you between the halves of the apple," said Lulabell. "Get a piece of paper and write the word "SCHEVA" on it, then wrap the apple in it. Don't be askin me what it means, because I don't know and it don't matter anyhow.

"Take it to the graveyard and hide it somewhere. No one must find it. Leave it there for three days. On the third day come back for it at midnight. Take it home and rub its juice all over your body, especially those places that think about me most, then put it under your pillow."

Alberto put his head down in embarrassment.

"It can also help if you eat some swallow birds," said Lulabell. "¿Me entiendes, Méndez?"

Alberto nodded. Lulabell picked up her super quesadilla and dug in.

La Pera

The Pear

EL QUE ESPERA, DESESPERA

HE WHO WAITS, DESPAIRS

DON PANCHO'S FLIGHT
FROM PURGATORY

It was the morning of her third full day in the pueblo, and Natalie didn't know what she liked best about the room Doña Elena had prepared for her—the white chenille bedspread with the red roses in the center and along the edges, the outdated calendar with the reproduced painting of *El Rebozo Blanco,* the glitter-covered picture of San Martín de Porres, the votive candles with other Saints and Jesus, the red-painted concrete floor, the green gauze curtains and the breeze that came through them, or the way the room smelled of gardenias. But she was sure of one thing: The framed photograph of Don Pancho sitting in the doorway of the white stucco house with his guitar in his lap, wearing a solemn countenance and a straw sombrero was the one thing that did not let her sleep at night.

Down the hall and around the corner in the kitchen, Doña Elena sat at the table drinking a cup of Nescafé®. "Buenos días," said la Doña as Natalie entered the room.

"Buenos," agreed Natalie.

"¿Cómo ameneciste?" la Doña said.

That was all it took, and it all came out, that Natalie was losing sleep even when she was sleeping, and she didn't know what to do. ¿Why hadn't anyone told her that it was fiesta week? Freeing Don Pancho from Purgatory required a concerted effort. ¿How was she to get the people away from the fiesta long enough to get Don Pancho out of Purgatory?

"Es más complicado todavía," said la doña.

"¡Ay! dios," replied Natalie.

La Doña quickly explained . . .

Angry, impatient, and always wearing a guayabera and huaraches, that is how Don Pancho appeared in the dreams of the women who had been his lovers. Over the gossip table, the ladies would curse him and his bad habits claiming they could smell his body odor. In nightmares he would wear his usual guayabera-based ensemble, but with the shirt in a shade of mustard, and his jeans glowing like Prestone®, as if he had peed himself. Huaraches in a shade of salmon would round out his clownlike combination. And the things he would say . . . Oh he would start with some standard come-on like, "Qué guapa andas, mi amor." The women would recognize his voice and remember his hot loving ways. From behind a bush or a blooming cactus he would spring, and there would be no hot loving, only insults and threats. He would call the women little fatty and tell them things like "There ain't nothing to do in this godawful place but practice inglés, gordita. ¡Get me out of here or else!"

Doña Elena divulged all of this causing Natalie to wonder: ¿Just how did she know so much about Don Pancho and the nighttime havoc he wreaked from his purgatorial place?

Natalie was aware that Doña Elena was the chief gossip in town, and that she was also Don Pancho's sister-in-law, but what Natalie didn't know was this: Doña Elena too had been one of his mistresses. Of course la Doña didn't share this with Natalie. Instead she explained that many of the town's residents felt that Purgatory was the second safest place for Don Pancho's soul. Not that anyone wanted him to go to that other place, but at least if he were down there, there would be no hope of him getting out. Considering all the trouble he made from Purgatory, imagine what he might do if he made his way to Heaven.

Natalie could hear the thud of a soccer ball being kicked back and forth outside, interrupted by the occasional automobile. Doña Elena stirred her coffee further contributing to the monotony of the moment. Then it occurred to Natalie: ¿What if Don Pancho came to her in a dream saying, "Get me out of here and nobody gets hurt"? ¿What if she told the entire pueblo a lie? That Don Pancho was good and angry and he wasn't gonna take it no more. He might have been stuck in the Perg, but he still had a few strings he could pull. If the people didn't come to his aid and rápido, he was gonna give them the worst curse of all: the curse of nightmares.

Natalie knew what she had to do, and instinct told her to shrug her shoulders, shake her head, and sigh in Doña Elena's presence, as if she had accepted that her task was impossible.

Natalie got up from the table, excused herself, then went about her day as if she had given up on the idea of releasing Don Pancho's soul. She played soccer, gave afternoon English lessons to the children and adults alike, and helped Doña Elena and the girls prepare dinner, before she headed out with La Marta, Doña Elena's eldest daughter, to walk the plaza. And when the day was finally up, she came home, sat down on her pretty blanketed bed, kicked her high heels off, and lay down.

And then a funny thing happened. Don Pancho appeared to her in a dream, just as she imagined he might.

He stood atop a high jagged cliff, his hair cut and combed beneath his sombrero, while Natalie waited all alone on a beach with the waves ripping and roaring behind her. She shaded her eyes with her hand, then looked up at the rocky precipice. Don Pancho strummed his Fender® guitar and sang her a song. Even though he was so far away, it seemed as though he were singing softly in her ear. The song was the most beautiful she had ever heard and it brought her to tears right there in her dreams. It said, I wish I had wings, so I could fly to your side.

Natalie ran toward the rocks, and tried to climb, but only succeeded in sleepwalking to the east wall of her room. The commotion was enough to awaken Marta, Natalie's closest neighbor, who walked across the hall to discover Natalie sprawled on the floor.

Marta's other six spinster sisters soon arrived on the scene, and sought to wake Natalie, but it was no use. They tried to subdue her, but these attempts were also in vain. Finally, one of the sisters walked up the stairs and roused the matriarch of the house, who quickly concluded: La Catrina is stuck in a fitful sleep provoked by some Demon or other.

Outside help was solicited as the sisters fanned out and spread the word. Within no time, the people of the pueblo began to arrive at Natalie's side.

When Natalie finally woke up, she was touched to see so many people had come to her aid. The crowd was so large, it spilled out into the street. She sat up in bed. Her luxurious curls had faded to frizz. Veiny purple bags sagged beneath her eyes. Her chapped and flaking lips were an unenticing lavender ringed in white, as if she had been foaming at the mouth. The crowd, torn and tattered itself, was in various stages of prayer.

Natalie was thankful for such a large turnout, all the better for her to put her plan into action, and then, all of the sudden, she was speaking perfect Spanish, telling everyone that Don Pancho had come to her in a dream. He was "bien enojado" and wasn't gonna take it no more. If somebody didn't get him out of Purgatory y ¡rápido! he was going to make them all pay, y que iban a pagar ¡bien caro! But if the people came to his aid, he would never bother them again, and would, in fact, consider each and every one of their requests since, being that he was a tiradito, he could perform miracles, if and when he got out of Purgatory, that is.

The men and women began to chitter-chatter. They liked the idea of these miracles. Natalie scratched her head with both hands and further frizzed her hair. She got up, didn't even bother to change out of her night-gown, and slipped on her high heels. The crowd followed her out the door. They headed for the railroad tracks, growing in numbers as they walked down the broken sidewalk, everyone blessing themselves en el nombre del Dios Padre, Dios Santo, y el Espíritu Santo as they passed the church of the pueblo.

In a few minutes, they reached their destination. The train tracks were unchanged from the day Don Pancho was run down. There were no crossing bars or lights to warn pedestrians, equestrians, or motorists of pending danger, just an abrupt change in slope on each side, then the tracks themselves, bordered by cacti of various genuses. A small rock mound still marked DP's burial site. The men, women, and children added to the pile one rock at a time, until it was so large, they had to start a new one.

The people immediately began to pray. Hail Marys and Our Fathers permeated the air as they chanted the Rosary. The voices young and old and out of sync pleased the ears of the Lord.

A little south of Heaven, Don Pancho sat in a white lawn chair watching the earthside goings-on. It is a common misnomer that white is the hue of Heaven. Heaven is a multishaded environ, while in Purgatory, the only thing that breaks up the whiteness of the place is the violet of the jamaica, nature's Kool-Aid®, and the only drink allowed in the Perg.

So there he sat, Don Pancho Macías Contreras, surrounded by white, dressed in white, kept prison, or rather, purgatorial-bound, not by white steel bars, but by a sea of white foam replete with floating icebergs, bordered by dunes of white sand. Even DP's knuckles were white, his hands being clasped so tight in prayer. And then came the realization that he was about to be set free. It was just a feeling, a premonition, a psychic moment on his part, but it was so full of certainty, that he began to jump around as if he were dancing a fast-paced quebradita. He even went as far as to curse the Saints and Angels Who ran the place. "Hijos de la chingada, ya me voy de aquí," he said rubbing his hands together, for he knew even Saints and Angels couldn't keep him in that horrible place any longer now that he had the prayers of four hundred and sixty-seven of his paisanos and one extranjera in his favor.

And then a strange thing began to happen: Don Pancho's hair began to shrink in length, thicken in girth, and change from white to black. His nails shortened, his skin unwrinkled, his back straightened. When his transformation was complete, he wore a pair of black western-tailored suit pants, a cream-colored long-sleeved dress shirt, a black leather western-tailored suit jacket detailed with brown crocodile skin which matched his boots of the same exotic leather, and a straw sombrero. His ensemble accented by a respectable, though ungaudy, amount of gold—around his neck, a twenty-four-inch serpentine with a cross dangling from it, a thicker serpentine bracelet on his wrist with his full first name—Francisco—engraved on it, and a horseshoe pinkie ring for good luck.

By the railroad tracks, the men and women were close-eyed and praying. They were approaching the six-hour mark, and still going strong, except for Natalie. She simply didn't have the prayer ethic they did. Her eyes were open, her hands unclasped, her mouth barely moving. But it was a good thing, since when Don Pancho showed up alongside the railroad tracks, in the middle of his very own dust devil, no longer looking like a don, but like some young guapetón, Natalie was the first one to see him. He clapped his hands, pointed an index finger at Nat, winked and said, "Papi's back in town," to which Natalie and the rest of the women replied, through sighs of longing, "¡Ay! papi."

And then, just like that, como si nada, Don Pancho snapped his fingers and said, "I be back later, mamacitas," and disappeared.

El Camarón

The Shrimp

CAMARÓN QUE SE DUERME SE LO LLEVA LA CORRIENTE

SHRIMP WHO SLEEP WILL BE SWEPT AWAY BY THE CURRENT

THE OTHER SIDE OF THE SPELL

Lulabell got home from Jaquería La Bamba just after 8:00 p.m. to find Javier already asleep on the couch. With his shirt untucked and unbuttoned, his belt buckle unfastened, and his boots in a pile on the floor, he looked drunk. But it was just as Lulabell suspected. His Bible lay beside him open to the book of Matthew; he'd been reading about the Betrayal, Crucifixion, and Resurrection of Christ.

Lulabell fell to her knees and leaned over Javier. He looked so handsome lying there, just like any one of hundreds of young men she'd run across on the dance floor over the years.

Lulabell had never been on the other side of the spell before, and she was more than a little afraid. If Alberto did everything right, in three days Lulabell would fall madly in love with him. To love one man and only one man for the rest of her life, was a concept Lulabell had heard of, tried once, failed at, and had since given up on.

She got up and headed for her room where she changed into her nightgown, then crawled into bed. She thought about the day in review. She'd given Alberto enough pieces of her person to do one over on her and good, and that was the one thing about brujería that Lulabell never understood. All love spells required the beloved's handwriting, hair, fingernails, and/or even more personal parts. If one could get that close to the beloved in the first place, then he or she ought to be able to win them over on their own.

When Lulabell was a child her grandmother told her that if she wanted to tame a bluebird, she would only have to sprinkle salt on its tail. Lulabell might only have been six or seven at the time, but even then she realized that if she could get that close, then she could pick the bird up and hold it in her hands, and brujería was the same way. If Alberto couldn't make Lulabell love him after forty years, then maybe he didn't deserve her. But if Beto didn't deserve her after loving her for so long, a pesar de todo, then ¿who did?

Sleep came before Lulabell could answer her own rhetorical question, and with it dreams. Lulabell dreamt she was at the Boardwalk in Santa Cruz. The rides were going, but no one was riding them. There were no ticket-takers or operators. Lulabell was all alone. It was close to either dusk or dawn, or perhaps just overcast. Lulabell looked out to sea and saw a tiny floating figure. She wasn't sure, but she thought whoever it was was waving to her. She walked up to the seaside telescope, stuck a hand in her pocket, came up with a silver coin, put it in the slot, then pointed the telescope out to sea.

It was Jesus floating in a black inner tube. Even with magnification, He was so small. He was waving at her, whether in SOS or greeting, she wasn't sure. Just as she finally got the telescope properly focused, her time ran out, the lens snapped angrily shut, and everything went black. She reached into her pocket, but found no more silver coins.

She walked on. The cotton candy stand was unattended, but well stocked, so she helped herself. The Boardwalk seemed never to end. Just as Lulabell reached the final attraction, the rides and other amusements repeated themselves. She looked down. Her only view of herself in the dream was of her feet, in blue flip-flops. She thought about boarding her favorite ride, the umbrella ride, but was sure she would lose her shoes. Perhaps it was this disappointment that woke her up.

She lay in bed at 1:53 a.m., wondering who she was in the dream. She was herself, but ¿which Lulabell had she been? ¿Was she a child, or already grown? If only she had known the denomination of the coin she had slipped into the seaside telescope, then she could have considered inflation, and arrived at some sort of estimate of the time frame in which the dream occurred. The coin was silver. It could have been a nickel, a dime, or a quarter. Her shoes might also have provided a clue, but flip-flops had been a constant in Lulabell's closet ever since she outgrew her huaraches.

Lulabell knew that Jesus was out to sea, far from shore, but ¿was He working His way back to her, or slowly floating away? If Lulabell had been a child in the dream, and if Jesus was indeed on His way back to her, perhaps He was almost there, or at least close enough to the wharf where He could boost Himself up, then walk the rest of the way. ¿Was He on His way back to Lulabell, or ¿was it adiós y suerte para siempre?—these were two separate scenarios Lulabell would contemplate all night long.

La Botella
The Bottle

LA HERRAMIENTA DEL BORRACHO
THE DRUNK'S TOOL

DON PANCHO'S FIRST MIRACLE

After freeing the soul of Don Pancho Macías Contreras, the crowd did not go back to the fiesta, or home to rest for it, even though six hours of perpetual prayer can really wear a soul out. After DP showed up earthside and as handsome as, if not handsomer, than he had been in his mortal life, the women sighed at his good looks, while the men breathed their own sighs of relief, for Don Pancho seemed in good humor and there was no threat, imminent or otherwise, that anyone was going to have their incisors knocked out, or their noses broken. The people surely didn't go home to rest. Sure they all set out for their respective households, and quick too—the women fleeing the scene as fast as their tight-fitting cut-along-the-bias dresses and high heels would allow, the men with their much less restrictive clothing already ahead of them. Everyone wanted to get in line for the miracles Don Pancho had promised.

Don Pancho, por su parte, stood in the midst of an uphill stretch of lush meadow, free to walk the requisite three paces north to get to Heaven. And that's just what he did to find that his theory was indeed correct. DP believed that Heaven and Hell were different for everyone, and this is what his Heaven entailed: His very own rancho with plenty of land, many head of cattle, and a variety of other farm animals.

He looked straight ahead and this is what lay in wait: a Spanish villa (¿Do they come in other styles? ¿Do the Turks and Chinese have their own spins? This narrator is unsure and unwilling to investigate.) with a courtyard in the center complete with a fountain and many beautiful girls washing their feet in its waters, all the while smiling wantonly at DP.

He began to feel a little weak, and not for the sake of the women either.

The color of the place was so vivid: the blue of the fountain water and the gold of the coins at its bottom, the cobalt of the tiled walkway, the red, blue, yellow, and black of the macaws, the chocolate of the servants' hair. It was a bit much to take for a man who hadn't seen a shade deeper than Antique White for more than twenty-seven years.

He stepped inside of what had to have been his living room. There was color in there too, but also a place to take it sitting down. He reclined in a leather armchair and put his feet up on the proverbial coffee table. The walls were persimmon, the floor tiled in terra-cotta, the kitchen a more stomach-able powder yellow, but in certain niches and enclaves there was the added ornamentation of a bouquet's worth of painted flowers.

There was industry in the kitchen. "¿Algo para tomar?" questioned one of the servants.

"Anything but jamaica," replied Don Pancho.

A few ranchos up the road, Jesús Malverde, Patron Saint of Drug Traffickers and Other Criminals, was getting ready. A tiradito like Don Pancho, the Saints and Angels had elected Malverde to welcome Don Pancho to Heaven and to otherwise show him the ropes.

In his earthly life, Malverde stole from the rich and gave to the poor, and like other doers of similarly good deeds, he was lynched. But, nearly a hundred years after his death, his memory lives on, and his likeness can be seen all the way from Cali to Culiacán to Califas, dangling from rearview mirrors, across belt buckles, but most frequently on the back of silk Sunday shirts worn by boys from Sinaloa and abroad every day of the week.

Malverde boarded his pickup truck, then stopped off to pick up Don Pancho's sidekick. Heaven, like earth, was divided up into barrios—places where people with stuff in common lived. On earth, what people from the barrios had most in common was poverty, but in Heaven, people were clustered together based on what they most desired. Don Pancho and Malverde were from that part of Heaven where everybody wanted things to be just like in an old Mexican cowboy movie, and ¿what good is an old Mexican cowboy movie without a good sidekick?

DP's sidekick was a shorter, fatter version of himself. His name was Juan Rosales González and he had DP's same honey-colored skin and gray-blue eyes. But that's where the similarity ended. He was chubby and short enough to be a midget, but since such a condition depends as much on proportion as it does height, he couldn't be clinically classified as such. He had a hearty mustache, big, bushy, and in every way overgrown, nothing like the wisp of upper-lip enticement Don Pancho wore. His jeans, bell-bottomed puddle jumpers, dangled a few inches above his snakeskin boots, which were so old and worn, his big toe poked out on the right side. To add a touch of elegance to an otherwise shabby ensemble, he wore a fancy belt with an oversized silver buckle displaying a bucking bronco across the front.

"Nice troca, patrón," said Juan as he boarded the Dodge Ram. It was low to the ground, so Juan had no trouble getting in. Not like some other trucks in those parts, lifted to the hilt with special kits and shock resisters.

They drove up the carretera until they reached the long road which led to El Rancho de Don Pancho. They arrived to find Don Pancho standing akimbo in front of the coral-colored stucco house, obviously in awe of the grand spread that was all of the sudden his. In front of the house there was a large cactus garden, the centerpiece of the polished rock, circular driveway. A twenty-foot, three-armed saguaro stood in the middle, surrounded by agave and yucca. There were the staple pitahayas, in semibloom, loaded with prickly pears, and many cascading donkey tail plants spilling from ornate planters. The ground was littered with the aptly named horse cripplers replete with intimidating spines and a sprinkling of deceitful magenta flowers.

As a whole, the landscape was a mixture of profusely overgrown greenery and sparse open spaces. Immense palm and banana trees bordered the cobblestone walkway, which led to the guest quarters, while the rest of the 1,200-acre hacienda where 250 head of cattle roamed freely was, for the most part, wide-open space with little plant life save for an occasional oak tree.

To the east of the house stood a barn for the horses. Behind that, a pen for the pigs and goats, and an attached coop where Don Pancho's prize-winning fighting roosters were kept.

On the west side of the property was the lienzo charro where Don Pancho intended to have bullfights, cockfights, charreadas, and other spectacles involving his livestock and brave men, including himself.

The ring around the arena was made of concrete, while the outer portion where the stands were located was constructed of wood painted fire engine red, and was equipped with enough bleachers to seat about eight thousand people.

Malverde approached DP, held a hand out, and said, "I am Jesús Malverde, El Santo Patrón de Los Narcotraficantes, and I have been sent to help you. You might consider me your mentor of sorts."

Malverde must have spent some time in the Perg, thought Don Pancho, for his English was quite good.

"¿Narcotraficantes?" said Don Pancho with a snicker.

"Heaven," said Malverde with his hands in the air. "It's a specialized place.

"And this here is Juan Rosales González, your secuaz."

"Mucho gusto. Please to meet jyou," said Juan Rosales González. He bowed, genuflected really.

"¿What do I need a sidekick for?" said DP indignant. "¿You see all of this? I get it all by myself. I don't need no secuaz." He kicked the dirt with his crocodile skin boots.

Malverde got near. "Listen my friend, here, in these parts, we all want the same thing. For our Heaven to be like in the old cowboy movies. ¿You know what I mean?"

They began to flash before DP's eyes, those old black and white películas with Luis Aguilar and Mantequilla, the former always getting the girl, his rooster always winning at the palenque, the latter always getting himself into some sort of trouble so that the former can ride to his rescue on his legendary horse.

DP nodded. "But ¿where is your sidekick?" He flared his eyebrows. DP knew he was the new vato on the block and for the time being the fuereño, and if this place was really like an old Mexican movie, for all he knew, Malverde could be his rival.

"Mine has the day off."

"All right," said DP. "I shall call you Márgaro." He grabbed Juan by his shirt collar, lifted him in the air, and set him down in front of him.

Márgaro was about to defend his given name, but there was no time for protest. A tour bus had just pulled up. Los Invasores de Nuevo León were there, bringing with them their very own brand of norteño music.

The band disembarked, then headed for the charro ring which was nothing more than an oversized gazebo-like contraption. The band quickly began, "Testing, un, dos, tres, testing."

People arrived by car, truck, bus, and burro-load. Everyone wanted to welcome Don Pancho to the neighborhood. For the occasion, the hired help had slaughtered a steer, as well as several pigs and a handful of goats, so not only were the people feasting upon such staple foods as carnitas y carne asada, they were also treated to the delicacy of birria de chivo, a goat-based dish, and a real crowd-pleaser.

Don Pancho and company made their way to the oversized gazebo contraption. Seeing Don Pancho arrive, Los Invasores de Nuevo León quickly cut into their hit "Mi Casa Nueva." The thrill of the parranda was coming back to Don Pancho—the delight he always took when he headed out for the cantina in his fresh-pressed best to dance the night away with dozens of women. It wasn't the women he missed, but the womanizing.

The men had a seat. "We need some women," said Don Pancho rubbing his hands together. DP eyed the servants. They were lovely, but he had seen enough Mexican movies to know that it's never a good idea to take up with the help.

"We need some ladycitas," agreed Márgaro.

"All in due time," said Malverde. He looked at Don Pancho. "First you must perform a miracle. These people want more than drinking, or dancing. They want a good show."

"¡My first miracle!" said Don Pancho. "¿Already?"

"Listen up, my friend. This place is like any other. You have to work hard just to get by."

"But, I wanna dance," protested DP. He cupped his hands around his mouth, then shouted to the band, which had taken a break, "Play more música."

They didn't oblige, but instead, the accordion player pulled a piece of yellow paper from the pocket of his slacks, then read, "Doña Rubi necesita una casa nueva."

"¡A new house! I don't have any new houses," protested DP. "And besides, I don't know how to perform a miracle."

"None of us do when we get here. But we figure it out and you will too. Otherwise They will send you back to the Perg, or worse." Malverde spiraled an index finger downward to illustrate his point.

Don Pancho looked toward Márgaro for help. "Don't look at me, patrón," he said, then he went where all sidekicks go when their main man is doing business. He went to check on Don Pancho's fighting roosters.

Another piece of paper was passed to the lead singer of the band. "Rickey quiere una bicicleta nueva," he read.

"That one sounds easy," said Don Pancho. If he were to be the world's latest miracle worker, he figured he oughtta start out small.

"Sorry," said Malverde. "Up here we don't consider requests for unnecessary material items."

"Don Filemón has fallen off of the roof and is currently convalescing in the town infirmary. Although he is not in danger of passing from his mortal life, his brother Ernesto respectfully requests assistance in restoring his ability to walk," read the drummer.

"You must use mucho cuidado," warned Malverde. "You don't want to move in on Anybody's territorio. I would hand that one off to San Martín de Porres or St. Jude if I were you."

"This saint business is not easy," said DP.

"No es nada de fácil. To work a miracle you have to really feel it," said Malverde.

The next request came from Don Eusebio, who was at the moment broken down in front of the train tracks with an empty bottle of Tequila de la Viuda® at his side. The accordion player read slowly:

Oye, Don Pancho, recuérdame un poquito
Tú ya estás en el cielo
Y aquí yo me quedo
Pero después de todo
Somos paisanos, ¿no?
Échame una

The man was asking for booze. Finally a miracle he could get behind. "I like that one," proclaimed Don Pancho.

"Consider it a maybe," said Malverde. "First you must review all the applicants, then decide. Rules are rules."

There was one more request that caught DP's fancy. It came from Doña Ruthi, the town whore. She had tried to dye her once long, thick, black hair blonde, and now, not only was she unhappy with the color (orange), but she was also displeased with its texture (burnt to a crisp) and worried that her new coif might cut into business. She had children to feed. ¿Wasn't there something Don Pancho could do?

"That one's pretty good too," said DP.

"Now you must choose," said Malverde.

"Hmmmm," said Don Pancho. He was stuck between the whore and the drunk. His indecision was brief. He cleared his mind and imagined himself as that drunk man all alone by the train tracks with nothing or no one to comfort him. All alone, ¡qué triste! And Don Pancho remembered how he had felt that way so many times in his life and how a wise woman once told him that sometimes a man feels most alone when he is surrounded by people that he doesn't love, and he knew just what she meant, but still he surrounded himself by, well, people que él no quería, and, of course, booze.

All of these thoughts rose and swirled in the Universe. They dissipated, then gathered before repatriating themselves not just to another place, but to another time and form, eventually causing the drunk's empty bottle of Tequila de la Viuda® to rise up in the air where it paused to turn over three times in its sleep, and when it awoke, it glided gently back to the ground and metamorphosed into a whole case of Cazadores®. The drunk quickly sobered up and grabbed his case of Cazadores® and headed for the plaza.

The guests who had crammed into the bleacher seating of Don Pancho's lienzo charro watched all of this unfold on the big screen which stood in the middle of the ring. The people applauded, held hands over their open mouths, and some even shed tears, for Don Pancho's first miracle was a thing of beauty, a work of art which reflected not just its recipient, his hopes, dreams, and disillusions, but Don Pancho's as well.

Struck by the success of his first miracle, DP didn't stop there. He looked down upon Doña Ruthi and her over-processed orange hair, then made it shiny and healthy once again before making her a redhead. Blonde, thought DP. Clearly, Doña Ruthi didn't know what was good for her, or her customers.

Around town, word spread and quick. Don Pancho was well on his way to becoming El Santo Patrón de los Borrachos y las Putas.

El Reloj de Mano
The Wristwatch

COMPAÑERO DE TODOS TIEMPOS

COMPANION OF ALL TIMES

THE PLAN

Lulabell couldn't sleep after her Jesus-out-to-sea dream, but rode it out until 4:33 a.m. when she rose, and walked to the bathroom. She washed her face, then, as part of her new routine aimed at thwarting the signs of aging, applied sunblock.

Up early for his route, Javier stepped inside the bathroom and grabbed his toothbrush. "Fires a Hell'll burn you worser, momma," he said.

"Got enough to worry about in this life," said Lulabell.

"You gotta start with your soul, then work your way outward," said Javier as he began to brush.

Lulabell bent down and grabbed the hem of her huipil, lifted it up over her head, and threw it on the floor, showing Javier what having the Devil on her side had done for her—the full upright breasts, the taut thighs and buttocks, the long legs—all of which went to waste, for Javier threw his arms up over his eyes, as if blinded by a great light, the likes of which he imagined would appear the day the Lord came again, as Javier knew He soon would. He ran down the hall with his toothbrush in his mouth. Lulabell stuck her head into the hallway and shouted, "Careful, hijo. You could choke on that."

Lulabell, all alone in front of the mirror, inspected her body. No signs of cellulite or varicose veins, her loveliness seemed as unchanged as when it had reached its apex. She picked up her huipil, put it back on, and headed toward the kitchen where Javier was now brushing his teeth.

"Forgive me, hijo. Sometimes I get carried away."

Javier spit in the sink.

"Your lunch is in the fridge. Chorizo con huevos just like you like," she said.

"Thank you, mother," he forced himself to say.

Lulabell opened the junk drawer, pulled out pen and paper, walked to the kitchen table, and sat down and began to plan what would quite likely be her final Dinner for Ranch Hands and Day Laborers. In just a few days, she was scheduled to fall madly in love with Beto, and she was sure he wouldn't allow her to throw a party with a guest list that included three hundred men and only four women.

Lulabell had come up with the idea more than a decade before. Each year, always at Christmas and Easter, and sometimes once or twice in between, Lulabell got together as many men as she could, and she made them all dinner—you only need be a ranch hand and/or a day laborer to qualify for an invite.

Through a series of inevitable bingo windfalls, Lulabell was always able to finance the event. She had always been lucky, perhaps not in love, but other things. With three pigs' worth of carnitas and a big pot of rice and beans, Lulabell would feed the masses. Each year, the guest list might have only included fifty or seventy-five men, but then it was a primo here, a compa there, and soon Lulabell had a backyard filled with three hundred ranch hands and/or day laborers.

Three hundred men and just one woman could have spelt trouble, but it never did. The men never fought over Lulabell, which was further evidence to her that not only did God exist, but He approved of her gesture. Either that, or the Devil worked in mysterious ways. Natalie, Consuelo, and True-Dee were inevitably called in for backup. The women gave the men one dance each, and didn't go to sleep until every last ranch hand had his turn.

There were so many things to remember. Paperplates, napkins, forks, Lulabell's list began. (A more comprehensive inventory follows this chapter.) No sooner did she get halfway done, when there was a knock at the door. She set her pen down, headed for the front door. Opening up, she was surprised to find Gilbert, the pompadoured day laborer she'd brought home from the lumberyard parking lot a few weeks previous.

"Hello, Osvaldo," said Lulabell as she swung the front door wide open.

"My name is Gilbert." He grabbed Lulabell and kissed her while Javier looked on through just parted fingers.

"¿What do you want?" said Lulabell when Gilbert finally let her loose.

"I want you," he said. "I think about you day and night. When I drink, I see you in the bottom of my glass. When I eat, I see you in my plate."

Those were the telltale signs of a puro. But Lulabell didn't practice the puro. It was a spell, she had heard, that involved a photograph and a cigar. It was strange that he was showing those symptoms.

"Listen, Gilberto," she said blending his name into Spanish, a language in which everything sounded better to her. "Sometimes the plan changes in the middle of the plans, if you know what I mean." She held her hands out to the air and shrugged.

"I want to take you to Acapulco," he declared. "¿Have you ever been there?"

Lulabell blinked three times, gathered her gaze, then said, "I was born there."

"Then we will live with your family."

"I ain't runnin off with a married man," said Lulabell.

"I got married in México. They don't keep good records."

Lulabell looked outside. His truck was loaded down and parked in front. From what she could tell, there was a kitchen table, a few mismatched chairs, a trunk, and a couple of bicycles in amongst who knows what else. She used to think about Mexico all the time. About going back. But now it seemed so far away, it was a dream, and since she had lived long enough to know that reality never lives up to dreams, the idea of going back frightened her.

She placed a hand on his right shoulder and said, "Try discoverin God, or dancin, or other women. I will light a candle for you. Everything will be all right. You'll see, cariño." She paused to caress, then gently slap his cheek as if he were a boxer she was sending out into the ring.

"Con permiso," she said with a slight bow, then raced to the kitchen for her purse and shopping list, before slipping out the back door.

"Brother, you're suffering from brujería," declared Javier once he heard the Cadillac speed off.

"¿Huh?" said Gilbert walking into the kitchen behind Javier.

"I knew something just wasn't right," Gilbert said as he sat down with Javier at the kitchen table. "But she must only have done it because she loves me just like I love her."

"My mother can love only one man. She is the Devil's faithful servant and lover, just as sure as He is hers."

Gilbert put his elbows up on the table and rested his chin in the palms of his hands. His pompadour was shoe polish black and shiny with pomade.

Seeing an opportunity to save another soul, Javier said, "¿Have you given your soul to Jesus Christ?"

Gilbert looked him in the eye. "I don't know. I made my First Communion, but we moved away before I could make my Confirmation, and since I married my first cousin, they wouldn't let us have a church wedding, but I pray sometimes, and I have a statue of the blessed Virgen de Guadalupe on the dashboard of my truck."

"You should give salvation some serious thought, because the end of the world is at hand."

"¿You're not part of that cult are you?" said Gilbert suspiciously.

"¿What cult is that?"

"The followers of San Narciso." Gilbert read the Sunday news magazine *The Lava Landing Outlook,* which included the investigative reporting of Olivia Quiñones, who had been monitoring the comings and goings of the Sons and Daughters of San Narciso for more than a decade, so he was well informed on the subject.

"I don't know what you're talking about," said Javier.

Gilbert leaned in. "San Narciso was a priest who lived here a long time ago and was able to predict things. He predicted the volcano and, on his deathbed, claimed that an event that would bring about the end of the world would happen right here in this town. Now he has a bunch of followers who live in the hills."

"A volcano conspiracy theory, ¿ay?" said Javier.

"I don't know about that. All's I know is, I'm in love with your mother, and I'm a married unemployed man with children I can't feed."

"Brother, just say that you accept Jesus Christ as your one and only Savior, and I can get you a job on my route," said Javier. But before Gilbert could say yea or nay, Javier rushed off. When he returned, he was holding one of his extra garbageman suits up by the hanger.

Gilbert squinted.

"Well, ¿do you, or don't you wanna come on over to Jesus?" Javier dangled the suit in front of Gilbert. It was army green with a zipper up the middle and a patch over the left breast showing the volcano in profile.

"I guess so, man," said Gilbert. To an unemployed man down to his last five-dollar bill and final pack of cigarettes, the suit looked better than he let on.

The men were headed toward the front door when it occurred to Javier, "¿Do you play soccer?"

"Sure."

"¡Terrific! Next Sunday after church, we're challenging the Janitors for Jesus."

"¿Will your mom be there?" asked Gilbert.

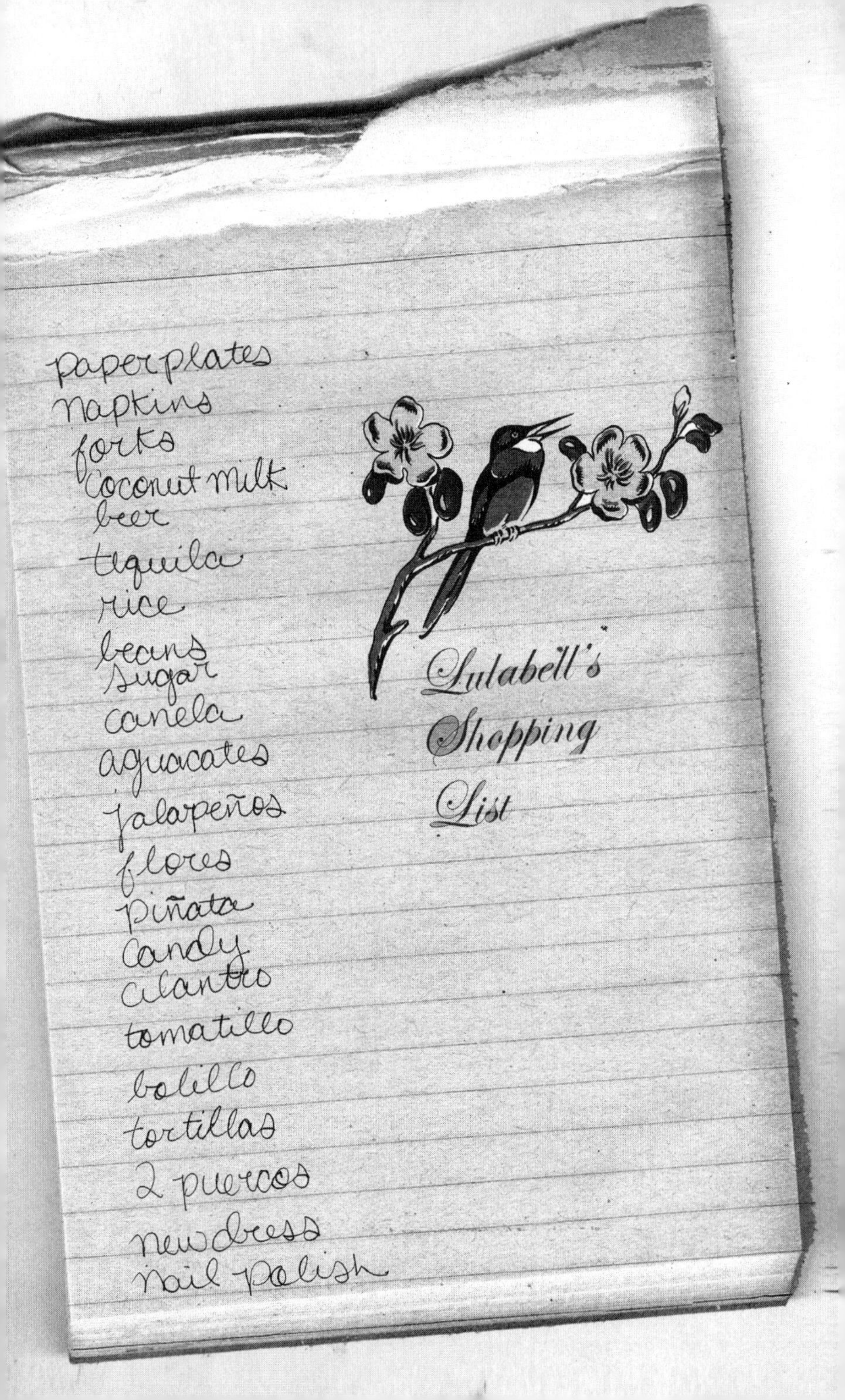

paper plates
napkins
forks
coconut milk
beer
tequila
rice
beans
sugar
canela
aguacates
jalapeños
flores
piñata
candy
cilantro
tomatillo
bolillo
tortillas
2 puercos
new dress
nail polish

Lulabell's
Shopping
List

El Mango

The Mango

RICO, SABROSO Y PARA LOS DIENTES, PEGAGOSO

RICH, DELICIOUS, AND VERY STICKY FOR THE TEETH

NATALIE'S DILEMMA

Two miracles in the books and all DP could think about was Natalie, who was at that very moment curled up in a ball on a park bench in the middle of the placita. Nat didn't know it, but Don Pancho's first miracle had occurred right before her closed eyes. Six hours on her knees in prayer had really worn her out, so after DP's soul was finally set free, she had lain down on a park bench in the middle of the placita and had fallen fast asleep.

Don Pancho looked down upon her from the comfort of his living room. He felt bad about the night before, the way he had kept her up even when she was sleeping, how he had been the cause of her constant crying. He didn't want to bother her yet again, but he had to thank her for all she had done for him. He grabbed his sombrero, then boarded the downward ramp toward the earth, and arrived in a flash.

It had been a little over twenty-seven years since he had visited the placita, but it remained, for the most part, unchanged. The grass was bordered by flowers and the flowers by cobblestone paths which all led to the same place: a gazebo where, in Don Pancho's day and age, a conjunto, mariachi, or banda played every Saturday night and Sunday afternoon. In one corner, there was a nonfunctioning well, good only for wishing. He looked across the street to the church, then blessed himself not once, but twice.

He tiptoed over to Natalie. Her hair was a wreck, her nails bit to the quick, and her knees were skinned. Yet she looked so peaceful lying there. He reached down and stroked her hair turning her frizz to pincurls. She was extremely pretty, but lacked the harshness often found in truly beautiful women. He slid her hair behind her ears, then caressed her from temples to chin. A smile slowly formed on her face. She stretched her arms out, sat up, rubbed her eyes, and promptly concluded that she was dreaming.

DP rose to his feet, removed his sombrero, and stood up straight.

"¿Don Pancho?" said Natalie with all the depth and wisp of a 1940s B movie queen.

"Yes. It's me," he whispered. He detected a craving in her tone, and moved closer. "¿What can I do for you?" he said. It was an open-ended question Natalie didn't hesitate to answer.

In that state of compromised judgment and with the lack of inhibition characteristic of dreams as her accomplice, Natalie went right straight to the point: She flung her arms around his neck, pulled him close, and kissed him. It was a long, sweet kiss, multilayered as an ice cream cake, and with the lingering presence of good, hot salsa, the kind that makes both tongue and mouth more acutely aware of one another for hours to come.

Don Pancho pulled away. Cuckoldry and womanizing were one thing, but his little girl's best friend and his favorite benefactor were another.

"Discúlpame. I don't know what got into me," he said.

Natalie said nothing. Her eyelids were weighed down by longing, her blink significantly longer in coming, and the bottom third of her face was formed into a subtle, yet unmistakable smirk.

Don Pancho tried to be official. "I have come to thank you for all you've done for me."

"It was nothin, really," said Nat with a flip of the wrist.

"Oh, it really was something. I have gone on to become the Patron Saint of Drunks and Prostitutes. Everyone needs representation, and it seems I have found my niche. To show my gratitude, I want to give you the miracle of your choice."

"You are my miracle, papi," she said. She got to her feet and headed toward Don Pancho set on giving him another long strong kiss, but he threw some leftover dream freeze on her and stopped her in her tracks.

They sat side by side on the bench. "I don't think you understand. I am offering you anything you want. So ¿what's it gonna be?" said DP.

Natalie licked her lips. "YOU don't understand. I want you." She fluffed her curls, rubbed her nose with a fist, then giggled.

Don Pancho looked at Nat. It was slow in coming, but DP finally got it: What Natalie needed was a big, strong, capable man, and DP was just the man to send him to her.

Natalie snuggled up next to Don Pancho and laid her head on his shoulder, letting it rest in that crevice created by chin and neck. It wasn't anything like the first time they'd met. He smelled so clean and sweet, like orange blossom water. It occurred to her that maybe that's all love really was: a set of sensations, the way a person smells, the feel of their skin, the sound of their voice, that something which puts one's heart at ease causing it to live between that state and longing.

Don Pancho draped an arm over Natalie's shoulder and did some thinking of his own. ¿Was that what it would have felt like to hold Consuelo in his arms? Natalie looked so innocent lying there and everything felt so perfect, he wished the world would stand still.

There was nothing but silencio for a spell until DP said, "¿You can't think of anything you want?"

"I told you," said Nat pausing to impatiently toss her head to and fro, "I want you, papi."

"Papi," repeated DP. "I like the sound of that. After all, you're like a daughter to me."

"¡Yúckate!" said Nat. She wrinkled her nose at the idea, the very prospect of having just kissed a man who thought of her "like a daughter."

"¿Why'd you have to go and ruin things?" she said.

"I didn't ruin anything, mija," he said, pleased not just with what he had up his sleeve, but with the way he had handled things. "Listen, mija," he continued. "I gotta run. But I need you to do a thing or two for me."

"Sure," said Nat. Suddenly she was all reluctance, indifference, and disappointment.

"Take care of yourself, and Consuelo. I love you two more than you will ever know, and I will do my best to take care of you both."

"Thanks," she said.

He put his sombrero back on, intent on sneaking off, but Nat grabbed him by the forearm. She was perturbed by his handsome presence, but still reluctant to let it slip away. "Before you go, ¿Can you tell me a story?" she said.

"Sure," said Don Pancho. That wasn't so much to ask, even with his busy schedule. She lay down on the park bench, resting her head in his lap. He began to stroke her hair, just like her father used to when she was a little girl. "I saw the Devil once and He isn't such a bad fellow. He came over to the Perg to recruit and He told us about His home."

"¿You mean Hell?" said Nat. She wiggled her feet and shivered.

"Yes. Only He referred to it as Hades. It's a place where you can have anything you want except two things: You will never know love and you will never achieve greatness."

"That's creepy," said Nat. She rolled over onto her side and brought her knees up to her chest and held them there. "¿Did He get anyone to go with Him?"

"A few people," said DP.

"I would never go," said Nat.

"That's what you say now, but you've never been stuck in Purgatory. You have to work hard day and night. There's no rest, not even on the day of the Sabbath. You have to prove yourself if you want to move on. But Hell, as Señor Satanás described it, is a place where you can eat, sing, and dance. It's a real free-for-all."

"Sounds like a big old smorgasbord to me," said Natalie.

"¿What's that?" said Don Pancho.

"It's a place where you go to eat. They have all kinds of food and it all looks really good and you can eat as much of it as you want. Only nothin is really good at all. You're lucky if you find one or two things you like because everything is just okay."

"Mediocrity, it's the enemy of man, if I didn't realize it before, I realize it now," said Don Pancho. He continued to stroke her hair. The moment was filled with silence. He looked down to find that Natalie had drifted off to sleep. He slid out from under her, letting her head rest gently on the park bench before he kissed her on the forehead, then headed back to Heaven.

After all was said and done, Natalie would forever remember the events herein described as the strangest, yet most pleasant and realistic dream she had ever had. She would never realize that what she had experienced was no dream, but a real bona fide apparition.

La Jarjeta Jelefónica

The Phone Card

LO QUE TODO HIJO BUENO TRAE EN SU CARTERA

WHAT EVERY GOOD SON CARRIES IN HIS WALLET

LA LARGA DISTANCIA

When Natalie woke up, she was surrounded by five happy and amazed drunks, a conjunto norteño, and a young man. All eyes were on her and with good reason. Gone was her gauzy lavender nightgown, her high heels, her sensible yet elegant haircut. Instead, she wore a long, light blue brocade evening gown with bustles and trains, roses and rosettes, but most annoyingly, a hoop skirt. She felt her chest. Sure enough, there was a corset under there, and a bit further down, bloomers. She struggled to sit up, but with all of that rigid and unyielding clothing, it was hard. She wanted to have a look at her glass slippers, but once she dominated her hoop skirt into submission, she was disappointed to find that she was wearing a pair of clear plastic pumps with gold vinyl heels that she recognized as decidedly de la Payless®. She touched her earlobes. Rhinestones. And the same could be said for her neck and wrists. She reached for the crown of her head. Her hair had grown significantly and was all piled up on top and held in place by a pompom of artificial flowers.

Natalie sighed. She knew what was going on and frankly, would have much preferred Cinderella's cleaning outfit, or even that little asymmetrical number she is left with after the evil stepsisters get done with her. Yes. That would have been much better. A single shoulder strap, a little ragged, but much improved.

Natalie knew that Don Pancho had to be behind all of this. There was no other explanation. She looked at her audience and wondered where her prince was. Surely he couldn't have been one of the drunks, and the musicians were far too old. That left a scrawny fellow in baggy jeans, a T-shirt and tennis shoes, with a backwards-turned baseball cap. That had better not be him.

It was one thing to mess up on the costuming, but to get the prince wrong, was another thing entirely.

The young man spoke up, "Usted, Señorita Catrina, tiene una llamada en la caseta."

"Consuelo," she whispered, then rushed to her feet.

Natalie made her way down the street, barefoot, and with her train in tow. She headed for la caseta de larga distancia. The sidewalk was more constant in the "commercial" as opposed to the "residential" part of town. She passed the jail, the joyería, and the tortillería. The storefronts were colorful, but dulled by the sun constantly beating down upon them.

When she finally reached her destination, she took a seat on a wooden bench in the fourth booth and waited for her phone to buzz (Mexican phones don't ring), and when it did, she picked it up immediately.

"¿Sway?" she said, her tone rigged with unnecessary suspense.

"Yep it's me." Consuelo sounded far away not just in distance, but in time, as if a four-hour plane ride wasn't enough to reunite them.

"I got your daddy out."

"I knew you would," said Sway. "But, ¿how'd you do it?"

"We just prayed is all. For a real long time. And then he showed up good as new in front of the train tracks. To tell you the truth, I was a bit worried he was gonna be all runned over, lookin like somethin the cat dragged in, but he's a handsome fellow."

"He sure is," agreed Sway.

"And what's more, he's already started with the miracles. Around here they're callin him the Patron Saint of Drunks and Prostitutes. It looks like he's blazin his own trail."

Consuelo didn't know what to say, so she said nothing, but Natalie could hear her gasping every now and then as she gave her the details.

"I got somethin else to tell you," said Nat segueing to another subject.

"Go right ahead," said Consuelo.

"¿Member that girl Olga Rosales we went to school with, and how once on the bus ride home she told us that Mexico was a different place with witches and magic everywhere?"

"Yeah, I do," said Consuelo.

"Well I think she was right because the strangest thing happened to me while I was sleepin."

There was pure silence on Consuelo's end as she imagined the worst.

"When I woke up I had on this fancy, poofy dress, my hair had grown, and I was wearin plastic pumps. The whole thing was just like in Cinderella, only my dress is way uglier."

"¡That's some traumatic shit!" said Consuelo.

"It looks like your daddy's doin fairy tales and I'm afraid he's gone and cast me as the princess."

"¡Chinga'o!" said Consuelo realizing in an instant that if Natalie was the princess, there had to be a prince out there somewhere. "Last thing I need is for you to go fallin for some vato over there and the next thing I know I never see you again."

"I don't see that happenin in the near or even distant future," said Nat. Her voice switched to the scheming tone—a little lower and markedly slower. "Listen, Sway, if you see your daddy, if he comes to visit you tonight or somethin, you tell him to pull the plug on whatever it is he's got up his sleeve."

"Will do," said Sway. "And for your part, you had better just watcha. Keep your eyes and ears open, and your skirt on."

"I always do," said Natalie. "Besides, I only got a few days left."

"Yeah. But the worst things always happen overnight. With all them young men, that music and dancin, and them singin in your ears, the goin can get rough."

"Don't you worry about a thing. This little dinghy can weather that storm."

"Just make sure you come back in one piece, by that I mean your heart too. ¿Okay, corazón? Don't be leavin even a little piece of it behind."

"Sí, mi comandante," said Natalie saluting the air for no one's benefit but her own.

"I love you baby, and see you soon," said Sway.

"Right back at you with twice the sugar," said Natalie. And with that, they both hung up.

Natalie walked up the street. Early August and it was just as hot there as in Lava Landing, but in Consuelo's pueblo, the sun seemed only to beat down from one particular spot in the sky. It must have been at least ninety degrees Fahrenheit, yet the sky was gray and the clouds were all clustered together. It reminded Natalie of earthquake weather.

She wanted out of those clothes and bad, but there would be no disrobing without help. Up ahead, the children were segregated by sex, the boys on one side of the street playing marbles, the girls on the other playing dolls.

Natalie wasn't sure if it was late morning, or early afternoon, she had no idea whether to say buenos días or buenas tardes, and some sort of greeting was in order for she was closing in on the girls.

"Buenas tardes, Señorita Catrina," they said rising to their feet.

"Buenas," said Nat trying to bend to their level, but her bodice wouldn't budge. ¿Why hadn't anyone told Natalie about the children, how lovely they were? Consuelo had gone to great lengths to warn her about the men of the land, but had mentioned nothing of the children. Had she known, she could have brought them something, dolls, marbles, clothes, or candy. They would have been happy with anything.

It occurred to Nat that she was wearing enough clothing to give something to each of the girls, to mention nothing of the hula hoop—she was sure that was a hula hoop under there, allowing her skirt to spread to unheard of circumferences.

"¿Ustedes me pueden ayudar?" said Natalie.

The girls took to unlacing, unhooking, untying, unbuttoning, and unsnapping, until she was down to her corset and bloomers. She looked so silly standing there, she was surprised no one laughed, not even the boys who had crossed the street to join them.

Natalie picked up her petticoat, and after a brief struggle with the wire caging and mesh netting, she came up with what was indeed a hula hoop right down to the pink candy stripe.

"Gracias, Señorita Catrina," said one, two, three little girls, followed by the rest of the children in unison. They lined up to hula-hoop.

When Natalie finally got home, the house with its many occupants was quiet. Even the perpetually busy stove was idle. She walked into her room to find that nothing was as she had left it. The bed was made, but judging by all the lumps, it wasn't the work of Doña Elena. Her high heels were back and they were shinier than ever. And there on the wall was a new framed photograph of Don Pancho with the inscription, "San Pancho, El Santo Patrón de Los Borrachos y Las Putas." Clearly Don Pancho had been there.

Natalie put on a red dress, then let her hair down. Her ringlets reached her waist. She was about to rush upstairs to ask Doña Elena or one of the girls for a pair of scissors, when there was a knock at the door. It was Marta and she had come to announce a visitor.

"¿Una visita?" said La Catrina. She wasn't expecting anyone.

She walked out of her room and down the hall to the sala where a tall, slim, pretty girl of perhaps seventeen waited. Mariana was her name. She took Natalie by the arm, and led her out the door. The young woman spoke quickly in Spanish as they walked across the street to her home. From what she understood, Mariana's big brother had been pining over Natalie since she'd arrived three days before. He had waited for an opportunity to introduce himself, but the occasion hadn't presented itself, so he sent his little sister over to do the job for him.

Natalie wanted no part of that. She wanted to turn around and scram. But it was too late. They had already crossed over onto another gardened terrace, the chairs were already arranged in a cozy conversation circle, the young men—there were two—were each scrambling to pull a chair out for their lovely visitor, their mother was already making her way out the door with a plate of antojitos, and a more substantial meal was already cooking in the kitchen. There would be no escaping.

Mariana pointed to each of her eager brothers and said, "Ellos son mis hermanos, Ernesto y Amador."

Natalie had no choice but to offer each brother a limp hand and say, "Mucho gusto, encantada," even though she really wasn't encantada. She was perturbada. She only had two days left in the pueblo. What had begun as a soul-springing expedition was now as close to a vacation as she had seen in the better part of twenty years, and she wanted to get to know the customs of the place on her own terms. She had a whole roll of film. There was no time for straying onto the neighbor's courtyard.

Natalie looked the boys over. At twenty-one (Ernesto) and nineteen (Amador), they were just that. Natalie wouldn't have to worry about Ernesto. He was a maricón if she ever saw one. That left Amador to contend with and with a name like that, she'd have to keep an eye on him. He was tall and thin, with bad posture. He sat slouched in his garden chair looking at her with aching eyes. His skin was light, his hair medium brown and curly, and his eyes were hazel. He wore jeans torn at the knees, and a Calvin Klein® T-shirt.

Natalie wished Consuelo was there. She would have gotten them both out of there with unrivaled efficiency and grace. It would all be over soon enough, but in the meantime, the very immediate meantime, she was being offered a plate of tostadas. She took one. Beans, pickled pig skin, cabbage, chile, and cheese. Everyone was watching and waiting, especialmente la Doña. The food wasn't bad. "Está muy buena, Señora, gracias," said Natalie.

The waiting Doña replied, "Oh, sí," then slid another tostada onto Natalie's plate.

The gardened terrace was lovely. Up above there was a lattice overgrown with plant life. The concrete floor below was edged in red and yellow mosaic tile. On top of that sat metal lawn furniture: a swinging sofa the size and shape of the back seat of a Volkswagen bus, and a few chairs and a table from the same set. To one side of the conversation area hung a cast iron birdcage—home of Pablo, an African Gray parrot purchased at market in San Luis Río Colorado—a necessary distinction since Consuelo wasn't really from SLRC after all. She was from a place called Cerro Verde, a mere rancho perhaps forty miles south of San Luís Río Colorado.

Surrounded by virtual strangers, and delicious, yet somehow unappetizing food, Natalie was overwhelmed. It came upon her like an ice cream headache: hard and sudden. Then more than ever she just wanted to go home. The intensity of the sun was trying on her even under the cover of all that greenery, for she knew it was beating down hard from its special place in the sky. She hated her hair, if not on the basis of style, or lack thereof, alone, then on the basis of practicality. It was heavy, hot, and itchy. More than anything, she missed Consuelo. Anxiety was hot on her tracks. It approached, then overtook her. She began to sweat. Things began to spin. ¿Was that the way Consuelo felt if she dared stray from her thirty-mile travel zone? Natalie's heart raced. Nausea came over her in a warm, uninviting rush.

It was all too much for her and it showed in her face. Mariana leaned in. "Señorita Catrina, ¿are you all right?"

"You speak English," said La Natalie in disbelief, and with that, she threw up.

How to see
TWICE AS MUCH
on your trip to Mexico

Tabla 4

THE PLAYERS PLACE *their* **BETS**

El Catrín
The Dandy

DON FERRUCO EN LA ALAMEDA SU BASTÓN QUERÍA TIRAR
DON FERRUCO WANTED TO TOSS HIS
CANE AWAY ALONG THE AVENUE

LA PURA NETA

*Nat wasn't the only one sufriendo a solas. Back in Lava Land-*ing, True-Dee was lying on her velvety couch with a pink tin of Almond Roca®, listening to the voices in her head, trying to solve her most trying problem.

True-Dee was a self-described chatter brain, not to be confused with a scatter brain—there were so many conflicting voices in her head, she often found their yakety-yak hard to keep track of. But that afternoon as she sat in a sea of gold foil wrappers, already feeling as if she had gained ten pounds, there amongst the hodgepodge of opinion givers, advice offerers, and harebrained scheme hatchers, emerged a calm and steady voice of reason which said, "Cariño don't be rash. Take it calm and easy, and get a second opinion."

It urged, if not beckoned True-Dee to do something she had for a long while contemplated: Sit down and write a letter to Querida Claudia, Lava Landing's most beloved advice columnist, soliciting what QC was famous for: únicamente la pura neta. (True-Dee's rather long-winded letter, with her innermost hopes and fears, follows.)

Querida Claudia,
                I was born a
boy, but I am a woman, but
not just any kind of woman.
You won't catch me in sweat
pants and tennis shoes. Not
that I have anything against
physical fitness. A girl ought
to watch her figure. Luckily, I
am not the sort of girl that
has to watch what she eats.
Nature has blessed me in that
respect. I am a beautiful
woman. I hope you don't
mind my saying so. Moreover,
I am an elegant lady which
is so rare in this day and
age. Notice the delicacy of my
hand. Why my handwriting is
straight off the third grade
learners chart!!!
            Harmones have given me
what nature didn't, but they
haven't taken away what
nature did give me, and
by that I don't mean facial
hair; for that we have wax!!!
            I have been completely in-
timate with men only a few
times. I attract men by the
dozen. See for yourself. Check

your archives. Last year I was the winner of the Thalia look alike contest!!! But, Querida Claudia, getting a man and keeping one are two seperate skills. That's not to say that I can't cook. And by the way, is it really true what they say about the way to a man's ♡ being through the stomach? I wouldn't know. I've never gotten close to a man's ♡, not even my own father's, but that's another story.

I am a fine cook, and as one of your biggest and most faithful fans, I cordially invite you to my home for a home cooked meal the likes of which you have never had. I am a state certified beautician and manicurist. At your convenience, come by my salon for a complimentary do, and by that I mean, when you walk out, you'll be done girl!!!

Querida Claudia, I wanna know what love is really like. But when I am with a man, I mean REALLY with him, as soon as he discovers nature's mistake, he's always promptly on his way. When given the opportunity, I have given men extreme pleasure, but they never come back for more. I am so confused. I feel like a volcano waiting to explode. Q.C. do you really believe what they say about the volcano getting ready to blow its top? I don't. I can recognize a petty vie for attention when I see one. After all, what's a better attention getter than a natural disaster? We educated types know better than to fall for that! Actually, if the truth be known, I'm not all that educated. Of course I passed the state administered Board exam and I participate in ongoing education for salon professionals, but what's the point in going to high school when you know no one is going to ask you to the prom?

At this point, I am faced with undergoing a costly and painful operation, the likes of which I have already been psychologically prepared for. But at what cost??? If I go through with it, I will no longer be capable of achieving complete sexual gratification.

To make a long story short, I am a woman under construction, not quite sure she is ready for the final phase of building, or should I say demolition? I'm not sure I'm ready to wreckon with the wrecking ball, if ya know what I mean. Maybe you do, maybe you don't, but whatever the case, I know you'll give it to me straight because you speak Unicamente La Pura Neta!!!

Write back quick.

Con Mucho Cariño

Really Super Confundida

La Luna
The Moon

EL FAROL DE ENAMORADOS

THE LANTERN OF LOVERS

LA FERIA

One might not think Nat would have headed out to the feria that evening after she had just thrown up, but it was precisely in that vulnerable just having vomited state that Ernesto and Amador were able to convince her to accompany them.

All parties had agreed, some reluctantly, that nine o'clock was the perfect time to head out and Amador proved himself punctual by showing up right on time.

When Natalie opened the door, she was pleasantly surprised to see a changed man. His posture was polished, the cock of his sombrero enticing, the ripple of his guayabera inviting, the smell of his cologne tantalizing.

Lifting his sombrero ever so slightly, he said, "Buenas noches, Señorita Catrina," then bowed his arm in invitation.

His Volkswagen Beetle, hereinafter referred to as the vocho, was parked in front. Ernesto and two cousins later introduced as Marcos y José waited in the back seat. Natalie took a seat in front and inhaled deeply. The vocho smelled heavily of men's cologne.

They headed noisily up the street. "You really should chew your food better, Señorita Catrina," he said once he'd gone through all the necessary gears. After Natalie had thrown up on his patio, he had stood with arms folded studying her vomit (as if it would give him some insight into what he had deemed her elusive character). Littered with chunks of pickled pig skin and strips of tostada, it looked as if it had been sliced rather than chewed.

Natalie shifted in her seat. The topic of vomit, especially her own, was an uncomfortable one. She switched the subject. "¿Does everyone in this town speak English?"

"Nope. Just us," said Amador pointing first to himself, then to his brother in the back seat. "Our parents sent us to the best schools. They wanted us to be prepared."

"¿For what?" said Natalie.

"For politics," said Ernesto from the back seat.

"Not me," said Amador. "I am taking my English north."

They had traveled perhaps four blocks, before they came to a stop at the mouth of another partially paved street.

"¿North?" said Natalie.

"To the United States," said Amador. He stepped out, then walked around to Nat's side, opened the door, then grabbed her by a hand and said, "Come on, mamacita, we got plenty of dancing to do."

Natalie watched Ernesto and the two cousins getting smaller in the distance as they went their separate ways.

The street was filled with double-, triple-, and quadruple-parked cars. Walking toward the feria, Natalie thought about what Amador had said about taking his English north. Handsome had always been in her head and in that moment she had imagined him in the midst of the mojado experience, struggling across the desert with everything of consequence strapped to his back, a gallon of water in each hand, and his eyes trained on the desert floor searching for snakes, lizards, scorpions, Border Patrol agents, and other dangerous creatures. That's what a trip north for a nineteen-year-old Mexican boy entailed. She had heard the stories before. Get a boy off the dance floor, then give him a chance to get all the ¡ay!-mamacitas out of his system so you can spend some quality time with him, and he'll eventually tell you about it—the mother's blessing, the hot sweaty bus ride to the border, the negotiations with the coyote(s), the trek(s) across the desert, the border crossing itself, followed by one-room accommodations until the other half of your passage is paid and you're driven to your ultimate destination. In Natalie's estimation, a trip like that was enough to make a boy a man.

The fiesta up ahead was small, but so crowded, it seemed big. On two sides it spilled out into a residential area where residents watched the goings-on from lawn chairs in front of their homes. On one end, there was a dried-up cornfield, on another, a chain link fence, and inside of that many tables and chairs, as well as a bunch of speakers. A conjunto norteño warmed up in the corner, readying for the dance.

There were many stands where games could be played and prizes won, lots of food for sale such as tacos, tamales, tortas, corn on the cob with chile y limón, and pan dulce. In the center of things sat a strange wood and metal contraption that reminded Natalie very much of one of the Wright brothers' first planes. She and Consuelo had recently watched a documentary about them.

Amador led her to a shabby stand with a hot pink spray-painted sign announcing REFRESCOS. He ordered two Fresca®s, handed one to her, kept one for himself, then opened up his wallet to pay. The drink came in a jarrito—a cute, fat, clay cup. Natalie was just as pleased with its contents as the jarrito itself. It was spiked with tequila. She pursed her lips after her first sip.

"You must be very careful," said Amador. They joined the assembled crowd. "Hay que poner mucho ojo." He pointed to his right eye. There was a man at the base of the earlier mentioned contraption. With a handful of matches, he was lighting a fuse of some sort. Amador put a protective arm around Natalie's shoulder as fireworks began to go off in a predetermined direction, then, after they ran that course, they went every which way including, but not limited to, right straight into the crowd. Natalie leaned into Amador. His chest was so sturdy and reassuring.

The festivities were to honor San Jacinto, El Santo Patrón del Pueblo, who Natalie was certain existed. If he didn't, then that cornfield most certainly would have gone up in flames. But the fireworks were soon over and with them that danger.

"You are really beautiful," said Amador to Natalie in the afterglow. "You are the prettiest girl I have ever seen in real life. I have seen some pretty cute girls on the tele, but they are all putas."

"¿Putas?" said Natalie.

"You see the way they dress. How they are always changing boyfriends. But you, my love, are such a lady, you could be a politician's wife."

A politician's wife. She let it sit in her head for a second, then said, "In that case, maybe I oughtta be hangin out with your brother."

Amador tossed his jarrito to the ground. He grabbed her firmly by the chin and raised her eyes to his. His grasp was so firm, she could feel the blood accumulating there. "Don't even say that," he said. "I am very jealous." He let go of her chin, then softly caressed it. The sensation was strange, but pleasurable.

"Besides," he said changing his tune. "My brother doesn't like girls."

She shrugged, finished up her Fresca®, then tossed her jarrito to the ground. It landed in a dozen pieces at her feet. It was so cute, she was sad to see it meet that end, but that's how the locals had been doing it all night long.

They were in the middle of the crowd. There was bustle all about. Amador leaned in close enough for Natalie to hear him, but spoke so softly she had to get even closer if she were to have a chance. They were so close she could feel his breath on her neck. "I must warn you, cariño," he said. "At some point during the evening, I am going to kiss you. I can do it now, or I can do it later." He caught her eyes and held her gaze as if he were about to make good on the promise at that very moment, then turned away.

She swallowed hard. She had never heard a kiss announced before.

They got in line at the chain link fence for the dance. While they waited, there was no conversation between them, but their silence was not empty. He had her by the hand and was rubbing her hard from palms to fingertips. She could feel herself being worked into a slight sweat.

Natalie watched the girls on the other side of the fence. They looked so expectant, as if the event held far more importance than she imagined it ever could. Natalie hoped that one day she wouldn't be dancing with one of their husbands. That's the way it usually went. Those girls would likely have babies far too soon. Their men would probably eventually head north to work eight or nine months out of the year in a town like Lava Landing. Any given Friday or Saturday night might find them dancing the night away at a place such as El Aguantador.

Once he paid their two-peso-apiece admission, Amador led Natalie to a corner table. "You are not feeling sick anymore, ¿are you?" he said, moving his chair closer to hers.

"I am okay. I just got a little nervous. Bein so far from home and all." She shriveled her shoulders and shivered.

"No need to be nervous, my love," he said. He pinched her by the chin, then urged her lips toward his ever so slowly. When they could get no closer there was a calculated pause where both knew what was going to happen, the only wondering was in to what extent.

He kissed her on the corner of the mouth. It would have been as unobtrusive as a kiss could have been, if Natalie wouldn't have flung her arms around his neck, pulled him close, and kissed him hard in what turned into a long, sweet kiss. When it was over, Amador had a very serious look and plenty of baby pink superfrost lipstick on his face. He stood up, pushed his chair clumsily aside, and said, "¿Bailamos?"

She got to her feet and giggled. She was just as drunk from Fresca® as she was from him and that place—being so far from home had led to careless abandon.

Amador took her in his arms and squeezed her tight as she kissed him again. They waited until the song hit a comfortable spot. They had no trouble finding their rhythm. The forthcoming fluidity of their perfectly matched steps was strangely familiar to her, as if she had danced with him in her dreams.

She rested her head on his shoulder and from that position decided that what a girl, namely herself, wanted was a boy with whom she felt safe, who offered her things she couldn't offer herself, who protected her from life's stuff: flat tires, cold weather, heavy things, mechanical devices, scary movies, and most of all, other boys and their bad intentions. She decided as judiciously as possible that in his arms, she felt just that: safe.

There were other things to consider. It could have been the Fresca® that was having its effect upon her, or the place, or DP's love spell, or ¿was it a miracle? That was interesting. When a person works love magic, that's a spell, when a Saint does it, it's a miracle. She hoped that whatever she was feeling for this Amador fellow was over and done with by the time her trip was.

She hadn't ached for a boy since she was in the ninth grade. His name was Johnny Sánchez and he played the electric guitar in a rock and roll mariachi band called Los Rok 'n' Roleros. He had curly hair like Frankie Avalon (and come to think of it, like Amador) and blue eyes. He rode a motorcycle and she and Consuelo (Consuelo was dating the group's drummer) would listen to "The Leader of the Pack" over and over on Natalie's wood cabinet stereo turntable. Eventually both drummer and guitarist dumped the girls for redheaded twins, causing Nat and Sway to contend that the ensuing heartbreak was more than just one of life's hard lessons, but another one of the factors that contributed to Consuelo's having dropped out of high school. Natalie didn't wanna go through that again.

The dancing and the prolonged dance floor kissing went on. Before either of them knew it, the feria was over.

People headed out toward the street at a slow, deliberate, drunk pace. It would be another year before such fun came to town again.

¿What do we do now?" said Natalie.

Amador petted her head and said, "We go home. Unless you have something else in mind."

They walked down the street the way they came, leaving the vocho behind for retrieval the following day. The stars were out in numbers and the moon was in its crescent stage. Between two houses there was a field with a corraled burro busy eating corncobs. Nat stopped for a visit. "All of God's creatures love me," she said as the donkey left his meal and walked straight over to her.

"I can see how they would," said Amador.

"Don't get too attached," warned Natalie. "I am leaving the day after tomorrow." She had wanted to broach the subject of her departure all evening, but hadn't found the right time.

"I know," said Amador, as they continued on their way. "But maybe I can come and visit you someday."

"Maybe," said Nat.

When they arrived at their respective homes, they sat down on a patch of sidewalk. It was after 4:00 a.m.

"Sometimes I feel like my life is spent at the quarter car wash and I have to hurry through everything otherwise my quarters are gonna run out before I do everything I wanna do. ¿Does that ever happen to you?" said Nat. She looked at her high heels, amazed that shoes could be so lovely. They were fashioned after Mary Janes with scalloped detailing, and peekaboo cutouts like men's wingtips, but with a fuchsia layer beneath.

"No, mija," he said, then paused to stroke her hair. She loved it when a man called her that, perhaps because her own father never had.

"Here there is far too much time and not enough everything," said Amador.

"There's a lot of nothin where I come from too, but you can always keep yourself busy lookin for somethin in nothin," said Nat. She was thinking of Consuelo, because being so far from home made Nat realize just how wide the world was.

"I wanna be close to your nothing," he whispered, then kissed her, but it was a different kind of kiss this time. It wasn't sweet so much as it was urgent, as if it were a prelude to something more substantial.

The true mark of a mujeriego, a ladies' man, is that he will tell you what you wanna hear in your lenguaje. He had spoken to her in her idiom, that mixed-up labyrinthine lingo that only she and Sway fully understood.

At that point they could have talked about things they might never get the chance to: favorite foods, books, sports, movies, songs, wants, desires, dreams, failures, accomplishments, or philosophies. Natalie would have liked to talk about these things, but Amador had other things on his mind.

"¿Do you want to come in?" he said.

She shaded her mouth with her hand, but he could tell from her eyes that she was smiling.

"You could take your shoes off and come in," he said softly and slowly, as if the steadiness of his voice could talk her into it.

It stood to reason that he would want her to take her high heels off. All of the floors in his house were tile. She couldn't begrudge him for trying, but she wanted something more substantial than a tiptoe across his living room floor, down the hall, and into his bedroom. She craved somebody who understood and appreciated all she entailed—her quirks, wisdoms, and misgivings. She hadn't found this man on home soil, and there was no reason to believe she would find him abroad. In fact, at no point during her life had the Universe ever indicated that this person even existed, except, of course, when It introduced her to Consuelo.

"I should go home," Natalie concluded.

She had expected, even wanted some protest from him, but he merely kissed her on the cheek, then said, "Good night, my love," and walked slowly away. Whatever they had started would have to linger until morning.

Span
the Gulf
and
Visit
MEXICO

El Cotorro
The Parrot

COTORRO DACA LA PATA Y EMPIÉZAME A PLATICAR

PARROT GIVE ME YOUR FOOT AND BEGIN TO CHAT WITH ME

MORNING

Natalie had woken up in that lovely room for five days straight, yet each time it surprised her—the light teal of the walls, the faint smell of gardenias, the glitter of the Saints and Angels, the gentle sway of the single-panel curtain suspended by the breeze, and the light that trickled in behind it. Each morning when she had woken up in that room, it had been jarring if not disheartening to know that she was so far from home, so imagine her added surprise when she woke to find Doña Elena and her seven daughters stationed throughout her room.

María del Carmen and Irma were on the floor braiding one another's hair. Doña Elena sat in a rocking chair in the corner with Lydia and Leticia at her feet. The twins, Beti and Esmeralda, slept in a bundle on the floor. And at the foot of Natalie's bed sat Marta.

At thirty-seven, Marta was the eldest of the bunch. She had always been her mother's helper. Maybe that is why she never got married.

Natalie blinked in an exaggerated manner, then collected her gaze. The scene was strange if not surreal. "¿Buenos días?" said La Catrina tentatively.

"Buenos," agreed the women.

Doña Marta stood up. She cozied Natalie's bedcovers from feet to head, then held a hand up to her forehead to check for fever. She took a seat at Natalie's side, then ran her hands through Natalie's hair. That's another thing Natalie had noticed about this land and its women. They were much more touchy-feely over here.

"¿Estás bien, mija?" Doña Marta inquired.

Natalie nodded. "Sí. Estoy bien."

The women had all gathered in La Catrina's room early that morning. In a house so full of women, nothing goes by unnoticed. The ladies were well aware that Natalie had gotten home after 4:00 a.m., and they were worried that La Natalie had gone lovesick, which is what usually happened when a girl got involved with Amador. Doña Marta did most of the talking.

Amador's name meant lover.

Natalie had figured that much out.

Around town he had lived up to it. Natalie should just see what happened to their first cousin Lupe Macías Alba. She had been named Miss San Pepito the year before last, but after Amador dumped her, she gained fifty pounds and completely cut off her once long and luxurious hair.

¿Natalie wasn't lovesick was she?

La Catrina thought it over and here is what came to mind: the previous night and its summery warmth, the smell of fire in the air, the pounding beat of the open-air speakers and how her heartbeat eventually adopted their rhythm, the way Amador danced her just right, the soft silky feel of his guayabera, the sharp crease in his slacks, the crisp point of his alligator skin boots, the enticing angle of his sombrero, the way he asserted himself upon her, the softness first of his words, then that of his lips kissing her hard, then parting just enough to allow his firm tongue to welcome hers into the open expanse of a French kiss.

Sure, Amador had what it took to knock a girl lovesick, but the previous evening was about as much fun as any one of many evenings spent in the company of Consuelo, dancing the night away with dozens of young men.

Natalie had a best friend, the car of her dreams, and thanks to her father's hard work, her house was humble, but paid for. She wasn't so worried about settling down with a man. This last part was a little hard to explain to the gathered congregation, so Natalie rationed her words and concluded, "No se preocupen. I will be all right." Of course she would be. She would return to the normalcy of her life: Consuelo, work, shopping, bingo, and the dance. Come to think of it, the Baile Grande was fast approaching. Los Huracanes del Norte were coming to town. ¿Did Doña Elena and the girls like Los Huracanes? Of course they did.

The ladies, Doña Marta in particular, were relieved to see what a get-back-in-the-saddle sorta girl Nat was.

Doña Marta reached for the silver platter that waited on the nightstand near the bed. On top there was a carafe of milk and a single red rose, compliments of Amador, Doña Marta informed her.

Natalie dipped a finger into the milk. It was warm.

"Está fresco," volunteered Doña Marta with a smile.

Fresh. That meant unpasteurized. "¡Yúckate!" Natalie said. She raised the rose to her nose and took a whiff. If that Amador wanted to be her bon-boncito, even if only for the rest of that day and on into the evening, then he would have to do better than fresh-squeezed milk and a homegrown rose. The women couldn't agree with Natalie more, but better would have to wait. Amador had gone to town—to San Luis Río Colorado. He had gotten up at the crack of dawn and had shoved two of his best cows into the back seat of the vocho. He was going to sell them at market in order to finance an evening out with La Catrina. He wouldn't be back until the afternoon.

Natalie smiled. A boy had never sold his cows for her before.

But by the time night fell, Natalie realized that Amador wasn't coming back. She sat on the couch in Doña Elena's living room saying goodbye to what had been her family for the past six days and would forever be a part of her. She had shown up in that dusty pueblo with half a dozen cashmere sweaters, four cut-along-the-bias dresses, two pencil skirts, two blouses, eight pairs of high heels, a boxful of costume jewelry, and four handbags. She was attached to each and every garment and accessory, but not as attached as she was to Doña Elena and her seven daughters. She left it all behind except for the clothes on her back and the memories the place had given her.

As for Amador, Natalie never saw his return, although the following morning when she awoke, then walked barefoot out to the living room and pulled the curtains aside, she would see the vocho parked in its usual spot across the street. But for the there and then, Amador didn't come back—not to say goodbye, or even to drop off a cookie to go with the lukewarm, unpasteurized milk he'd left her. It was the least he could have done.

In the morning just before she walked out the door onto the sidewalk in front of the old stucco house where Don Lalo was waiting in his flatbed Chevy to take her to the airport, Natalie scribbled out a note on a piece of binder paper, then pressed it into Doña Marta's hands, telling her to give it to Amador. Brief and to the point, it read, "Sorry I missed you. If you ever take your English north, look me up. Give your mother and sister my love, and wish your brother luck in politics."

She wrote down her address and both her and Consuelo's telephone numbers, then signed it love—a closing comment she had yet to find any meaning in, unless of course as it applied to Consuelo.

La Bota
The Boot

UNA BOTA, IGUAL QUE LA OTRA
ONE BOOT, THE SAME AS THE OTHER

GIRL TALK II

¿You know how when you get off of a boat, you feel like you're still rocking back and forth? Well for some reason, that's just how Nat felt when she got off the airplane. Since a serious haircut was in order, she rushed to the nearest pay phone, called Consuelo, and told her to meet her at True-Dee's Tresses ¡inmediatamente!

And boy was Nat ever consoled when she arrived and found Sway's yellow five-speed parked in front of the salon. She scarcely got the door open before she was enveloped by Consuelo and Lulabell in a three-way hug. Lulabell had shown up earlier that morning to announce her Twelfth Annual Dinner for Ranch Hands and Day Laborers, which would be celebrated the following evening. When Lulabell heard that Nat was on her way, she decided to stay on as part of the homecoming.

True-Dee waited her turn, then hugged Nat gingerly. She was debuting her Hair Growth Accelerators. At least that's what she was calling them for now. The system employed fishing weights, which True-Dee was sure would stretch the hair as well as improve circulation at the scalp, all of which would in turn promote faster-growing hair.

"¿Whatever on earth has happened to your hair?" said True-Dee sizing up Natalie's hair, which was past her hips headed for her knees.

"I might ask you the same question," said Nat. True-Dee's bangs were divided into equal sections and rolled under with two #7 egg sinkers held in place by sturdy bobby pins. From each side of her head swung a single, two-ounce bullet weight she had to venture into the deep sea fishing section at the Super Kmart just to find. And from the back of her head dangled so many BB shots, just like a bunch of beads.

"It's a hair growth system I invented myself and I'm savin my money to have it patented," said True-Dee, a bit proud and a bit embarrassed.

Nat dipped into the mesh Mexican market bag she had brought home, came up with the framed photograph of Don Pancho Macías Contreras that he had left in Natalie's room, then handed it to Sway. "Sorry I didn't bring you a present, but there just wasn't time. I was gonna get you a belt with your name on it, but seein as how your name's so long and your waist's so small, I didn't figure it'd fit."

Consuelo studied the picture, then looked up at Nat and said, "You brought me my daddy, a girl can't ask for more than that."

It was a moment that could have stood still and lingered, but didn't, a space in time that could have been filled with thank yous and you're welcomes, but wasn't. The subject was quickly switched to a more pressing matter.

"¿Can you fix my hair?" said Nat to True-Dee.

"Why sure. But I don't know what I can do for you that you haven't already done for yourself." True-Dee circled Nat, assessing her hair from every angle.

"I just want you to make it like it was before," said Nat.

"So ¿you want that intelligent elegant look?"

"I guess I do," said Nat. She took a seat as True-Dee reached for a smock. Consuelo and Lulabell occupied the neighboring styling chairs.

The women were anxious to hear the details of Nat's trip, and since Consuelo had already given Lulabell and True-Dee the basic lowdown, Nat began with her impressions of the land and customs, saying, "Over there they get to have more fun because they have a lot less rules and people don't hardly ever sue each other.

"They let the bulls run wild in the streets at 11:00 every morning during fiesta week and anybody that wants to can ride them," said Nat.

"I seen a documentary about them bulls runnin in the streets before," said Sway. She was sucking on a Smarty® sour lollipop. She took it out of her mouth and gazed at it for a moment, marveling at its beauty: It was marbled green and yellow and plenty shiny from use.

"You've seen far too many documentaries," commented Natalie.

"¿Did you get any pictures?" said Lulabell. She too was sucking on a Smarty®—a red and orange one.

"Nope. Not a one."

"¿You didn't take no pictures?" said Sway yanking the Smarty® from her mouth.

Natalie wiggled just enough to get a look at Sway. "No pictures," confirmed Nat. "With the way everybody was callin on me just like in an old

British novel, it was kinda difficult. I was always goin here and there, and every time forgettin the camera."

"I remember them books from high school and they were dreamy," said True-Dee.

"But I told you I wanted pictures," said Sway and she was stern about it.

Nat wiggled some more.

"I can't work if somebody won't be still," said True-Dee. She set her scissors ever so calmly on the counter in front of the styling station. Nat's hair was a little under a quarter done.

"Now look what you did," said Nat to Sway.

"I didn't do nothin."

"You never do. ¿You know what, Sway?"

Consuelo took the Fifth.

"That trip meant nothin to me. It was just a lot of hard work and awkward situations. But I did it. I got your daddy out of Purgatory and you're whinin about pictures."

Sway didn't say nothing and it was a good thing because Nat was hardly finished.

"We sold stuff we really loved. That we can never replace, so I could make that trip. I want those cow horns back. You know how I get attached to things and I really loved the cow horns."

"¡You sold the bull horns!" said True-Dee. Both True-Dee and Lulabell were familiar with that set of horns. They had been proudly displayed in Nat's living room for years, and both True-Dee and Lulabell had hung their coats upon them during more than a few occasions.

Nat nodded.

"¿How much did you get for them?" said Lulabell. She was all calmness and serenity.

"Thirty-eight dollars," said Nat.

"We were askin forty and some guy tried to talk us down to thirty-five, so we settled on thirty-eight. And besides, we made a profit."

"Some profit," said Nat doing the math. "We had them for ten years and sold them for eleven dollars more than we paid, so that's, ¿what, a dollar and ten cents a year?"

"That's not even worth it," said True-Dee. She put a consolatory arm around Nat's shoulders. "To think, you could have put them on the Cadillac. Imagine that. They would have looked so snazzy."

"I would have given you fifty bucks," contributed Lulabell.

"At least that way they would have stayed in the family," said Nat.

"Sway, ¿do you think we can live our entire lives like this, workin in a cheese factory?" said Nat.

"Sure we can. It's not like we're poor," concluded Consuelo.

"Nope. Poor is when you start thinkin about everything you don't have, then bustin your ass tryin to get it." All four women nodded in agreement.

"And besides," said Sway. "I never met nothin I loved so much I couldn't wait to get it out of layaway."

"You're not poor until you try to have everything everybody else has. When you try to be like normal people."

"In case you haven't noticed, Nat, we ain't normal."

"Thank the good Lord for that."

True-Dee and Lulabell breathed easier; it seemed Nat and Sway were yet again seeing eye-to-eye.

"Least we're not shaggin shoppin carts in the Kmart parkin lot," said Sway.

"That would suck," said Nat. "But not as bad as bein a secretary. I would really hate that."

"Me too, and besides all that typin might lead to carpal trouble."

"I hear that shit is real bad," said Lulabell. "Makes your fingers tingle and not in a good way either."

"Anything that lists trouble as its last name has got to be real bad," said True-Dee. She picked up her scissors and started in where she left off.

"I wanna get away from things every now and again," said Natalie. "I wanna go to a place where the sun occupies a different space in the sky, where things smell different. I wanna get away from here." She pointed down at the floor.

"Then maybe you should get away," said Sway. She stuck the Smarty® back in her mouth with renewed interest.

"But I wanna get away with you. We don't never leave. We just watch the come and go of the crops and the men that come and go with them. We don't got no new stories. It's always the same. I met a boy, Sway, and maybe some-day I might wanna go and visit him."

"¡¿¡You met a what!?!" said Consuelo.

"A boy," repeated True-Dee, her voice loaded with longing.

"A boy," declared Lulabell.

"Yes, a boy," said Nat. "I wanna go and see him someday, and I want you to go with me."

"But we promised we'd never run off and leave each other for a boy," protested Sway.

"We made no such promise," said Natalie.

"Well let's," countered Sway.

"I ain't makin no promises until you say you're gonna get some help and at least try to get rid of that unreasonable fear of yours."

"Maybe I don't want to. Maybe I'm happy just like I am." She folded her arms. If there was one thing Sway hated, it was being ultimatumed.

"But it's not always about you. ¿Why don't you ever think about me?"

"I always think about you," said Sway.

"I'm askin for more than a donut in the mornin and free rein of your closet. I wanna go some place. I'm tired of bein stuck."

"But it ain't that easy. Say we get in the car and we get down the road, and I start to thinkin and worryin that maybe my house is on fire, or that your house is on fire, or that we're gonna get a flat tire and some creepy scary guys are gonna haul us off to the forest, have their way with us, then chop our arms off."

"You've got to have more faith in yourself," said True-Dee to Consuelo.

"But you gotta admit," said Sway. "Such a thing has happened before."

"But that sort of thing would never happen to you, as big as you are." Lulabell, who was a mere five-foot-three in heels to Sway's five-eleven-and-three-quarters in bare feet, shook her head.

"You guys act like it's like quittin smokin or somethin."

"Sway, I bet your daddy pays one of us a visit, and when he does, we can ask him to help you. Simple as that," said Nat.

"That's an idea," said True-Dee. She was putting the finishing snips on Nat's hair. "I mean look what he did with your hair. If he can do somethin like this, he must be mighty powerful."

"I'll think about it," said Sway.

"That's all I'm askin," said Nat.

"Well I better git," said Lulabell. "But ¿do you girls mind swingin by tomorrow afternoon to give me a hand?"

"Sure thing," said Consuelo and True-Dee, who were quick to inform Natalie of Lulabell's impending Dinner for Ranch Hands and Day Laborers. "Sounds like a plan," said Nat as Lulabell rushed out the door to do some last-minute shopping.

Nat fluffed her curls, then said, "Good as new."

Sway removed the beige scarf she had ponytailed around her hair, then shook her head as in a shampoo commercial and said, "Take mine too."

"¿Come again?" said True-Dee.

"Get rid of mine as well. Take it up to about here. Blunt. No bangs. All one length," said Sway holding a hand up to her chin.

"¿You want me to bob you?" said True-Dee in disbelief. Sway's hair was three quarters of the way down her back, headed for her nalgas.

"I sure do," said Sway.

"All right then." True-Dee went to work. It was a swift process. She put Sway's hair back in a ponytail, cut it off, then touched up the ends.

And when it was all done and Sway looked in the mirror, she realized that the bob was the coif that best suited her straight, thick, jet black hair, the tips of which pointed to her blossomy lips, her high cheekbones, poignant nose, and those gray-green eyes.

With their haircuts, Nat and Sway looked just like they had as kids. Sure they were taller and they had grown breasts, but they were still as united and just as girly as they had been back then, even though that afternoon they had come closer to a fight than they ever had since the second grade.

El Nopal

The Cactus

LO QUE TODOS VAN A VER CUANDO TIENEN QUE COMER

WHAT EVERYONE WILL SEE WHEN THEY HAVE TO EAT

LULABELL'S TWELFTH ANNUAL DINNER FOR RANCH HANDS AND DAY LABORERS

"No matter what anybody says, there ain't nothin wrong with Connie Francis," said Natalie turning up the AM radio. Looney Bugsy McCray was spinning oldies having to do with the life and times of Connie Francis.

"She's enough to get my shoulders shakin anyday," said Consuelo proving the point. The girls were at Lulabell's, aproned and in the kitchen, slicing and dicing jalapeños and tomatoes, respectively.

True-Dee was also present, but she was so excited about spending the evening with three hundred ranch hands and/or day laborers that she had spent the majority of the afternoon in the bathroom primping. True-Dee had gone blonde for the event, donning a bouffant from the Dolly Parton wig collection, and what's more, she'd gone vaquera, adopting a cowgirl style, realizing that all ranch hands and the vast majority of day laborers prefer el estilo vaquero.

"¿How do I look?" she said making her entrance in a pair of tight-fitting polyester jeans, cowboy boots, and a pink sleeveless frilly blouse.

"Like a million pesos nuevos," said Lulabell handing True-Dee a paring knife and a bag of avocados.

The radio cut into "Where the Boys Are" anticipating the arrival of the guests just as the doorbell sounded the first seventeen notes of "La Cucaracha." Lulabell opened the door to a handful of sombrero-ed gardeners. "Amor de mis amores," she said embracing Don José, the eldest of the bunch. Don José was responsible for the flora and fauna which overgrew

Lulabell's front, back, and side yards. He'd started the gardening project more than twenty years before when he'd kissed Lulabell for the first time in front of the succulents she mistook for cacti.

The men came in. True-Dee ran up, pulling her apron off on the way. "¡Ay! mamacita," said Juan when he got a look at True-Dee.

"That's what he thinks," said Consuelo under her breath. She and Natalie were watching the scene unfold from the kitchen.

True-Dee made eye-to-eye contact with Juan, but that was the extent of her coquetry, for the other four men promptly pulled Juan away.

"No es mamacita," said one of the gardeners.

"A ¿cómo no?" said Juan. "Se parece una botella de Coca-Cola®." He made the shape out with his hands.

"Es mamápa," announced one of the men.

"¿Mamápa?" repeated Juan. "¿Qué es éso?"

"Part mamacita, part papacito," they said in unison.

"¡Ay! no. So many curvas and me without brekas," said Juan.

It wasn't that True-Dee didn't look like a woman. The other four men were regulars at the Thursday night show transvestis. True-Dee, in her parts as Thalía and Paulina Rubio, was their favorite impersonator. Juan never attended the Tuesday night event with the other men due to a serious tele-novela habit which kept him glued to the television set five nights a week.

Lulabell led her first group of guests through the house and out the back door, which opened up to the backyard deck. All along its perimeter, there was a built-in bench so there would be plenty of seating, but just in case, there were several brightly colored picnic tables in the center of things, each complete with a fresh bouquet of homegrown flowers. At its southmost point, the deck jutted out into an ornate gazebo. It was nearly 8:00 p.m. and had just begun to get dark. Lulabell plugged in the Tiki lights. She stood with her arms folded, at once pleased, yet surprised by how lovely they looked. It was amazing the stuff you could get at the one-dollar store.

In no time, the party was underway, and the backyard was overflowing with guests. The men ate, drank, laughed, talked about their families at home, and argued about their favorite soccer teams—things men such as themselves generally do if given the chance. Lulabell, Natalie, Consuelo, and True-Dee milled about, playing the parts of perfect hostesses.

All of this was momentarily interrupted by the sounding of a trumpet as Mariachi de Dos Nacimientos marched single file into the backyard, just as they had for the past twelve years. During the event's history, Javier and the boys had had marginal success, and had, to date, made off with over twenty souls for Jesus. But that evening, soul saving wasn't the only thing on Javier's mind. He had brought Lucha along as his date and could hardly wait for her to meet Lulabell. He spotted his mother in the distance, looked down at Lucha, smiled, then said, with an inordinate amount of enthusiasm, "Come and meet momma."

Lucha furrowed her brow and crinkled her nose. Not another momma's boy, she thought, as Javier grabbed her by the wrist and dragged her toward Lulabell.

Lulabell was taking a break, seated on a bench amongst a handful of janitors. Javier straightened his sombrero, then said, "Momma, meet my girlfriend."

Hearing this, Lulabell nearly choked on her carnitas. Javier's declaration came as a surprise to Lucha as well; she had no idea they were officially novios.

"Mijo, ¿Tienes novia?" said Lulabell.

"Yes I have a girlfriend," said Javier. He threw an arm momentarily around Lucha's shoulders, pulled her near, then kissed her on the cheek.

Lucha looked so innocent standing at Javier's side dressed in an embroidered peasant top and flowing skirt—an ensemble Javier had deemed befitting her debut as Mariachi de Dos Nacimientos' new vocalist when he'd hauled it off from Lulabell's closet earlier that afternoon. In spite of Lucha's innocent appearance, Lulabell still had cause for alarm. She got to her feet, took both of Lucha's hands in her own, and studied her hard before smiling, then saying, "Let's go for a walk."

The women looped arms. They passed the rosebushes in the side yard heading away from the crowd and toward the front of the house while Javier stood watching and wondering in the distance.

"You're wearin my clothes," Lulabell said after a spell of silence.

"Javier said dressin decent like this would bring me closer to Heaven," said Lucha.

"They suit you. They would look ridiculous on anyone but a divine young woman such as yourself. But you could use some earrings."

Lucha felt her ears. "¿You think?"

"Yes, mija," said Lulabell holding the front door open, inviting Lucha in.

The women went into Lulabell's room, which spoke of years of accumulation. The bed was covered with a velvet patchwork quilt from the 1970s. The pillowcases, which read "Buenas noches mi amor," were left over from the time when Lulabell's bed was a marriage bed, and hence predated even the quilt. The walls were painted avocado green and were covered with yet more old Mexican calendars, these from the 1960s, which looked the same as the more current ones, and original framed prison drawings (Lulabell had many "pen" pals) from the 1970s depicting buxom Aztec princesses, but with feathered hair, tattoos, and other evidence of homegirlhood. Lulabell had an armoire which held her regional costumes from regions unknown to her, a large collection of shawls, a sizable accumulation of huaraches of various colors, some with wooden heels like the ones Lucha wore, others embroidered Sinaloan style. (Paper dolls of Lulabell's regional costumes follow The Big Cheese Plant, The Big Five-Four, and The Baile Grande: A Present-Tense Account.)

Lucha sat down on the bed while Lulabell headed for her jewelry box. She pulled out a pair of gold earrings, grabbed one of Lucha's earlobes, then the other, outfitting them with a shiny pair of extra-large coquetas. The earrings felt heavy hanging from Lucha's ears. She looked in the mirror and smiled.

"We have to talk en serio," said Lulabell taking Lucha's hand and caressing it.

"All right, Señora," said Lucha tentatively.

"¿Did you know I knew your father?"

"No," said Lucha shaking her head.

"I mean I KNEW him," reiterated Lulabell.

"I hardly did," said Lucha. He had commuted between Lava Landing and Tecalitlán for most of Lucha's childhood, until he had found sedentary work at The Sausage Factory. The family immigrated permanently to the United States when Lucha was nine years old, and her father had died shortly thereafter. According to Lucha's mother, Doña Violeta, the absence of her father was just one of the reasons Lucha had turned out to be "such a bad girl."

"When I say I knew your father, I mean I really knew him and I loved him, but I didn't realize it until after he was gone."

"You mean ¿you and my father were like that?" said Lucha crossing two fingers.

"Sí, mija. When I met your father, he was married to your mother, but she was far away in México. A man far from his country and his family gets lonely.

"I was married too, but men and women can get restless in marriage. My husband started runnin around on me, and a woman can only take so much. I resigned myself to get back at my husband. To do to him what he had done to me.

"I was only lookin for an aventura. No quería nada en serio. But I fell in love."

"I understand, Señora," said Lucha. "I have never been very good at bein faithful myself."

"Thank you, mija, but I need to ask you somethin very important," said Lulabell.

"Adelante," said Lucha.

"Mija, tú y Javier, ¿han tenido relaciones?"

Lucha laughed. "¿Have we had relationships? ¿You mean like sex?"

Lulabell nodded.

"¡Ay! no. I mean I wanted to, but he said we had to get married first and that sex outside of marriage era un pecado mortal."

The ease with which Lucha spoke about sex amazed and frightened Lulabell. Maybe Lulabell would have found this capacity admirable had Javier not been involved.

"Listen, mija," said Lulabell taking both of Lucha's hands in her own. "Be glad you and Javier haven't been intimate with one another. Trust me, it's for the best. There is no easy way to put this . . ." She squeezed Lucha's hand tight. "Your father might very well be Javier's father too." She let go of Lucha's hands, closed her eyes and clenched her fists, expecting the worst.

Lucha stood up and began to pace. First it hit her that she might not be an only child. Well at least it was a brother. Even though they were cousins, Favy was all the sister she could ever want or need. It was a novelty, more than anything else, the thought that she might have a sibling.

"Tell me more," prompted Lucha resuming her seat on the bed.

Lulabell sat down next to her. "Sometimes I see your father in Javier, but I get confused because I hardly even remember my husband. When a thing like infidelity makes its way into your bed, you do your best to forget about it and everything associated with it. It's really strange."

"Maybe. But not as strange as goin out with your own brother and not even knowin it," said Lucha, then she hunched down, as if to gather strength, before she laughed, not just any laugh, but a big, scary, crazy Devil-just-let-loose laugh that startled even Lulabell.

Lulabell cleared her throat. "It's best that I told you, mija, because you and Javier, you can't go on, así como andan. You have to end things for good and ASAP."

Lucha nodded.

"And one more thing," said Lulabell.

Lucha was all ears.

"¿Don't say anything about this to Javier. I wanna wait for the right time, then tell him myself."

"All right, Señora," she agreed.

"I'm sorry if this comes as a shock to you. Pero la vida está llena de sorpresas. Maybe you and I can get to know each other. Maybe we can be friends. ¿Do you like bingo?" said Lulabell.

"I have never been," said Lucha.

"Someday we can go. But let's not think about all of this right now. We got some dancin to do," said Lulabell.

"¡Ándale chiquilla loca!" said Lucha, shouting her newfound favorite refrain. The women looped arms and headed for the backyard.

When Javier saw Lucha heading his way, he picked up his guitarrón and led the mariachis unknowingly into "Qué Bonito Amor"—an agnostic number, and a love song for sure. Lucha had to stop and think. ¿Was that the same song Cheque had serenaded her that fateful night just before they consummated their love in the rear quarters of the lonchera? Indeed it was. Goose bumps rose on Lucha's arms as she remembered it all over again, only this time she put Javier in Cheque's place.

Javier was crooning, Lucha was swooning, and from a distance things looked as they should be—the handsome Javier in his traje de charro, Lucha looking at once innocent and seductive, but Lulabell, knowing better, walked up to Lucha, grabbed her firmly by the forearm, and muttered the acronym "ASAP."

Lucha merely nodded. The second verse of the song had arrived. It was the perfect time for Lucha to make her debut as the mariachis' lead singer and she did so in resounding fashion. Ranch hands and day laborers alike were impressed. The mariachis had to significantly slow the serenade down, allowing Lucha extra time to show off the range of her voice, to ride out all of the notes in the song. She looked so lovely in the glow of the Tiki lights with her full skirt billowing in the evening breeze.

After the song was up, the crowd gave Lucha a standing ovation and began to chant, "Otra, otra, otra."

Lucha bowed cordially, but at the moment, music was the last thing on her mind. She wrapped her arms around Javier's neck. Now that she knew that he could very well be her long-lost half-brother, he was no longer the clumsy missionary out to save her soul, but a thrill waiting to be had. Lucha had an insight: She would dangle her unsaved soul in front of him until he pounced upon it, then, when he went after it, she would go after him. It sounded like such fun, she could hardly wait, and wouldn't hardly have to either—their roller-skating date was less than a week away.

Javier, a missionary and a mariachi, but foremost a man, was suffering an internal struggle. Lucha appealed to him even more after he heard her in song. But as he looked around at the men assembled before him, he realized how many souls there were to save and the missionary in him was soon awakened. It wasted no time usurping the mariachi and the manly part of his manhood as he embarked upon the first few notes of "Just a Closer Walk with Thee." The other mariachis were quick to join in.

Javier gave Lucha the nod and she began to sing the song, but somehow her voice had lost its power and it no longer cast its spell on the audience. The men were less interested in the soul-saving message than they were in their buddies and their booze. But as Javier saw it, the only thing that could have made Lucha's debut stronger was a tambourine.

About three quarters of the way through, the soul-saving serenade was interrupted by a banda which arrived playing the classic love song "Mi Gusto Es." The mariachis all agreed that it was a good time to take a break and eat.

Meanwhile, Lulabell was in the arms of Carlos, a bricklayer from the state of Michoacán. He was singing quite capably in her ear. She was so involved in the moment that she didn't even notice Alberto, who had just arrived.

He wanted to be at Lulabell's side the moment the spell took effect. He paused to sniff the air. The scent of carnitas was enticing, but he wasn't about to let a love song like that go by without a dance with his beloved Lulabell. "Con permiso," he said wedging his short fat body between Carlos and Lulabell.

Carlos pushed him away, and held Lulabell tighter.

"She's mine," protested Alberto stomping his feet.

Lulabell put her hands on her hips and said, "¡Mentiroso! I am not." She had a point. Beto's spell wouldn't take effect until the final stroke of midnight, if at all.

Carlos didn't give Beto a chance to argue. He knocked him out with a single chingazo, in such resounding and efficient fashion Lulabell could hardly believe it. Well at least he was considerate enough to drag him off to the corner and prop him up against one of the fence posts, thought Lulabell.

It was a little after 11:00 p.m.—way past bedtime for the average ranch hand or day laborer. The party had hit a lull. Only the janitors were going at it full force, their energy owing to the fact that they were swing-shifters. A handful had Natalie and Consuelo all to themselves.

"Cómo que estás chula, mi amor," said Carlos as he held Lulabell once again in his arms. They were dancing slow to a fast song. She let him kiss her on the cheek, then ease his way toward her lips. They were so close she could feel the firmness of his most private part brushing against the softness of her own. Carlos ran his hands up her bare back—she was wearing a sequined, backless, purple, spaghetti-strapped dress. She was about to say, "Vamos pa' dentro," about to invite that young man in, offer to fix him a cup of coffee or some other refreshment, then move to the couch, start something there that could only be finished in more intimate quarters, lead him to her bedroom, and do what comes natural. But then she started to itch. A little at first, but then all over. She scratched her head, and her chonguitos came tumbling down. She scratched her legs, leaving white tracks all over her brown skin. She sighed, wiped the sweat which had accumulated on her brow, looked around as if confused, before whispering, then shouting Alberto's name.

Lulabell left Carlos in a similar state, hot, sweating, with an itch that needed scratching, more than a bit confused by her sudden departure, and even more so when he got an eyeful of what Lulabell had abandoned him for. There, in the distance, was Lulabell, lying on the ground cradling Alberto's bald head in her lap.

"¡Despiértate, mi amor! ¡Despiértate!" She slapped his cheeks until he came to, then placed her lips on his. It was the first kiss they had shared and it was the softest sweetest kiss Lulabell had ever experienced. How strange that it should remind her of her sons, their first words, their first steps, single milestones amongst many others to come whose beauty was at once transient, yet permanent.

Lulabell and Alberto walked hand in hand to the front door, all the while staring at one another, then made their way inside where Lulabell offered him a cup of coffee. He declined and they headed for the couch and started something that could only be finished in more private quarters.

And so it was that Lulabell's Dinner for Ranch Hands and Day Laborers came to an abrupt end. With the early departure of its lovely hostess, the party simply unraveled. Natalie and Consuelo, barefoot and blistered, limped out to the front yard, got into the Cadillac, and drove off. Juan and True-Dee headed for his house to watch prerecorded episodes of *Amor y Pecado* with the intention of cultivating the one (love) by partaking in the other (sin).

The other mariachis, including Lucha, got into Raymundo's station wagon and went home as well, leaving Javier all alone, so he took his boots and his sombrero off, then reclined in a vinyl chaise-lounge on the deck. The nighttime weather was in the low if not mid-seventies. The crickets creaked in the distance.

Aside from the smell of burnt corn tortillas still lingering in the air, there was little evidence of the party. It always amazed Javier how little there was to clean up every year after the event. If anything, the yard was always in better condition after those men left. Not only did they clean up after themselves, but they pruned the trees, weeded the garden, fixed the fence posts, fertilized and seeded the back lawn.

Javier remembered something Lulabell had once told him. She had stated simply and succinctly that when Jesus said to feed the hungry, He meant more than that. At the time, Javier couldn't have agreed with Lulabell more since he thought she was talking about visiting the sick and imprisoned, about clothing the naked. But as he sat there, hot and sweaty with his traje de charro itchy against his skin, it occurred to him that Lulabell was talking about something else entirely: There were so many different varieties of hunger, and each year when Lulabell brought those men together, she was trying to feed them in more ways than one. It made Javier proud of his mother. And to think for so many years he had been against the event, had looked upon it as nothing more than another occasion for Lulabell to cavort and carouse.

Lying there under a handful of stars with his boots in a pile on the floor, and the jacket to his traje de charro slung over a nearby lawn chair, Javier had to admit: There were so many things in the world he didn't know whether to file under "good" or "evil," his mother being foremost amongst them, and now, there was Lucha.

La Peluca
Blonde Bouffant
The Blonde Bouffant Wig

STYLE
707

LO QUE USA LA CASTAÑA, Y

A TODO EL MUNDO ENGAÑA

WHAT THE BRUNETTE USES TO FOOL THE WORLD

NO LO PUEDO BELIEVE

True-Dee and Juan sat on Juan's living room couch. They had left Lulabell's shindig early and were watching recorded episodes of *Amor y Pecado*. They were all alone. Juan couldn't keep his eyes off of True-Dee, her big blue eyes, her big blonde hair, her big melones de chichis, her big round nalgas. From his vantage point he couldn't see her nalgas, but he could remember them, and as he did, as they flashed before his eyes, he could think of only one phrase to describe what he considered his immense good fortune: "No lo puedo believe."

The two were close together, very, very close together. Juan caressed the back of True-Dee's neck, and she did the same. They were face-to-face, eye-to-eye, moving toward one another just like in any given episode of any given telenovela and Juan couldn't help but think, "No lo puedo believe."

He knew what came next. Their lips touched ever so softly. Their eyes shut. True-Dee slid her tongue into Juan's waiting mouth and did the things she had learned over the years, over the men, the many, many men, and Juan thought over and over again, "No lo puedo believe."

"¿You hungry, mi amor?" said True-Dee. She wanted to slow things down. She wasn't sure Juan was ready for what lay in store. He seemed a tender soul, an understanding type, at least judging by the way he had cried during the finale of *Amor y Pecado*. Juan's smile waned to a grin. Come to think of it, he was hungry. "Sí, mamacita. I got a little bit of hungry."

True-Dee made for the kitchen, and once she was out of listening range Juan muttered another, "No lo puedo believe," for not only was that ruca lovely, she was also domesticated.

And ¿why was it that Juan no lo podía believe? Guys like Juan just don't get dates like True-Dee. Juan was by no means ugly. He was average—of average height, or maybe even a little tall for a Mexican. His facial features normal, perhaps even slightly handsome. He had all of his hair and a few well-developed muscles. He made twelve dollars an hour, cash, a necessity since he had no papers, no Social Security number, not even a fake one, mucho menos una driver's license. He had a bicycle, a VCR, a television set, and a stake in next week's tanda—he had given his hundred dollars a week for the past several weeks, and what went around was about to come around to him. Even so, True-Dee was far too lovely. As Juan saw it, she could have her pick of starring roles in the telenovela of her choice.

After a spell, True-Dee returned with chorizo con huevos and a glass of milk. Juan took his first bite. With his mouth full he couldn't help but mutter, "No lo puedo believe," for the chorizo con huevos tasted just like chorizo con huevos.

Juan snatched the plate from True-Dee's hands and dug in. He was hungry all right, not for chorizo per se, menos por huevos, but for some more of True-Dee's tender loving ways.

He put the empty plate on the floor, finished his milk, wiped his milk mustache on the back of his sleeve, then grabbed True-Dee by the hair in a dame-un-beso-¡pero-rápido! sort of way. He came up with a whole lot of blonde bouffant and no True-Dee whatsoever. He looked at the bouffant, then at True-Dee, then back again before saying in a tell-me-it-ain't-so sort of way, "No lo puedo believe."

True-Dee took the pins out of her updo letting all that shiny, long black hair come tumbling down. She swung her head and tossed her hair in a cuz-I'm-a-woman sort of way, and Juan couldn't help but say, "No lo puedo believe," for True-Dee was even better with black hair.

"Believe it," said True-Dee.

Juan grabbed True-Dee by her real hair this time, and started in where he assumed they had left off, but True-Dee wasn't playing that way. If they were playing a game of Candy Land®, then by Juan's estimation they had made it at least to the Lollipop Woods, if not as far as the Ice Cream Sea. But it looked like he had picked up a Candy Cane card somewhere along the way, and now he found himself back at the Peppermint Forest, him trying to unbutton her shirt, and her insisting, "No, no, no."

They sat lip-locked and tongue-tied for a time until Juan said, "Vamos a mi cuarto, mamacita."

"¿You wanna go to your room?" guessed True-Dee.

"Sí, honey. A mi room let's vámonos."

"Okay, papi. But you gotta be a good boy."

"¡Oh, my!" said True-Dee when she got a look at Juan's room. The floor was covered with twin mattresses, seven True-Dee could see, and one in the closet she couldn't. It didn't shock her that so many men kept such close quarters. It thrilled her knowing that she was about to lie down in the same space where so many men had laid themselves down to sleep and she could only imagine what else.

Perhaps that was all it took to loosen True-Dee up. They lay down on Juan's mattress and crawled under the blanket and True-Dee allowed Juan to unbutton her pink frilly blouse, to unhook her matching lacy brassiere, and to uncover her pride and joy, her bosoms, her boobis, her chichis. She had developed them herself, really developed them. They were not falsies. She had done with hormones what some women can only do with silicone and payments. All the more proof that she was indeed a woman trapped in the trappings of a man's body.

Juan buried his face in her breasts, all the while thinking, "No lo puedo believe." He examined them, held them, beheld them, admired them from every angle before whispering, "No lo puedo believe."

They made their way to the Lollipop Forest without incident. Juan was happier than he had ever been with his True-Dee, his Princess Lolly, if you will. He licked and sucked at True-Dee's breasts as if they were his favorite lollipops, the watermelon ones covered with chilito y limón, and a little bit of salt and tamarindo.

Juan dipped his tongue in True-Dee's belly button, all the while struggling with the buckle of her fancy belt. It was an effort peeling those tight pants off. True-Dee wasn't about to help. There she was on her back on Juan's humble twin mattress, forget the box spring, just a mattress thrown on the floor, and a secondhand one at that. She was naked or nearly so—just her panties stood in the way of delights Juan could only imagine, delights he had seen the prelude to countless nights between the hours of 7:00 and 11:00 p.m. And now he was on the verge of finding out what happens after the telenovela is over. He was about to see what goes on during strategically timed commercial breaks. "No lo puedo believe," he said as he unbuckled his belt, as he unbuttoned and unzipped his pants, as he pulled his underpants down, and let his most manly part spring loose. True-Dee held her breath. Juan had his hands tucked under the elastic band of her panties, he was pulling and they were coming down—down over the hips, down over the tip. The tip. There was something under there that shouldn't have been. And as the panties came further down, it didn't go away. It got bigger, and bigger, longer, and longer, it seemed to have no end. True-Dee was about to explain, about to exhale and say that Nature, well sometimes Nature makes a mistake, but it was already too late, for Juan screamed, "¡Ay! buey," and then, just like in the telenovelas, he rolled over sideways and fainted.

True-Dee shrugged her shoulders, grabbed her blonde bouffant, and made a beeline for her 1972 Chevy Malibu Super Sport. It wasn't the first time such a thing had happened to her, but it still wasn't easy. If tears were in order they would have been spontaneous, but True-Dee had something to console her: Querida Claudia had written back.

Revista La Guía
P.O. Box 9069 ♦ LAVA LANDING
CALIFORNIA 95027-0909

DIRECTOR DE ARTE
Elizabeth Sánchez

EDITOR/DIRECTOR
Rogelio Mora

GERENTE DE VENTA
Orlando Ortega, Jr.

FOTOGRAFÍA
Eduardo Medina

Dear Reader,

Thank you for writing to Querida Claudia and her column "La Pura Neta". We are pleased to inform you that an edited version of your letter will be included in next Tuesday's column. Enclosed please find a copy of your original correspondence, our edited version of said correspondence, Querida Claudia's response, as well as a personal note from La Doctora.

Thank you for your interest in Querida Claudia's column.

Atentamente

Rogelio Mora
Editor in Chief

Dear Reader,

Thank you for your recent letter. To answer your question, I do believe that the volcano is about to erupt. I am one of many local descendants of the man who predicted the volcano when it first came into being. If you would like to know more about us and our mission, then you may call me at your convenience at 546-2493.

Atentamente

Querida Claudia

¿¿CONFUNDIDA??

Querida Claudia,

I was born a boy, but I am a woman. Hormones have given me what Nature didn't, but they haven't taken away what Nature did give me, and by that I do not mean facial hair. I have been completely intimate with men on very few occasions. I attract men, but getting a man and keeping one are two separate skills. Querida Claudia, I want to know what love is like, but when a man discovers Nature's mistake, he is promptly on his way. I am so confused I don't know what to do. I feel just like the volcano waiting to explode! I am faced with undergoing a costly and painful operation, or living as I do now. To make a long story short, I am a woman under construction, not quite sure she is ready for the final phase of building, or should I say demolition? I know you'll know the answer, Querida Claudia, and that you'll give it to me straight because you speak únicamente la pura neta. Write back quick.

Really Super Confundida

RESPUESTA

Dear Volcano Waiting to Explode,

I hope you don't mind my changing your name—it's a right I reserve. I don't think you are, as you say, confundida. Let me tell you a little secret, mi querida volcáncita. On a weekly basis I receive dozens of letters from women who are on the verge, who are outraged, and downright asustadas by their husbands who beg, plead, and sometimes even insist that they concede to anal sex. I receive just as many, if not more letters from pregnant women abandoned by their boyfriends, or sometimes even their husbands, who insist that they had nada que ver con el asunto. Sometimes I even receive correspondence from the grown children of these sinvergüenzas. While I would not wish these fellows on even my worst enemiga, it would seem that with the proliferation of men obsessed with anal sex, and the equally abundant number who seem to have no qualms with abandoning their children, that you would be a hot commodity.

You say you wanna know love. I say, cariño, you will know love when you find a man who accepts you as you are. I am not sure that is what you wanted to hear, but don't forget you heard it here con Querida Claudia, únicamente la pura neta.

¡¡Suerte!!

La Bandera
The Flag

VERDE, BLANCO Y COLORADO, LA BANDERA DEL SOLDADO

GREEN, WHITE AND RED, THE SOLDIER'S FLAG

A SADNESS

There was a sadness in the way a man always fell asleep before Lulabell, leaving her all alone, sad and lonely, with nothing to do but think about the difference between the two, and wonder if there was one at all. Inevitably she always concluded the same thing, that all sadness was the result of one thing: loneliness.

But that night and that man were different. She was neither sad, nor lonely, and even though they had already made love, Beto was wide awake.

"Platícame algo," said Lulabell lying there in Beto's arms.

"¿Qué quieres que te platique?"

"Tell me about you."

"Soy del rancho," began Beto.

"The world is full of ranchos," said Lulabell. She wiggled and squirmed in a way she knew would conjure a caress.

Beto nodded, smoothed her hair, and said, "Es cierto. The world is full of ranchos. But rule number one, a man must never forget where he came from. Never."

"Yes. I know, mi amor."

"Mi papá era vagabundo, but he wasn't your average vagabundo with a woman in every pueblo and abandoned children all over the place. He was a man that liked to travel. To always be on the move. He was from Guanajuato, but he met my mother in Aguascalientes. He was seventeen and just passing through, on his way to Nayarit where there was a job waiting. Era de pura suerte that he happened to pass through Aguascalientes because it's not really on the way."

"Probably it was meant to be," said Lulabell.

"He took one look at my mother and knew she was the one he wanted for his wife. He didn't bother to ask permission. He just threw her in his truck and drove off."

"¿Se la robó?" said Lulabell.

"Sí. Se la robó. And that's what I thought about doing with you all these years."

"I wish you would have," she said.

"I know, mi amorcito," he said. The word made her shiver. She loved the way Beto used every sort of cariño, all kinds of sweet names, and their diminutive as well.

"Your mother must have been real beautiful for your father to have carried her off like that," she said.

"Not beautiful, just sturdy. She was short and she had muscles. Maybe my father thought she could survive his life on the road."

"That's not very romantic," said Lulabell.

Beto kissed her. "Not like waiting forty years for the woman you love to love you back."

Lulabell sighed. "Tell me about your rancho," she said.

"My father was headed south when I was born. My mother had already had eight children in eight different states.

"I was born in Tabasco and I lived off of coconut milk for the first year of my life. That's why my mother said I turned out to be such a cachetón."

Lulabell paused to pinch Beto's fat cheeks.

"After we headed north, first to Puebla to harvest the corn and the wheat, then to Veracruz where my father worked as a fisherman."

"I bet it's real purty there."

"Not really," said Beto. "There's too much industry and the air is very ugly, which is sad because you listen to Agustín Lara singing "Vera Cruz" and you think it must be the nicest place on earth.

"In Veracruz the tourists were always getting their dune buggies stuck in the sand. My father said that a man could make a living towing people out of the trouble they'd gotten themselves into. He decided we would make our way across the country and save up enough money to buy a tow truck. Since there was a lot of sand in the deserts of Chihuahua and Sonora, that became our destination.

"In San Luis Potosí, my father worked at the tequila plant while the rest of us picked potatoes.

"Then he heard about a job on an oil rig in Tamaulipas. My mother cried every night he was gone until my brother drove her out to where they were drilling and she dragged him off.

"People talk bad about the old ways. My father was the only man my mother ever knew, and my mother was the only woman my father ever knew. My father might have carried her off kicking and screaming, but he always took care of her, and he loved her until the day he died, and that day my mother kicked, screamed, and cried more than ever.

"It wasn't until we got to the state of Nuevo León that we had enough money to buy the first tow truck.

"But when we got to Chihuahua, there was nobody to pull out of the sand. That's when my father started talking about coming north, not just north to Sonora, but north to Los Estados Unidos. He had mentioned it all along, but no one ever thought he was serious. He was a forward-thinking man.

"Back then, things were different. A man could get a passport if he wanted to come over and work, or if he didn't want to deal with the paperwork and the waiting, he could just sneak over the border through a hole in the fence at night. My father said that one day that would all change, and that we had to take advantage of the opportunity while we could.

"We headed for Sonora on the off chance that there might be some people to pull out of the sand, but mostly because my father wanted to see every state in his homeland, and it was the only one he hadn't seen.

"My mother cried all the way across the state of Chihuahua, which is the biggest in all of the republic. Back then I thought she was crying because I had gotten carsick. She always cried when any of her children were sick and she didn't know how to comfort them.

"It's funny how you hold memories in your head for a long time, or forever for those things that you never forget, and then one day when you're old enough, you finally understand them. It wasn't until a long time after that I realized that my mother was crying because she was leaving her homeland.

"Then we came here and a funny thing happened. My father changed. Se le quitó el vagabundo de plano. Maybe because life is easier in this country, he didn't feel like he always had to be moving around. Either that or he'd already seen his entire country so he felt he could settle down.

"His towing business picked up little by little, and in the meantime, the rest of us worked in the fields. We got by all right. My father was the only Spanish-speaking tow man in town. Back then, a tow man was respected. He didn't make his living pulling people out of parking lots or out of fire lanes. A tow man came to somebody's rescue."

Beto looked down at Lulabell. He had been so caught up in his story that he hadn't noticed that she was crying, and that she had been since the state of Nuevo León. There was a sadness and a truth in all that Beto had told her, and behind that, yet another sadness—the sadness of finally knowing and hearing all the things she could have known and heard, but hadn't, over the better part of the last forty years.

In the morning, when Lulabell woke up to find Alberto in bed next to her, she didn't feel awkward like she thought she would. He didn't look handsome lying there, but cute, his moderately bald head gleaming in the morning sunlight. She nudged him just enough to get him to open his eyes, then said something spur-of-the-moment, without ulterior motives attached, that came straight from her heart: "Beto, I want you to stay."

"¿Quieres que me quede, aquí contigo?" he repeated. It was one of his more endearing habits, the way he reverted to Spanish when he was nervous or otherwise unsure of himself.

"Sí, viejo. I want you to stay with me. With us." She petted his head and smiled. "You can think about it if you want. But I just think it would be nice. Javier has always wanted a family. He has always wanted a father. I know it's a little late, but it's never too late."

It took Beto about thirty seconds to think things over and decide: "I guess I can stay, but only if Javier says it's all right. A man can't go moving in on another man's territory, and in case you haven't noticed, your son's not a little boy no more."

"All right, viejo," said Lulabell.

"I don't think you oughtta be calling me that until I have that talk with Javier," said Beto. He was right. When a woman called a man viejo, she was playing for keeps.

La Sirena
The Siren

CON LOS CANTOS DE SIRENA NO TE VAYAS A MAREAR

WITH THE SONGS OF THE SIREN, YOU WON'T SET SAIL

THE MIDDLE OF THE ROAD

What Javier knew about women was as brief and enigmatic as any one of the 150 Psalms. Women were strange creatures, constantly changing, especially directly before and during menstruation, but more importantly, a woman, any woman could be the downfall of any man, no matter how righteous or fortified by the Holy Spirit he might be. Even with said knowledge, so basic, yet vague, and by that virtue malleable, Javier couldn't understand what was going on with the women around him.

Take Lulabell, por ejemplo. She was in love. It wasn't as if Javier hadn't seen that happen before, at least a hundred times. But love, for Lulabell, was again, like the Psalms, brief, and for her sake he hoped, poignant.

Four days had passed since Lulabell's Dinner for Ranch Hands and Day Laborers, and Beto had spent all four of those days, and five nights with Lulabell. Javier couldn't remember a man who had lasted under the same roof with Lulabell for that long, other than his father. And if that wasn't a sign of permanence, Lulabell had pulled the Cadillac out of the garage to make room for the tow truck. While Javier might have been against sex before marriage, and undecided about it afterward, he was still glad to see his mother giving in to sin with just one man instead of pulling scores of others down with her.

Under Beto's influence, Lulabell started cooking on a regular basis, and dressing like a lady. But the very most strangest thing of all was this: Lulabell had gone to Mass, and even stranger yet, she'd taken Lucha with her.

Things being as such, that Wednesday, when Javier went to pick Lucha up to take her to Christian Music Night at The Lava Landing Roller Palace, he shouldn't have been surprised that she was wearing a long, loose skirt with a baby blue crocheted shawl draped over her shoulders, her hair in two loose braids.

"Buenas tardes," said Lucha.

"Buenas," said Javier.

They walked to the waiting Monte Carlo, stepped in, buckled up, and locked their doors.

Down the road, Javier spoke up. "Sister Lucha, ¿is something bothering you? You seem changed."

Lucha liked being called Sister. She wanted to utter an "¡ay! papacito" right then and there, but instead she paused to translate her enthusiasm into something Javier would understand.

"Brother Javier, I am just so happy to be in the company of a true Christian, to be on my way to a Christian event, and to be on the path to the Lord after havin sinned so long. What great joy it brings me knowin that my love of the Lord shows," she said.

Javier sat silent. Lucha looked at him and thought of her father. Try as she did to remember tender moments—her sitting on his lap, him boosting her up onto the pony at the County Fair, him carrying her upstairs to her bedroom after she'd fallen asleep on the couch, she could only see herself at Javier's side, her tongue in his ear, her hands beginning at his neck, tracing his torso, then, going their separate ways—one down his pants, the other unbuttoning and unzipping, until they came together once again, as if in prayer.

"¿En qué piensas, Hermano Javier?" asked Lucha.

"I think always and only in the Lord."

Inside that missionary there was a man. Lucha was trying to appeal to the missionary in order to get to him.

"I too have begun only to think in Him."

He looked over at Lucha. "I pray that what you speak is the truth." He was used to Lucha in high heels and tight jeans, her hair teased to unknown heights and widths, but there she was, looking so lovely, her cheeks glowing with the glow of the Holy Spirit, so innocent, like a little lamb, and so appealing.

For a moment their thoughts coincided. They imagined the lights dimming at the roller rink, the music slowing, the strobe light in the center of the ceiling spinning, its reflection carrying to every corner of the skating surface, the announcer announcing, "This one's for couples only," Javier offering Lucha his hand, or perhaps turning backwards and placing his hands gently on her shoulders, he skates backwards, while she goes frontwards. That is where Javier's imaginings ended and he swung his arm across the seat.

Lucha sat still and continued her private thoughts. She saw herself in Javier's arms, him picking her up after a fall, helping her to the snack bar area, lifting her skirt to carefully clean her skinned knee with a damp, lukewarm napkin, then placing his mouth over her wound and licking, quoting the old belief that saliva takes away the sting and prevents infection, then Lucha losing it, wrapping her legs around his neck, and Javier breaking loose, looking Lucha in the eye, the warmth of his hand on her cheek, him asking her for forgiveness—thinking their near brush with sin was all his fault, then Lucha saying, "My little shepherd, I know you'd never let me lose my way."

Lucha rolled the window down to get some air, but it was a little late, or perhaps just in time, for they had arrived.

Javier pulled the keys from the ignition. He rushed to open Lucha's door. They paused at the trunk where Javier pulled out his skates. He had bought them upon April May's suggestion, and he wasn't sorry either. Anything was better than rentals. He was taking weekly artistic dance lessons with none other than Miss Magma herself, whom Javier and Lucha met at The Lava Landing Roller Palace entrance.

"Good evening, Sister April May," said Javier.

April May only grunted. She took the $5.50 admission fee times two, tore their tickets, and let them in.

They walked up to the rental counter. April May beat them there. Lucha asked for a size 7.

"¿Isn't she something?" said Javier admiring April May.

Lucha's jealousy flared. Javier continued as Lucha laced up. "You do know who she is, ¿don't you?"

"Not really," said Lucha.

"She is the queen of Lava County, ¡Miss Magma herself!"

"Oh, sí," said Lucha.

"Yes. And the very best news of all is this, ¡I just about got her soul!"

"Sí, Hermanito," said Lucha.

"Yes. I have been attending lessons every Tuesday night. I can do a double Axel, but most importantly I have been able to persuade April May to come to services next Sunday," said Javier. He bent to his knee and helped Lucha with her roller skates. "Imagine it, this Labor Day at the parade, ¡Miss Magma carrying the banner for Jesus!"

Lucha looked down at Javier. She touched his cheek with her entire palm and as Javier looked into her eyes, he felt as if he were looking into his own, he was filled with warmth and comfort, and was simultaneously reminded of his most pleasant moments of childhood: trimming the Christmas tree, his just made bed, the sound of mariachi music coming from his Fisher-Price® record player, the smell of Lulabell's shawl as he laid his head on her shoulder to fall asleep.

"My little Savior," said Lucha.

Javier swallowed hard. She could have afforded him no greater compliment. And then, all of the sudden, April May stepped into the announcer's booth and said, "This one's for couples only."

Javier took a deep breath. He looked down at Lucha, offered her his hand and said, "¿Patinamos?"

They made their way out to the floor, then slowly around the skating surface, and it was nothing like either of them had imagined. Javier had an arm around Lucha's waist to keep her from falling down, and with his free hand, he held her by an elbow. As they circled the rink, slowly, but by Javier's estimation, surely, Lucha was gathering up her courage, for she was about to take a spill, and it occurred to her that she should undermine Javier's balance as well, so that she might have the added pleasure of healing his wounds, and within seconds they were both splayed on the skating surface. April May came speed-skating up, and stopped in a hurry with her arms outstretched, giving Javier a vision of the crucified Christ. She was merely doing her job, blocking the fallen skaters off from further harm, while protecting the upright ones from an unnecessary collision.

Javier got to his feet, then helped Lucha to hers. They made their way to the snack bar area where April May provided them with a handful of napkins, their corners dipped in lukewarm water. Javier tended to Lucha's wounds for he was unscathed. He wiped the blood from both knees, she looked down at him and muttered a non sequitur: "My little shepherd, I know you'd never let me lose my way." Her imagination was running wild and she was dreaming of things as she wanted them to be, not as they were. But with those words she'd roused the man in Javier, and all of the sudden his warm hand was on her cheek, and she was moving closer to him, and his eyes, previously wide open in fright, suddenly closed, as Lucha's lips touched his. His body warmed and tingled in every possible place, for it seemed Lucha's unsaved and cunning soul had played its part perfectly, and Javier, seeing and desiring this little lamb and its unsaved soul, decided to give in to the woman in Lucha in order to get to the soul, and it was in that manner that the two set their differences aside, and met in the middle of the road in a brief but profound kiss.

They opened their eyes simultaneously, one muttering, "Brother Javier," the other, "Sister Lucha."

"Tell me what we did is not a sin," said Lucha.

Javier was speechless.

"¿Should I take your silence to mean that we have sinned?" said Lucha.

"No, Sister Lucha. What we did is not a sin. But just in case, let us bow in prayer and ask the Lord for forgiveness. When it comes to the soul, it's always good to practice preventative maintenance."

They knelt down and closed their eyes. Seeing them on their knees in prayer in front of the snack bar, the rest of the skaters joined them.

"And ¿to what do we owe this occasion of spontaneous prayer, Brother Javier?" said Minister Harold as he speed-skated by, then sharply turned the corner, past the guardrail, and straight onto the carpet where he came to an abrupt halt.

Lucha grabbed Javier by the hand and proclaimed, "We are in love."

"¿Is this so, Brother Javier?"

Javier nodded.

"Then we must do something about it," said the minister.

"Amen," said the others in unison.

"Marry them," suggested one parishioner.

Lucha was taken aback, but her stance on the issue softened when she thought of the delights their marriage bed might bring. Besides, once she got tired of Javier, she could send him on his way—an annulment would likely be forthcoming once it came to light that they were brother and sister.

Javier received the idea with guarded enthusiasm. "We must do things right," he said. "And these things take time." He imagined himself bringing Lucha serenatas, asking for her hand on bended knee.

"Whatever you say, papacito," said Lucha slipping up. "I mean, yes, of course, Brother Javier." She had him in her snare, and it was only a matter of time before she would have her way with him.

The skaters headed back out to the skating surface. Javier did a double Axel for he knew women appreciated a show-off. Lucha's subsequent skating performance was nothing less than a miracle for she made her way around the rink with confidence to "The Lord Is in the House Now," a spin-off of some hip-hop tune or other.

Watching his little lamb rex her way around the roller rink, Javier concluded out loud, "There's no end to the power of the Lord and His instrument the Holy Spirit."

El Diablito
The Little Devil

PÓRTATE BIEN CUATITO, SI NO TE LLEVA EL COLORADITO
BEHAVE YOURSELF WELL, LEST THE LITTLE RED ONE MIGHT
CARRY YOU AWAY

A STRANGE ONE

"Evenin, son," said Lulabell to the just getting home Javier. His face was red, and not just from roller skating. Lulabell was lying down on the couch, her head in Beto's lap, they were watching the baseball game. She sat up.

"You look a bit flushed, son. ¿Wanna talk about it?" said Lulabell.

"No thanks, momma," said Javier.

He still hadn't gotten used to the new Lulabell. In fact, he found Lucha's and Lulabell's combined behavior so strange, he wondered might it be a sign leading to the Second Coming of Christ. He walked into his room, shut his door, and picked up his Bible intent on looking for something he might have missed, but he could only think of Lucha. He set the Bible aside, and turned on the AM radio. It played a slow waltz; Javier imagined himself under Lucha's window serenading—her soul coming closer and closer, while the Lord watched from above.

Javier found it hard to sit still, and finally gave up trying. He grabbed his guitarrón, then walked to his closet to look for something appropriate for a one-man show. He pulled out a pair of Wrangler®s and a fancy belt Lulabell had bought him several Christmases before. With the tags attached, they were unworn and still in their box. He put on the white shirt he always wore under his traje de charro, his cowboy boots, the belt, and the jeans. He looked in the mirror. Something was missing. He needed a hat, but his wardrobe only offered his big fancy sombrero and a selection of baseball caps. He smoothed his hair, and headed for the living room.

"Loan me your tejana," he said to Beto.

"A man don't loan his hat or his gun," said Beto, his eyes fixed on the television set.

"Momma, I need a hat," said Javier.

"Maybe Santa'll bring you one," said Lulabell not paying her son proper attention—the home team had the bases loaded and nobody was out.

"I can't wait that long," said Javier.

Lulabell looked up. "¡Ay-ay-ay!" she said getting to her feet, grabbing Javier by an elbow, leading him to the back room saying, "About time you started dressin like a young man should."

She took another look at Javier, shook her head, and said, "Son, there must be somethin wrong with you." She stood on her tippy toes and reached up to the top shelf where Beto kept his Stetson®, then pulled the fancy hat box down, and handed it to Javier.

"Thanks a bunch, momma," he said. He put the hat on, looked in the mirror, and positioned the brim. Then he did something he hadn't done in a long time: He kissed Lulabell on the cheek.

Lulabell stood still, touching the warm, damp spot on her cheek. "¿Where are you goin, son?" she said.

"Going to get me a girl," said Javier.

"Been meanin to talk to you about that," said Lulabell. But it was too late. Javier was already out the door.

"¿What's gotten into him?" said Beto as Lulabell took her place on the couch.

"I don't know," said Lulabell. "He always has been a strange one."

On the way to Lucha's, Javier turned over a dozen songs in his head trying to find one perfect for serenading, but each time he thought he had come upon the perfect song, he would disqualify it on the grounds that it either mentioned the act of love, or getting drunk. Finally, as he pulled up in front of Lucha's house, he decided on "¡Ay! Jalisco No Te Rajes" based solely on the fact that Lucha's family was from said state. He grabbed his guitarrón, placed himself under Lucha's window, and began in the middle of the song, "¡AAAAAAAAY Jalisco, no te rajes . . ." But all was in vain.

Javier was shocked by Violeta, Lucha's mother, pulling the curtains back, opening the window, sticking her head out, cupping a hand over her eyes, then saying, "Oh, it's only you."

"Sorry, ma'am," he said standing up straight. "And ¿Lucha?"

"Oh, she has gone to the dance," said Doña Violeta.

"¿En serio?" said Javier.

"I'm afraid so. I thought she'd given it up, but it's worse than ever."

"Just ¿what do you mean by that, ma'am?" said Javier removing his borrowed hat.

"Well," said Violeta motioning Javier closer, then whispering in his ear, "You should have seen what she was wearing."

"¿Really?" said Javier.

Violeta nodded. "Do have a talk with her ¿won't you?"

"Sure will."

"You are the best male influence she has had since my late husband," said Violeta making the sign of the cross, then continuing, "Que en paz descanse."

"Don't you worry about a thing. I'll have her back here in no time, Señora," said Javier putting his borrowed hat back on.

Javier arrived at El Aguantador in a hurry. Seeing Javier's guitarrón, the man at the door let him in free of charge, realizing that live music is good for business at the bar.

With a drink in one hand, and a cigarette in the other, Lucha was surrounded by men. She didn't readily recognize Javier. She was used to him in his traje de charro—elegant, extravagant, and enticing. Or Javier in a button-down shirt and jeans—not tight enough to entice, but not baggy enough to be fashionable either. But there, in the distance, was Javier in Wrangler®s and a Stetson®, fitting right in. She took one look at him and thought, "Looks familiar," then concluded, "Must have danced with him before," before realizing just who he was and how much trouble she was in. She repositioned the shawl, which had shamelessly fallen from her shoulders.

"¿What are you doing in a place like this?" said Javier to Lucha.

"Hermanito, save me," pleaded Lucha feigning tears. "The Devil came unto me, and temptation He did bring."

"When the Devil comes, temptation is always in tow," said Javier shaking his head.

Lucha's whimper escalated to a wail. The truth of the matter was, after their roller-skating date, Lucha had gone home and changed into her dancing duds, then headed out to El Aguantador looking for someone to finish what Javier had started.

"No llores, Hermanita," said Javier taking Lucha in his arms.

"Take me home," said Lucha gazing up at Javier. He got a little closer, then a little closer, until he took the initiative and kissed her, softly and sweetly. They broke apart just when the kiss was about to escalate, then joined hands, and headed for the door.

Once inside the Monte Carlo and down the road, Lucha slid up to Javier, nibbled on his ear, put her hands on his neck, traced his torso, then her hands went their separate ways, one down his pants, the other unbuttoning and unzipping, until they came together once again.

"Hermanita, ¿what are you doing?" said Javier.

"The Lord made man and woman different for a reason," she declared.

"But the Lord set down rules on how man and woman must negotiate their differences." He pushed Lucha aside and zipped up.

"This soul comes with a body, Hermanito, and if you want the soul, then you've got to give the body what it wants, needs, and deserves." Lucha moved on over to her side of the automobile and folded her arms.

"Sounds like a threat to me, Sister."

"I'm a woman, y como una mujer, I got my necesidades. If you don't give me what I want, I get it elsewhere. Así de fácil. But if you see to my needs, I give you my soul, then you give it to the Lord, and boy don't that ever make Him happy."

"Only the Devil makes deals."

"And maybe I'll make one with Him," said Lucha unlocking the door, for they'd arrived curbside. Then she laughed a big scary laugh that gave Javier goose bumps.

"I knew your soul was too far gone to save," said Javier.

"You might be right, Hermanito. But ¿aren't you forgettin about your own soul? ¿Who's to say it ain't out of danger?"

Javier's eyes widened.

"¿What if I make that deal with the Devil? The Devil'd give a girl like me just about anything she wants, and ¿what if I tell Him what I want is you, body and soul?"

"You wouldn't."

"¿Won't you come inside, Hermanito? Promise I'll be real gentle with you."

Javier killed the engine and decided to go in and try to buy himself some time.

They walked up the hall hand in hand, headed toward Lucha's room.

"Take your hat off, Hermanito. Everything's gonna go real suave, just you wait and see," said Lucha as they set foot into her bedroom.

Javier set his hat on a nearby nightstand. He had never been in Lucha's bedroom before, but had seen the pink and white candy stripe of the wallpaper from the window when he had serenaded her. The room set Javier at ease. There was nothing intimidating about it, in fact it looked like he imagined an eleven-year-old girl's might: She had a twin bed covered with a fuzzy pink spread, and on top of that, many stuffed animals and rag dolls. There was a white vanity table against one wall, and a dresser against another.

"Let's pray," said Lucha grabbing Javier's hand. She figured prayer was foreplay a missionary could understand.

They knelt down bedside, closed their eyes, and placed their folded hands atop the pink fuzz, but Javier wasn't praying, and neither was Lucha.

Javier was suffering with his inner trichotomy. The man in him said, "Ut-Oh," the mariachi, "Be a man about it," and the missionary, "Lord forgive me," and with those final words he commenced his prayer which went like this:

Lord, forgive me for what I am about to do. I love this woman and feel her soul is both salvageable and worthy to take its place in Your kingdom. Also rest assured in knowing that I intend to make this woman my wife in accordance with Your most Holy Word. Lastly, please help to make our first love encounter a success so as to bring Lucha one step closer to myself, Your willing and faithful servant. And I promise just as sure as You are my witness, that once I have this woman, her soul is Yours, Lord.

Amen

Javier made the sign of the cross. Lucha did the same, then jumped up onto her bed. Off went the high heels, the pretend python jeans, and the red velvet panties. Lucha crossed her arms, grabbed her halter top by the hem, and pulled it up, over, and off. She lay there naked, waiting for Javier to make his move.

Javier had never seen a naked woman until very recently when Lulabell had pulled her huipil off as he stood innocently in the bathroom brushing his teeth.

Lucha patted the twin bed beside her, and said, "Lie down, Hermanito."

She pulled off his boots, then his socks, unbuckled his belt, unbuttoned and unzipped his pants, took them off along with his boxer shorts, two undershirts, and his fancy white dress shirt. She pulled a condom from her bedside drawer, opened the foil package, and gestured toward Javier's erect penis.

"¿What do you think you are doing, Sister Lucha?" said Javier. He grabbed the fuzzy pink bedspread and covered up.

"¿Tryin to prevent an unwanted pregnancy?"

"Let nothing get in the way of the Will of the Lord." Javier took the condom in his hands and pulled it back like a second-grader ready to shoot a rubber band, and let it go.

"Whatever you say," said Lucha. She wasn't at the fertile spot in her cycle anyway. She had learned about natural family planning while she was in the

Lava County Women's Correctional Facility. And with regard to sexually communicable diseases, she wasn't worried. Javier was a virgin and Lucha couldn't hope for safer sex than that.

Javier lay back on the pink fuzz of the bedspread. He closed his eyes and thought of Lucha's soul, which he imagined changing from one form of matter into another. It began as a deep pink, almost red colored liquid, then solidified into the most beautiful shape he had ever seen—a hybrid between a rose and a heart.

Lucha took the dominant position, and in that moment, as Javier lay on his back with his eyes closed imagining that hard heart-shaped rose, he felt Lucha's warmth all over and around him. The image of her soul behind his closed eyes lost its solidity, but kept both its lovely shape and color. It changed to a gas and floated upward slowly but surely toward the heavens. Javier too felt as if he were about to lose his solidity and float somewhere far away.

¿And Lucha? She worried the whole event would be over in a matter of seconds. Even as inexperienced as Javier was, he somehow held his own. That was good enough for Lucha, who was convinced that she was making love to her long-lost half-brother. That thought alone with all of its nasty and naughty implications was enough to make her feel as if she were changing from one form of matter into another, then back again.

As Javier lay there, he was sure that Lucha had discovered a part of him he never knew existed, and that she had been directed to it by none other than the Lord. Within this new place, there was one spot in particular she was concentrating on. She caressed it little by little so that in moments of respite it became more delicate, sensitive, and vulnerable—just like Lucha's soul.

Lucha's soul in its gaseous form continued its climb toward the sky, stopping occasionally to rest along the way, allowing Javier to get a good look at it in all its beauty, before it resumed its flight toward the heavens. Finally it was so close that it could rise no more. It was as vulnerable as a canoe full of wayward pioneers approaching the waterfall during a Saturday afternoon television matinee. Javier too felt this same helplessness as if he were about to succumb to a force greater than himself.

Lucha's soul made its final ascent toward Heaven. Once it got there, it was blown to bits by a single sudden burst as it became one with God.

Javier breathed deeply for a few moments before opening his eyes to find Lucha sitting at the edge of the bed, reaching into a dresser drawer for her nightgown.

Javier lacked the energy to put his clothes on, to say good night, give Lucha a bedtime kiss, whisper his prayers, or even wipe the smile off his face. He drifted off to slumber, and so deep was his sleep that he didn't even wake up at 3:30 a.m. for his garbage route. Instead, he was roused by Violeta shortly after 8:00 a.m. when she stuck her head in the doorway and said, "Lucha, get up and have some breakfast before your probation officer gets here."

It was the first day of work Javier had missed in over nine years of faithful and dedicated service to the Lava County Waste Management Company, and he was well aware that it would cost him a perfect-attendance plaque at the year-end awards banquet. He got to his feet, got dressed, then jumped out the window. In his haste, he forgot all about Beto's Stetson®, which he left resting atop Lucha's dresser. For that and other reasons, when Javier got home, he would have plenty of explaining to do.

Tabla 5

THE CARDS *are* DEALT

La Calavera
The Skull

AL PASAR POR EL PANTEÓN, ME ENCONTRÉ UNA CALAVERA

UPON PASSING THE GRAVEYARD, I ENCOUNTERED A SKULL

THAT TALK

"¿That you, mijo?" said Lulabell. She was washing the dishes. "¿You just gettin home? You had us worried sick."

"¿Where's my hat?" said Alberto.

"Momma, I'm ready to have that talk," said Javier. His shirt was unbuttoned, his hair messed up.

"¿You mind tellin us where you've been first?" said Lulabell turning around with a spatula in her hand.

"¿And telling us where my hat is?"

"Momma, I'm in love and I really wanna have that talk."

"¡Ay-ay-ay!" Lulabell set her spatula down and untied her green and white checkered apron. "And just ¿what talk is that?"

"¿Where is my hat?"

"¿Would you shut up already? ¡My son is in love! ¿Just what talk is it that you wanna have, mijo?" Lulabell put an arm around Javier's shoulders.

"You know, the one you mentioned the other day. The one about girls."

"¡¿¡You spent the night with a girl!?!"

"That's what happened to my hat." Beto pushed his plate of tacos aside.

"¿Did I do something wrong? I mean, momma, you're always saying I oughtta act more like boys my age."

"Mijo, you're twenty-seven years old. You're a man already. So, ¿when do we get to meet this girl? ¿She go to church with you?" said Lulabell.

"She didn't used to, but she does now, and you've already met her. It's Lucha." He held his upturned palms to the air, as if he were proud of himself.

"¡¿¡You spent the night with Lucha!?! ¡I told her to stay away from you!"

"¿Why would you do a thing like that? I thought you liked her. She told me about all the time you two have been spending together while I'm away on my route. The way you go to Rosary meeting and how you've been teaching her special stitches. She even showed me the shawl you made her." It was true. L and L had been spending time together, but not for any of the reasons Javier might have thought.

"Son, you had better sit down," said Lulabell.

"Take my seat," said Beto trying to sneak out.

"¿Can't you see I need you here with me, Beto? This is a family discussion so ¡sit your ass back down!"

Javier sat down next to Lulabell at the light green Formica® kitchen table, and she got started with that talk.

"Mijo, things aren't always as they seem," she began.

"¿You mean like sometimes there's a wolf in sheep's clothing?"

"Kinda. I know I don't talk much about my husband, but the man I was married to changed on me, and then I changed too."

"¿You mean my father?"

"No, I mean my husband. He was everything I thought a man should be, and I really loved him. He whispered the sweetest things in my ear at night, and he was the best dancer you could ever imagine. But that's not what love is. It's not dancin or sweet words, it's what a person is, and what someone will do for you with or without the askin."

"Momma, ¿when we gonna talk about girls?"

"Just wait a minute, mijo. Let me finish. We had only been married a few years when he quit comin home after work, and for all I know he quit workin too because I never saw any of the money he made. I was so used to his sweet words in my ear at night that I couldn't stand to be alone without the affections of a man. So, I found another."

"Momma, you broke the Seventh Commandment." He put a hand up over his open mouth.

"I know, mijo."

"But ¿what does all this have to do with me and girls?"

"There is no gentle way to put this, son. Lucha's father and I were together for many years, and it all started when my husband took up drinkin and womanizin. He was drunk almost every night of the week, and durin those nights, Lucha's father kept me company."

"He kept you more than company, mujer," said Beto getting the picture long before Javier.

"Yes, he kept me more than company." Lulabell looked down at her hands. They looked much older than the rest of her and she supposed there wasn't a lot that could be done about that.

"It's okay, momma. Just because there is a bit of discord between our families doesn't mean we can't love each other and get married. I seen it in a movie before. I seen it in lots of movies, only we don't have to go around killing each other like they do on the Saturday afternoon películas, or in the telenovelas, and besides, Lucha doesn't have any brothers or even any uncles that I know of, so there is no one to go around killing anyway, and since we are all Christians we would never dream of acting like that anyhow."

"You don't get it, son, ¿do you?" said Alberto grabbing Javier by the shoulders. He held him firmly and looked him in the eye. "You don't get it at all. Lucha's father and your father are the same man. She's your sister. ¿You ever seen a movie like that? I have and it don't have a happy ending."

"I don't know that she's your sister, but she might be," said Lulabell. She put both elbows up on the table, hung her head low, then ran her fingers through her hair.

There was a long pause before Javier said, "¿Does that mean that I have a father now?"

"I'm afraid not. Lucha's father is dead and he has been for goin on fifteen years. I'm sorry, hijo." She went to put her arms around Javier, but he wouldn't allow it.

Lulabell watched as Beto exited the kitchen headed for their bedroom. She could hear the angry clang of his keys as he picked them up off the dresser and it made her heart beat so fast, she felt as if she were going to throw up. As he stormed through the kitchen on his way out the door, she knew better than to try to chase him down, and felt guilty for even thinking about trying.

"¿How could you, momma?" said Javier. Lulabell didn't know what to say, and wouldn't have to fumble for words either. Javier followed Beto's lead and rushed back for his own keys, before marching out the door, leaving Lulabell all alone to think things over.

Once on his way, Javier did something completely unexpected and uncharacteristic: He headed for The Big Five-Four, walked through the swinging bar doors, cleared his throat, took a deep breath, and ordered, "Una botella de la tequila más fina."

THE BIG FIVE-FOUR

"¿Una botella de la tequila más fina?" repeated Consuelo from behind the bar. As Cal McDaniel's Girls Friday, Natalie and Consuelo served Cal in a variety of different capacities, and that morning, they were filling in for the regular barmaid, who had called in sick.

"¿Are you sure that's what you want?" said Natalie with her hands on her hips.

"I'm sure," said Javier.

It was mid-morning and the bar had just opened. The Big Five-Four looked different at that hour. Everything seemed so faux without the glow of the candles and the jukebox, without the regulars lined up at the bar, without the sparkle of the strobe light.

Consuelo grabbed a bottle of Cazadores® and three shot glasses. She could tell by the look on Javier's face that not only was he in need of good, hard liquor, but of company to share it with. Natalie saw to the lime and salt.

"Let's all have a seat over here. ¿More cozy don't you think?" said Consuelo taking a corner booth, sliding over to make room for Javier. He took one look at Sway and signaled for Natalie to move over. There were no hard feelings on Sway's side. She knew that Javier had always preferred Nat, at least to the extent that it was Nat's panties he snuck a hand down on the bus ride home when they were in the third grade.

Javier was still in last night's outfit. Nat and Sway had never seen him look so secular. His shirt was untucked and half unbuttoned, his hair in a matted mess. He filled the three shot glasses, and readied the lime and salt before he realized he didn't know what went first.

"It goes like this," said Sway licking the salt, downing the liquor, then sucking the lime. Javier followed suit.

"¿What's a young man like you doin behind a bottle anyhow?" said Natalie.

"I get to know you better, maybe I tell you," said Javier.

"All the years we got between us, I hardly think it's possible, but whatever you say," said Natalie pinching Javier's cheeks until he grinned and hung his head from embarrassment.

"Oh, my," said Consuelo. She could have sworn Javier was flirting with her best friend.

Consuelo got up and walked to the jukebox. She picked six selections for a dollar: G47, B13, A17, Q19, and L42 twice (See pages 16–17 for "Guide to the Rockola at The Big Five-Four"), then returned to find that the bottle was nearly empty. She drank the remainder of the tequila in a single swig, then went to the bar for more.

Javier and Natalie sat right up next to one another and from the looks of things, Javier had begun to open up to Natalie, a contarle sus penas, if you will.

"I never thought I'd fall in love," said Javier.

"¡Ay! cariñito," said Natalie, getting the wrong idea.

"Con todo el respeto, I'm not in love with you. I am in love with somebody else."

"I see," said Nat.

"I admit that I was crazy for you when we were in school, and that I prayed day and night that the Lord would take you out of me." He pounded his chest. "And He did. For a long time there was an empty space there." He hit his chest again. "But now it is so full it is overflowing like the bountiful love of the Lord."

"¿Who's the lucky girl?" said Consuelo arriving at the table with a fresh bottle.

"She's my sister," said Javier.

"Everybody's your Sister," said Natalie. And all of the sudden things made perfect sense: Javier had hooked up with a church girl.

"That's really nice to hear. You gone and found yourself a Sister," said Sway. It was kind of cute, Javier cuddling up with one of his fellow churchgoers.

The jukebox cut into N44, and Consuelo grabbed Javier by the hand and said, "Let's dance."

"But, it has been so long since I've danced," he said stumbling to his feet.

"Don't worry about it, lady-killer," said Natalie getting up to go to the bathroom.

By the time Natalie got back, Javier and Consuelo were two-stepping confidently around the dance floor. The jukebox cut into F37, and it was Natalie's turn.

Natalie had thought about dancing with Javier for years, if not decades. She had known him since kindergarten and had had a crush on him straight up through junior high, and the first two years of high school.

Javier stared at her hard, slurring first his eyes, then his words. "The Lord took you out of me, but I bet He could put you back in." He licked his lips, leaned in, and kissed her.

She kissed him back, or at least tried to. But she found his method completely lacking, like dancing with a man that don't know how, it was frustrating. His tongue prodded when it should have swirled, poked when it should have stroked. His technique was so obtrusive it barred participation. Natalie pulled away. If there was one thing she hated, it was a boy that couldn't kiss. She stranded him on the dance floor.

"¿How was it?" said Consuelo expectantly.

"Not good. At least I don't think it was, then again, I can't rightfully say. He's the third boy I've kissed this week."

Consuelo got her fingers out. She could only account for two men. ¿Who's the other one?" she said.

"Your father," said Natalie. She was semi-fortified by the tequila, but not so much so that she could actually look Sway in the eye when she said it.

"¡¿¡My what!?!"

"He came to me in a dream and he was so handsome. He said he would give me anything I wanted, and in that moment, I wanted him. Sometimes I feel lonely, Sway. Like I'm the sorta girl that can't do without the affections of a man. It don't even have to be the same man either. Just so long as he's not too painful to look at and he knows how to put the touch on me."

"Sometimes I feel the same way, ¿but my father?"

"I'm sorry. It was a spur-of-the-moment thing."

"It always is," said Consuelo shaking her head, then throwing her hands up in the air.

Javier walked over to the bar, pulled his wallet out from the back pocket of his jeans, opened up, and removed the biggest wad of money Consuelo and Natalie had ever seen. He placed a hundred-dollar bill on the table.

"It's on the house," said Consuelo giving him his money back.

"¿You always carry that much money around?" said Natalie.

"No. I was gonna buy my girl a ring. We were gonna get married," said Javier.

He walked out the door, and up the street, and then all the way home thinking not just about Lucha, but about the entire afternoon. Javier had danced for the first time in nearly twenty years, and for some reason, all of the sudden he liked it.

China poblana—
national costume

Maya Indian—Yucatán

Indigo *enredo*
(wraparound skirt)

Folk dance costume

El Anillo de Compromiso

The Engagement Ring

PÓNTELO AL LADO DE TU CORAZÓN

PLACE IT ON THE SIDE OF YOUR HEART

LULABELL'S SIXTEEN
GOLDEN RINGS

"*Momma, I'm home,*" *said Javier, sticking his head in the door*way of Lulabell's bedroom. He was just getting back from The Big Five-Four.

"¿Have you been readin your Bible?" said Lulabell. She was lying down in bed, but still wide awake.

"I'm drunk," he declared.

"¡Ay! mijo. Come in and sit down." She pushed the covers aside, swung her legs around, and sat up. Her bedside lamp was on its dimmest setting lending a warm glow to the room.

"¿What are you doing with Beto's jumpsuit?" said Javier noticing the dark blue heap next to Lulabell.

She was vaguely embarrassed. After Beto had walked out on her, Lulabell had curled up with his work clothes in his absence.

"It smells like him," said Lulabell. She took a final whiff of the greasy jumpsuit before she threw it in a pile on the other side of the bed. "If you ever fall in love, you'll understand."

"I am in love and I do understand," said Javier. He reached into his pants pocket and pulled out a wadded-up napkin stained with Lucha's blood, a souvenir from their roller skating date. "I have her blood." He clicked his tongue twice.

"I know, and I'm sorry, but you're gonna have to forget about that woman para siempre."

"I won't ever," said Javier. He had a seat at the edge of the bed.

"Mijo, ¿do you know the difference between querer and amar?" said Lulabell.

His expression answered the question. It was as Lulabell suspected; he didn't know the difference.

"Querer is to love someone," she began. "But amar is to feel them right down to your soul, to not be able to exist without that person, to want to die in their arms and at the same moment. ¿Is that how you feel about Lucha?"

"I don't know, but I want her. I really, really want her."

"But that ain't love."

"Then ¿what is?"

"I'm the last person you should ask."

"But you love Beto, ¿don't you?"

"Of course I do, mijo. But what you don't know is this: I told Beto how to put a spell on me so I would love him, and now I don't know if I really love him or if it's just brujería. And if I really do love him, to think I could have loved him for forty years."

"¿Do you think you could teach me how to put a spell on Lucha?" said Javier, his eyes wide with optimism.

"You don't love Lucha. What you are feeling is puro deseo. And when I feel like that, I just sleep with a man. Then I go to the taquería and I order two tacos de tripas." Lulabell held her right index finger in the air as if she were giving good, sound advice. "And when you order tripas, make sure you tell them to cook them real good, otherwise they are bien yúckate. Just tell them that you want them bien doradas.

"I drink some jamaica. If I can afford it, I go shoppin. Then I go to bingo. After, the feelin goes away," said Lulabell.

"¿Are you saying I should sleep with Lucha some more?"

"Of course not. But you should find another girl and sleep with her." Lulabell smiled.

Javier thought about telling Lulabell that Lucha was the only woman he wanted to go to bed with, but he knew Lulabell wouldn't understand, or worse yet, that she would understand completely. Besides, sound advice and big smiles aside, Javier knew Lulabell was plenty worried, not just about him, but about Beto as well. ¿Who knows?, maybe Beto would never come back.

"Brujería only causes problems," said Lulabell. "Look at this." She held up a piece of wrinkled paper she had found in the pocket of Beto's jumpsuit. It wasn't another woman's phone number, but a list written in black ink with the headings "Pros" and "Cons," words Beto had learned in a civics class he had taken in preparation for his citizenship exam. ("Beto's List of Pros and Cons Acerca de la Lulabell" follows.)

After reading the list, Lulabell realized that to Beto, she was nothing more than an inventory of body parts and labor-intensive regional dishes.

"I thought he loved me for four decades, but now I just don't know and I'm gonna have to put a spell on him to be sure that he will love me like I love him. ¿How would you like to do that for the rest of your life?"

"I guess that's what brujería gets you," said Javier sympathetically.

"All those years. So many men. It was like not bein able to sleep. If you couldn't sleep, you would take a sleepin pill. That's what I did. I took a sleepin pill."

"¿What are you gonna do if he never comes back?" said Javier furrowing his brow. "You're all alone with no ring on your finger, no plans, no nothing." He spoke at a whisper.

Lulabell could tell that he was genuinely concerned. She sat there for a moment and looked at Javier, then smiled as she rose to her feet. "If I wanted that life, if I wanted a husband, I had plenty of chances." She spoke softly and deliberately.

She walked to her vanity table and opened the bottom drawer. And there, at the bottom of the bottom drawer, was evidence of just what a divine woman Lulabell was, for there at the bottom of that hardly ever opened drawer were seventeen engagement rings and their accompanying wedding bands all strung on a piece of purple yarn.

"This is the best one, or at least the most valuable one." She held up one of the rings. "It's two carats. I kept them all in case you ever decided to go to college. I knew I didn't have that kind of money." Lulabell removed the ring, tried it on, then held her hand out in front of her. After so many years, it was still as shiny as ever.

"¿You did that for me, momma?"

"Of course. You were the only sure thing I had." She rubbed the crown of his head and tousled his hair.

"Well ¿can I have them now?"

"¿Huh?" said Lulabell.

"¿Can I have my college education now?"

"Oh, sí," said Lulabell. She bent down and picked the rings up, surprised by how heavy they felt. "Just make sure that when you go to pawn them, you don't go downtown to Benny's, ¿all right, mijo?"

"All right, momma. ¿Is it because you and old Benny had a thing going?" said Javier gesturing toward the rings.

"No, actually his cousin. One of the Calderón brothers." Lulabell scrunched her shoulders and demurred, at once proud yet ashamed of her exploits. "He gave me the only platinum one." (As the title of this chapter indicates, the other sixteen were gold.)

Javier looked at the ring, then at Lulabell. He could tell by the expression on her face that that Calderón fellow actually came close.

"At least he knew you liked platinum better than gold," said Javier.

"Yes, mijo. I actually thought about it. To think, he would have been your father."

"Either him, or maybe Beto. But I'm glad things worked out the way they did. I got to have you all to myself all these years," Javier said taking his mother in his arms.

It was enough to make Lulabell cry, and it took everything she had not to. Instead she laughed in his ear and said, "Don't lie, mijo. You know you always wanted a father. But thanks for saying that." She slapped him on the back as they disembraced.

Javier picked up the pile of rings. "Thanks, momma," he said.

"Put them to good use. Buy yourself a new car or go back to school, even if it's only part-time," she suggested. She knew how much he loved his job as a garbageman.

"I will," he said walking out into the hall headed toward his bedroom. As he turned the corner he caught a glimpse of Lulabell leaning against the door jamb. She was dressed in one of her huipiles (she had a total of twenty-two, in fourteen distinct colors, each uniquely embroidered with flowers and/or birds and butterflies), her hair dangling in a single braid over her shoulder, her right foot propped up, resting on her left calf. She looked beyond beautiful standing there, and even after years of what Javier would unequivocally classify as immoral behavior, there was still that unmistakable light that always shone through her sinful veneer. ¿How, he had to ask himself, would he ever find a woman that could even come close to Lulabell?

He walked into his bedroom, felt around in the dark for his bedside lamp, turned the switch three clicks to the brightest setting, then set the rings in a pile next to his Bible. And even though it was against his better judgment, Javier spent half the night examining the rings and otherwise holding them up to the light, trying to decide which one Lucha would like best.

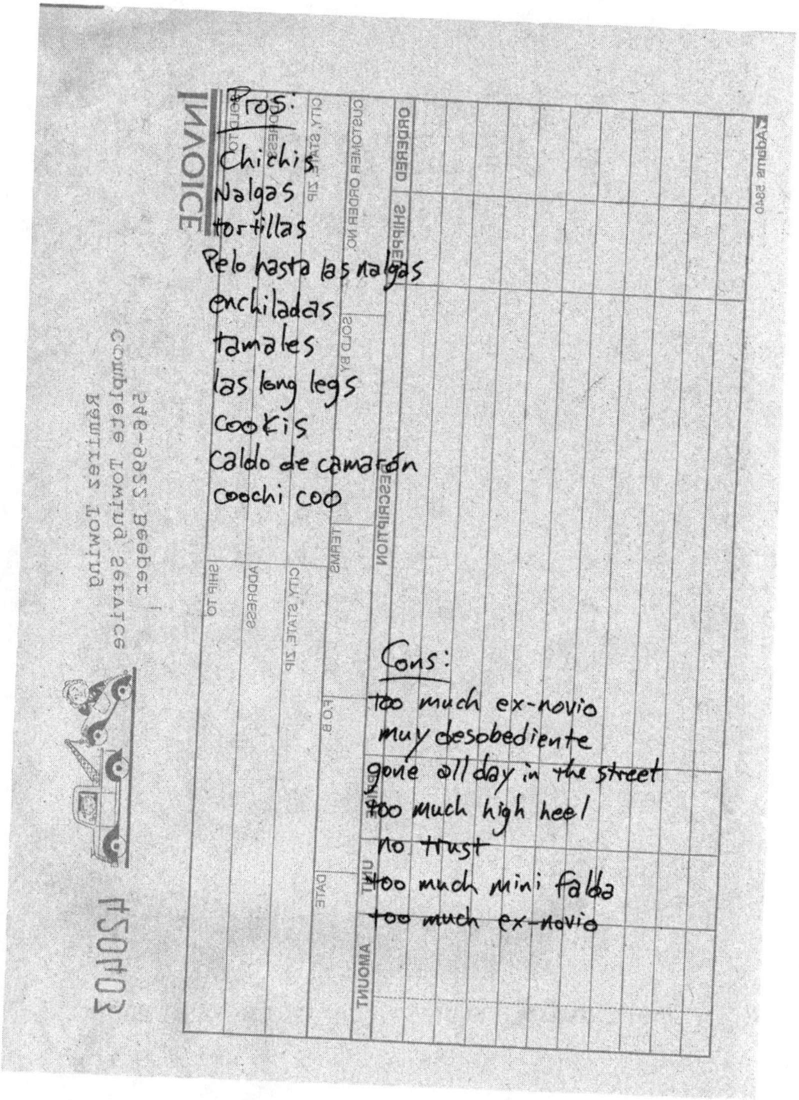

Pros:
Chichis
Nalgas
tortillas
Pelo hasta las nalgas
enchiladas
tamales
las long legs
cookis
Caldo de camarón
Coochi coo

Cons:
too much ex-novio
muy desobediente
gone all day in the street
too much high heel
no trust
too much mini falda
too much ex-novio

Menudo

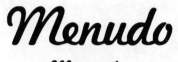

Menudo

PARA EL CRUDO, ES EL MENUDO

FOR THOSE WITH HANGOVERS, THERE IS MENUDO

BREAKFAST OF CHAMPIONS

*Of all of Lulabell's seventeen engagement rings and their accom-*panying wedding bands, Javier thought Lucha would like the simplest ones best—the engagement ring, a one-half-carat marquise diamond in an unopposing setting, and the wedding band, a simple band of gold. Collectively, the rings were marketed as the Princess Set, a classification Javier surely would have approved of were he privy to such information.

And now it was morning. Javier headed for the kitchen, made himself a cup of coffee, then sat down at the table. Even though, or perhaps precisely because of the fact that she might be his half-sister, Lucha weighed heavy on his mind, and elsewhere.

"¿Missing work again?" said Alberto entering the room.

Javier blew coffee out his mouth—he was in mid-sip and Beto's sudden arrival had startled him.

"I called in sick," said Javier once he recovered. "Glad to see you're back. Momma and I weren't sure if you were ever coming home." Home. It sounded funny in relation to Beto, and Javier was vaguely embarrassed by his choice of words.

"I needed a little fresh air last night. When a man gets angry, he has to cool off. Otherwise he might do something he'll regret."

"My head hurts," said Javier kneading his neck muscles.

"That's what happens when you drink too much." Beto put a firm hand on Javier's right shoulder. "I think we better go out for menudo. It's the best thing for la cruda. My treat." He patted Javier's shoulder. His hands were so solid it hurt.

Beto grabbed the keys off the hook, then pulled up his jeans, which, in spite of his belly, always tended to sag.

"¿You and momma fix things up last night?" said Javier once they were on the road.

"Me and your momma may never fix things up. ¿Who'll ever understand that woman?"

"My momma loves you," said Javier.

"Don't know about that. Sometimes I think about going back to my old life. To the trailer with the little frigerator, eating wienies and beans every night, watching the tele, but once a man has a woman like your momma, there ain't no going back never."

"I know what you mean," said Javier. He stuck a hand into the pocket of his Lava County Waste Management Company jacket and caressed the Princess Set.

Alberto looked at Javier and read his expression. "You've got to give up on that woman, son."

"I already have, but we better stop off for your hat. ¿Don't you think?"

"Good idea," said Beto. "I was thinking about taking your momma to the Baile Grande next weekend. Gonna need it."

Javier gave Beto directions to Lucha's house.

"Be back in a flash," said Javier once they pulled up at the curb.

He ran to Lucha's window and pounded. She emerged in her night-gown—a see-through red fur-trimmed spaghetti-strapped number. Javier watched intently while Lucha stretched and yawned. Temptation personified, she embodied everything he had tried to avoid for the better part of his twenty-seven years.

"Mornin, hermanito," she said. It was strange to hear her call him that, for the word "hermanito" had taken on an entirely different meaning in the past twenty-four hours.

"Look what I got, honey," he said pulling the Princess Set from the pocket of his jacket. "It's a nice pretty ring for you. It means we're novios." He pressed it into her hand.

"That's nice," said Lucha accepting the engagement half of the Princess Set. She had held much more valuable items in her hand, namely a kilo of high-grade cocaine, so she was hardly impressed, but she readily recognized and never turned down anything she could, with certainty, get at least a few hundred dollars for.

"We don't have to get married or nothin, ¿do we?" she thought twice about it and said.

Javier hadn't considered that. The Universe had put those rings on his platter just as surely as It had Lucha, and that's what you did with fine jewelry, ¿right? You gave it to girls you liked. "No, chiquita, we don't have to get married, but tonight I want you to come out with me and the boys. We are going out to herd up some souls."

"I really can't," said Lucha. "The conditions of my probation don't allow me to go out after 10:00 p.m.," she said, then demurred, her chin pitched down toward her left shoulder, her lips in a pout.

"I understand," said Javier. "Perhaps another time. Now give me a kiss . . ." He closed his eyes, got on his tippy-toes, and puckered up.

Lucha leaned out her first-story window, getting close enough to catch a whiff of Javier. "You stink. Have you been drinkin?" she said.

"Sure have," said Javier.

Lucha swatted the air in front of her, pulled her hair to the side, then leaned in and gave Javier an innocuous kiss on the cheek.

"I gotta run now," he said with undue enthusiasm. "Don't forget about the fund-raiser car wash tomorrow."

"I will most definitely see you there," she said. "I always look for opportunities to serve the Lord, and besides, I can knock off a few hours of community service."

"You can kill two birds con un solo tiro," said Javier. "Now ¿do you mind passing me my hat?"

"Sure," said Lucha. She had forgotten about the Stetson®, which was still sitting on her dresser.

"Me and Beto are gonna go and have menudo. He says it's the best thing for la cruda," said Javier.

"Breakfast of champions," said Lucha handing him the Stetson®.

El Camarón
The Shrimp

CAMARÓN QUE SE DUERME SE LO LLEVA LA CORRIENTE
SHRIMP WHO SLEEP WILL BE SWEPT AWAY BY THE CURRENT

QUERIDA CLAUDIA

That same morning, True-Dee had an important meeting with Querida Claudia, scheduled for 10:30 a.m. at the Lava Landing Bowling Alley Café. True-Dee was beside herself with flattery that Lava Landing's most beloved advice columnist had called for a face-to-face with hers truly, and for the occasion True-Dee had slipped on a pair of conservative, tan, fitted slacks, a gold chain link belt, and a long-sleeved, silk, suburban housewife shirt circa 1974, complete with a tie at the neck in an eye-catching, bright graphic print. Her hair was up in a sloppy bun, on top of which rested a pair of gold-framed sunglasses with a rhinestone butterfly hovering in the bottom corner of the left-hand lens.

True-Dee was oh so nervous as she walked into the Bowling Alley Café. Someone bowled a strike. The sound of the pins tumbling down and the congratulatory cheers that followed made her jump. She took several deep breaths, checked her makeup in her compact without breaking stride, then put on a fresh coat of lipstick and gloss. This made her feel better. Another deep breath and she was opening the door to the bowling alley coffee shop.

She was on time, or nearly so, perhaps three minutes late according to her timepiece. Her heart sank once again. The place was nearly abandoned, save for a man sitting in the far corner. He peeked out from his booth to have a look, then got to his feet and walked her way. "You must be the volcano," he said.

True-Dee held a palm to her chest. "Why yes, I am."

"Come this way," he motioned.

She followed along. There was something about his air, about the situation itself, that made True-Dee at once suspicious, yet enticed. All of her dealings with Querida Claudia had been conducted under a veil of secrecy, causing her to wonder if she was about to brush elbows with the members of a secret society, and ¿was this gentleman in the red and black checkered shirt just another obstacle in her path to that secret society and Lava Landing's most adored advice columnist?

They sat down at the booth. Several moments of silence ensued as they summed one another up. "¿Would you like some coffee, something to eat?" said the man. He put his hands up on the table and folded them.

"No thank you," said True-Dee. "I would really like to see La Doctora," she added, lowering her voice.

The man leaned in. He was big and tall, his complexion ruddy. He wore his mustache in the handlebar fashion. With that shirt, he reminded True-Dee of a lumberjack. His voice was very deep. "I am La Doctora," he said.

True-Dee grabbed at her ice water.

"My name is Larry," said Querida Claudia. "Larry," he paused, contemplated, and said, "Perhaps we oughtta just leave it at that."

"True-Dee," she said. "True-Dee Spreckels."

"¿Like the sugar company?"

"Yes. Like the sugar company." Indeed there was a defunct sugar factory a few miles away, and an entire town named after it.

"¿Are you an heir? Or, an heiress I suppose. Perdóname."

"No. I'm a hairdresser."

"Oh, yes. I know. I remember from your letter," he reached over and cupped a hand over True-Dee's folded hands. "You won't tell anyone about me. I can count on you. ¿Can't I?"

True-Dee looked down at his hand. It was enormous. She said nothing. She was waiting for a good reason why she had been so cruelly deceived.

"I am a doctor," said the doctor. "A real bona fide medical doctor. Even with all of my education, I never wanted anything more than to be an advice columnist. And ¿who asks for advice, but women? And ¿what do women want advice about? About love, about men. And of course, a woman will only take another woman's word. A woman will not accept advice from a man. He is after all, in the other camp."

"Yes. The other camp," agreed True-Dee.

"Forgive me if I have disappointed you. But there was something in your letter that isn't in just every letter. A dedication and a passion hard to come by. That's why I called you here today, because you have evidenced yourself as a person who can be wholeheartedly dedicated to a mission."

"But I reached out to you," said True-Dee leaning over the table.

"Yes, that's what you think. But here I am the puppeteer," said Larry.

"From your letter I gathered that you are a dedicated and passionate individual with the spirit of a volcano."

"That I am," said True-Dee.

"We need individuals such as yourself for our cause."

¿Cause? ¿Did he say cause?

He said cause, and True-Dee sat straight up. She balled her fists up from the excitement. "A cause, oh, do tell me more."

"Padre Narciso, the founder of this town, ¿ever heard of him?"

"No. I'm afraid I haven't."

"He was a priest and an all-around powerful man. No use beating around the bush," said Larry.

"No. No use," said True-Dee. The tension was already built.

"He was a prescient," announced Querida Claudia.

"A prescient," whispered True-Dee. It sounded so glamorous. French even.

"¿Was he a Canadian?" asked True-Dee.

"No. A Mexican."

"Oh, yes. With a name like that, one would figure. Perdona my oversight, and while you're at it, kindly define the word 'prescient.' "

"He saw the future."

"I see," said True-Dee. "And ¿what did it look like?"

"¿What?"

"The future, ¿what did it look like?"

"I'm getting to that. But first things first. Padre Narciso predicted the spread of disease, he predicted wars, he predicted infidelities and other chaoses, but he was most gifted at the prediction of natural disasters."

"Oh, my," said True-Dee.

"Most importantly, and I need you all the way with me on this one," said Larry looking True-Dee in the eye, "Padre Narciso predicted the volcano, but he didn't stop at that. He said that one day it would come back to life."

"¿The volcano?"

"Yes. The volcano. And that those who knew his word, those who listened when he spoke, only they would be saved. The volcano is gonna go. It's gonna go one day real soon, and we're ready for it."

"Please explain who the we is."

Larry looked both ways, then straight ahead, lowered his voice and said, "Us. The Sons and Daughters of San Narciso."

"Sons and daughters, but he was a priest."

"Yes, but Church records indicate that he had a number of mistresses."

"That explains it," True-Dee muttered.

"We go underground every Sunday. We don't come up until Tuesday. At 12:01 a.m. we come creeping out. That doesn't interfere with your salon schedule ¿does it?"

As a matter of fact it didn't. True-Dee's Tresses was closed on Sunday and Monday.

"Nope," said True-Dee.

"You see, Padre Narciso was clear about one thing. Any duress would occur on the day of the Sabbath. But we stay underground until Tuesday just in case. Besides, there's plenty of work to do down there."

True-Dee's eyes widened. "I can just imagine it," she said.

"I knew you could," said Querida Claudia. "And about your little problem."

"Yes," said True-Dee. "I thought you would never get to that. I greatly appreciate the advice you have already given me, but I was lookin for some sort of hope, some light at the end of the tunnel. I know that you are right, about everything, about love bein a blind thing, that I will only know love when I find a man that loves me as I am, but that don't help me cope with the here and now."

Again, he put his hand over hers. Again, he lowered his voice. Again, he leaned in. "Down under there's plenty of forward-thinking people. People from all over the world. People as you have never seen or known in your life. Down under you are sure to meet the one that will love you as you are. I am certain of it. ¿How's that for esperanza?" said La Doctora.

True-Dee sighed. She said nothing, only nodded.

"So, ¿will we be seeing you next Sunday?"

"You can be certain of it."

Querida Claudia provided True-Dee with the necessary information: the where and when of it all, and her own special password, which she was to share with no one, which she would share with no one, not even her best friend, the most elegant poodle in all of three counties, Miss Miranda.

La Herradura
de la Suerte
The Lucky Horseshoe

LO QUE VA Y VIENE
THAT WHICH COMES AND GOES

THE LORD'S WORK

That evening, everything felt different in Javier's pants—*the new* horseshoe key ring that rested in his front pocket, that held the keys to the house, the backyard shed, the Church of God and His Son Jesus Christ, the office at the garbage company, that led to the yard, that held the garbage truck, the keys to the garbage truck itself, to the Monte Carlo, and Javier's skate key as well; the ostrich skin wallet that rested in his back pocket, that held the ninety-two hundred-dollar bills that would have went, to wine, dine, and woo the girl that was Heaven-sent; the fancy boots that hugged the ankles and pinched the toes, that went with the suit that Javier had to have, but most of all, that part of Javier that most made him a man, which, due to all the room in that suit, enjoyed both lateral and longitudinal movement. Everything was different that night, and not just in his slacks. The Stetson® resting confidently on his head, light like the pants, not ever-present like a baseball cap, or over-present like his fancy mariachi hat; but back to the pants that gave Javier something that both his traje de charro and his garbageman suit lacked, room and freedom of movement, but more than either of the two, that suit and its accoutrements gave Javier attitude.

After their menudo in the morning, Javier and Beto had done a little shopping at the Lava Landing Western Store, and presently it was Friday night and Javier and Gilbert were in the Monte Carlo, headed toward town on their way to Raymundo's to fetch the other mariachis. It had been a little over two weeks since Gilbert had settled into a position on Javier's garbage route, during which time he had demonstrated himself not just as a capable soccer player, but also as an accomplished accordionist. Accordingly, Javier wasted no time incorporating him into his musical ensemble.

"¿Are you feeling better, my man?" said Javier. He glanced over at Gilbert, who was wearing one of his old trajes de charro, which fit him far too snuggly. It appeared that Gilbert was cured of Lulabell's love spell. He ate heartily and regularly, and was in prime physical condition. At work, Gilbert had proven himself a natural can man. With Javier behind the wheel of the garbage truck, and Gilbert riding the stepside, they were able to shave a full hour's time off their route.

"Thank you for asking, Brother. I am feeling great. I only think of Lula-bell when I make love to my wife. And since I like to think about her, I have mucho más interés en mi esposa. This has really helped to improve our marriage. Everything has worked out."

"How odd. All the result of brujería. This is very strange," said Javier. "But I am glad for you."

"I have just one complaint," said Gilbert hesitantly. "Sólo una queja." He repeated himself in Spanish, and in that he was like scores of other bilinguals who reiterate their sentiments in a second language when they get nervous.

"I don't want to sound like an ingrato, but . . ." Gilbert started, then stopped.

"Con confianza, Brother, you can tell me." Javier put the transmission in park and killed the engine. They had arrived in front of Las Tres Palmas Apartment Complex where Raymundo and the other mariachis lived.

"I am not comfortable with all of this soul-saving business. I am a Catholic to the best of my ability. Every night I pray to the blessed Virgen de Guadalupe, El Gran Señor, and sometimes even El Santo Niño de Atocha. But I am not a Christian soldier like you. I am a simple man with an acordeón, but my heart is not in this musical misionero thing."

"I understand," said Javier. "Yo te comprendo, Brother. Don't worry. No te preocupes." And now Javier was doing it too—repeating himself in Spanish, and questioning whether or not he was a musical misionero, or just a mariachi, or a man in love, or a man in love with his own sister, or perhaps all of the above.

Once the mariachis were all together, they headed for El Aguantador night-club where they were, allegedly, going to flex the prevention prong of their three-pronged attack upon sin. Once there, Javier swaggered through the nightclub door, grabbed his guitarrón by its neck, gave it a spin, and without a word said on either end, the doorman waved him and his mariachis through.

Once inside, Javier took a deep breath and a profound look around, then said, "Let's start off with a little something to pierce the Devil's armor," then cut into "Prieta Linda." The mariachis watched suspiciously as Javier scanned the nightclub looking for a woman he could rightfully dedicate a love song of that nature to. He was greatly disappointed. The women were all older than he thought they would be. More than old, they looked tired, as if their lives had been one big perpetual parranda from which they never fully recovered. The women were likely there every night, or at some similar establishment, so used to the routine of putting on the mini-falda, the high-heel vinyl pumps they'd bought years before, the low-cut blouse and the push-up bra from La Family Bargain, sprinkling the dime store glitter glaze across their cleavage, making themselves up with Wet 'n' Wild® cosmetics, then curling and teasing their over-processed hair, that they were tired of it. There was no longer the anticipation—Wednesday afternoon calling the bar to see who would be play-ing on Friday and Saturday night, Thursday going shopping for the perfect blouse, bringing it home, deciding between boots and jeans, or mini-falda and high heels, trying it all on for size, standing on the toilet, trying to get some semblance of a full-length-mirror view, thinking you should have splurged for that $9.99 door mirror, then Friday or Saturday night, putting it all together with the lipstick, plugging in the curling iron, fixing the hair con La Aqua Net®, spritzing yourself with perfume—expensive or cheap just so long as it smells purty, then running out the door with two or three girlfriends. No, for these women there was nothing left of that. It all boiled down to rummaging through the dirty clothes pile, sniffing the armpits of blouses to see which one smelled the least, wiping the spots off the skirt with the dishrag, squeezing into the clothes on the premise that they might land you a decent dancer on the grounds of what might come after the dancing is done, looking in the mirror, telling yourself not to worry—it's dark in there.

And indeed, it was dark in there. The mariachis huddled at song's end.

"Let's get out of here," said Kiko. "I'm getting scared."

"I think the men are right," said Raymundo. "Best we move our message elsewhere."

Javier stopped in his tracks. "Boys, keep in mind that the Devil sees the world as one big unincorporated area, and He is there with a survey crew of His leading Demons set on incorporating all the world's lost souls into His Kingdom. And when the Devil sees a saved soul, He brings His bulldozer set on demolishing the fortress the Lord has built. No, Brothers. We must stay where we are needed."

Javier reached into the inside pocket of his suit coat and pulled out a pile of Bible pamphlets and passed them around. "It's time to separate and circu-late," he said.

But it had all been a soul-saving ruse, Javier's way of throwing the other mariachis off his scent. He grabbed Gilbert by the elbow and said, "Let's blow this joint," and the men headed for El Zarape.

El Zarape was the new, hip place in town. It had been open just three weeks, and Radio KAZA was there with its radio-móvil and spotlight, celebrating the estreno of a brand-new club.

"¿How do I look?" said Javier as they walked in. "Maybe Lucha will be here."

"You look different," said Gilbert.

"Different." Javier freshened his Stetson®, furrowed his brow, then said, "¿In a bad way?"

"No. Just different."

Gilbert was on to him. Javier had been a changing man ever since Lucha had given him his first kiss. The missionary in Javier had been receding slowly at first, then, after their recent love encounter, at an exponentially accelerated rate so that at this juncture, the missionary in Javier was in complete remission. As he stood up against the nightclub wall with his guitarrón at his side, eyeing the girls as they went by, Javier was all man and mariachi.

"¿What do we do now?" said Javier.

"I told you, I'm new to soul saving," said Gilbert.

"We ain't here to soul save. ¡Agarra la onda! We're here to pick up girls, and so I can practice my dancing to impress Lucha."

"Right on, Brother," said Gilbert with a nod. He was doing it, catching the onda, agarrando la wave.

¿Y Javier? He knew a mutineer when he saw one, and he thought about telling Gilbert that Lucha was his sister with a lower-case "s" as opposed to his Sister. If only he and Lucha were cousins, then their union would have equaled straight-up, good old country incest. But as it were, there were just too many maybes in the gravy; Javier kept his mouth shut.

"Let's get a table and order a beer," suggested Gilbert.

"Now you're talking," said Javier.

By the time their beers arrived, the banda was in full swing, and the tables were all occupied.

"I think it's about time we find some girls," declared Javier. "But remember, when the band breaks we grab our instruments and make the rounds. Girls just love musicians."

"Whatever you say, jefe," said Gilbert taking a drink of his beer.

Javier walked over to a nearby table, held his hand out to a pretty little redhead, and said, "¿Bailamos?"

She got to her feet. The banda played a ranchera. Javier grabbed her hand, and rushed her to the floor where he exhibited dancing moves aplenty. When he was just seven years old, Lulabell had taught him how to dance claiming it was a skill all men should have, and over the years she had forced him to be her partner at countless quinceañeras, birthday parties, baptisms, and the like, and now Javier was making up for lost time as he moved that red-headed mamacita to every squeeze of the accordion, every tremble of the drums. The dance floor exchange began:

"¿Cómo te llamas?

"Teresa."

"Qué bonito nombre." Her eyes met his before vergüenza got the best of her and she leaned her head into his shoulder. She was quite lovely, a güera in a frilly dress.

"¿Vienes muy seguido?" he wanted to know.

"De vez en cuando," she replied.

"Y tú ¿cómo te llamas?"

"Javier."

"¿En qué trabajas?" she asked.

"Soy carpintero." It was the lie he'd always wanted to tell, to cast himself in the same trade as Jesus.

She demurred, lowered her head más, and due to their difference in height, her head rested on his chest, and he was thankful for all that room in his pants.

The song ended and the band took its break. "Gracias," said Javier before stranding her on the dance floor.

He fetched Gilbert, they fetched their instruments, and deposited themselves in front of Teresa's table for a serenade. They cut into the Ramón Ayala classic "Piquito de Oro." Teresa sat with eyes wide open and watching, while the other three women at her table were left similarly in awe. The music was lovely, with just the accordion and the guitarrón, in the northern style. Teresa didn't downright smile, and a few minutes later when Javier and Gilbert began the second half of the serenade, Javier knew why. She was a lovely woman, bordering on the beautiful, but also on the equine, for her teeth were large, crooked, and gold-capped, so big in fact they reminded Javier of a mule.

Nervousness and anticipation got the best of her. She began to gently gnaw at her fingernails as Javier and Gilbert segued to their norteña version of "Despacito, Muy Despacito," the same song Javier had serenaded Lucha one not so distant summer afternoon.

After the serenade was over, the men headed back to their table. "¿Who's that bigotón over there?" Gilbert pointed out a big mustached man.

"¿How am I supposed to know?" said Javier popping the top on his latest beer.

"He keeps looking over here," said Gilbert.

The mustached man soon arrived. "¿You been messing with my ruca?" He pointed an accusatory finger in Javier's face. After hearing Javier's serenade, the mustached man realized that as he had made love to Lucha despacito, muy despacito, it had been Javier who had showed up windowside serenading her the song of the same name.

"The only woman I've been messing with is my own," said Javier. He finished his beer, licked his lips, then set the bottle on the table.

Joaquín was still pointing fingers. "You have really big fingers. ¿Ever consider taking up the accordion?" said Gilbert.

"¡Hijo de puta!" said Joaquín. He flexed his jailhouse muscles, then grabbed Gilbert by the collar, and lifted him from his seat.

"Put my Brother down," said Javier. He was about to attempt to employ some diplomacy, but Joaquín dropped Gilbert to the ground before he had the chance.

"I ain't your Brother," said Gilbert as he hit the floor.

"In God's family we are all one," said Javier. For old times' sake, he was about to elaborate, but was broadsided by Joaquín's fist, and soon found himself right there on the floor next to Brother Gilbert.

Javier touched his nose and was surprised when two fingers came back bloody, but not nearly as surprised as when he heard a familiar feminine voice say, "¿Qué chinga'os andas haciendo?"

There, hovering behind Joaquín, stood Lucha. She was wearing Lulabell's white peasant blouse, the one with the red flowers embroidered across the front, that tied around the neck, but Lucha had opted to start her bow significantly lower—in the middle of the V that was her cleavage—a pair of Wrangler® jeans, calfskin boots, a matching belt and a heart-shaped silver buckle with a cursive "L" in the middle. Her hair was in two braids with red ribbons woven in that trailed down her back, and in the front, her bangs were curled and teased early 1980s homegirl style.

"¿Lucha?" said Javier, his head still ringing from the recent chingazo.

"¿Javier?" said Lucha. El Zarape was the last place she'd expect to see the likes of him.

"Yes, my little lamb, it is me." He got to his feet, freshened his suit, then grabbed her left hand, isolating the ring finger. "You're not wearing the ring and you're violating your probation," he said, his tone switching from disappointed to accusatory.

Joaquín pulled the engagement half of the Princess Set from his pocket, then attempted to make a move toward Javier, but Lucha stood in his way. She grabbed Joaquín by an ear, pulled him near, and reminded him of the importance of keeping a low profile and staying out of trouble, then whispered, "Keep your mouth shut and I'll explain it all later.

"I gave the ring to my brother. You see, our uncle is a jeweler and I wanted to have it cleaned," said Lucha. She squeezed Joaquín's forearm and smiled up at him.

"¿He's your brother?" said Javier pointing at Joaquín.

"Yes, but you are my favorite one." She cocked her head convincingly to the side.

"Come on let's dance." Javier reached out for her hand, but Lucha raised it to her mouth and feigned a yawn.

"I'm gettin tired and if I'm to make it to the church fund-raiser tomorrow, I better get home and get to bed," she said.

"Good point. I'll take you home," offered Javier. He grabbed her by the wrist, anxious for a repeat of the other night's fun.

"That's okay," she said busting loose. "My brother can give me a ride."

"Well all right," agreed Javier semi-reluctantly. He would be content to spend the rest of the night perfecting his dancing ways and getting to know La Teresita. In order to win a woman, Javier knew he had to have something to offer her. With a steady job, a substantial savings, and a nice car, he was off to a good start. But his dancing/romancing skills still needed honing.

Javier sent Lucha on her way, and once outside, she whispered to Joaquín, "Vamos al Aguantador," and they took off in Lucha's pickup truck.

Javier and Teresa resumed the dance floor, and in no time, the dancing gap closed. What Javier had worked so many years to suppress, now flowed freely. Stooping over to compensate for their difference in height, Javier was soon dancing cheek to cheek with her. Despite her dental imperfection, she was beautiful, though she lacked that certain je ne sais quoi that Lucha had in abundance. She was good to practice on, but something just wasn't right. They were dancing to a slightly different rhythm. Once in a while Javier looked down at Teresa's feet, trying to figure out that rhythm, and for a few paces they would be completely in sync, only to lose the pace moments later. Javier imagined that dancing with a perfect partner was like dancing with yourself, only not being alone while you were doing it.

The baile came to an abrupt end as it always does. Javier didn't know what to do, but say thanks, then walk off and fetch Gilbert, who was asleep with his head on the table, and his hand around his beer.

"Come on, man, let's go," said Javier.

"¿It's over already?" said Gilbert.

"Yep. Se acabó. Now let's vámonos."

"Man, you look like shit," said Gilbert.

Javier swatted the air in front of him and said, "Not only do you look like shit, you smell like it too."

Javier helped Gilbert to his feet, then to the parking lot, and finally, into the Monte Carlo.

Once inside himself, Javier had a look in the rearview mirror. He didn't look like shit per se, but he had two black eyes, which could only indicate one thing: He had a broken nose.

"¿Did you get her number?" said Gilbert.

"¿Was I supposed to?" said Javier as they drove off.

"If you ever wanna see her again."

"That's okay. Plenty more where that came from. Besides I'm only practicing up for Lucha."

"It's hard loving just one woman. A man's better off with two or three," said Gilbert.

"I suppose he is. The Baile Grande is coming up next week, and I'm gonna invite Lucha."

"I'm a married man and I'm gonna stay home with my wife and kids," declared Gilbert with a fist to the air. "I don't want no more of this staying out all night. I don't want no soul saving. I just wanna work and be a good father."

"Wise decision, my man," said Javier. "But Los Huracanes del Norte are coming. I sure do like conjunto music. As a matter of fact, I think we go over better with the ladies as a conjunto norteño. ¿What do you think?"

"That sounds good to me and besides, we're already two fourths of the way there," said Gilbert as they arrived in front of his apartment complex.

Javier shook his head, for Gilbert had it all wrong. "One half," he said. "A man always oughtta reduce his fractions."

Los Botes
The Cans

AL REVISAR LOS BOTES, ME ENCONTRÉ UN TESORO

UPON INSPECTING THE GARBAGE CANS,

I CAME ACROSS A TREASURE

THE CANS

Javier slept through the morning and well into the afternoon, missing the church fund-raiser car wash. He would have slept longer had he not been interrupted—first by a knock on the door, then the ringing of the doorbell, both of which were easy enough to ignore, but then, there was a tap on his windowpane, decidedly feminine, or so he thought when he sat up in bed, tamed his hair, then, better yet, grabbed his hat, and went rushing to see who was there.

Javier slid the window open, and there stood Pablo, Mariachi de Dos Nacimientos' trumpet player. He had his hands in his back pockets and his white car washing rag in his front one.

The men met on the front porch.

"Sorry I missed the car wash," said Javier stepping outside. "Gilbert and I ran into a little trouble."

"I can see that," said Pablo gesturing toward Javier's two black eyes.

"If you've got a minute, I'd like to talk to you about something," said Pablo.

"¿What's on your mind?" said Javier having a seat on the porch swing. He was still in last night's suit pants and a white undershirt, his loose-fitting pants ballooning at the pockets.

"¿You know how you always say you're más misionero que mariachi?"

"Sí," said Javier.

"Well I always thought it was the other way around for me. That I was more mariachi than missionary."

"¿Are you losing faith in the Lord, Brother Pablo?"

"No. I just wanna write a song is all. And I want your help."

Javier chuckled. "I hate to disappoint you, but since the beginning of time, all the songs have already been written. If I were you, I wouldn't waste my time."

Pablo's countenance crumbled in disappointment. "I don't get it, jefe."

"Piénsalo. ¿What are all songs about?"

Pablo shrugged.

"They are about love. Maybe the songs we sing are gospel in nature, but they are still about love, the love of the Lord. Books are the same way too. Like when you were in high school—"

"I didn't go to no high school," interrupted Pablo.

"Well I did, and they taught us what books are about. They're about man against man, man against Nature, against himself, against God, and other things. Things they call conflicts. If a book is really good, it's about all them things, about all them so-called conflicts."

"¿Like the Bible?" questioned Pablo.

"Actually, I was thinking more along the lines of *The Treasure of the Sierra Madre*. That's a real good book. I think if I wasn't a garbageman, I might have been a gold prospector."

"¿A gold prospector?" repeated Pablo.

"Sure, but being a garbageman is sort of like that because you can find lots of good things in the cans."

"¿Really?" said Pablo, his eyes wide with surprise.

Javier looked at him, squinted and said, "¿You mean to tell me you don't look in yours? ¿You just pick them up and dump them?"

Pablo nodded.

Javier was confounded. He got to his feet, then led Pablo to a large shed located at the foremost corner of the property, where he opened the door to more junk than Pablo had ever seen in any single place in his entire life.

Javier stepped inside, then said, "Take a look at all the fine items a man can find in the cans.

"This here's the fiesta section." He gestured toward two piñatas in the corner—one a three-tier cake adorned with paper roses, the other a banana.

Javier walked past sporting goods, art, and trophies, before he finally pushed the bicycles and Big Wheel®s out of the way, making a path for himself to the book department. It took him a while before he found what he was after—a tattered copy of *The Treasure of the Sierra Madre*. "Read this," said Javier handing the paperback to Pablo. "It has plenty of truth in it, and can only help you with that song you wanna write."

"Thanks, jefe," said Pablo gazing at the worn cover.

"If you're not much of a reader, there's a movie. But the book is always better."

The men stepped outside.

"Say, Brother Pablo, ¿do you think you could make the transition from the trumpet to the saxophone?" said Javier locking up.

"I suppose I could, but ¿why would I want to?"

"Me and Brother Gilbert are thinking about starting a conjunto norteño and we could use a sax player."

"In that case, I don't think so," said Pablo. "Soy mariachi."

"I can understand and respect that," said Javier.

"I better get going," said Pablo.

"Que te vaya bien," said Javier. "And remember, always check the cans."

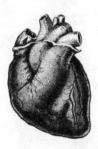

La Muerte

Death

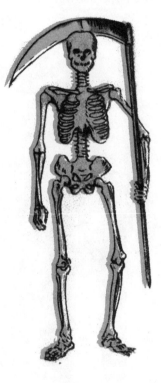

PELÓN Y FLACO
BALD AND SKINNY

EL RE-ENCUENTRO

Consuelo's house began with a mailbox at the end of a dirt road bordered by a barbed wire fence which confined cows, horses, mules, goats, sheep, and donkeys, which faced first a prune orchard, followed by a tomato, then bell pepper field. At that time of year, everything was in season or just about, so only after you smelled all the different scents, after the prune segued to bell pepper, then to tomato, and after you carefully zigzagged your way down the long dirt road avoiding all the potholes—assuming you were concerned with the alignment of your tires and the front-end suspension of your vehicle—would you arrive at la casa de Consuelo.

The house was yellow, Consuelo's favorite color, of wood construction, with white trim. First came the porch steps, then the porch itself, a screen door which opened to a wooden door with the earlier-mentioned brass lock set that was never locked, and then there was the living room more often referred to as the sala, adjoined by a dining area which opened up into a kitchen, which turned the corner to the hall where there were two bathrooms whose toilets mustered a flush every twenty minutes, and three bedrooms, the very last of which had a back door that opened up onto a concrete patio with plenty of plants, some potted and stationary, others basketed and dangling, and an unplugged old pink refrigerator, circa 1953, that the girls kept around on account of the fact that it was "so cute" and one day they were gonna have its guts replaced bringing it up to modern-day energy efficiency.

But let me direct your attention to the washer and dryer because it was Monday and Nat and Sway were in the midst of doing a week's worth of laundry. The washer was avocado in color, the dryer almond. They were mismatched because, as luck would have it, Consuelo's avocado dryer went kerplunk about the same time Nat's almond washer gave out, so instead of getting angry about it, they decided to synthesize the set.

"I'll be damned if this don't remind me of earthquake weather," said Natalie shaking first her head, then the bedsheets. The weather was strange for any time of the year. It was cloudy, hot, and humid all at the same time.

"I do agree," said Sway, "but if there was really one on the way, then the goats would have told us about it."

"That sets my mind at ease," said Nat. Animals have senses humans don't, and that's just one of the reasons why Nat and Sway considered them the best earthquake detectors known to man.

"Earthquakes don't scare me. In fact, now that I know my daddy's safe, nothin scares me no more."

"Except travel," corrected Natalie.

Consuelo frowned, then pursed her lips as if she had just applied lipstick. "Except travel," she concurred.

The washing contraption was on the verge of its rinse cycle. With an illuminated control panel that flashed and sometimes even shocked you as you went to give it a start, this was no mere machine. It had a hose the girls referred to as the "tailpipe" from which it spilt its dirty water into a nearby wash basin, and the machine was known to migrate three feet in any given direction during the spin cycle.

Something began to rumble, but Nat and Sway couldn't blame the Maytag® because the sound was coming from beneath the house. For a moment, they thought it was an earthquake, because that's the way the biggest baddest ones begin, with that far-off unmistakable growl.

But no. There was definitely something under the house. Consuelo grabbed a baseball bat, and Natalie reached first for the broom, then for Consuelo's elbow, as they tiptoed around the perimeter of the house, following the underground commotion as it headed toward the front porch.

And then came a voice, "Mija," said Don Pancho Macías Contreras, "Ayúdame. Estoy e-stuck."

"¡Ay! papá," said Consuelo throwing the bat—a habit she had held since grade school which had gotten her called immediately out on more than a few occasions. (See Rule Number 14, Section 3, of the *Official Rules of the Game of Softball*.)

"Don Pancho," proclaimed Natalie letting the broom rest against the side of the house. DP was stuck all right, or wedged rather, between an air vent and the porch.

"Don't just stand there, Sway," she said. "¡Ayúdale!"

"You speak a very good e-Spanish," said DP.

"You are always gettin stuck, papá. You must learn to be more careful," said Sway. She passed him the broomstick and said, "Jálale." But no matter how hard he pulled from his end and Consuelo and Natalie pulled from theirs, no progress was made.

"I will get the Vaseline®," declared Natalie. Momentarily, she showed up with a vat to last a lifetime, something the girls had brought home one afternoon from the Humongous Bargain One Dollar Store.

The Vaseline® was passed to DP. "Now put it on your shoulder and your arm, all over, and we will pull you out of there," instructed Consuelo.

"But this is my favorite shirt," said DP.

"We will get you a new one," promised Nat and Sway in unison.

DP did as he was told and the girls were able to retrieve him from his stuck place. Tattered, slightly bleeding at the shoulder and with his sombrero smashed, Don Pancho eventually emerged. He swung an arm around each of the girls and they staggered up the porch steps arm in arm, then entered the house, looking just like a cowboy and a couple of saloon girls busting through the swinging cantina doors.

Don Pancho sat down on the couch, then set his beat-up sombrero on an end table. He grabbed his earlobes and said, "You two have been talking about me. My ears have been itching all week."

"We miss you," said Nat.

"And we want to ask you a favor," added Sway.

"Anything you need, mija." Don Pancho clasped his hands together, then bent them backwards and away from himself until a good portion of knuckles cracked.

"I want you to cure me of my unreasonable fear of public transportation and long car rides," said Sway.

Don Pancho took a deep breath. "I cannot help you with that. Remember, I am the Patron Saint of Drunks and Prostitutes. To cure your fear would be a little far from my calling. ¿Can't you ask me for something else? ¿How about a man? I can send you un hombre, hecho y derecho. Just ask Natalie."

"That didn't work out," said Nat referring to her short-lived liaison con El Amador. She looked down at her fingernails, and thought about biting them, ashamed and embarrassed that DP's love miracle didn't pan out.

"Sure it did. Amador thinks of you all the time, especially when he goes 'e-sleeping.' " He wagged a pair of finger quotations in the air.

"He has sold all of his cows and he is coming to see you very soon," said DP.

"If he cared, then he would have come back when he had the chance," said Nat with her arms folded.

"Circunstancias beyond his control did not allow him to return."

"Death is the only thing that ought keep a man from a girl like Nat," said Consuelo. "Look at her." Consuelo pulled Natalie to her feet and she, Nat, turned and twinkled, demurred and allured, in a way that only a bona fide divine woman can.

"He had not one, but two flat tires," said DP with a fist to the air.

"A man that can't deal with that has got no place in my future," said Natalie.

"Mine either," seconded Consuelo.

Don Pancho lifted his hat, then smoothed his hair. "I gave you the most desirable young man in town, the one with the most animals and the only one who speaks English."

"We don't choose our men by their animals, papi," said Sway.

He looked at Natalie. "I don't understand. I saw the look in your eyes and knew you needed love."

"There's a big difference between needin love and needin lovin, and I'd think you of all people would know the difference," said Sway.

He shook his head. After so many years, women were still a mystery to him.

Natalie stood up. "I wanna show you somethin," she said to Don Pancho. He followed her to the living room window where she pulled the lavender pin-striped curtains aside, and pointed to the volcano. "It might not look so menacin, but they don't call it El Condenado for nothin," she said.

Don Pancho cleared his throat.

"¿Did you know that even a small volcano can wipe out a hundred-mile radius and can cause worldwide climatological changes?"

DP wasn't aware.

Consuelo stayed put on the couch, watching genius unfold as she slowly caught on to what Natalie had up her sleeve.

"On the upside, in its aftermath, an eruption leaves behind extremely fertile soil complete with all the necessary nutrients which are readily separated into essential compounds," continued Natalie.

She brought it down to a whisper. "A hundred and fifty years ago our volcano wiped out a good portion of the area's livestock. Luckily there were no human casualties, but now look at the verdant splendor of our farmlands."

Don Pancho looked out at the bell pepper field which fanned out into a tomato field. The volcano stood in the distance, as if proud of itself for having employed so many people in the fields and the cannery.

The look on Don Pancho's face was wide-eyed and surprised. Natalie flashed Consuelo, who stood wisely aside, a smile. They had him right where they wanted him.

"Our volcano is dormant, but not extinct," continued Nat. "Just a few days ago we experienced an earthquake cluster event with magnitudes between 1.1 and 1.7, too small for us to feel, but enough to get the geologists worried. Even though seismic activity isn't always a sign of an imminent eruptive event, it's a purty convincin precursor." Nat let the curtains fall back into place.

"There are hundreds of volcanoes around the world, only a small portion of them active, but what sets ours apart is the prophecy attached to it." A calculated pause ensued during which Don Pancho swallowed hard.

"A long time ago in this very town, there lived a priest who not only predicted the volcano, but said that one day our modest little volcán would set every volcano in the entire world into motion."

"¿You mean it's the detonator?" said DP. Nat had drawn him into the narrative and now he was its captive.

She flared her eyebrows. "Exactly. There's a local cult that lives up in the hills. They believe these volcanic events will bring about the end of the world, but modern science disagrees. Vulcanologists can predict eruptions, thereby minimizin casualties. Here in Lava Landin we have an emergency plan. If one day our volcano were to get feisty, I don't know what I'd do with Sway." Natalie put her arm around her best, and in fact only friend in the world. "With her fear of public transportation and long car rides, she wouldn't be able to get far enough away to escape the danger and I just couldn't leave her here to get all burned up. I guess I'd have to get burned alive too."

DP sat down on the couch. He sighed, then did that sombrero-removing/hair-smoothing thing again. He was looking increasingly more his age. "I'll think about it. See what I can do," he concluded.

Nat and Sway hugged him.

"I gotta go. Lots of people depend on me and I have lots of work to do. You girls behave yourselves, ¿ay?" He kissed them both on top of the head, then walked through the front door (without opening it).

Once he was gone Sway said to Nat, "Just ¿how'd you know so much about volcanoes?"

"I like documentaries too," said Natalie.

El Baile Grande
The Big Dance

AHÍ NOS VEMOS EN EL BAILE GRANDE

OVER THERE AT THE BIG DANCE, WE WILL SEE ONE ANOTHER

TROUBLE IN PARADISE
AND HOW IT HELPED LULABELL
BECOME A DECENT WOMAN

"Jú y yo, ya no somos novios," said the just-getting-home Alberto to La Lulabell. He had had a hard and heavy day towing and it showed in his demeanor.

It was Friday, early afternoon, the day before the Baile Grande, and Lulabell was just putting the groceries away. She paused, put her hands on her hips, and said, "¿What'd you say that for?"

Beto was feeling a little uneasy, used to Lulabell in her huipil and huaraches, her hair in two tame trenzas, one at each side of her head, but there she was, obviously just having gotten home herself, in lipstick, minifalda and high heels, and con el pelo suelto.

"You're mine now, mujer," said Beto with another pound of the fist. "Somos esposos. ¿Me entiendes?"

Lulabell nodded, even though she didn't rightfully understand. Beto, being from the rancho as he was, and thinking as he did, what he and Lulabell had embarked upon was nothing less than matrimonio.

"¿How am I supposed to work all day knowing you're roaming the streets looking like that, giving gusto to cualquier cabrón?" he said taking note of Lulabell's bare legs. "A skirt goes down to here." He pointed to his own ankles. "You better put yourself right, woman, o ¡yo te pongo! Te meto una chinga."

"¡Ay-ay-ay!" said Lulabell. A man had never threatened her with physical violence before. The thought of Beto coming home, sweaty, tired, and impatient after a long day towing, grabbing her by the greñas, dragging her into the bedroom, or better yet, bringing her to her knees right there on the cold kitchen floor, then taking off his belt and giving her a good one, was novel if not appealing.

"¡Te acabo el cinto, mujer!"

"¡Ay-ay-ay!" said Lulabell yet again as she imagined Beto wasting an entire belt on her bare nalgas.

Lulabell had been all shawls and long skirts for at least two weeks, but with the way her suitors called at all hours of the night, it wasn't easy to keep the domestic tranquillity. (She had told them not to call, to leave her in paz, pero no le hicieron caso.)

But Lulabell was really trying to be a good mujer. She got up every day to make two home-cooked meals—one for Beto and one for Javier—since she knew that good motherhood was a sign of decent womanhood. And ¿the lunches? They weren't just cold meat between two pieces of bread, but rather, chiles rellenos, three-cheese enchiladas stuffed upright into a thermos so that they were still hot at whatever hour. She made all kinds of meat in any sort of sauce, and rolled it up in a corn or flour tortilla, and even sometimes stuffed it into a tamal.

Beto's tow truck was in the garage, his toothbrush in the jarrito atop the medicine cabinet, his robe hanging from the gancho on the bathroom door, his chanclas at her bedside, and from the looks of things, Beto was there to stay. But that afternoon, Lulabell's miniskirt sojourn had been the straw that broke the burro's back. Everything had happened so quick. No, wait, Beto had waited around for Lulabell for forty years, and then all of the sudden she was his, so it was a bit hard for him to take, and de vez en cuando, his jealousy got the best of him.

And now Beto walked calmly to the bedroom, where he began to pack his extra jumpsuits, along with his one good go-to-the-baile outfit and Stetson®. He grabbed the keys to the tow truck and headed for the door.

Lulabell threw herself to the floor and wrapped her arms around Beto's knees. "Don't leave, mi amor. I will be good. Te lo prometo."

"You don't know how to be good."

Lulabell momentarily was at a loss for words. "I will go to church, and I will learn how to be good. We can get up early on Sunday and go to misa."

"¡Pa' que sacas el pinche Demonio!"

Lulabell clasped her hands together. "I will go every day."

"It would do you good to suck the Demonio out of you, woman, ¡porque lo tienes bien clavado!"

"Mi amor . . ." pleaded Lulabell. "Put your keys down and let's go to bed."

"No," said Beto. "Ya me voy. The day you learn how to act like a Señora, una Señora de respeto, you let me know."

"Por favor," said Lulabell. "Pégame, pégame, pero no me dejes."

"Hit you. ¿How could I ever raise a hand to you?"

She shrugged. She didn't know, but had merely muttered the refrain she had heard a dozen times on the Mexican radio station as a last-ditch attempt to keep her Beto.

Beto took her in his arms. "Ay, cariño, I could never leave you."

"You had better not, because I'm in this thing for the long haul."

Beto smiled. Not only did he share the sentiment, but Lulabell had employed a metaphor only a towing man could fully appreciate.

"Prove it to me, viejo. I want you to show me that you will love me forever and never leave me," said Lulabell.

"¿Qué quieres que haga?" said Alberto.

"You're the man. You think of somethin."

"I will tell you a story," said Alberto running his hands through Lulabell's long hair.

"Sí," said Lulabell. They sat down on the couch.

Beto began, "Soy del rancho."

"I know. You have told me so a million times."

"Because I am from the rancho, I know how all of the animals make love." He grinned in a way that Lulabell found extremely attractive and enticing.

"¿Every single one?"

"Sí, mi amor. Every single one."

"Y ¿los burros?" said Lulabell.

"Oh, they are the ugliest ones of all, for el burro, has it really big, lo trae pero bien grande, and the burra, she cries when he does it to her."

"Oh," said Lulabell disappointed.

"It is the same with the cows, only it takes them days."

"That is worse yet. Y ¿los gallos?"

"They do it very quick. It is over in a few minutes, or even less."

"Y ¿los caballos?"

"Same as the burros."

Lulabell thought hard. She wanted to come up with an animal that Alberto didn't know anything about.

"¿How about the guajolotes?" she said with a smile, as if she had finally stumped him.

Beto smiled. "The turkeys are the best of all. The turkey gets on top of the guajolota, and once they are as they should be, he opens up all of his feathers, and he wraps them around her, until you can only see her face."

"Es bonito," said Lulabell.

"Sí. Es bonito," agreed Beto.

"I like the turkeys the best," said Lulabell. "You are my turkeycito."

"And you are my guajolotita," said Alberto, taking her in his arms, covering her up, carrying her off to bed.

Once they were on the way, Lulabell said, "Viejo, ¿do you think you can take me to the Baile Grande?"

"Claro que sí, mi amor. I have been planning on it."

CHARACTER

Lucha sat on her fuzzy pink bed, filing her silver fingernails to a seductive point, when she was interrupted by a stirring near her open bedroom window. So many had trod the beaten path to her sill, but still, a girl can never be too careful. She reached under her bed, grabbed the .45, then tiptoed to the window with the gun at her side, only to be surprised by a mariachi all fanned out in the perfect position for a serenade. It was a real mariachi this time, for there, in the corner, stood a harp—the instrument which separates the boys from the mariachis.

Lucha was so shocked to find such a grand ensemble assembled on her behalf that she dropped the .45 carelessly in the geranium-filled window box. She looked left, right, then straight ahead, trying to find Javier. He was certainly behind all of this, even though he wasn't behind the guitarrón—that spot being filled by a short, chubby, pudgy-fingered middle-aged man.

Her suspicions were momentarily confirmed as Javier emerged from behind the hydrangeas and gave the mariachi a start with a fist to the air. That evening seven bows stabbed the just setting sun as the violin section strummed out the opening notes of "Entrega Total."

Lucha was no connoisseur of mariachi, but she had a working knowledge and a commensurate appreciation for the classics. It was a song that Javier's namesake had made famous and it conveyed approximately the same sentiment as the Marvin Gaye hit "Let's Get It On," only it went about expressing it in a more elegant and antiquated fashion.

Javier's voice commenced velvety smooth, but by the second verse, it had taken on an air of urgency, and now he was singing through clenched teeth, his back arched in an exaggerated fashion so that he might gather air to propel his vocal momentum. And then just as quickly as it began, the song was over and with it the serenade. Lucha watched sadly as the twelve-piece mariachi ensemble walked bowlegged into the sunset. Javier got on tippy toes, grabbed the wrought iron flower boxes for balance, and rose to give her a kiss.

"Evening, princess," he said, his eyes poised in a squint.

"¿What the hell happened to your face?" It wasn't exactly the response he'd hoped for, especially given that Lucha had been, at least in part, responsible for the bruises he still bore beneath his eyes.

"¿You don't like it? Beto says it gives a man like me character," he said proudly.

"You already got too much character."

"¿You really think so?" He took it as a compliment. "Look what I got," he said reaching into the pocket of his suit coat. "Gran agarrón de tuba y acordeón," he said, holding up two tickets to the Baile Grande.

Lucha stared at him long and hard. He was right handsome and a musician no less, but still plain old goody-two-shoes Javier. It was this very two-out-of-three-ness that led her to conclude, "I ain't goin."

"Sure you are." He slid the tickets back into his pocket and smiled. But that reminded him of something. "Just ¿who is that vato you've been keeping time with?" The rumors now were rampant. Lucha'd been seen all over town with Joaquín.

"I told you, he's my brother," she said raising her eyebrows and her voice.

"Let me tell you something, mujer. Yo no soy ningún pendejo."

"¿Oh, no?" The window screen was absent allowing Lucha to lean out toward Javier. "That's what we all say. That we're not pendejos." She tapped an index finger against her head. "We go through life thinkin we got a big 'S' on our chests como el Superman, when en realidad we got a big 'P' across our foreheads."

"Cálmate," said Javier. He raised his arms up offering to lift her out.

"I ain't goin nowhere with you." She leaned backwards.

Javier looked down and saw the .45 lying innocently in the flower bed. He dipped two fingers into the window-side geraniums and came up with the gun, which dangled from his thumb and index finger. "Sister Lucha, ¿what is this doing here?"

Lucha considered two equally implausible lies:

1. It belongs to my cousin, and he has been looking everywhere for it.
2. I have absolutely no idea how that got there.

She chose number two. Javier put the .45 in his pocket, then said, "Ándale, mamacita, the Lord brought us together for a reason."

Lucha kneeled down, then rested first her hands then her chin on the windowsill. "One minute it's Ándale, mamacita, the next it's The Lord wants it like that. ¿Which is it gonna be, hermano? Because it sounds like you're tryin to serve two masters."

"¿Which way do you like better?" he queried.

"I like, we had our fun y todo se acabó. Cada quien por su lado y que te vaya bien."

"But, you were born to be mine. That's why the Lord crossed our paths."

"He crossed more than our paths, little brother."

With such a knowing twinkle in her eye, Javier had to wonder: ¿Had Lulabell shared with her the secret she'd shared with him? And if Lucha knew, ¿did she know he knew? And if she knew he knew, ¿did she also know he knew she knew he knew? My, what a tangled web he'd woven. No. Javier stood corrected. The web'd been woven years before and he wasn't its weaver, but its victim.

"Big brother," he countered.

"Little."

"Have it your way," said Javier cool and collectedly. Then he did a strange thing. He sat down right smack dab on the ground, fancy western-tailored-about-to-debut-at-the-baile suit and all, facing the hydrangeas, with his legs folded under Indian style—at least that's what they called it when Javier was in kindergarten and he played his first game of Duck, Duck, Goose. Natalie had been It, and she had walked tentatively around the circle perhaps three or four times, until finally she named him Goose. He chased, then caught her, and felt so bad when she had to go in the middle of the circle to be cooked.

From that moment on, he never looked at her in the same way. About a week later, he dreamt about her. When they were in the second grade, he cried when she danced the Mexican hat dance with another boy. (In Lava Landing, every second grade class for more than fifty years had had to learn el Jarabe Tapatío.) In the third grade he stuck a hand down her panties because, well, he was curious about little girls' underpants. In the fourth grade, he turned mean and made fun of her until she cried, Consuelo beat him up, and then he cried. To get beat up by a girl. ¡Qué horror! ¡Qué vergüenza! ¡Qué . . . ¿bonito? ¿Was that what it was like for Beto and Lulabell? ¡Ay! ¡Qué beautiful! to have loved the same woman for so many years.

But Javier didn't love Natalie anymore. At least not like that. Their recent fish kiss was enough to prove it to him. But he did ¿love her?

So many things had changed, so many had remained the same. Now he ¿loved? Lucha. He looked over his shoulder. She was sitting on her windowsill with her legs dangling over the edge. She looked so luscious, every article of her clothing at least a size too small, readily betraying what lay beneath.

He stared at her so intently he failed to blink long enough for his eyes to water, and his vision to blur. Then his mind did a cruel thing: It went on a treacherous tangent and pretty soon Javier was imagining a very bad scene which was seemingly unfolding right before his very eyes.

He saw himself walking out to the Monte Carlo to fetch his guitarrón, then serenading Lucha, not a love song, but a tragi-corrido about a man and woman who fall madly in love with one another, but kill themselves after they discover that they are, in fact, brother and sister. There was such a song, and it had been so popular during its day and age that a movie based upon it was eventually made.

Javier had seen the movie. It was called *La Hija de Nadie* and it starred Yolanda del Río, the singer who had made the song of the same name famous.

This is what happens in the movie: Yolanda is born in the Mexican state of Hidalgo along with her twin sister, Inés. Their father abandons them and their mother because he doesn't want a daughter let alone two, but he is not entirely against the idea of fatherhood, so he takes his only other child, a son, with him.

Yolanda and Inés grow up poor in Mexico, without the benefit of a father, in a time and place where having one's father is such a given, the children at school make fun of them because theirs isn't around.

When the girls are teenagers, they immigrate to the United States with their mother. All three work in a factory. Things are looking up for the family when Yolanda enters and wins a singing competition. But then her mother falls down a flight of stairs and dies suddenly. Inés goes blind from the shock.

Yolanda has little choice but to concentrate on her music. She starts crying as she sings, a surefire way to launch a career as a ranchera singer. Pretty soon she is able to afford an experimental operation for Inés. The operation is ultimately unsuccessful, but one day while on her daily walk around the hospital grounds, Inés runs into the gardener. They knock heads and she is thus returned to the world of the seeing. After not having set sight on anything for so long, she falls madly in love with the gardener. The two are set to get married, but find out that ¡they are brother and sister! Ashamed of their unspeakable sin and well aware that their illicit love affair can't go on, they kill themselves leaving Yolandita all alone in the cruel, cruel world with nothing to do but sing about it.

Javier blinked several times to clear his vision, then put his hand over his heart, which was beating far too fast for its own good. A little below his heart, he could feel the outline of the .45 lying in the interior pocket of his suit coat. He rose slowly to his feet and dusted off his slacks. Methodically, he took his sombrero off and wrangled his hair into place, then put the hat back on and cocked it. He stared at Lucha, stroked his mustache three or four times with thumb and forefinger, then said, "I wanted us to live happily ever after, para siempre."

Lucha pulled the cigarette she had discreetly stashed behind her ear, then reached into her cowboy boots for her Zippo®. She ran the lighter southbound along the length of her thigh, then held the ensuing flame up to the Marlboro® Red that dangled from the corner of her mouth. She closed her eyes as she inhaled deeply. "¿What do I want with happily ever after? It's Saturday night and I am going to the Baile Grande. By myself," she declared.

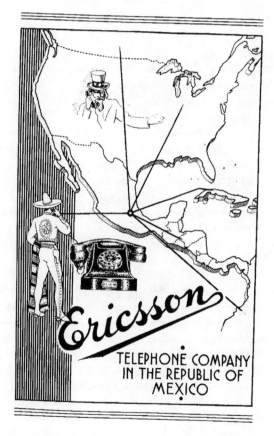

THE BAILE GRANDE:
A PRESENT-TENSE ACCOUNT

Natalie and Consuelo

"Sometimes, Sway, I swear to God, I wish, we were bears, so we could hibernate the winter," says Natalie to Consuelo. She is painting her nails, pausing between brush strokes. The girls are making final primperations for the Baile Grande.

"That would be a disastrophe," says Consuelo. "Imagine me goin about tryin to find food. The fish would likely swim upstream out of my range. But I do like the bit about hibernatin."

In Lava Landing, there is a mixed message in the air. The BG is a joyous event, make no mistakes. Imagine this if you will: five thousand ranch hands and day laborers from the tri-city area that is Lava County dressed up in their very best, piling into an exhibit hall at the Lava County Fairgrounds, which, earlier that year, held home-baked, thick-crusted apple pies, jams and jellies, gingerbread men and houses, candy and other such confectionery delights, quilts, pillows, sweaters, science experiments, and prize-winning flowers put on show by county residents. But the exhibit hall named after some white, wealthy, upstanding onetime resident of Lava County, a Jones, Murphy, Kennedy, or other, has all of the sudden become the site of un Gran Bailaso.

But once the dance is over, so is summer. Sure the Indian summer pow-wows until December, but summer is more about footloose fancy freedom than it is about weather. The day after the BG, everyone rushes to the taquería and orders menudo so as to cure their crudas, but after, the ranch hands and day laborers put their heads down and it's puro trabajar from there on until diciembre when they all board Mexicana® flights home.

Nat leans over the bathroom sink toward the mirror, squints and applies a bit of Superfrost® to her left lid. "Winter is way too borin for my taste," she says.

"Mine too. And I just hate the way we can't convertible no more."

Lucha y Fabiola

After Lucha leaves Javier fiddling with her pistola, she heads first for El Charrito Market where she buys two tickets to the Baile Grande, then for Fabiola's. She walks through the door, and into the kitchen where Doña Lupe is doing dinner's dishes.

"¿Cómo 'stás, tía?" She pauses to give her aunt a kiss.

Down the hall the walls are lined with Favy's school pictures: Favy with more freckles than usual, missing one front tooth, in stripes, in a foo-foo-rufoo dress, going through an awkward stage, her hair the color of urine and carrots, then Favy all of the sudden point-of-no-return lovely, with dark hair and honey-colored skin.

Fabiola is on her bed watching *Sábado Gigante*. Ana Gabriel is singing "México Lindo," and ¿wouldn't ya know it? La Favy is singing along. "México lindo y querido . . ." she trails off as the door opens full swing.

Lucha hasn't heard Favy sing in more than fifteen years, and all she can do is stand by with arms folded, listening, watching, and wondering how many times Favy has sung alone without anyone knowing about it. ¿Is this something that has happened all of the sudden, or something that happened a long time ago, but never got noticed?

Fabiola watches intently as if the television set is teaching her something. Her singing is lovely, yet methodical.

Lucha grabs Favy by the shoulders so that she is facing her and says, "¿You wanna go home, Favy? That's it, ¿isn't it?"

Fabiola nods. "I wanna go to Metzico."

Not Mexico, or even México, but Metzico, a place that's on nobody's map.

Favy opens up her bedside drawer and pulls out her .45.

"You wanna kill him, ¿don't you?"

"Sí. Lo quiero matar," says Favy.

Lucha begins to remember things: the way Favy always turned the radio up in the truck when a good rollicking corrido came on, how much she loved her gun, the way that, when they went to rent movies at Video Azteca on Tuesdays when they were dos por el precio de una, Favy always chose the modern-day shoot-'em-up películas as opposed to the old funny black and white movies Lucha loved. It all of the sudden makes sense. La Señora Linda was right all along. What Favy needs is good old-fashioned venganza.

"First we finish our business, then we head south. Anything you want, Favy."

"I wanna kill him bien dead," repeats Favy. She flares her eyebrows and smiles.

"We will," Lucha reassures. Maybe somebody will even write a corrido about them.

Lucha flashes two tickets to the BG. "Look what I got, prima. Vamos al baile."

"Cosa segura," says Favy. She gets to her feet. She is in jeans, a V-neck T-shirt, and her fuzzy pink slippers. She walks to the closet and pulls out a pair of studded, purple bell-bottomed jeans, and a pair of suede high-heeled cowboy boots. Her candy-striped T matches just fine. She puts on a thin, metal gold-toned belt with a heart-shaped buckle. Her sense of style is situated in the same decade she stored her speech so many years.

Beto y Chulabell

"You are my Chulabell," says Beto to Lulabell. It's what he calls her when mi amor, cariño, mi vidita, or vieja simply won't do. He has his Stetson® on, his good silk Sunday shirt, his jeans, and his fancy boots, which are no longer fancy, and haven't been for about fifteen years.

"And you are my gordito," she says. They are still high from the mutual love spell they put on one another two days previous when, in the morning, they had gone their separate ways as though they were Christmas shopping for each other at the same store. With a list in hand, they split up to perform their private chores, only to meet again in some predetermined spot with a matching grin on their faces, before they fell into bed and enjoyed the spoils.

And now Beto is putting on his cologne, the Brut® from the five-piece gift set his mother gives him every year at Christmas, and they are getting ready to go not just to the baile, but the Baile Grande. To think they haven't danced together since the second grade.

Nat and Sway

The drive to the dance is uneventful, the line to get into the fairgrounds parking lot backed up for two miles. A narco-corrido plays from the Cadillac's stereo. Nat and Sway look so unexpected, two divine women singing along to a polka about drug traffickers in an out-of-date luxury car.

Once inside the parking lot, Sway dips down into her pocket for two dollars to pay the attendant. They walk to the dance hall, their cowboy boots hitting the pavement with an impressive thud as they head toward the entrance. If a girl wants a good dancer, then she wants a boy bien ranchero, straight from the rancho, ¡sí señores!, and for that, she has to dress the part.

Nat loops her arm in Sway's drawing a strange look from Consuelo. They have been best friends for twenty years and counting, but have never looped arms like that before. For Sway it's strange and kind of freaky, like holding hands.

"Sway, this is how they do it in Mexico. All the girls. Someday we might go back together and you oughtta know how to act."

Consuelo agrees. They bypass all the taco and souvenir stands arm in arm until they enter the dance hall where Banda El Mexicano is on stage, and even though the quebradita is several years out of vogue, everyone is going at it as if it were 1993.

Toda la Bola
Los Huracanes del Norte take the stage and it's what everybody is waiting for. The man behind the guitar is about to bust the lapels on his fancy leather, western-tailored suit from having consumed too many tacos, tortas, chiles rellenos, tostadas, enchiladas, tamales, sopes, gorditas, hamburguesas, hot dogs con tocino, from having hunched over too many cazuelas de menudo (¡Ay! qué rico), pozole, cocido, y caldo de camarón, from having dipped too many pieces of pan dulce in too many tazas de chocolate. That's why he's such a gordito, pero un gordito bien alegre y de buena onda.

El momento que everybody has been waiting for, ya llegó. There are laser lights, drum rolls, videos, smoke, rocket launcher noises, and things that even onomatopoeia cannot describe. A voice refined in broadcaster school echoes and Dopplers proclaiming that en el año mil novecientos something or other, ¡llegó una sensación norteña! Then comes the popurrico (un potpourri bien rico) of Los Huracanes' greatest hits. The gritos fly. There are recorded bits and pieces of songs about drug traffickers ("Clave Privado"), cuckoldry ("El 911"), las queridas madres ("Por el Amor a Mi Madre"), about being ranchero and proud ("El Ranchero Chido"), about the parranda ("El Troquero"), love lost, love gained, love gained then lost, lost then gained ("Volver, Volver"), about overcoming poverty by whatever means ("Doble Fondo Carga Pesada"), about death ("Cruz de Madera"), fast horses ("La Leona y El Carcomido"), about patriotism/regionalism ("Hijo de La Sierra"), about witchcraft ("Embrujado"), revenge ("Venganza del Viejito"), about back-stabbing soplones ("Informe del DEA"), about las grupis ("La Musiquera"), about a bad childhood ("Huérfano y Perdido"), and about loyalty ("Los Tres Amigos").

The introduction is done. The live music begins as the rhinestone-encrusted accordions (there are three) wax and wane, the saxofón does its saxofón thing, the drums don't stop, the bajo sexto thumps, and it's so rock and roll it's más rock and roll que el mero rocanról.

The crowd begins at the stage and extends two thirds of the way throughout the hall, headed for the back wall. One song keeps all in awe. Everyone looks straight ahead with subtle smiles upon their faces. The saludos come in between songs: Un saludo pa' toda la gente de Guanajuato; los amigos de Durango, ¿dónde andan?; y ¡arriba Sinaloa!; no se me raje Jalisco; a mis amigos de San Luis Potosí, la raza de Michoacán no se me queda, y arriba México, compa. En fin, ¡qué viva México!

And all of the sudden you're not a gardener, a "yanitór," a cook, a maid, un carpintero. You don't work at the car "watch," or en la canería, in the fields piscando las strawberries, los tomates, chiles, and whatever else is in season, en las huertas pulling, shaking, then bucketing the fruit from the trees. You don't fry up the tortillas todo el pinche día from the small confines of the lonchera. You're not a stucco slapper, a tile layer, a paver, a jackhammer operator. You're not somebody that does what no one else will do. But most of all: Ya no eres un pobre muerto de hambre sin donde cayerte muerto (You are not no more a poor dead of hunger without no place to fall you down dead . . .) You are whatever you wanna be.

And why even bother being beautiful when you are as pretty as Natalie and Consuelo. With beauty comes harshness and unapproachability. Being lovely is all about being delicate, soft, and sweet, about being a surprise every time. Beautiful you come to expect. It gets boring after a while, if it's not too busy taking years off a man's life, or a woman's for that matter.

There is nothing false alarm about Natalie and Consuelo. When the boys turn to follow their silhouettes, they are never disappointed by ugly faces, or flat chests.

Favy and Lucha arrive and prop themselves up against the wall, one sipping jamaica, the other horchata. If one had to choose, Favy is the pretty one. She is tall and the kind of thin that if you put a thumb and index finger around her wrist, you'd be surprised when they met, the kind of lithe your grandmother would call dainty. Her hair, hip-grazing, straight, fine, and the color of rust. Hers is a lovely that comes from the epoch of the high cheekbones.

Lucha's skin is copper, her eyes deep, dark, and almond-shaped. It's her body that's most impressive. It comes in spurts: an enormous head of thick hair, a graceful neck, jutting breasts, a slim abdomen, billowing hips, rounded out by a pair of slender legs. She is like a poem where every other line rhymes. She has always been so plentiful and therefore can't remember a time in which men weren't reaching out for her.

There are other women too. The one-dress ladies, wearing the same taffeta dress with the shoes dyed to match that they wore to Magda's quinceañera, Leti's wedding, uncle Pato's retirement party. The girls with the shirts so short they show their ombligos, who will empty out to the parking lot upon invitation to show the boys other things as well. The girls that came with boys, the ones that didn't. Las muchachas recién llegadas de México, much shyer than the rest of the bunch and with their hair still so long, it's past their nalgas. The transvestis, stuffed into their outfits, sparkling from head to toe, trying to make up for what nature didn't give them. (And by the way, ¿where is True-Dee? Natalie and Consuelo wonder out loud as they pass the transvestites who are clustered in the corner by the men's rest room.)

And then the boys . . . Los muchachos nacidos en Los Estados Unidos who have all of the sudden taken a liking to la música de sus papás. The rockeros with their fresa attitudes, pierced ears, and slicked-back hair. Los cholos rancheros with the cowboy boots and hats y los baggy pants. Everyone is there. Even the no speak a nada Spanish, country 'n' western set can appreciate the accordions of norteño music.

No three months pass quicker and none are more work-ridden than September, October, and November. Es for eso que everybody goes to the BG.

Los Huracanes are three songs into their set. There is a point during every dance, be it a dance hall dance, a quinceañera, a boda, or even a big dance, when the boys just arrive and they are shy. But give them an hour or so in Compalandia, that fictional place which really exists, where there is drink, food, and more than anything else paisanos, and they really let loose. This is the best part of the evening. Their inhibitions are down just enough to ask a divine woman to dance.

And two are knocking on Nat and Sway's door, arms extended they are saying, "¿Bailamos?"

No sense in being picky. Just so long as he's tall enough, he doesn't stink, and his intentions seem honorable, go right ahead, chiquita. You don't want to wait too long. Leave a man in Compalandia and he's bound to fall in love with his buddy and his beer instead of you.

Natalie grabs the hand that reaches out for her, and Sway does the same, and they dance, right there, no making their way to the designated area, because everyone is dancing everywhere.

In its going on four-hundred-year history, the waltz has never been treated like this. The boys grab the girls, and if the girls like the boys, they get close, very very close. Hips sway to the sound of the accordions and saxophones. Boys sing in girls' ears. The rhythm moves to a polka, the gritos fly.

Gustavo, Natalie's dancer, says to her, "¿Cómo te llamas?" as they bounce to the twang.

She tells the truth.

He squeezes her hand and opens up the dancing bridge just long enough to look at her and say, "Ay, mamacita, chula de mi vida, lánzame los ojos."

Nat knows just how to do it. The way the eyes bow down, open slowly, then come straight up, before batting, then staring longingly at their subject.

"¡Estás re-cáte-chula!" he says through his teeth as he hungry-eyes her. His eyes are handsome and she likes the way he wears the hair on his face. She guesses he is from the state of Jalisco.

It occurs to Nat that she is in the happiest place in the world.

Sway thinks the same thing and it shows as she smiles and beams until her dancer declares that she has una sonrisa de Colgate®. All night long he proclaims it, una sonrisa de Colgate®. And even though Sway can scarcely make it around the block without getting bored, and/or even sometimes winded if she tries to get the task done too soon, she manages to dance zapateados, quebraditas, cumbias, rancheras, and norteñas for more than an hour without so much as stopping to wipe the sweat from her brow.

His name is Erubiel and Sway wonders if she called him Rubi, ¿would he be offended? Both she and Nat know they can dance with any boy in the place. The realization makes them ever more aware of themselves. They can feel the swing of their hips as they dance arm in arm, as they twirl in and out of the vueltas.

La Lulabell is beautiful, and couldn't be more so even if she were penned and painted by Jesús Helgüera. She is learning how to curb this tendency, this blessing, curse, or whatever it is, which is becoming more fierce with age. She wears little makeup, combs her hair into braids, and uses a shawl for its intended purpose. Lulabell knows that if a beautiful woman is careful, she can become pretty with age, instead of ferocious.

But Beto seems most concerned with his platter of super-nachos. Lulabell fiddles with the fringe of her shawl as they sit as near the snack bar as possible. All of the sudden Beto licks his fingers and surprises her. He grabs her hand and rushes her to the floor. It's frightening at first. Her heart starts to beat so fast, that if it kept it up, it would surely wear itself out. Beto wipes his hands on his pants a few times, then drags the back of his right hand across his mouth, stands up straight, then takes her in his arms. He moves her with confidence. Dance floor equality hasn't progressed. A woman still must follow a man's lead, and Lulabell is surprised how well Beto maneuvers her. It's all strangely familiar. Suffice to say, he isn't the best dancer she has ever had. She misses the flash she once encountered in earlier arms, the way a young man will make a vuelta last forever, how he will spin you and spin you before finishing you off by dipping you down toward the floor.

"Beto, ¿have you ever watched old people dance?" she says.

"I don't think so, vieja. Not really."

"Well I have watched them a lot. That's how I feel with you. Like we've been dancin together forever."

He looks down at her. "I have been dancing with you forever, mi niñita." He has taken it as a compliment. Lulabell might have prefaced her comment with, "I hate to say it, viejo, but . . ." But she didn't. His response is sweet, but boring. Lulabell is too comfortable, perhaps even restless in his arms. ¿Is this really what she's cut out for, or does she need always to be seeking out nuevos horizontes? In that instant she imagines a horizon which doesn't have Beto's short, fat self rising to meet it, and it frightens her. She squeezes him tight.

Lucha and Favy are still propped up against the same wall. Lucha has all the tools necessary to a lady, but she has chosen a different path. No dancer is good enough for her. She sums the men up through squinting eyes. One is too corriente, the other too indio, another too ranchero, and yet another is just plain naco.

Los Huracanes finish their set to a chant of otra-otra-otra-otra. They oblige with a couple more songs until the DJ puts on a Chalino Sánchez tune. This gets the gritos going.

And now Favy all of the sudden wants to dance. Chalino Sánchez has been dead for more than ten years. Born en el estado de Sinaloa, when he was just eleven, his fifteen-year-old sister was kidnapped and raped. Chalino waited until he had fifteen years himself, then he hunted that bad man down and killed him, dándole dos tiros en la pura cabeza. But the thing is this: You don't just go kicking up dirt with one man, but his entire familia. Chalino had to put some distancia between himself and his pueblo. He headed pa' el otro lado where he worked doing what one does: picking this and that. He wrote songs on the side. Le sorprendía que las peoples would pay him to write songs about sus vidas. Vendían su música en la Swap Meet. Pretty soon he was famoso. En Los Angeles, he sold out every baile he played. He never took the stage without his pistola and it was a good thing on more than a few occasions. They wanted to see him back in Sinaloa, and even though he knew it wasn't such a good idea, he obliged. His show was sold out by 6:00 p.m. They had to close the doors, and this in Mexico, a place where the Fire Code is either ignored, bought, or nonexistent. After the show, they pulled him from the arms of a beautiful woman, blindfolded, then shot him twice in the head. The next morning, he was found in a ditch by two campesinos.

Chalino wasn't handsome and he sang like a goat con la gripa. Pero ni modo. The kids started playing him from the stereos of their lowered pickups, they started wearing their hats cockeyed like he did, as if the carefully placed plume of feathers on the side of the Stetson® had somehow weighed it down.

Fabiola knows and appreciates Chalino's story, but she doesn't know how to dance. ¿What is she thinking? Go figure, she can hardly speak. One-two, one-two, one-two, put a little bounce in it if you so desire, or be straight up, rigid, and elegant, depending on your mood, chiquita. In this and other things, you will do fine.

And this is the Baile Grande, damas y caballeros, where everything and nothing happens. When it is all over, there are hundreds of pieces of gum stuck to the hardwood floors, and thousands of scuff marks from so many cowboy boots y high heels. A sea of Stetson®s heads for the parking lot. The next day people begin the figurative packing of their bags, those left behind have to wait until next spring when there is a new crop of ranch hands and day laborers that flood the dance floors every Saturday night yet again, and who do all of the things no one else will do the rest of the week, and sometimes even on Sundays.

Tarascan Indian—Michoacán

THE DRIVER'S SEAT

Javier sat in the Monte Carlo in front of Lucha's house long after she sped off. He held the .45 in his hand. Right-left-right-left-right-left. He had never held a gun before, not even a squirt gun, and he was surprised that it felt just as heavy in his hand as his Bible, but unlike his Bible, the .45 fit comfortably in the inside pocket of his suit coat.

He turned the Monte Carlo over, turned it around, and headed up the street. He might have had two tickets to the Baile Grande, a nice new suit, exotic-skin boots, an expensive hat, a pocketful of cash, and a pistol in his pocket, but missing was the most important element of all: the girl.

He headed for El Zarape where he muttered an inert "darn" as he read the sign on the nightclub door. "Sorry. We're closed para el Baile Grande."

He made a U-turn and headed to El Aguantador and a different scene entirely. The parking lot was overflowing, not just with cars, but people. He pulled into the first available space, then cupped an imaginary hand to his ear. ¿Was that live music he heard? He rolled the window down. Sure enough, there was a conjunto norteño in the parking lot.

Inside the nightclub proper, things were in full swing. Javier had probability on his side. There were so many people there and he needed just one little chickadee, a single lone chiquitita to use his extra ticket and his newfound moves upon. Everyone was there it seemed—everyone who couldn't get a date to the Baile Grande, or who was too cheap to pay for a ticket, that is.

Javier wanted a beer—to have something to hold on to, to give his hands something to do. But there was no stray mesera to flag down, to grab by an elbow and say, "Me traes una cerveza cuando tengas tiempo, ¡mamacita!"

He slumped up against the nightclub wall, causing a stir at a nearby table where seven older women pointed and giggled. He put his hands in his pockets, then removed them, shifted his weight from his left foot to his right, then back again. He had never gone to the Baile Grande before and knew that if he missed it, he would have to wait another year for the chance to make his debut.

There was a banda on stage, hardly Javier's preferred musical genre, but the delicacies of last night's dancing were coming back to him nonetheless: the delight of holding a strange woman in his arms, of breathing in deeply with his nostrils dangerously close to her neck, moving in closer and closer as the song progressed, then putting it all on hold to put some distance between the two, to pause to dance a cumbia or a quebradita, then waiting, even praying, for the banda to switch to a ranchera rhythm so he could take that young thing in his arms once again. Young thing. That was funny. Javier hadn't seen a single young thing all night, and now three women at the aforementioned table were looking his way, their upturned index fingers curling-and-straightening, curling-and-straightening, curling-and-straightening, beckoning Javier their way.

There was an empty seat at their table, from Javier's vantage point, the only one in sight, and a lingering mesera bent at the waist muttering the telltale phrase: ¿Algo para tomar? He walked over, sat down, ordered, "Una cerveza and whatever these nice ladies want, por favor," then opened up his wallet and placed a crisp one-hundred-dollar bill on the corner of the white tableclothed table.

Someone passed him a shot of tequila. He drank it down while the women rattled off their introductions. Clockwise, beginning at noon and going on into the live-long day: Marta, Janet, Cristina, Celia, Paula, Inés, and Carmelita. Javier announced his name. The women closed in. He slid his chair away from his two closest contenders, but audacity was seated clear across the table. She got up, walked around behind Javier, placed a hand on each of his shoulders, leaned over and said, "¿Bailamos?"

Never de los never de los neveres had a woman asked Javier to dance, not even when he put himself in Harm's way and went out with his mariachis to serenade at nightclubs, pool joints, penitentiaries, and other sinful spots. He downed a second shot of tequila, then followed his partner to the dance floor.

By Javier's estimation, she looked about seventy. Plug that into the standard dance floor formula (Apparent Age (.7) + seven years for extra wear and tear = Actual Age) to arrive at her true age of fifty-six. She was short and chubby—which is to say neither fat, nor pleasantly plump. Her hair, a mistake shade, a home hair dye disaster in an awful hue of orange—the telltale result of a brunette trying to go blonde with one fell swoop of the applicator bottle, failing, then not doing anything about it. To add insult to injury, she had a perm, presumably another home job. What was left of her hair looked like it had been through the sizzler, and to make it even crispier, she had applied several fare shares of Aqua Net®, extra-super-hold. Her clothing—the usual dance floor attire for a woman of her stature, of her combined state of deterioration and desperation: a miniskirt, a low-cut blouse in a shimmery synthetic fabric, seamed stockings, and a pair of toe-pinching pumps. Luckily, Javier wouldn't have to get close to her. They would be dancing within the safe confines of a cumbia.

In that moment it occurred to Javier that if Lulabell hadn't found true love, then maybe she might have ended up just like those women. ¿Was that what she was thinking when she gave Beto a chance? It saddened Javier and made his heart sink to think of his mother twenty years down the line, dressed like that, in a place like this.

They reached the dance floor. Javier looked Celia over. ¿Why such audacity? The answer: Women like Celia were an important part of the dance floor diaspora. A ranch hand of even slight savvy knows that a man gets further quicker with a woman like Celia. And with a woman like that, he runs less risk of falling in love—a time-and-money-consuming pursuit, and a big bad no-no for one who has a woman waiting for him patiently, albeit far away, at home. With all the lonely young ranch hands and day laborers in town with no intention of sticking around, but still looking for some short-term fun with neither promises nor demands, Celia was a hot commodity. In the Animal Kingdom, this dance floor phenomenon would be known as symbiosis.

Javier scanned the dance floor, but there were still no young chickadees in sight and Celia was getting closer, and closer, until pretty soon she was right up against him. "Mantenga su distancia, ¡Señora!" he said holding up his third-grade safety patrol sign for ¡Stop!—an extended arm with an upturned palm.

To Javier's relief, Celia merely wanted to do a vuelta, a mainstay move of the cumbia—she wanted to get just close enough to Javier to brush shoulders before turning around and switching places. With this accomplished, Javier got another view of the nightclub and there, at a far, far-away table was the prettiest, youngest thing in the place.

That was more like it. Javier didn't wait for the cumbia to end. He muttered a "gracias ay," then marched off.

In his fancy suit and hat and with a beer in his hand, Javier felt invincible. He made his way to that far, far-away table tucked conveniently in the corner. "¿Está ocupada?" he said gesturing toward an empty chair at her table. She turned around and smiled. A full head of shiny, just dyed hair can be so deceiving. Javier's countenance dropped. She was no young thing, but a middle-aged mamacita.

Her name was Xochitl. Hmmm . . . thought Javier. So-cheel, the word for flower in the ancient Aztec tongue. Another sign from the Divine. Javier sat down, scooted over, and threw an arm around his little buttercup.

She spoke English well, and it was a good thing because Javier didn't speak very good Spanish. Au contraire. He spoke near perfect Spanish which gave the listener every indication that he was book taught. Yet, his accent was off, he had an exceedingly difficult time riding out all of the diphthongs, and he occasionally even fell into the classic amateur's trap of literal translation.

Xochitl's English was rattled with all sorts of endearing little imperfections. Like when she haphazardly slipped a needless "e" before an "s." There was rhyme to her reason however—she only added the "e" when the "s" was followed by a consonant. That was the rule in her native language. Her tongue so used to rattling off especiales, estrellas, escándalos, and other et cetera, et ceteras, it was no wonder, when the mesera lingered over their table and said, "¿Algo para tomar?" Xochitl smiled and said, "Una e-Squirt® por favor."

Javier shook his head, and waved the mesera off. He knew when to say when—for a man who didn't drink, Javier'd had more than his share.

"¿What do you do?" asked Xochitl.

Javier wasn't about to give in to English. His tongue took a dive into literal translation as he claimed, "Soy un hombre de basura." A man of trash. Xochitl snickered. Javier should have stated simply and succinctly and with all the shoulders-back, head-held-high-in-the-air pride that his station in life deserved: Soy basurero.

There was renewed activity up front as the banda was replaced by five men and a woman. Then the music began. Javier had never heard anything like it. Seeing the eyes-wide-open-in-surprise look upon his face, Xochitl leaned in and said, "¿Te gusta la música de recuerdo?" So that's what it's called. Javier nodded.

The dancers flooded the floor. Javier paid close attention. "Let's get a little closer to the action," he said succumbing to English. He grabbed Xochitl by the hand. The musicians moved back and forth on stage with all the synchronicity of the Spinners. Javier had seen them on TV numerous Saturday mornings during his childhood on the Souuuuuul Train. Lulabell would slap the sofa and insist with her hands squeezed together in feigned prayer, and her head cocked convincingly to one side, "Please, mijo. Sit down and watch Donnie with me." Javier would have much preferred the other Donnie, the more wholesome Osmond over the Cornelius any day, the latter being so at the edge of something scary and unknown, he made Javier wriggle in his seat every time.

Xochitl and Javier stood at the edge of the dance floor, Javier watching the action, Xochitl frowning with arms folded, shifting her weight from one high heel to the other. Javier lowered his voice, looked Xochitl in the eye, and said, "¿Bailamos?"

They stepped off the carpet, over the aluminum threshold, and onto the dance floor. There was no sense in putting off the inevitable, of working up to that which comes only after several songs' worth of eager anticipation and numerous moments of crucial decision making. He took Xochitl in his arms and held her tight, so very, very tight. One inevitability led to another and pretty soon she put an open palm on the back of his neck, then laid her head on his shoulder, making it ever so convenient for him to let his own head hang low, first to rest an innocent chin on her shoulder, then to let his nose linger on her left clavicle, before his lips made their way to her neck where they initiated something even a cumbia couldn't break up. Javier was practicing the Golden Rule, he was doing unto her as he would have her do unto him. His prayers were answered momentarily as reciprocation began.

But with all that up close contact, pretty soon Xochitl was reaching inside Javier's suit coat trying to get a handle on what had been stabbing her in the ribs all night long.

"It's a gun," whispered Javier raising an index finger to his parted lips. He tried to scoop Xochitl up again, but she wouldn't have it.

"¡¿¡Una pistola!?!" said Xochitl—not with the eager enthusiastic curiosity of a young girl, but with all the alarm of a middle-aged mother of three.

"Don't worry about it, chiquita," said Javier.

"But ¿what are you doing with a gun?"

Javier paused to think before deciding to tell the truth. "I took it away from my sister. It's gotten her into trouble more than once. Now let's dance." Since the truth was so unbelievable it had to be true, Xochitl believed him. They resumed their dancing position.

"¿You have something else in your pocket you want to tell me about?" said Xochitl raising her eyebrows at Javier.

"No nothing, just my keys, my wallet, and two tickets to the Baile Grande."

"¿The Baile Grande?" said Xochitl. She came to life, then turned sad.

"Sí. El Baile Grande. But you wouldn't want to go because it's too late."

"No," said Xochitl. "It is late and you wouldn't want to take me anyway." She laid her head on his shoulder so that he couldn't see the sadness in her eyes. The place was filled with middle-aged dancers and those even old enough to qualify for a discount at a diner. If the BG hadn't been in town, they might have been younger, but at fifty-one, Xochitl knew she could only rely on hooking up with a hot young papacito if he had just one thing in mind. Pobre de La Xochitl. Gone were the days in which she would have her choice of handsome young things with whom to go to the Baile Grande.

"¿Who was the extra ticket for?" asked Xochitl as they made their way back to the table.

"It was for my sister," said Javier.

"Your sister ¿ay? I've never heard that one before, and I have heard lots of sad and sometimes crazy e-stories from young men like you."

"It's sad and it's crazy, but it's true. I didn't know she was my sister when I met her. I found out later."

"You met a girl, maybe even at a place like this." She gestured to their surroundings.

"I met her when she was in jail and my mariachis went to the prison to play for the lady inmates."

"You don't look like a mariachi," said Xochitl.

"When I put on my traje de charro, I do."

"That's not what I mean. You might be dressed like some of the other guys in here, but you are not one of them even with a gun in your pocket."

"¿You don't think so?" said Javier, unsure if he should be flattered or offended.

"No," said Xochitl. "And I have been doing this for a long time. Coming here for a long time."

"But ¿why would you want to keep coming to a place like this?" said Javier.

Xochitl leaned in closer. "Because it is fun. Because I like it when a man I hardly know pays attention to me." There was absolutely nothing apologetic in her tone.

"That might be fun for a little while," said Javier. "But ¿don't you get bored?"

"A woman like me doesn't change. For me this never gets old."

"¿You never got married or anything?"

"Yes, I did, and I have three beautiful daughters to show for it."

They stood up. They walked to the dance floor. They danced. There was no more kissing, no more neck licking, no more firm squeezing, no more restless hands all over either of their bodies, there was just dancing.

At the end of the night when the lights came on, Xochitl looked even older, even tireder. The band said good night as everyone rushed back to their tables to finish off their high-priced drinks, before the nightclub personnel told them something they already knew—that it was time to go home.

Javier held Xochitl's hand as they walked toward the exit. "¿Can I take you home?" he said.

"I would appreciate it," she said. "But only if you let me drive."

"Of course." He gave Xochitl the keys as they approached the Monte Carlo.

"Nice car," she said unlocking the doors, Javier's side first.

"A classic," said Javier.

They boarded the MC. Xochitl lived just around the corner, so close, in fact, she had arrived at the nightclub earlier that evening on foot.

"I will walk you to the door," said Javier.

"Okay."

They lingered at her front door for a moment before Javier leaned over and gave her a kiss on the cheek, followed by another, and another, and another, until they finally led to a kiss on the lips.

"¿Do you think you could give me your phone number?" he said.

"I don't ever give anyone my phone number." She stepped into her apartment.

"Maybe I can come and visit you sometime," said Javier.

"I would like that," said Xochitl.

Javier leaned over and gave her another kiss on the cheek. "Thank you," he said. "I had a wonderful time."

"I did too."

Javier headed for the stairs, then paused to look over his shoulder. "Thank you," he said again, even though Xochitl had already shut the door. She had soothed something in Javier, really soothed something in him, and for that he was grateful.

Promociones de Oro Presenta

UN BAILASO DE CALIBRE

⋆ Gran Agarrón de Tuba y ⋆
Acordeón

LOS HURACANES DEL NORTE

BANDA MACHOS

Los Cadetes de Linares

BANDA EL MEXICANO

EN LOS TERENOS DE LA FERI

DE AGOSTO DESDE LAS 7:00

MÚSICA DE DJ EN LOS INTERMEDIOS

Boletos en Lugares de Costumbr

ONLY!

Sábado
24

Call Para más información 546-2397

Tabla 6

THE PLAYERS SIT *in a* CIRCLE
FACING EACH OTHER WHILE
the UNIVERSE WHISPERS,
"YOU'RE GONNA HAVE TO PAY TO SEE MY HAND"

El Tocadiscos
The Record Player

TÓCAME UN DISCO BONITO, AUNQUE SEA VIEJO

PLAY ME A LOVELY RECORD, EVEN IF IT'S OLD

THE LAST DANCE

When Javier got home, he was surprised to find Lulabell still awake and lying on the couch.

"¿That you, mijo?" she said.

"¿What are you still doing up, momma?"

"Oh nothin, hijo. I couldn't sleep that's all." The phonograph was going. She was listening to Agustín Lara.

She took hold of Javier's chin, then moved his face from side to side. He had had those black eyes for over a week, but she still couldn't get used to seeing him like that. "I'm sure thankful they didn't get to your teeth because I left every single one of them for the ratoncito," she said.

"¿The ratoncito?" repeated Javier.

"Sí, mijo. ¿I never told you about him?"

Javier shook his head.

"Well get comfortable and I'll tell you the story."

Javier pulled the .45 from the inside pocket of his suit coat, then took his hat off and set both down on the coffee table.

"¡Ay! mijo. ¿Now you're carryin a gun?"

"Don't worry. I'm not gonna do anything with it."

"It's not the gun that worries me. Lots of people carry them. Beto has two or three. Of course, in his line of work it's necessary. But, mijo you're changin overnight."

"Just tell me about the ratoncito," said Javier.

He lay down, resting his head in Lulabell's lap, letting his legs hang over the sofa armrest, and his boots dangle.

"When a child loses a tooth, his mother puts it in a rathole where Mr.

Ratoncito is sure to find it. This is so the ratoncito will carry it off. If Mr. Ratoncito, his Señora, or any of their ratoncitos eats the baby tooth, then the child's new tooth is sure to come in straight and beautiful."

Javier smiled.

She grabbed him by the jowls and squeezed. "Mr. Ratoncito and his family must have eaten every single one of your baby teeth, porque ¡mira qué bonitos dientecitos tienes!"

"Thanks for telling me such a nice story and for leaving my teeth for the ratoncito," said Javier.

"It's the least a mother can do."

Javier looked up at Lulabell. "¿You feel all right, momma?"

"Sí, mijo. ¿Why, don't I look okay?"

"You look okay, just a little different."

"¿You mean old, don't you?"

"No, just different," said Javier. Lulabell didn't look old, just older, as if she had finally turned into the beautiful woman all beautiful girls want to grow up to be.

"Somethin's happenin to me," she said. "I used to think that it was all those young men that kept me young. Either that or somethin they represented. To make things easy, let's call it love."

"Okay," said Javier. "We'll call it love."

"Love wasn't a thing that came and went. It wasn't somethin that actually happened, but somethin waitin to happen."

"You still love Beto ¿don't you?"

"Sí, mijo. Más que nunca. And if I didn't, then I would make sure I did."

"You're talking about brujería ¿aren't you?"

"Somethin like that. I'd fix things is all, because that's what I've gotten us into. It's not just about me and Beto, or me and you, it's about all of us. I know you've always wanted a family."

"The Lord gave you something He don't give many, and I'm glad to see you're finally putting it to good use. The Lord's ways are bien mysterious, momma, and He picked you to carry out His greater purposes, just as sure as He picked me."

"¿Would you stop it with that crap?" said Lulabell. "¿Who are you tryin to fool?" It was plain to see, Javier had taken a break from the Lord, whether it would be a sojourn or a permanent leave of absence remained to be seen. Lulabell only wished Javier would be honest with himself about it.

As far as Javier was concerned, he wasn't trying to fool anyone but the Devil. Sure he'd be the first to concede that he and his mission had hit a curve in the road, a hairpin turn to be exact, but once he came around the bend and headed into the straightaway, the Lord would be waiting for him, and with open arms.

"Maybe the Lord picked Beto to carry out His greater purpose," said Lulabell. "¿Have you ever thought of that?"

"I don't think so," said Javier. "But you and me, we got gifts."

"¿What good are gifts if you don't know how to use them? Sometimes we need somebody to come along and teach us all the things we should have learned a long time ago."

Javier couldn't help but feel jealous. All those years he'd tried to reach his mother's soul in vain, and little bitty Beto had done the job in no time.

"I used to think that love was just gettin dressed up, stayin out all night dancin, feelin like you're on top of the world. But that's not it at all. Love is a lot of hard work and sufferin, and it don't never end," said Lulabell.

"I think you're right," said Javier.

"Hard work and sufferin are the enemies of youth and physical beauty," continued Lulabell. "¿Do you ever watch the women comin out of the cannery or comin home from the fields? ¿Do they look young to you? ¿Any of them? No they don't. They never do. I used to look at them and say, 'Now there's a woman who hasn't taken care of herself, who has let the years get the best of her.' But it's not like that at all. Try lookin lovely if you've been workin out in the sun all day, or if you've been up all night cryin."

"Love sure takes its toll ¿don't it?" said Javier.

"Yeah. And it changes you, not for better or worse, but because it's the only thing it can do, the only thing you can do. Look what it's done to you. I assume all of this is about love," said Lulabell pointing to the gun and the Stetson® lying side by side on the coffee table.

Javier said nothing.

"Men don't look at me the same way anymore, mijo. And if they do, it scares me, really, really scares me. And the craziest thing is, I can't even look at another man. Imagínate."

"I have. And I've been praying for this for a long time."

"Thanks. When we were kids in Catechism, the Sisters told us that that was the nicest thing you could do for someone. Pray for them."

"I think they were right, momma." Javier sat up. Agustín Lara was playing the piano, just his piano and his voice this time, for he was in the midst of the introductory notes and the introductory words of Javier's favorite waltz, "Santa."

Javier stood up, grabbed his hat and put it on straight. He swallowed hard. "Let's dance," he said as the rest of Agustín's orchestra joined in.

Lulabell stood up. She was wearing her red huipil. Her hair hung loose and long. Javier took her in his arms. He had heard that waltz hundreds, or maybe even thousands of times during his childhood. He knew the song by heart, but could only bring himself to whisper its refrain softly in Lulabell's ear.

The song was simple. A violin and percussion, a piano, a man, his heartfelt emotions, and his voice. Agustín Lara banged hard on his piano, then faded away. And indeed, as Javier held his mother in his arms, it was just as he had imagined, the perfect timing of dancing with yourself, only not being alone while you were doing it.

El Oro
Gold

TODO QUE BRILLA . . .

ALL THAT GLITTERS . . .

THE STRAIGHTAWAY:
JAVIER'S DREAM

Javier went to bed and dreamt about the straightaway, but not straightaway. First there were the blind curves and hairpin turns of a never-ending, two-lane mountainous country highway.

Javier was headed southbound with one hand firmly on the wheel, and no idea as to where he was going. He was all alone, or so he thought, when he heard a noise coming from the trunk. He pulled over to investigate, opened up, and there, bound and gagged, was Lucha. He lifted her out, then carefully lowered her to the shoulder.

"My little lamb," whispered Javier as he untied her. Once free, she slapped him across the face.

"¿Why must you call me that stupid name?" she said. She got up and started walking before he could answer.

Javier opened his mouth and tried to scream. He wanted to shout, "Mi amor, wait. This road, it could be dangerous." But all was in vain. He tried to walk, but his effort got him nowhere. He heard a growl coming from behind the brush. His heart raced. He thought it was the Devil Himself. He began to pray and in no time he was again behind the wheel of the Monte Carlo, and the Monte Carlo, through no effort of Javier's, was making its way around the curves.

He checked the rearview mirror to find that Xochitl was in the back seat idly filing her fingernails.

"¿Where are we going?" he asked.

"We are headed for the e-straightaway," she proclaimed.

"Come up here with me," said Javier. "I'm afraid."

"There is no reason to be," said Xochitl and in that instant things got even scarier as they entered a long, dimly lit tunnel.

The road inside the tunnel narrowed to a single lane. Javier took charge of the wheel. The ceiling got lower and lower, the lane, narrower and narrower. The end of the tunnel was just up ahead, and then it was right in front of them, or rather, him—Xochitl had disappeared.

It was dark on the other side, nighttime dark, and peaceful. Javier was no longer afraid. He looked around for Lucha, hoping that she had done a full circle and that she would eventually catch up with him, even though, considering the valley that lay ahead, his theory didn't make sound geometrical sense.

There was no Lucha in sight. Javier could live with that. But ¿where was Jesus? ¿Where were His open arms? Jesus was nowhere to be found, but in the distance there was a mariachi and they were playing the instrumental "El Niño Perdido."

Javier walked down a small hill to discover a river. In the moonlight, something sparkled at its bottom. "¡¡¡Gold!!!" he proclaimed, then dove down after it. That river wasn't deep enough for diving, and even though he landed with a painful thud, he still managed a handful of sparkly nuggets.

"That there's not gold," warned a deep voice from a shaded grove.

Javier spotted a bearded prospector in the corner.

"See it sparkle," said Javier.

"Pyrite," said the man. "Fool's gold, but don't be fooled, son. There's plenty of the real thing deep in the hills. Far away and deep."

The man raised his right hand. It trembled. It shook. The man pointed, but there was a bend in his finger that didn't straighten, it went south, then bent sharply east at the knuckle. Javier didn't know if he meant south, or east, or southeast. The man went back to his panning, and no matter how loud Javier tried to yell, or how fast he moved his legs in the prospector's direction, the man neither saw, nor heard him, nor did Javier gain any ground. He finally gave up trying, and woke up instead.

He had reached the straightaway and this is what it held: a mariachi, a handful of fool's gold, and some sound advice on where to find the real thing.

ASAP

Javier knew about the maps Lulabell had slowly been shading in for the better part of twenty years, and he considered them more than just geographical aids. To Javier they were mysterious blueprints of what a man might be.

In the morning when he woke up, he rushed into the kitchen where Lulabell was preparing Sunday breakfast. "Momma, I need a map of Mexico," he said, out of breath.

"¿A map? ¿Where would I get one of those?" Lulabell wiped her hands on her apron.

Javier got close and whispered. "I know about the maps you've been keeping and coloring all these years. I've seen them both."

Lulabell lowered her voice accordingly. "They're stored away. Hidden better than the treasure of the Sierra Madre."

"The treasure of the Sierra Madre," repeated Javier. It was another sign. "Get them out when you get a chance, because I wanna look at them."

"¿What do you need a map for?" She set her spatula down.

"I'm looking for a spot south, maybe southeast of here, a place with plenty of mountains. I dreamt about it last night."

"¿Are you thinkin of movin out or somethin?" It was a prospect Lulabell had been waiting years for, but now, somehow, something had changed and the thought that Javier would one day set out on his own saddened her.

Javier didn't answer. He'd spotted his traje de charro hanging innocently from the kitchen door jamb. "Mi traje de charro," he said reverently.

"Sí, hijo. Tu traje de charro. With all the work I put into it, you really should take better care of it. The cleaners have been callin all week," she scolded.

"Yes," said Javier. "But ¿do you think if I brought you a suitcase full of gold, you could take these crosses off, and you could put some gold conches on my traje de charro?" He spoke in spurts, his speech gaining both momentum and volume as he progressed.

"Sure, but I don't know where either one of us is gonna get a suitcase full of gold," she said.

"There's gold in them hills. Real gold. Not pyrite. And I'm gonna go and get it."

"That's nice, mijo." She served Javier a plate of huevos rancheros, then sat down beside him at the kitchen table. "I think it's time me and you had another little talk."

"If it's about Lucha, you don't have to worry. Last night I met a real nice lady." He ripped off a piece of tortilla and scooped up his first bite with it.

"¿You met a girl, mijo?"

"A lady, your age or maybe even a little older, but of course not as pretty."

"¡¡Ay!! hijo."

"¿What is it, momma?"

"Sometimes a boy becomes a man overnight," said Lulabell going right straight to the point.

"¿You think that's what happened to me?" He pushed his plate aside.

"No. You were a man even when you should have been a boy. You were always the man of the house."

"Somebody had to be," said Javier.

"Sí, mijo. You became a man too soon. You never had time to be a boy. But sometimes a man can become a boy overnight."

"Ut-oh," said Javier. "I think that's what's happening to me."

"I do too," said Lulabell. "And that's okay. Only you're twenty-seven years old and you oughtta think about becomin a man again ASAP."

"ASAP," repeated Javier.

"And another thing," said Lulabell, "about this lady you met. Be forewarned. There's lots of things an older woman knows that can drive a boy crazy, so watcha. ¿Okay, mijo?"

"You worry too much about me, but okay, momma."

"Now eat your breakfast, it's almost time for church."

"I ain't going," said Javier.

"Somehow that don't surprise me. Bingo's at one if you're interested."

"I am," said Javier. "And thanks for the talk. I'll get on that man thing ASAP."

After his huevos rancheros, a shower and a shave, Javier grabbed his hat and keys, and headed out the door. The Monte Carlo was parked at the north end of the property, on its windshield a note folded carefully in half to protect the confidentiality of its content. Javier stretched out and grabbed it, mindful not to get his Sunday clothes dirty. He read the note out loud, "You been dancin with the viejitas"—a question or statement he wasn't sure, for the note was completely void of punctuation, but it was signed with a single cursive "L." Javier wadded it up and stuck it in the front pocket of his pants.

He was about to fish through his keys, isolate the proper one, stick it in the keyhole, open the door, and step into the driver's seat, when he noticed that the entire side of the Monte Carlo was scratched, and not with the ear-aching handiwork of a key either, but with something significantly more substantial. He muttered a "chinga'o."

Javier was certain that someone had defiled his precious automobile, and that someone was Lucha. (Actually, as Javier slept, the Monte Carlo was side-swiped by a tractor on the way to do its early morning chores.)

Javier got in, slammed the door, and headed for Lucha's. But everything was different. His hands weren't sweaty against the steering wheel. He wasn't worried about whether his guitarrón was properly tuned in case he should have to serenade. Lucha had stood him up for the Big Dance, had left him plantado, and in so doing she was the real reason why he hadn't gone, and that, in Javier's mind, was unforgivable.

He arrived at Lucha's, walked around to her window, and roused her with a whistle.

"Mornin, hermanito," she said.

"Morning." He was showered, shaved, and cologned, but all business.

"Turn the can over and come on up," said Lucha referring to the empty white five-gallon plastic paint bucket tucked conveniently behind the bushes.

"No thanks." He pulled the wadded-up piece of paper from his pocket. "¿Is this your doing?"

"Yep," said Lucha. "You been dancin with the viejitas ¿ay?"

"¿How would you know?"

"I got feelers," said Lucha. "You know. Antennae." She held her index fingers appropriately above her head. Lucha knew a thing or two about the secret world of insects and arachnids. She had been watching the Discovery Channel, a habit she had formed while locked up.

"Last night you didn't want nothing to do with me, ¿and today you've got feelers?" said Javier.

"Absence makes the heart grow fonder," said Lucha rocking back and forth on her heels. "¿Won't you come on up, hermanito?" It had been nearly a week since anyone had stepped on her bucket.

Javier paused. Absence ¿ay? ¿Was that the key to the parable he was looking for? The reason why Jesus wasn't waiting for him with open arms at the straightaway. ¿Was His absence designed to make Javier's heart, or rather, his soul grow fonder?

Lucha leaned over the windowsill. It was a one-story. But still. Her breasts nearly spilt from her chocolate-brown negligee. "Come on up," she beckoned.

Javier brought the bucket out from behind the bushes, then stepped on it. He could smell last night's perfume on Lucha's neck.

He got close, pulled her near, and whispered his one-word response in her ear: "No."

"Ay, hermanito," she said, four fingers of her hand resting on his right cheek, applying constant pressure, urging his lips her way. Javier didn't fight it. He put an arm around her neck, pulled her near, then kissed her softly and slowly on the lips before deviating to her neck, up along her jawline, then around to the back of her ear, then the ear itself.

Lucha leaned back and stepped aside. Javier could see the fuzzy pink bedspread lying across the unmade bed, could imagine its softness grazing rhythmically against his thighs. Lucha walked backwards to her bed and lay down. The silkiness of her negligee gathered in ripples between her legs.

Javier placed his palms on the windowsill, and rested his chin on his hands.

"Ándale, hermanito," said Lucha patting the bed beside her. "I miss you."

Javier missed her too. He missed his constant struggle to save her soul, the way she looked in Lulabell's borrowed clothes with her hair tamed into two braids. The way she always damsel-in-distressed him. He missed trying to talk her into doing what was good for her, trying to haul her off to church, to practice with his mariachi, to the Baile Grande. He missed other things as well: like the way she looked in her pretend python jeans, high heels, and halter top, a shawl flung deceivingly over her shoulders, or just in red velvet panties, lying on her bed propped up by her elbows and desire alone. The way he felt lying beneath her rhythm. But more even than any of that, Javier missed the prospect of dancing with her. They had never gone arm in arm to a ranchera—a magic moment Javier had imagined perhaps a hundred times in the short time since he had discovered the joys of norteño music and the delights of holding a woman in his arms and moving to the rhythm. Lucha lay on her twin bed offering him delights hard to turn down, and Javier could only think of taking her in his arms and dancing with her. He looked at her and knew that they would never share in that simple pleasure and it made him sad.

Lucha scissored her legs, then let them linger in an open position forming what Javier estimated at a 120 degree angle. She was not the type of woman that took to courtship. A serenade here and there was fine, but Lucha was not the sort a man took to dinner and a dance, the type of woman who appreciated flowers.

In that moment Javier realized that what he knew about women was just as brief and enigmatic as any one of the 150 Psalms, and that perhaps his limited knowledge of the female species was even bite-sized enough to fit within the tiny confines of a single Proverb.

Then he began to mumble, his chin still resting on his hands, his hands still resting on the windowsill. *"Deliver thee from the strange woman, even from the stranger which flattereth with her words; which forsaketh the guide of her youth, and forgeteth the covenant of her God. For her house inclineth unto death, and her paths unto the dead. None that go unto her return again."* He had perused if not downright read the Bible so many times looking for all he'd found lacking in life, namely a father's love and guidance, that he knew much of it by heart.

His musings were permeated by a dab of agnostic wisdom. Con los cantos de la sirena no te vayas a marear. With the songs of the siren, you won't set sail. Number six of the game La Lotería. Lulabell used to play with Javier. She'd insist that they play. The game was like bingo, except the numbers came with pictures and phrases. Sometimes they would make one or two lines, or go on to a blackout. Javier always got nervous when number six came out. His shoulders would tighten. He would cringe. The card showed a long-haired topless temptress—a mermaid on the open sea, her hair nighttime black just like Lucha's.

"¿What are you doin, hermanito?" said Lucha. "¿Are you talkin in tongues? Come on up here and do that," she said as she gently gnawed her fingerips.

Her evil knew no end, her perversity no bounds. But still, Javier couldn't take his eyes off her.

Lucha got to her feet and came to the window. Few are the men who can resist the charms of a charming and beautiful woman—her hands in his hair, her lips running the length and width of his neck, her fingers unsnapping the first few snaps of his fancy western-tailored shirt, her fingernails gently clawing at his torso, her tongue making its way slowly toward his ear.

But Javier was no wildebeest naively lapping at the banks of the Nile. He was no antelope on the open African plain waiting to be run down by a hungry cheetah. He knew that women were strange and needy creatures, constantly changing, but most importantly, Javier knew that any woman could bring about the downfall of any man, no matter how righteous or fortified by the Holy Spirit he might be.

Javier pushed Lucha away. Her once straight hair lay in the wavy aftermath of last night's braids, except for in the front where it was teased high and wide, so high and so wide, Javier thought it capable of blocking out the sun, hence preventing the Lord from casting His shadow upon the earth the day of His Second Coming.

¿Was that what had happened? ¿Was the shadow Lucha had cast upon Javier both big enough and dark enough to prevent the Lord's loving light from shining through? ¿Had Lucha led Javier down the wide path to destruction with the tip of her tongue?

Javier pointed a finger at Lucha and said, "Stay away from my ride, ¡¡¡woman!!!"

He jumped off the paint bucket, didn't bother to put it back, and walked slowly away.

Lucha stuck her head out the window. "You'll be back," she called to him.

"I don't think so," said the already-on-his-way-far-away Javier.

Javier walked to his Monte Carlo, wrote Lucha a note, then placed it on the windshield of her pickup truck.

DEAR LUCHA,

FORGIVE ME FOR NOT FINISHING WHAT I STARTED. I AM OFF TO THE MOUNTAINS NOW TO FIND GOLD; NOT FOR THE SAKE OF RICHES, BUT TO SOLVE THE RIDDLE OF WHAT IT MEANS TO BE A MAN. REMEMBER THE LORD'S LIGHT ALWAYS SHINES, IT IS AS SUBLIME AS ANY SUNSET AND JUST AS BEAUTIFUL, AS SURPRISING AS THE CLOUDS PARTING ON THE RAINIEST DAY AND THE SUN SHINING THROUGH, WHETHER YOU CHOSE TO STEP INTO THE LIGHT OR REMAIN IN THE SHADOWS IS UP TO YOU.

FOREVER YOURS,

Javier

EL BIG CHEESE II

If Natalie and Consuelo regularly read the *Lava Landing Lookout,* then they would have already known what it took a Monday morning telephone call to inform them of. Cal McDaniel, local businessman and entrepreneur, had been found dead over the weekend at his hillside home.

That morning, Consuelo had received a telephone call from Henry Kellenberger, Jr., a local attorney who specialized in everything, but nothing in particular. He wanted to see Consuelo and Natalie in his office as soon as possible, preferably that very morning.

And now Nat and Sway were grabbing their purses, running out the door, and piling into the Cadillac. Once they were on the road, Consuelo said, "¿Think maybe there's a curse on us?"

Natalie coughed. "¿What the hell kinda curse you talkin about?"

Consuelo hung a hand out the window and raised it to the wind, then said, "A curse that kills men. Look what happened to our daddys. They didn't stick around nearly long enough, and now Cal's dead too."

"Your daddy more so than mine," said Nat.

"I'll say," said Sway.

"I don't know about that curse, but it seems to me that the Universe is a damn efficient place, and if I'm not mistaken it's one-stop-shoppin us with the way everything's happenin all at once."

"I think you're right about that, Nat, but right now I wonder if we still got jobs with Cal bein gone. And I sure hope he didn't suffer none. Maybe he was short, and a shade creepy, but he was always a gentleman."

"That he was," agreed Nat as they pulled into a parking space right in front of the downtown law office of Henry Kellenberger, Jr. Cal was plenty thoughtful with the way he always brought Sway something, whether it be donuts, flowers, or tacos. And not only did he think of her, but also of Natalie by extension. Sure her bouquets were smaller, her donuts were never sugar-coated, and her tacos were regulares as opposed to Consuelo's supers, but that was just his way of showing who he preferred, and Nat, recognizing it as such, was never offended.

The girls took the stairs up to the third floor. The door to the law office was heavy and required a concerted effort to open. Nat and Sway were met in the lobby by Mr. Kellenberger, Jr., himself.

"Ms. Vergüenza," he said offering a hand to both girls until Consuelo stepped forward, then to Nat, "Ms. Steven.

"Come into my office." He sat down at his solid oak desk, which was, by that time, an antique—it had been there since his grandfather started the practice more than sixty years before. The girls had a seat as well. Mr. Kellenberger fiddled with his tie. "Please accept my deepest condolences. Every death is a great tragedy, but we, the living, must go on.

"Pardon my haste, but I am about to go on a highly anticipated and carefully planned vacation." He got up and walked to a nearby bookcase, lowered an urn from the top shelf, then set it in front of Consuelo, before reaching for an envelope, which he handed to Natalie.

"¿What's this?" said Consuelo. She tried to pop the top on the urn, but it didn't budge.

"The deceased," said Mr. Kellenberger lowering his voice. "He passed over the weekend, but we've kept it private until now."

"¿How'd he go?" said Consuelo wrinkling her brow.

"In his sleep. A heart attack."

"It could have been worser," said Sway with a sigh.

"You mean worse," countered Mr. Kellenberger.

"English is a live language," said Nat. "It's always changin. I think she meant worser."

"I see," said counsel. He tapped the envelope that waited in front of Nat. "Go ahead, open it, dear."

Nat opened and read the note contained within: "Send me out in style as only you two can, but make sure at least a teaspoon of me gets to the sea." It was signed and dated by Cal McDaniel. Natalie recognized Cal's signature in an instant, for it was the same chicken scratch that had appeared at the bottom of her and Consuelo's paychecks for over ten years.

"Look, Sway. He knew he was gonna go," said Natalie to Consuelo. The note was dated just two weeks before.

"¿Ain't that the darn strangest thing?" said Sway.

"You'd be surprised how often that happens," said Mr. Kellenberger. "People often know when their time is near."

He opened another drawer and came up with two envelopes filled with cash. "And here's a little something to cover your time and expenses." Each envelope contained $1,199.00 in big and small bills. Cal wanted Natalie and Consuelo to have the largest amount of spending money without creating a tax liability, Mr. Kellenberger explained.

The girls shoved the money into their matching macramé bags and Nat grabbed the urn and held it tight, as if their windfall somehow depended upon it.

"¿Is there anything else you need from us, Mr. Junior?" said Sway.

"I'm afraid we have only just begun. Mr. McDaniel elected you two as the executors, or rather, executrixes of his will, and you are also his chief heiresses. He leaves no living relatives. You ladies are soon to be the proud owners of The Big Cheese Plant, as well as his other holdings."

Natalie looked at Consuelo. They said nothing. Consuelo bit her bottom lip, and Nat did the same. They wrinkled their foreheads. And then it occurred to Natalie that the whole thing was just like in a movie, and ¿how strange was that? since their lives were like anything but movies. And then Nat stopped to think just what their lives were like, after all, and she concluded that they were like dreams. This made her happy, so she smiled, and Sway followed suit.

Then Nat said, "Oh my gosh, Sway. This so reminds me of *Willy Wonka and the Chocolate Factory* and how when they're in that elevator and Willy gives everything to Charlie, except in this instance, Willy's dead."

Mr. Kellenberger swallowed hard. It was obvious that Natalie had just stepped into her own private universe, and Consuelo was soon to follow.

"I don't know about you, Nat. But every time we watched that movie, and I put myself in Charlie's shoes, I was never really excited about the prospect of owning a big old chocolate factory. Then again, I ain't too much for chocolate and never have been. I'm more the fruity-nutty type."

"And them ooompa-loompas always really creeped me out," added Nat.

"Me too," concurred Consuelo.

"¿What if we don't want The Big Cheese Plant?" said Nat to Mr. Kellenberger.

"An investment firm is already expressing interest in Cal's holdings. We could broker a sale," said Mr. Kellenberger.

"That sounds like a great idea," said Nat. "¿Can we be in touch?"

"Sure. I understand completely," said counsel. "Our office will handle everything and then get in touch with you when we have further details. At any rate, probate is at least thirty days. And until then, it was very nice to meet you both . . ." He got to his feet and shook both girls' hands.

And once they were out the door and safely taking the stairs so as "to burn some extra calories," Natalie said to Consuelo, "Everything is happenin all at once. First your daddy gets Himself stuck in Purgatory, then He gets out. Now Cal is gone and instead of just jobs, we got a whole cheese factory."

"The Universe is purty trippy," agreed Consuelo. "¿But what are we gonna do with all that cheese money?"

"Somethin good," said Nat. She paused to think when all of the sudden it occurred to her, "Maybe we oughtta sponsor True-Dee and her Hair Growth Accelerators, or whatever she decides to call them," said Nat.

"I think you may be right. Looks like she's on to somethin."

The girls ran all the way down the stairs, and out the door. It was no longer cloudy, hot, and humid, but sunny, hot, and dry. Nat and Sway stopped off at the Cadillac to deposit the urn containing Cal Leroy McDaniel's ashes on the front seat, before they headed toward Leroy's.

There was nothing that could be done for Cal, so the girls might as well shop. But first, since they were in the area and hadn't seen her in at least a couple weeks, they dropped by True-Dee's Tresses, but they were shocked, dismayed, and plenty worried when they read the sign on the front door: CLOSED FOR REMODELING.

"Looks more like de-modeling to me," said Consuelo as they took turns pressing their noses against the window. The whole place had been gutted. The styling chairs were on their sides, the shampoo basins were uprooted and stacked on top of one another, and the perm rods were thrown on the floor like pick-up-sticks.

"Somethin is very wrong," said Natalie. She looked down at her right arm to confirm that it had given her goose bumps, the very thought, or ¿was it a premonition? that True-Dee was in trouble.

"And it's funny how she wasn't at the Baile Grande either," added Consuelo as they continued on their way. The girls were of the same mind and opinion that it would be a good idea to check in on True-Dee soon, but Leroy's was just up the street.

They walked into the store with no idea that in addition to The Big Five-Four and The Big Cheese Plant, they had also inherited Leroy's Footwear and Apparel. And it had also yet to cross their mind that the ocean was forty-nine miles away, and Consuelo's travel zone fanned out to an even thirty.

Cal McDaniel, 53,
entrepreneur and community leader

Outspoken and tenacious businessman created more than a thousand jobs for community

BY RAYMOND CAMINADA

LAVA LANDING – Cal McDaniel, resident of Lava Landing since 1963, businessman and community leader, was found dead at his hillside home late Saturday afternoon by his gardener. The official cause of death is under investigation by the County Coroner, but no foul play is suspected.

Mr. McDaniel, a native of Miami, Florida, came to Lava Landing in 1963 to assist his cousin Rufus Wayne McDaniel (also deceased) with the operation of his cheese factory. Within the year, Cal McDaniel had turned the tiny cheese plant into a thriving business known as The Big Cheese Plant. The Big Cheese Plant was one of the first cheese companies to specialize in prepackaged, grated mozzarella cheese, which became a favorite amongst pizzerias. Under Cal's direction, The Big Cheese Plant also packaged and marketed the popular snack food known as "String Cheese." Once a tiny company, the BCP now employs more than 1,400.

Mr. McDaniel made his first and most indelible mark on the community after the dairy tragedy of 1965. Bacteria in improperly treated cheese caused widespread listeria and claimed the lives of 105 people. Mr. McDaniel created a scholarship fund for the orphaned children of listeria victims, bringing higher education to dozens of youth. Mr. McDaniel continued his lifelong support of higher education through several scholarships he offered to FFA members.

He ran a successful nightclub known as The Big Five-Four. Owing to his short stature, he was often heard saying, "I might only be five-four, but I'm a big five-four." Short in stature, but an enormous individual, Cal McDaniel will be greatly missed by our close-knit community.

LAST WILL AND TESTAMENT OF CAL MCDANIEL

I, CAL LEROY MCDANIEL, a resident of and domiciled in Lava County, California, being of sound mind do hereby make, publish and declare this to be my Last Will and Testament, thereby revoking all wills and codicils at any time heretofore made by me. I give my body to the sea and my soul to God Who gave it. My property and other worldly possessions I distribute as follows:

I

I declare that I am unmarried and have no children living or deceased.

II

I direct that there be no funeral service or memorial service of any kind for me and that I be cremated and my ashes scattered at sea.

III

I direct my EXECUTORS to pay all my debts and cremation expenses as soon after my death as may be practicable.

IV

A. I give, devise and bequeath all of my right, title and interest in and to a certain portion of my real property located at 333 Granite Rock Drive in Lava Landing, California, and all structures and improvements located thereon, to CONSUELO CONSTANCIA GONZÁLEZ CONTRERAS also known as CONSUELO SIN VERGÜENZA, and hereinafter referred to as CONSUELO.

B. I give, devise and bequeath all of my right, title and interest in and to a certain portion of my real property located at 224 Main Street in Lava Landing, California, and all structures and improvements located thereon, known as "The Big Five-Four" to CONSUELO.

C. I give, devise and bequeath all of my right, title and interest in and to a certain portion of my real property located at 679 Fallon Road in Lava Landing, California, and all structures and improvements located thereon, known as "The Big Cheese Plant" to CONSUELO.

D. I give, devise and bequeath all of my right, title and interest in and to a certain portion of my real property located at 337 Main Street in Lava Landing, California, and all structures and improvements located thereon, known as "Leroy's Footwear and Apparel" to CONSUELO.

E. I give, devise and bequeath all of my furniture, furnishings, clothing, jewelry, fishing and hunting trophies, my automobile, and other household effects, and all other tangible personal property located at my residence at 333 Granite Rock Drive in Lava Landing, California at the time of my death to CONSUELO.

F. I give devise and bequeath the following sums to such of the following persons as shall survive me:

1. Three Hundred Fifty Thousand Dollars ($350,000) to my assistant NATALIE STEVEN.

2. Fifty Thousand Dollars ($50,000) to my barmaid BETHANY STUART

3. Fifty Thousand Dollars ($50,000) to my gardener IVAN MORALES SMITH

G. I give, devise and bequeath to each other person who shall survive me and who my EXECUTORS shall determine in their absolute discretion shall be on my payroll at the time of my death, a sum of one hundred dollars ($100) for each full year of such employment prior to my death, rounded up to the nearest five hundred dollars ($500), but in no case less than one thousand dollars ($1,000).

V

I give, devise and bequeath all of the residue and remainder of my Estate, after payment of all my just debts, expenses, taxes, administration costs, and individual devises and bequests to CONSUELO.

VI

A. I hereby nominate and appoint CONSUELO CONSTANCIA GONZÁLEZ CONTRERAS also known as CONSUELO SIN VERGÜENZA and NATALIE STEVEN to act as EXECUTORS of this will. If either of them shall be, or become unable or unwilling to act, then the survivor shall act with my attorney HENRY KELLENBERGER, JR. No bond or other security shall be required of any person who acts as EXECUTOR herein.

B. I hereby expressly authorize and empower my EXECUTORS to sell and dispose of the whole or any portion of my estate, real or personal, and wherever situated, as and when and upon such terms as my EXECUTORS deem proper, at public or private sale, with or without notice, and without first securing any order of court thereof.

\\

IN WITNESS WHEREOF, I hereunto set my hand and affix my seal to this my Last Will and Testament on this 18th day of August, 2000

Cal Leroy Mcdaniel

CAL LEROY MCDANIEL

On the date above written, the Testator, CAL LEROY MCDANIEL, declared to us, the undersigned, that the foregoing instrument was his Last Will and Testament, and requested us to act as witnesses to it. The Testator thereupon signed this Will in our presence, all of us being present at the same time, and we now, at the Testator's request, in the Testator's presence, and in the presence of each other, subscribe our names as witnesses.

Each of us observed the signing of this Will by the Testator and by each other subscribing witness and knows that each signature is the true signature of the person whose name was signed. Each of us is now more than eighteen (18) years of age, and to the best of our knowledge, is of sound mind and is not acting under duress, menace, fraud, misrepresentation, or undue influence.

We declare under penalty of perjury that the foregoing is true and correct, and that this declaration was executed at Lava Landing, in Lava County, California, this 18th day of August, 2000.

Florence Sánchez

FLORENCE SÁNCHEZ
residing in 1292 Seventh St.
Lava Landing, California 95763

Edith Papangellin

EDITH PAPANGELLIN
Residing at 3257 San Pedro St.
Lava Landing, California 95763

On this 22nd day of August, 2000, CAL LEROY MCDANIEL declared to us, the undersigned, that the foregoing instrument was the First Codicil to his Last Will and Testame and he requested us to act as witnesses to the same and to his signature thereon. He thereupon signed the said Codicil in our presence, we being present at the same time. And we now, at h request, in his presence, and in the presence of one another, hereto subscribe our names as witnesses, each of us declaring that the Testator is, to the best of our knowledge, of sound mi and memory.

Florence Sánchez

FLORENCE SÁNCHEZ
residing in 1292 Seventh St.
Lava Landing, California 95763

\\
\\
\\

Edith Pangelli

EDITH PAPANGELLIN
Residing at 3257 San Pedro St.
Lava Landing, California 95763

El Traje de Charro
The Charro's Suit

¡AY! QUÉ MARIACHI TAN ELEGANTE, CON SU TRAJE
DE CHARRO SE PARECE A PEDRO INFANTE
¡OH! WHAT AN ELEGANT MARIACHI, WITH HIS CHARRO'S SUIT
HE RESEMBLES PEDRO INFANTE

SETTLING ACCOUNTS, OR WHAT A DIFFERENCE A DAY MAKES, OR HOW JAVIER SPENT HIS FINAL DAY IN LAVA LANDING BEFORE HEADING FOR THE SIERRA MADRE TO SEARCH NOT JUST FOR GOLD, BUT HIMSELF: A PRESENT-TENSE ACCOUNT

Headed down Highway 33 with the red slash of speedometer needle teetering between 90 and 95, Javier laments not his and Lucha's parting of the ways, but the Oil Embargo of 1973.

It is Tuesday afternoon; approximately forty-eight hours have transpired since Javier last saw Lucha.

After he left Lucha lingering on her windowsill Sunday afternoon, Javier put her in his in-box with other things to be contemplated later, then he headed for Taquería La Bamba where he ordered tres tacos de tripitas y una agua de horchata grande. It is true what Lulabell says. You have to ask for them well cooked, otherwise cow intestines are simply unpalatable. But cooked golden crispy y con plenty of chilito y limón, they are delectable.

That very evening, once he was under the covers and his prayers were said, Javier had thought on Lucha for half the night before deciding to file her away once and for all with other things he'd just as soon forget: when he peed his pants in kindergarten, the time Consuelo beat him up in the fourth grade and made him cry, how he had, at the age of twenty-two, brought home 350 chocolate bars to sell for the church fund-raiser, only to let 347 of them melt carelessly on the front seat of the Monte Carlo.

And now he laments a long-gone oil embargo which robbed his automobile of a potential extra 104 cubic inches under the hood and their accompanying 50 horsepower.

The first Monte Carlo hit showroom floors in September of 1969 as Chevrolet's late-in-coming market response most notably to the Ford Thunderbird, but also to the Buick Regal and the Pontiac Grand Prix. Javier's is a 1976 Landau model with a 350-cubic-inch, V8 engine, modified by Rochester dual carbs, an Offenhauser dual-intake manifold, a high-lift cam, high-compression pistons, and tweaked valves. The MC was souped up by its first owner and for that Javier is grateful. In its modified state, the automobile achieves slightly greater than the factory-promised 165 horsepower at 3,800 rpms.

Javier speeds down the highway thinking about the extra cubic inches and horsepower that might have been. After the oil embargo, Chevy had little choice but to turn the Monte Carlo from a muscle car into a gentleman's touring coupe. Javier is most certainly a gentleman, but he is going to Mexico, and he suspects horsepower is something that can come in handy in a foreign land.

At the moment, he is on his way to Consuelo's to bid Nat and Sway hasta luego. He will leave for Mexico in the morning because today is Tuesday, and if you believe what they say, it is a notoriously bad day to either get married or embark upon a trip. Javier raises an index finger above the steering wheel, and he reminds himself of this little piece of wisdom, "Hoy es martes, no te cases, no te embarques."

Javier stands on Consuelo's doorstep shifting his weight from one foot to the other. He lifts a ready-made fist to the door where it lingers indecisively before knocking. The presence of pretty girls makes Javier nervous. It always has.

Consuelo comes to the door in a floral sundress, which is completely apropos. It's the last day of August, and, as Natalie has been known to put it, it's "suntan-in-an-instant" weather. Nat stands behind Consuelo, dressed just like Sway—same dress, different color. Both girls are barefoot. Natalie holds a box of Screaming Yellow Zonkers®. Her mouth is full, her jaw is moving.

Consuelo glares at Javier. There's definitely something different about him. For starters, he has missed four consecutive days of work, and sometimes a thing as simple as rest can fortify a man in unexpected ways, allowing him to do things he never would. Javier walks past Consuelo, and grabs Natalie. He embraces her, but keeps heading forward, causing her to stagger backwards, as if they are doing some sort of awkward dance. He runs a hand up her back, allowing it to ride the ripples of her well-toned muscles until it arrives at the base of her head where it stays and squeezes. His lips pause at her ear. "I am leaving tomorrow. I have come to say goodbye," he whispers, then he kisses her ear and her neck, headed down toward her chest, then up again. It feels so good, she pitches her head backwards. He sucks, then bites on her chin, then kisses the side of her mouth, then her lips, and it is nothing like that fish kiss. Everything is smooth, sweet, and synchronized.

Consuelo stands back and doesn't rightfully know what to do, but furrow her brow.

Then Javier lets go of Natalie, at which point she says, "¿Are you drunk?"

"Nope. I have just always wanted to do that. I want you to know how I have felt about you all of these years."

Nat and Sway stare. Consuelo has her hands on her hips. How dare he barge in and sweep Natalie off her feet like that.

Consuelo grabs Natalie by an elbow with undue force, as if she is in trouble, and she drags her to the kitchen table where she pulls out a chair, then forces her to have a seat.

Once Consuelo is certain she has put a safe amount of distance between Natalie and Javier, she says to Javier, "¿How exactly do you feel about Natalie?"

Javier sits down on the couch. He pinches his bottom lip, then fiddles with his mustache. "I don't know," he declares. "But I am going to Mexico and I am leaving tomorrow." He has a look around. The place is a mess. There are boxes, bags, and pieces of different-colored tissue paper everywhere.

"¿What the hell happened in here?" says Javier.

"We've been shoppin. ¡So what!" says Sway. There has always been friction between her and Javier. He has never forgiven her for the time she beat him up, she has never forgiven him for always considering Natalie the saint, and her the sinner.

"Listen, I'm sorry for all of those years I was so hard on you," Javier says to Consuelo. "God is much more complicated than I thought." He shrugs.

"He is very complicated," says Natalie. Then she goes on to yet again tell the story of how she went down to Mexico to get Don Pancho out of the Perg and how he has gone on to become the Patron Saint of Drunks and Prostitutes, and ¿how odd is that? because you wouldn't really think the Good Lord would be lookin out for those types, now ¿would ya?

Consuelo leans her backside up against the sofa armrest allowing her long legs to sprawl halfway to the kitchen. "All right," she says to Javier after Natalie concludes her musings. "I forgive you for everything, even the time you pushed me into that mud puddle when we were in the first grade and you were still bigger than me.

"Now please answer my question. You can start out by explainin exactly how you've felt about Natalie all of these years, and then you can update me on how you feel about her now." Consuelo puts the tips of a few of her long, pearly pink nails into her mouth, and nibbles on them. When it comes to Natalie, jealousy has always been an issue for Consuelo. It's one thing to watch Nat kickin up her heels dancin the night away with some stray cute thang on a Saturday night, but to have a young man standin in her very own livin room declarin long-felt feelins for her best friend is another thing entirely.

"I don't know how I feel," says Javier. "I used to think that everything was a sin, and that my life should be spent trying to wipe out not just my own sins, but the sins of the world. I don't feel that way anymore. Now I think the real reason why Jesus only got to be a man for such a short time is because it's so hard. That's why I'm going to Mexico. To figure things out. And besides, I have always wanted to be a gold prospector.

"And as far as Natalie goes, I think she is the prettiest girl I have ever seen in my life, and the nicest one too. I have thought that since we were in kindergarten and I don't think I could be wrong all of them years. And I love her, just like I love you," he says to Consuelo. "I love you both because I know that you love me, that you love my mother, and because of time. It's what we got together."

"But I thought you were in love with a Sister," say Nat and Sway in unison.

"That is long gone and over with," says Javier.

And now, Natalie and Consuelo, but especially Natalie, are about to cry. They have watched Javier grow up. So what if they are the same age. For so many years they thought of him as nothing more than a charade of an overgrown boy, and now he has become, dare they say it, ¿a man?

What Javier has said is so true, it overwhelms all three of them and all they can do is hug each other in a three-way embrace. "Friends to the end," says Javier.

"Friends para siempre," says Sway.

"Friends for always and forever," says Nat.

And then Javier is out the door and on his way. He feels, to quote Natalie, like he is washing cars at the quarter car wash and he has to hurry because he wants to get all of his scrubbing and rinsing done before his time runs out, because he has no more quarters jingle-jangling in his front pocket, and his wallet holds only large bills.

The seven-mile stretch of Highway 33 which leads from Consuelo's house to his is pure straight, unabashed asphalt. Javier gets the MC up to 103 before he eases back and heeds the 35 mph speed limit in town.

He parks in front of the house, then runs up the porch steps, before barging through the door.

Lulabell has the laundry all spread out on the couch. She scarcely looks at him as he comes flying around the corner.

"Momma, I was thinking . . ." he begins, then pauses to catch his breath. "¿Why don't you come with me?"

"¿Are you gonna start that again?" she says. He has told her about his plans at least a dozen times, but she still doesn't believe him. She has two socks in her hands and she is about to turn them into one another, to form them into a ball. "I have some bad news for you, son," she says. "Te corrieron de tu trabajo." These are not words she can bear to say en inglés. She stretches her lips into a half frown which resembles a half smile.

"¡¿¡They fired me!?!" Javier's countenance drops.

"I'm sorry, mijo," she consoles, then she raises a hand to the air and begins to speak at an accelerated rate, you know, that pace one employs when giving good, sound advice. "If you ask me, it is for the best," she says. "You will see. You will find another, better job. ¡Por dios! You can't spend your entire life as a garbageman. No, mijo. The world meant more for you than that."

"But, momma, ¿where are they gonna find another can man like me?"

"I don't know, but that's not all. They kicked you out of the mariachi. Pablo came by and gave me the news a few days ago. I just couldn't find the way to tell you. He left a couple of things for you as well." Lulabell marches over to the kitchen, then returns with Javier's weathered copy of *The Treasure of the Sierra Madre* and a piece of coffee-stained paper.

"That is my mariachi. They can't kick me out. I'll show them. They just wait." He starts to pace. "When I come back from México I will start another, better mariachi."

Lulabell hands Javier the book and the sheet of paper. It seems Pablo has written that song he was talking about, and he has entitled it "El Corrido de Javier el Desgraciado."

Javier looks it over. It is written in red ink on a piece of legal-sized binder paper. He skims the lyrics, then lets it fall to the ground. "Amateurish," he concludes.

"I'm leaving at dawn tomorrow," he says.

"That should be no problem for you with the way you're used to gettin up early for your route," says Lulabell. She won't look at him, but continues folding the bath towels. "I will make you lunch. ¿How about chorizo con huevos?"

"You know it's my favorite."

And now the laundry is all folded. Lulabell hasn't much choice but to look up at Javier, and when she does, she realizes that he really is going. Her baby boy is leaving. She blinks several times in rapid succession as if she doesn't believe her eyes. She is seized with worry and begins to speak a mile a minute. "Promise to call me so I know you're all right. You don't know how much a mother can worry. You are my only son, mijo. Don't you ever forget it." She grabs him by both arms and shakes him as best she can a man of his size. "And promise you won't forget about your mother."

"Of course I won't."

"And there is one more thing . . . ," she trails off as she rushes to the back room. She returns carrying Javier's traje de charro. "I took the crosses off just like you told me to, and I replaced them with gold conches. Of course, they are not the real thing, but for now, they will have to do." The suit is so heavy it must weigh thirty pounds. She holds the hanger with one hand, then lets the pant legs hang over her arm as she passes the suit to Javier.

"Mi traje de charro," says Javier. He walks over and sets it down on the kitchen table.

"Si, hijo. Tu traje de charro. Be sure to take it with you so you can find some work if you have to."

"It looks beautiful, momma, really it does. But it's so heavy, and I already got the car loaded. My guitarrón is already packed and you know how much room it takes up."

"All the more reason to bring your traje de charro along," says Lulabell gesturing toward the suit, which sparkles nearly as much as a matador's suit of lights.

"No, momma, really," he says. "With all due respect, it's not the clothes that make the man, but the man that makes the man."

Lulabell rubs her eyes.

"¿What's the matter?" says Javier. He puts an arm around her shoulders.

"My eyes hurt. They water. I think I have allergies. And then I get these big bags under my eyes. I look so old." She puts her face in her hands and sighs.

"Maybe you need to cry. Those bags under your eyes, maybe they are filled with llanto."

Lulabell looks up at Javier and squints. She has heard of sueño viejo. That's when you are so tired, even if you sleep soundly for two weeks, you will still be exhausted. ¿Is Javier advocating the existence of such a thing as llanto viejo? ¿Old pent-up sadness that should have been cried out years before?

Javier rubs the small of Lulabell's back. "It's okay, mamá. Go ahead and cry."

Mamá. ¿Did he call her mamá? He never called her that. And then she started to cry because her life had been hard, very hard, and nothing like the way she had imagined it would be. She thought she would have her husband para always y siempre, that those pillows they slept on which read "Buenas noches, mi amor" and "Que suenes con los angelitos" really meant something. And ¡she had lost one of her sons! ¡Ay! ¡Qué dolor! like no other pain and sadness in the world. And she almost lost Javier too. And to think, he had never called her mamá. That is how she thought her life would be: one husband, two sons who call her mamá, and a nice warm sweater with just one Kleenex® tucked into the pocket.

"Don't cry, mamá," says Javier.

But it is the nature of things that when you are crying and someone tells you not to, this only makes you want to cry more. "But you just told me to," Lulabell says through sobs.

"I am going to come back a man and I am going to make you so proud of me," he says.

"¡I am proud of you, dammit! I am more proud than you will ever know."

"Thank you. Now that I know that you are all right, that you are in good hands with Beto, I can go away for a while. He might be short. He might be bald. He might be fat."

"And he can't dance," interjects Lulabell.

"I already had a talk with him about that, but if you like, I can have another."

"That's okay. Just do what you have to do."

"One more thing," says Javier. "I am sorry I was so hard on you all of those years."

"Somebody had to be," says Lulabell wiping her eyes with the sleeve of her shirt.

"It's only because I love you so much," says Javier.

"Yes. I know. Now get to bed before you make me cry more than you already have," says Lulabell and Javier does as he is told.

El Volcán y su Reina

The Volcano and His Queen

CADA VOLCÁN, SU REINA

TO EACH VOLCANO, HIS QUEEN

WHERE THE LAVA LANDED II

"*I thought they wanted me for me, but they just used me for my* salon," says True-Dee to Natalie and Consuelo. True-Dee has only just begun to explain to the girls how she was duped by the Sons and Daughters of San Narciso.

The radio plays in the background. Looney Bugsy McCray is broadcasting live from the umpteenth Annual Lava County Labor Day Parade. "Ninety-seven degrees and there's nothin but clouds in the sky," he declares. "Dare I say it. ¿Could this be earthquake weather?" He takes time out to howl, then puts on Martha and the Vandellas' 1960s hit "(Love Is Like a) Heat Wave." Looney Bugsy McCray is spinning oldies having to do with climatological phenomena.

True-Dee pulls a Kleenex® from the nearby box. "I barely got the secret password before they showed up with a jackhammer and started tearin the place apart."

Nat and Sway gasp. "That's one wreckin ball of a tool," says Natalie.

"When they got done, the only thing left standin was my clientele." True-Dee wipes her nose, which, judging by the manner in which it is chafed and peeling, is something she's been doing a lot of lately.

"But ¿what were they after?" says Sway.

"They believe in sacred geography."

"You must mean sacred geometry," says Consuelo as Natalie nods her agreement. "That's somethin we've heard of before seein as how we just watched a documentary about it the other day."

True-Dee throws her hands up in the air. "Geography. Geometry. All I know is, it's sacred somethin I never passed in high school."

"Don't feel so bad," says Sway. "I never passed nothin."

"... Viejo, ¿how many times have I told you, the kitchen table's no place for your cachucha?" Lulabell picks up Beto's fluorescent towing cap and places it backwards on his head.

"¿What's for breakfast?" says Beto.

"¡¿¡Breakfast!?! It's nearly lunchtime. Come on, get ready, so we can go," she urges.

"¿You wanna go to the parade?" says Alberto picking up a green apple from the nearby fruit bowl.

"No, viejo. I wanna go on a trip. I wanna get out of here."

"All right," says Alberto with his mouth full. "But ¿what's your hurry? I'm hungry."

"I miss Javier. He has never been gone before. I don't know what to do. The house, it just doesn't feel right without him."

"Slow down. You're going way too fast," says Alberto.

"Our bags are packed. ¿Why don't you go and take a shower?"

"You wanna go look for Javier ¿don't you?" he says.

"Maybe. Or we could go to your rancho."

"All right, vieja. Whatever you say. Just let me take that shower." He takes another bite of the apple. He has been up since 6:00, first on an emergency call, then towing leftover cars off the street downtown in preparation for the parade.

"¿That's it?" says Lulabell. "You're not even gonna argue about it."

"¿Don't you know that you are the only thing that has kept me here all these years?" says Alberto with his mouth still full.

He finishes off his apple and throws the core into the kitchen garbage can.

"Ay, viejo," says Lulabell. She gets up close to him, throws her arms around his neck, and kisses him.

Beto goes to the bathroom and turns the hot water on in the shower. In the bedroom, he opens up the underwear drawer and pulls out the last pair of briefs, then the sock drawer for the last pair of socks, the undershirt drawer for the last undershirt. From the looks of things, Lulabell has planned a long trip. Only one shirt and one pair of jeans remain in the closet. His boots and his Stetson® are gone, but his tennies wait by the bed.

Downtown, April May is in her one-piece, the one she has worn ten years in a row, the one with the red, yellow, and orange flames shooting up the side. She already has her expensive roller skates with the sparkly red laces on. The volcano tiara rests proudly on her head.

One would never know it, but April May has the pre-pageant jitters. She waves confidently to the crowd as she parades down Main Street in the volcano float. She knows she has her detractors, the out-with-the-old/in-with-the-new crowd that would like nothing better than to see her ousted. She has obtained a copy of the minutes from the panel's last pre-pageant meeting, wherein and whence Judge Number Three stood up, raised a finger in the air for emphasis, and said, "April May might represent our volcano, but she does not represent us." That comment has kept April May up every night this week. She smiles for the photographers as she steps carefully from the volcano float.

It is just about time for the swimsuit parade. This year seven bikini-clad challengers will walk the swimsuit parade, while the incumbent skates it in her one-piece.

Mariachi de Dos Nacimientos stands at the corner of Main and Calderón playing "El Corrido de Javier el Desgraciado" over and over. With the departure first of Javier, followed by that of Kiko, who cited poor leadership as his reason for leaving, the quartet has disintegrated to a hybrid between a mariachi and a conjunto norteño.

Lucha and Fabiola linger on the northbound side of Main sharing a plate of tacos. The final kilo rests in Lucha's purse. The girls have a noon appointment with El Mago de Michoacán, who this week is known as El Guerrillero de Guanajuato. The girls watch the swimsuit parade, then turn their attention toward Mariachi de Dos Nacimientos, which is taking a break. Lucha grabs Fabiola's arm and they walk over to the mariachi.

"¿Where's Javier?" says Lucha. She directs her question to no one in particular.

"His whereabouts are unknown. We only know that he has stepped out of the loving light of the Lord," says Raymundo. In Javier's absence, he has taken over as leader.

"That's the way it goes sometimes," concludes Lucha.

"Like I was sayin, the Sons and Daughters of San Narcisco are a cult. They are not a club or a cause, but a cult that takes advantage of well-intentioned individuals who want to make a bona fide difference in the world such as myself. They believe in sacred somethin or other. Apparently my salon runs right through the volcano's line of fire, so they had to dig a tunnel so as to let some pressure off and save the world," says True-Dee.

"That's some purty trippy stuff," says Consuelo.

"Purty trippy indeed, but you gotta stop your cryin," says Natalie. "Nothin undermines a girl's appearance like sufferin."

"And besides, we got some news for you," says Sway.

True-Dee perks up. She turns her neck to the left until it pops. Then to the right. She takes a deep breath. "¿Good news or bad news?" she wants to know.

"A little of both," says Sway.

"Cal McDaniel is dead," whispers Natalie.

"¿However on earth did that happen?" True-Dee's eyes open wide. She puts a hand over Consuelo's and gives her a look of heartfelt sympathy. "Dear, I am so sorry," she says to Sway.

"No need to feel so bad. He didn't suffer none, and seein as how he didn't leave no livin airs, he's gone and left his everything to me and Nat."

"Lucky you," True-Dee says and smiles. "That's just what I need to get me, an oldie with no livin heirs. ¡You girls are heiresses! It's got such a glamorous ring to it, it makes me wish I were an heiress too."

"Actually," says Natalie about to get down to business, "we came by because we have a proposition for you."

True-Dee wrinkles her nose.

"We wanna finance your Hair Growth Accelerators," says Nat.

"We think you're on to somethin," adds Consuelo.

"That would make me an inventor, ¿wouldn't it? or better yet, an inventress. ¡That's even more glamorous!"

All three women wrap their arms around each other.

"You two are the best friends a girl can have," declares True-Dee as she squeezes Nat and Sway, who look at one another and remember the time when they were in the third grade and tried to add another best friend and were taught one of the most important lessons of their lives: A girl can and only should have one best friend. Nat and Sway head for the Cadillac.

Lulabell and Alberto meet in the kitchen. He grabs his keys and his baseball cap. "¿Where's my Stetson®?" he says.

"I packed it."

"You think of everything."

Lulabell grabs her keys. "We're takin the Cadillac," she declares.

"No, vieja. Not a good idea," he says holding up his own keys. "We take the truck, that way we can make some money along the way." He tosses the keys in the air and catches them.

"Good idea, viejo," agrees Lulabell.

Javier is in Uruapan, in the Mexican state of Michoacán. It is his second day in town and he roams the streets looking for a cantina called El Oso Negro.

Without the routine of his route, without the regularity of Sunday services, Javier has lost track of time. Only after thinking about it for several minutes, does he deduce that it is indeed Labor Day. He thinks about what is going on in his hometown: the parade and how he loved it as a kid, especially the volcano-making booth and the cinnamon snow cones, hot and cold all at once. He is rooting for April May. He knows how much that tenth crown means to her. He wonders if Lulabell and Beto are going to the parade. If they are already there. He thinks about Natalie and that kiss, then forces his mind to move to another subject.

Nat and Sway are half an hour into their trip to the coast and already Consuelo has traveled further away from home than at any other time in the last twenty years. She holds the urn of Cal's ashes in her lap. She seems completely at ease on the open road. As if to prove herself so, she stretches and lets her free hand dangle out the window.

Whether they will scatter Cal's ashes on the beach or in the water itself, is still up for debate.

The Cadillac is silent, except for the steady hum of the eight-cylinder engine and the sound of the AM radio, which is tuned to Radio KAZA. Since it's a holiday, the station is on a Sunday schedule and is playing nothing but old-time singers.

Natalie trades Highway 33 for the windy Coastal Highway. The Highway is slightly scary even for her. It is super-curvy and surrounded by tall pines so the sun never really gets to it. As if to enhance this sense of danger, there are roadside signs at every bend warning of deer, slippery conditions, and hairpin turns.

They travel a few miles, perhaps five, and the trees dissipate and the sun is all of the sudden visible. The road has gone straight and there is a valley in front of them.

"Stop," says Consuelo. She holds her hands out as if for balance.

Natalie signals, she slows down, she pulls the Cadillac to the shoulder, puts the transmission in park, and kills the engine. She takes her time doing all of this, for she fears the very worst—that Consuelo has had enough, that they have come too far, and that she must go home.

The Lava Landing Disposal Site is in the distance. The girls get out and lean up against the Cadillac looking toward the county dump. Natalie is nervous. She fidgets her fingers back and forth, then folds them all under and says, "¿Remember this, Sway?" She raises both index fingers into an isosceles triangle. "This is the church and this is the steeple, open the church and look at the people." She flips her wrists and shows all her raised-up fingers.

"Of course I remember that," says Consuelo. "Sister Mary-Harry taught us that in Catechism."

"Be nice. Not her fault she had a mustache and besides, it's probably against some Church mandate to wax."

"Maybe."

"Say, Sway," says Natalie looking off toward the dump. "¿You think dumps smell the same everywhere, or do you think they just smell that way here?"

Consuelo doesn't know.

"Like if we went to a place in Asia, say Thailand or somethin, ¿do you think their dumps would smell any different than they do here?"

Consuelo still doesn't know.

"Maybe they would smell way different over there as compared to the way they smell here, seein as how they use way different ingredients in their cookin."

"Maybe." Consuelo pays mild attention to Natalie's babble because she always blabs when she is nervous, and she has every reason to be nervous. Consuelo has gone beyond her travel zone and Natalie must wonder and worry that Sway can't handle it and now wants to turn back.

"Then there would be the added question as to whether or not the dumps would all smell the same in that country or even that region of the world," continues Natalie. "Maybe they would smell different than they smell here, but in that part of the world they would all smell the same."

It gets quiet. Without the bustle of Natalie's conversation, it was quiet all along, but in a moment, the girls notice that quietness. A single-engine Cessna® flies up overhead. Natalie looks up. "¿Ain't that somethin?" she says.

"Yep. Amazin what man can do."

"And ¿ain't it peace-bringin lookin up there in the sky realizin how big and wide the world is?" adds Natalie.

"And crazy," concludes Consuelo.

"Yep. That's one thing I never really understood."

"And ¿what's that?" questions Consuelo.

"Well, they got all kinds of statistics for all kinds of badness. They keep track of how often somebody is raped, murdered, or robbed, but nobody thinks to keep tabs on just how often it is somebody goes crazy."

"Yeah but you have to consider," says Consuelo. "All that badness has got to be the result of some kinda insanity ¿no?"

"Yeah," agrees Natalie. "That would make for plenty of overlap, at least statistically speakin, but you can't overestimate the importance of mathematics. Mathematics is the real reason you can never get your house clean no matter how hard and long you scrub. Things can multiply and divide themselves into so many pieces, you can never get rid of them."

"Never," says Consuelo idly.

"Most of the great mysteries of the world can be explained mathematically. Sway, ¿what'd you want me to pull over for? ¿You ready to go home?" Natalie has calmed down considerably. Somehow during the course of her contemplations, she has managed to prepare herself for whatever is in store.

"Not in the least," says Consuelo.

"No," echoes Natalie.

"Actually I was figurin we could go somewhere. On a trip or somethin, seein as how we've already come this far and you've already packed our bags."

Natalie makes a face. "¿How'd you know?"

"You can't fool me, Nat. Me and you, we think alike."

"It's because we're like-minded individuals," agrees Natalie.

"That we are," says Consuelo. "We don't even have to go to the ocean. We can find a nice place on the way and we can dump the ashes there. I can just pop the top and let them go."

The girls get back into the Cadillac. As Natalie pulls out onto the Highway, Consuelo says, "¿You think maybe someday you can teach me how to drive?"

"Course I can. You know I'd do anything in this big, old, wide, crazy, world for you, Sway."

"I know. You've already proved that to me more than once."

"Just let me know when you're ready, and don't let this big machine intimidate you," says Natalie tapping the steering wheel.

Lulabell lives in that part of town where all the streets are named after gems and precious metals—on the corner of Platinum and Emerald. She and Alberto stand in the driveway and take a long look at their surroundings before getting into the tow truck. Alberto starts the engine. Come to think of it, Lulabell has never ridden in the tow truck before. She sits next to Alberto, their bags piled up on the seat and floor beside her.

The engine heaves and wheezes, the gears pop into and out of place. The tow truck has no get-up-and-go. After every stop sign, after every red light, it is like starting over again. All those gears. All that slowness. Yet there is a comfort in the bigness and safety of it all.

They get onto Highway 33, which turns into the Coastal Highway, before turning back into itself then connecting to Highway 54, to the Mexican border. "Now that we're on the road, ¿you mind finding my hat?" says Alberto.

"¿Right now?" says Lulabell.

"Sí, vieja. I'm going home. Really going home. I might have been here," he points down, "forty years, but a man's home is where he was born. And if I'm going home, I wanna look good. It might be a long way off, but still. I wanna be ready, so that when we cross over, I look right."

"Okay, viejo," she says. "But if you look at it that way, then I guess I'm goin home too, only I don't see it like that. This is my home." She points down. "This is where my children were born, where Javier grew up. But I'll find your hat for you. I suppose you want me to find your boots too."

"If it wouldn't be too much trouble."

Lulabell takes off her seat belt and starts digging into the bags until she finds the Stetson® and the boots.

"That's better," says Alberto putting his hat on.

"You can put the boots on when we stop to eat," says Lulabell.

"Sounds good to me, vieja." He guns the engine, brings the tow truck up to 85 mph, then turns on the cruise control.

On Highway 33, Natalie says to Consuelo, "¿How will we know where to dump the ashes?"

"I'm waitin to get a feelin."

"¿What sorta feelin?"

"The right sorta feelin," says Consuelo.

"But ¿don't you worry that maybe Cal'll get mad at us, or somethin? He did leave instructions."

"Yeah, but it ain't like he's comin back or nothin."

"You never know," says Natalie.

Javier continues to wander the streets of Uruapan. He cannot find a cantina called El Oso Negro. Pretty soon he gives up trying and wanders into another called La Tenampa where he sits down and orders a small bottle of tequila and a beer.

The cantinero slides the beer onto the counter. He reaches for the bottle opener. He opens the bottle. He goes to the back of the bar for the bottle of tequila, to the corner for the lime, to the other side for the salt, then back behind the bar for the glasses. He takes his time every step of the way. Javier does not get impatient. He has heard about something called Mexican time. After all of this is done, the cantinero says, "¿Algo más?

"Sí," says Javier. "¿Quién es?" He points to a makeshift altar behind the bar. There are two candles burning, one black, the other white, and behind them a picture of a man in a guayabera, sombrero, slacks, and huaraches, with a guitar in his lap.

The cantinero stands up straight and says proudly, "San Pancho. El Santo Patrón de Los Borrachos y Las Putas." He is filled with a sense of urgency as he grabs a barstool, moves in close to Javier, then begins to tell his own version of how a humble campesino such as Don Pancho became the Patron Saint of Drunks and Prostitutes.

Natalie has swapped the Highway for the Interstate.

"It's time," says Consuelo.

"¿For what?" says Natalie expecting the worst.

"To let the ashes loose," says Consuelo with a smile.

"¡Consuelo Constancia González Contreras! We only have three more miles until the sea. You will wait. It's the least we can do considerin all Cal did for us."

"Guess you're right," agrees Sway. "I didn't think you still remembered my full name."

They arrive at the sea and take their shoes off and run down the hill—a soft dune really, which doesn't hurt the soles of their feet in the least. And even if it were rocky, they wouldn't have felt a thing. ¡Consuelo has never been to the ocean before! She has done it. She has strayed a full nineteen miles beyond her travel zone.

Consuelo carries the urn of ashes under her arm the way a lady carries a sequin-covered clutch when she is out for a night on the town. She pops the top on the urn and begins to sprinkle the ashes as she dances and prances about. "Angel dust," she declares. "Ascend and be one in Heaven. You are free." Free. What a word. After all of these years, it actually means something to her.

Back in Lava Landing, it is almost noon. Lucha and Fabiola are seven kilos into the deal, and from the looks of things, they haven't a care in the world. This late in the game another fifty grand is neither going to make nor break them. They are still in last night's outfits—Lucha in pedal pushers, platforms, and a halter top. Fabiola wears jeans, black high-heeled cowboy boots, and a fringed black shawl with colorful flowers embroidered across the breast. The shawl is long enough to conceal the shiny silver pistol she has tucked into the waistband of her jeans. Fabiola has her long, straight, fine auburn hair parted down the middle, and two daisies tucked behind an ear.

Last night's glitter lingers on both girls' eyelids. Last night's lipstick stains their lips. Last night's mascara has begun to flake and settle below their eyes. Yet they both look like two Aztec princesses waiting to be saved from the volcano. Never mind that the final kilo lies beside Lucha's shiny silver pistol in her purse. Never mind that they are about to make the last of a series of big deals. Lucha has told Fabiola once if she has told her a hundred times, "Favy, life gives out very few good opportunities, so when one comes along, a girl's got to make the best of it."

A mariachi waits silently at the corner. The girls have half an hour before it's time to do business. April May has begun to exhibit her talent, but no one, not even the judges pay attention. The needle has been dropped on the phonograph, Billy Lee Riley has made his most famous declaration, that his girl is red-hot, that anybody else's ain't doodley squat. April May has speed-skated, she has gathered momentum, for the first double Axel. The bearings in her twelve-hundred-dollar roller skates are humming. But all of this falls on blind eyes and deaf ears.

Lucha and Fabiola walk over to the mariachi. Lucha passes the man behind the guitarrón a hundred-dollar bill. "La Cigarra," she asserts. The man behind the guitarrón inspects the bill for authenticity. Satisfied, he lets the violins loose. April May is three double Axels into her skate-dance routine. The fat man behind the guitarrón lowers his chin the way all fat men behind guitarrones do when they are getting ready to sing. Lucha waves a finger in the air. She shakes her head no. Fabiola has already taken the bubblegum out of her mouth. She has taken a big, big breath, as if trying to make up for more than just lost time.

At first, she sings slowly and softly, all the while gathering up momentum and volume, like Beto's tow truck just after the light turns green, like the pace at which Javier's drunkenness approaches, like the manner in which Natalie and Consuelo get further and further down the road, the way True-Dee rolls her perms, the way Lulabell starts her spells, like the way Don Pancho cranks out his miracles, Fabiola sings slowly and surely, but moreover inevitably, so that by the second verse her voice is as loud and as sure of itself as Beto's tow truck, as inevitable as Javier's fast-approaching drunkenness, as textured and tapered as any one of True-Dee's coiffures, as enormous as Natalie and Consuelo's ever growing fascination with the wideness of the world, as reliable as Lulabell's spells, and as beautiful and unexpected as any one of Don Pancho's miracles.

All eyes turn to Fabiola. The panel of judges mistake her for a contestant. They get up and walk her way. They surround her. Never mind that she wears neither a one-piece, nor a bikini. Disregard her lack of the proper paperwork.

The judges see her in her pretty embroidered shawl, the wind sweeping her long auburn hair aside, big gold coquetas dangling from her ears, with a mariachi in the background and a single well-rendered observation lingers in each of their minds: APRIL MAY MIGHT REPRESENT OUR VOLCANO, BUT SHE DOES NOT REPRESENT US.

April May has finished her skate-dance routine. She comes speed-skating up. Her volcano tiara sparkles in the sunlight. It has been hers nine years in a row. Nobody knows it, but she has slept with that tiara every night for just about ten years, and now she senses she is in danger of losing it.

Fabiola's song has ended. The crowd is silent. Even Mariachi de Dos Nacimientos has ceased to play. Lucha and Fabiola loop arms. They are surrounded and it has to feel uncomfortable, each packing her own private pistol, and Lucha, still on probation and with a kilo of high-grade cocaine in her purse.

Judge Number One raises his hands in the air and addresses the crowd. He bites his bottom lip in a moment of indecision. He was an April May backer, but in an instant he switches tickets. In a move of classic political strategy he polishes his posture and declares, "April May might represent our volcano, but she does not represent us. We," he says holding his arms out wide for inclusivity, "are more than just a volcano."

The crowd claps. The crowd cheers. April May stands aside. April May with her long, thick, wavy, fiery red hair, her translucent skin with the veins and arteries showing through, her freckles now so abundant they form several distinct blobs across her face like continents on the globe, her teeth so crooked she can no longer fully close her mouth, has begun to hyperventilate. The children in the crowd begin to cry. Judge Number One reaches for the rhinestone-encrusted tiara. He tries to take it off of Miss Magma's head, but with all that thick, fiery hair, he cannot do it all by himself. Judges Four and Five come to his aid, but even with all the help, the tiara will not come out of April May's hair. It is as if it has set down roots there.

April May has had enough. She throws last year's crown to the ground. The judges rush to pick it up. They inspect it for damage. Seeing none, they walk over to Fabiola. One of the judges removes the daisies from behind her ear, the other slides the tiara onto her head, but her baby-fine hair is just too thin to fill the slots in April May's crown. That can be fixed, thinks Judge Number Three as he holds the crown in place while the photographers' strobes go off. Just one of many adjustments to be made.

On the Interstate Consuelo slides into the driver's seat for the very first time. In her entire life, she has never boarded a play car, or a motorcycle at an amusement park, or even in front of the Kmart. She has never so much as entered a car on the driver's side and lingered on the driver's seat while sliding over.

"Pull it in and bring it down to the 'D,'" says Natalie.

Consuelo puts the transmission in drive and without further instruction she pulls out into traffic. In no time she is in the fast lane. They are in the fast lane.

Lulabell and Beto are several miles behind on the Interstate. Lulabell snores on Beto's shoulder. The reliability of that big engine and its monotony motoring them down the highway has put her to sleep.

Fabiola and Lucha are still surrounded. Fabiola takes the volcano tiara from her head, takes one look at it, and throws it to the ground. Rhinestones. ¿What does she want with rhinestones when she has the means to get the real thing? And besides, Favy has unfinished business to take care of in Metzico. She hasn't the time to don the sashes and tiaras, to give the grade-school pep talks, to smile and wave for the crowd.

And now the judges rush to the crown's rescue, but it is too late. It has been lost. Lucha has already come down hard on it with her platform huaraches.

All eyes turn toward April May. They wait for her to save the day, but she is off and skating. She speed-skates to the far corner of the blacktop. She does a triple Axel followed by a double—an exceedingly difficult move since she does not give herself time to build up momentum, but somehow she pulls it off. Her body is working as a complete unit. Her artistry and athleticism are excellent. She goes into a Camel spin. Her left leg hovers parallel to the blacktop, her fierce red hair completely parallel to her left leg. She spins faster and faster, her hair threatening to whip anything in its path out of existence. All of those hours of silent and demanding practice have paid off. Her form is exceptional, her fall so unexpected. Down she goes. Her size 13 feet fold under her, the wheels on her twelve-hundred-dollar roller skates are still spinning, their bearings still humming. April May is in a heap on the blacktop. She balls up her fists and shows her chagrin. Her roller skates with their sparkly red laces look as out of place and essential as the mermaid's tail. She throws her head back. Her large Adam's apple sticks out like a goiter. Her long fiery hair has never been longer, has never been thicker, has never been fierier. It trails behind her like, well ¿what can I say? It looks just like lava lying there on the blacktop. April May fills her large lungs with air. She screams, a scream many years in the making, so long and prolonged, the parade goers duck and cover their ears, a scream so full of everything that screams are made of, a scream such as the Earth, even in Her many, many years of existence, has never ever heard, and the Earth responds in kind.

Author's Note

Don Clemente Jacques, a Frenchman, arrived in Mexico on the 11th of November 1880 with the intention of setting up a business dedicated to the production and sale of cork. He soon realized there was little demand for his product, so he switched his operation to the sale of packaged foods. Around the turn of the century, he began attending World's Fairs, bringing with him decks of cards he passed out as gifts to potential clients. This was not far from his calling, since part of his business was already dedicated to selling party supplies.

Shortly after arriving in Mexico, he noticed the popularity of a game known as Lotería Campechana that resembled Le Lotto, a game very similar to bingo played in his native France. Historians believe that the game was descended from beano, a game played by the ancient Romans. Beano later spread throughout Europe. In France it was played by members of high society. The Germans put a didactic spin on the game, using it in their classrooms to teach children everything from mathematics to history. It eventually arrived in Spain, then Mexico, where it was and is still known as Lotería.

In 1887 Don Clemente fashioned a deck of Lotería cards based on Mexican culture that included dichos, brief but poignant sayings and plays on words. Sometimes being an outsider can enable a person to make acute observations about his new environment, and such seems to have been the case with Don Clemente. At the World's Fairs, he soon found that people were more interested in this little deck of cards than they were in his packaged foods. He shifted his business operations accordingly and Don Clemente's Lotería has been going strong ever since.

Many of the Lotería images in this book are part of Don Clemente's original deck. But just as Don Clemente was moved to fashion a deck specific to the place and time in which he lived, the author was also inspired to create a few cards as part of the Lava Landing Lotería.

It should be noted that the creation of these new cards could not have been possible without the hard work, vision, and dedication of Peter Mendelsund, to whom the author extends her sincerest thanks and gratitude.

¡CARAMBA!

El Paraguas	*The Umbrella*	Don Clemente
El Músico	*The Musician*	Don Clemente
La Sirena	*The Siren*	Don Clemente
La Lonchera	*The Lunch Wagon*	Lava Landing
El Diablito	*The Little Devil*	Don Clemente
El Salón de Belleza	*The Beauty Salon*	Lava Landing
El Volcán y su Reina	*The Volcano & His Queen*	Lava Landing
La Mano	*The Hand*	Don Clemente
El Queso Grande	*The Big Cheese*	Lava Landing
El Ajolote	*The Axolotl*	Lava Landing
La Muerte	*Death*	Don Clemente
El Camarón	*The Shrimp*	Don Clemente
El Tupperware®	*The Tupperware®*	Lava Landing
El Pino	*The Pine Tree*	Don Clemente
El Cazo	*The Pot*	Don Clemente
El Árbol	*The Tree*	Don Clemente
El Avión	*The Airplane*	Lava Landing
La Dama	*The Lady*	Don Clemente
La Grúa	*The Tow Truck*	Lava Landing
La Pera	*The Pear*	Don Clemente
La Botella	*The Bottle*	Don Clemente
El Reloj de Mano	*The Wristwatch*	Lava Landing
El Mango	*The Mango*	Lava Landing
La Tarjeta Telefónica	*The Phone Card*	Lava Landing
El Catrín	*The Dandy*	Don Clemente
La Luna	*The Moon*	Don Clemente
El Cotorro	*The Parrot*	Don Clemente
La Bota	*The Boot*	Don Clemente
El Nopal	*The Cactus*	Don Clemente
La Peluca Blonde Bouffant	*The Blonde Bouffant Wig*	Lava Landing
La Bandera	*The Flag*	Don Clemente
La Calavera	*The Skull*	Don Clemente
El Anillo de Compromiso	*The Engagement Ring*	Lava Landing
Menudo	*Menudo*	Lava Landing
La Herradura de la Suerte	*The Lucky Horseshoe*	Lava Landing
Los Botes	*The Cans*	Lava Landing
El Baile Grande	*The Big Dance*	Lava Landing
El Tocadiscos	*The Record Player*	Lava Landing
El Oro	*Gold*	Lava Landing
El Traje de Charro	*The Charro's Suit*	Lava Landing